The Sword

Guinevere
Book Three

Fil Reid

DRAGONBLADE
PUBLISHING, INC.

Dragonblade Publishing, Inc. is an imprint of Kathryn Le Veque Novels, Inc.
P.O. Box 23
Moreno Valley, CA 92556
ceo@dragonbladepublishing.com

Produced in the United States of America

First Edition May 2022
Trade Paperback Edition

ARE YOU SIGNED UP FOR DRAGONBLADE'S BLOG?

You'll get the latest news and information on exclusive giveaways, exclusive excerpts, coming releases, sales, free books, cover reveals and more.

Check out our complete list of authors, too!

No spam, no junk. That's a promise!

Sign Up Here

www.dragonbladepublishing.com

Dearest Reader;

Thank you for your support of a small press. At Dragonblade Publishing, we strive to bring you the highest quality Historical Romance from some of the best authors in the business. Without your support, there is no 'us', so we sincerely hope you adore these stories and find some new favorite authors along the way.

Happy Reading!

CEO, Dragonblade Publishing

Additional Dragonblade books by
Author Fil Reid

Guinevere Series
The Dragon Ring (Book 1)
The Bear's Heart (Book 2)
The Sword (Book 3)

Dedication

With heartfelt thanks to my editor, Amelia.

The Legend of King Arthur

Long ago, after the Roman legions abandoned Britain to defend their city of Rome, a time of turbulence came upon the land, and many men fought for the right to rule. A proud tyrant named Vortigern seized power, making himself High King above all other kings. At first, he ruled well, but when he was old and beleaguered on all sides by his enemies, he retreated into the mountains of Wales. Here he planned to build a great fortress and lock himself safely inside, leaving his people to their fate at the hands of the invading Saxons.

Each morning, the workers found the walls they'd built the day before had fallen down, and they had to start again. After many days, despairing, Vortigern called his wise men to him and sought their counsel. They told him to find a boy born with no mortal father and sacrifice him, and only then would the walls of his fortress stay standing.

Vortigern sent his knights out to search the length and breadth of Britain for a boy who fitted this description. At last, they brought such a boy to him, who, when questioned, answered that he had no mortal father, being supposedly the son of a demon. His name was Merlin Emrys. The wise men were about to sacrifice this boy when he asked why they had need of him. On being told that the walls would not stay standing, he informed Vortigern and his wise men that if they dug down into the hill, they would find a lake. Vortigern ordered this done, and the wise men found a lake beneath the hill.

Merlin then asked the wise men what was in the lake, but they knew not. So he told them that if they had the lake drained, they would find two dragons fighting – one white and one red.

The wise men did so, and sure enough, there were the two dragons, fighting. Some of the time the white one gained the upper hand, and some of the time the red one appeared to be winning.

Merlin asked the wise men if they knew what the two fighting dragons meant, but they knew not. So he told the High King that the white dragon represented the Saxons, and the red the British who would eventually, under a great leader, defeat the Saxons.

Vortigern was able to build his fortress and, needless to say, he didn't have the boy sacrificed. Instead, he named the fortress Dinas Emrys after the boy. And thanks to the High King's patronage, young Merlin Emrys became the king's chief advisor and enchanter.

When Vortigern died, a new High King came to power – Uther Pendragon, who was a brave and successful warrior, and was also, in his turn, advised by Merlin. He ruled for many years from his capital in London, with much strife against the enemies of the British: the Saxons from the eastern seas, the Irish from the western seas and the Picts from beyond the wall.

At Pentecost one year, Uther called together his knights for a tournament in London. Gorlois, Duke of Cornwall, left his home of Tintagel Castle in Cornwall and journeyed to London to take part, bringing his young wife, Ygraine. At the tournament, King Uther fell deeply in love with Ygraine, and seeing this, Gorlois fled with her back to Tintagel.

Uther was angry, and ordered Gorlois to return, but the duke did not. So, taking his army, Uther marched into Cornwall and fought against Gorlois at his castle of Dimilioc. Desperate to have Ygraine for himself, Uther persuaded Merlin, his enchanter, to help him. Merlin said that he would as long as Uther gave him the child who would result from this union to bring up himself. Consumed with lust, Uther readily agreed, and one night, while Gorlois was engaged in battle at Dimilioc, he came to Tintagel disguised as Ygraine's husband. Allowed inside by the unsuspecting guards, he spent the night with Ygraine and his son, Arthur, was conceived.

The following morning news came to the castle that Gorlois

had been killed, and Ygraine realized she had been fooled by Uther. As the victor, he now took her as his wife, but when her child, Arthur, was born, Uther had to fulfill his promise to give the child up to Merlin as the price he paid for the enchanter's help.

Merlin took the baby far away to the home of the knight Sir Ector for the boy to be brought up as his own son, stepbrother to Kay. And there Arthur grew to be a young man of sixteen. Sir Ector was ignorant of who his young ward was.

King Uther, meanwhile, took a wound in battle that was incurable, and eventually he sickened and died without ever seeing his heir. On his death there was dispute as to who should reign after him, and to settle this, Merlin set up a sword embedded in a stone, with the instruction that whosoever could draw the sword from the stone was the true-born king of Britain. Many came and tried their hands, but none could draw the sword.

A tournament was held, to which all the knights in the land were invited. Sir Ector came with his son, Sir Kay, and young Arthur accompanied them as Kay's squire. On the morning of the tournament Sir Kay realized he'd left his sword in their lodgings and sent his squire to fetch it. On the way, Arthur spied the sword in the stone, and thinking to be quicker, drew the sword and brought it back to Sir Kay. The young knight recognized the sword and asked his father if this meant that he was king, but wise Sir Ector realized his stepson was the one who should be king. The boy was taken back to the stone, and the sword returned to it. Before all the knights in the realm, Arthur drew the sword a second time and Merlin proclaimed him king.

Arthur became a great king, ruling wisely for a long time from his capital of Camelot. Many great knights came to his castle – Bedivere, Gawaine, Agrivaine, Tristan and Percival, to name but a few. At length the sword from the stone broke in battle, and riding past a lake Arthur saw a hand rise from the water holding a new sword – Excalibur. Taking a small boat he rowed toward the hand, and took the sword for himself. The hand retreated into the water.

For a wife, Arthur took the beautiful Guinevere, daughter of King Leodegrance, and for a long time they were both very happy. He fought many battles against the Saxons, culminating in his famous Battle of Mount Badon, where he bore the image of the Virgin Mary upon his shield and drove the Saxons back once and for all.

But he had two sisters, born of his father's marriage with Ygraine: Morgana and Morgawse. And unwittingly, before he knew Morgawse was his sister, he lay with her and the boy Mordred was born. Morgawse married King Lot of Lothian and bore other sons, and eventually these sons all came to Camelot to become knights of the Round Table which Merlin had provided for Arthur.

When Arthur took his army to fight in Gaul, he left Mordred as his regent, and Mordred, knowing his parentage and thinking that the kingdom could be his, seduced Guinevere and took her for his own. When Arthur returned, he and Mordred came to the final battle of Camlann, where Mordred was eventually slain, and where Arthur was sorely wounded.

Dying, Arthur called his faithful knight Bedivere to his side and, giving him the sword Excalibur, asked him to take it to the nearby lake and throw it in. Bedivere went to the lake, but he could not bring himself to throw away so beautiful a sword. He returned to Arthur and told him he'd done as he'd asked. Arthur asked him what had happened, and Bedivere could not say, so Arthur knew he had lied. A second time he sent Bedivere to the lake, and a second time that knight could not throw the sword away, and Arthur knew he lied. Finally, on the third time of asking, Bedivere threw the sword as far as he could into the water and a hand emerged to grasp it by the hilt. As he watched, hand and sword disappeared beneath the surface of the lake. When Bedivere told him what had happened, Arthur knew Bedivere had at last done as he was asked.

The dying Arthur was then carried to the edge of the lakes around the Island of Avalon. Here, a boat bearing three queens came to carry him away from the land of the living to be cured of his wounds and put into a deep sleep from which he would only waken when the island of Britain was in dire need of his help. To this day, he sleeps there still, waiting for the moment when he is needed again.

Place Names

Din Cadan South Cadbury Castle in Somerset, refortified Iron Age Hill Fort

Ynys Witrin Glastonbury, which once was an island surrounded by marshes

Viroconium Wroxeter Roman Town (near Shrewsbury)

Caer Baddan Bath (Roman Aquae Sulis)

Caer Ceri Cirencester (Roman Corinium)

Caer Gloui Gloucester (Roman Glevum)

Caer Luit CoytWall (Roman Letocetum)

Caer Legeion guar Uisc Caerleon (Roman Isca Silurem) South Wales

Caerwysg Exeter (Roman Isca Dumnoniorum)

Castle Dore Stronghold of King Mark of Cornubia (Cornwall) near Fowey

Tintagel North coast of Cornwall

Caer Pensa Ilchester (Roman Lindinis)

Caer Gwinntguic Winchester (Roman Venta Belgarum) Hampshire

Caer Lundein London

Caer Ebrauc York

Caer Ligualid Carlisle (on Hadrian's Wall)

Caer Lind Colun Lincoln

Linnuis Kingdom centered on Lincoln

Sabrina Sea Estuary of the River Severn (Sabrina)

Metaris Estuary The Wash

Chapter One

HE WIND HAD blown bad weather down from the north, and fine rain hung in the late autumnal air. Dirty clouds scudded across a slate grey sky where a single red kite wheeled on the shoulders of the wind, its mewling cry plaintive as a cat's. I drew my cloak closer around my body and leaned into the gusts, damp strands of hair that had come loose from my long braid whipping across my face.

I stood alone on the wall-walk of the fortress of Din Cadan. Before me stretched the plain of what would one day be called the Somerset Levels, stained a colorless grey by the wintry light. Smoke, from the small farmsteads that dotted the plain right as far as the dark line of the distant forest edge, curled up to be snatched by the cruel north wind. Beyond the forest, the hump of Glastonbury Tor rose out of the flat landscape, the expanse of watery marshes that surrounded it here in the fifth century hidden from view.

Once again, as I'd been doing every day, I'd come up here to be alone. To think. God alone knew how much I needed to think, and this was one of the only places within the fortress I could do it by myself.

I narrowed my eyes, staring out across the plain toward the Tor, my jumbled thoughts turning to how that far-off, marsh-encircled hill might mark the way back to my own world if I so chose. Ten months ago, I'd gone there with Arthur, my husband

and my king. He'd taken me because he loved me too much to ask me to stay with him, and, as I'd hoped, a portal in time had opened. Presented with the choice I'd needed, between returning to my life as Gwen the librarian or remaining with the man I loved, I'd been able to choose to stay. But events had moved on since then, and now I no longer felt so sure of my decision.

Now I didn't have just me to think of. I had my baby son.

The bitter wind made my eyes water. I put a hand up and brushed back my hair, drawing the hood of my fur-lined cloak further forward. If I looked to left or right, I'd see my husband's armed warriors on sentry duty, stamping their feet to stave off the cold, wrapped up tighter than I was. They were used to seeing me up here and no longer came to ask if I needed anything. I was their queen, and they respected and perhaps loved me, but it hadn't taken them long to work out that I wanted to be alone.

A gust of rain spattered across my face. Finally defeated by the weather, I turned around. Hunching my shoulders, I stared up the slope at the buildings, clustering like barnacles on an upturned boat, that occupied the fortress of Din Cadan. On the highest point, the whale-like hump of the Great Hall, its thatched roof dark with age, rose above the smaller buildings, as though some spring high tide had deposited it there.

Scattered across the hilltop lay houses and huts, barns and byres, pig pens and vegetable patches in a glorious hotchpotch of life. Warhorses grazed in small, fenced paddocks, pigs rooted in the muddy fields where vegetable crops had already been brought in, and smoke rose from a myriad of rooftops as dark as the Hall's.

One day, long in the future, this windy hilltop fortress would become known as South Cadbury Castle. Scholars would dig it up and argue about whether it could ever have been King Arthur's stronghold. Only I knew that was true.

The sharp tang of the woodsmoke, the damp earthiness of the ground, the underlying aroma of the animals and middens, and the scent of the mizzling rain, filled the air. Voices carried from amongst the buildings: men called to one another, a boy whistled for his dog, two women harangued each other in a shouting match, and in the byre the cows waiting to be milked lowed their impatience.

This was the place I'd called home for a year, the place I'd come to love. Yet now my own doubt hung like a funeral shroud over everything.

A wagonload of brushwood creaked in through the main gates, swaying precariously even though roped down. In the courtyard in front of the Great Hall, in defiance of the rain, they were preparing a bonfire for the harvest feast of Samhain that would begin this evening at sunset. My friend Merlin, who apart from Arthur was the only one who knew of my other-worldly origin, had explained there would be a great fire again, as at the spring feast of Beltane, and after that all of us would have to stay shut inside. Tonight, the dead could walk again on this curious mix of harvest festival and Hallowe'en.

I'd been standing here long enough. In the west, hidden by the banks of cloud, the sun must be nearing its rest, and Samhain would begin soon. Not that I believed the dead could really walk. I descended the wooden steps to the foot of the wide earthen bank that supported the outer wall of the fortress. The short grass, wet from the rain blowing across the hilltop, soaked into the hem of my gown as I headed uphill toward the Great Hall.

A pall of foreboding enveloped me, the nearer I drew.

In front of the Hall, men were unloading the brushwood from the wagon and stacking it onto the pyramidal bonfire with the help of half a dozen eager boys. I recognized one of them, who seemed to be getting very much in the way of the adults, as Arthur's seven-year-old illegitimate son, Llacheu. He spotted me as I rounded the corner of the stable block and, abandoning his self-appointed chore, came running to meet me.

"Gwen!" He fell in by my side. "Look how big the bonfire is. It's going to make a huge blaze." Normally his enthusiasm would rub off on me, but today, as yesterday and the day before and the day before that, I wasn't in the mood.

He had to do an extra skip to keep up with my fast walk. "My mother's baked some special loaves for the feast. She let me help her with the decoration – one of them looks just like a sheaf of wheat. It's huge and beautiful, and it smells delicious. Cottia saw it and said it was a work of art."

I didn't really want to hear what his mother, Tangwyn, had been doing. I already had my suspicions about that. Arthur had not been to my bed since the day Melwas died. I'd slept alone, waking in the darkest hour to feed my baby, Amhar, in solitary sadness. Where else could he have gone if not back to the woman who'd been his mistress until I came along? The mother of a child he knew for certain was his.

For just before he died, Melwas had whispered to Arthur with his last breath that my newborn baby, Amhar, was not Arthur's child, but his, and sown the seed of terrifying doubt in my husband's mind. We'd argued, and he'd assured me he believed me when I swore Melwas had never touched me. But had he meant it? His absence from my bed gave the lie to that.

However, it wasn't just that. If it had been, perhaps I could have won him back. I could have argued with him until he accepted my word concerning what had happened when I'd been Melwas's prisoner, nine months before Amhar's birth.

But another thing troubled me – a terrible thing to suspect my husband of, and guilt racked me that I'd even given it house room. The fact that I knew all the legends didn't help.

When Morgana had been our prisoner, after the battle of Bassas, the thought, perhaps picked from my brain and redirected with her mastery of magic, that Arthur was the father of his sister Morgawse's son, had risen in my heart. Medraut, then a cheery eight-month-old, appeared forged in the image of Arthur's son Llacheu, from his dark brows and thickly curling, almost black hair, to the curve of his baby mouth.

I'd spoken to no one about this, keeping it tight in my heart, festering like a pus-filled sore. And the longer it stayed there, the more it raised its ugly head and insisted on me taking notice of it. For this reason, I'd been disinclined to go running after Arthur and asking where he was spending his nights. If he suspected me, then I suspected him back, and in the four days since Melwas had died, all I'd done was brood.

"I love Samhain." Llacheu was nothing if not determined. "I love the feast food. This year I'm old enough to come to the feast instead of having to eat the cold leftovers tomorrow. And there's going to be a minstrel. He came up from the village carrying a lyre."

We'd reached the hall doors, which stood wide open. Inside, the torches in their iron brackets burned with a fierce yellow glare and the aroma of roasting meat spilled into the night air, funneling out through the doors on a wave of heat that overpowered the usual stench of damp dog and musty floor reeds.

I stopped. "Oughtn't you to be helping your mother?"

His small face, so like his father's, puckered in a frown. "She doesn't need me. She has Tulac." His body slave, a boy of thirteen. "And she's in an awful mood. She always is when she has to cook for something special. She has been for days. Can't I come with you and see my little brother?"

My ears pricked. Why would Tangwyn be in an awful mood when presumably she'd had Arthur in her bed these four nights? Surely she'd be smug with self-satisfaction that she'd won him back from me so soon after the birth of his son. Perhaps she hoped that now he had a legitimate heir he no longer needed me? Perhaps he'd told her his suspicions. But maybe not. Her bad mood might indicate something quite different.

Well, if she could pinch my husband, I could do the same with her son.

I forced myself to smile at him. "Of course you can. Come along."

We made our way across the crowded hall, full of noisy servants preparing for the feast, past the huge ox roasting over the glowing coals in the hearth, spitting juices and fat into the flames.

5

The same Saxon slave boy I'd seen on the first day I'd come to Din Cadan was tending the roasting meat, clad only in his braccae, sweat running off his scrawny body.

I led the way past the raised dais where the top table stood and through the door behind it, Llacheu at my heels.

Immediately, the noise of people talking as they worked muted. In the square chamber I normally shared with Arthur, furs and thick rugs lay spread over the flagstone floor. A large bed stood against the far wall, with the big wooden chests that held our clothes to either side, and a table near the glowing brazier. Close beside the bed stood Amhar's crib, made of dark wood and set on rockers. Maia, my young maidservant and now Amhar's nurse, sat on a stool, gently rocking the crib.

Llacheu ran across the room to stand looking down into the crib, and I followed him more slowly.

Amhar was sleeping, his tiny, rosebud mouth working as though in his dreams he suckled. His already plentiful dark hair haloed his head on the linen sheet, one fisted hand peeking above the blankets covering him.

"Was I ever that small?" Llacheu asked, in wonder.

Maia, never stopping her rocking, laughed gently. "Indeed ye were, my little lord." She put an arm round him, drawing him in close. "I remember well when yer mother birthed ye. A noisier babby it would've bin hard to find. Ye wanted all the fortress to know ye were here." She gave him a squeeze. "T'were a great day fer yer father."

Maia seemed to know instinctively that Llacheu might have been feeling elbowed out by his new brother, legitimate when he was not, and hit upon the exact right words to make him feel valued still. If only I possessed her natural feel for getting things right. So far, I seemed better at getting things wrong.

Llacheu, bolstered now by the knowledge that his father had been happy when he was born, looked up at me with a wide, gap-toothed grin. "I know he's small yet, but when he's older I'll show him how to do things – how to climb trees and fish, how to ride a pony and spear targets, and how to fight with a sword." He paused to think. "Although by then I think I'll be a warrior myself. With a proper sword and not a silly wooden one."

The thought of Llacheu fighting by his father's side evoked mixed feelings. The thought of any child armed with a sword and spear and fighting to the death was abhorrent even after a year in the fifth century, but that seemingly unavoidable fate lay ahead for both Llacheu and Amhar.

I gazed down at my little son, so small and vulnerable in his cot. Every instinct told me to do everything I could to protect him from what the future might hold. Arthur's mother, Eigr, who possessed the Sight, had seen her son Arthur's end in her scrying glass, when he was just a child, and fought to protect him from it. But she'd only brought about her separation from him when he was seven years old.

Yet I was different. I had no need of a scrying glass. I might have the power at my fingertips to save Amhar from whatever fate had in store. On Glastonbury Tor, within the ring of ancient stones, the doorway I'd turned away from might still exist. A doorway I could take Amhar through before he was old enough to fight.

The thought intoxicated me, making my head whirl. Perhaps, even, I could take Llacheu as well, save him from the almost inevitable death that lay ahead of him.

"Would you like to hold him?" I asked Llacheu.

MUCH LATER, WHEN Llacheu had reluctantly gone back to his own house to change his clothes for the evening celebrations, Arthur came to our chamber. Although he hadn't been to my bed, I'd seen him from time to time during the day, and he kept coming back to collect things he needed. He arrived just as Maia was braiding gold thread through my hair. I glanced up at him from where I sat on one of the benches at the table, noting the heavy frown I'd grown accustomed to seeing since Melwas's death.

Maia tied up the end of my braid with the gold thread and stepped back hastily. She was always a trifle tongue-tied and awkward in Arthur's presence. He was her king, after all.

"You may go." He waved her away imperiously.

With a glance at me, Maia scuttled from the room. Not to go far though. One of the storage rooms beside the Hall had been turned over to her so she could be close to me and help with Amhar whenever I required.

Arthur turned his back on me and went to his chest of clothes. The hinges squeaked as he raised the lid then silently rootled through his belongings searching for what he wanted. I remained seated at the table, twirling the golden, dragon-headed bracelet that Merlin had given me back in my world, long ago before I even knew his identity.

Without looking, I could tell exactly what Arthur was doing from the faint noises he was making. His four-days-worn workaday tunic came off, and then his undershirt. Probably they'd been thrown onto the flagstones for Maia to pick up later, as was his habit. A clunk signaled his boots coming off. I pictured him wriggling out of his trousers.

It was at this point, when I knew he'd be at his most vulnerable, that I chose to turn around. He was naked, picking up his clean linen undershirt from the bed.

I got to my feet and stood staring at him. We were only ten feet apart, but it might have been a thousand. He held the undershirt in front of his nakedness as though it needed protecting, as though a frosty discomfort existed between us. With good reason.

I steeled myself to face him down. "Where have you been these last four nights?" It came out much colder than I'd intended, and I bit my tongue in regret.

His dark brows lowered in a look that reminded me of Llacheu. "Is that any of your business?"

Understandably, I was affronted. Despite this being the fifth century, I'd so far viewed our marriage as being one of equals, as it would have been where I'd come from. I suppose I knew in my heart that it wasn't, or rather that he didn't see it like that, but this was the first time it had been borne in upon me. "You are my husband." My voice was as frosty and full of contempt as his was. The air between us thrummed with unspoken words of mutual anger.

"And you my wife." His brow furrowed as though it hurt him to say this. "It is I who rule not just this kingdom but also this household. If I choose to absent myself, it is no concern of yours."

I set my teeth over my lower lip, biting down into it, in an attempt to give myself time to think before I spoke. But my words came falling out, unbidden, uncensored. "Were you with her? With Tangwyn?" Regretted as soon as uttered. I didn't want him to see my jealousy, my anger, my sorrow.

He stood there, naked and ridiculously handsome, his dark hair brushing his shoulders, his eyes flashing anger back at me. In the moment before he replied, I took in his long limbs, the muscles of his arms and legs, his taut belly, the curling hairs on his chest, the dressing on the wound Melwas's mother, old Olwyn, had given him after he killed her last remaining son. Whatever he'd done, however he'd treated me, I still loved him, only now that love was painful.

A heavy scowl shaded his hostile eyes. "Do you care?" The three words hung between us.

I wanted to shout out *yes*, tell him that I loved him still, tell him again that Amhar was his son, and Melwas a nasty, scheming liar. If only Olwyn had not died, and could have told Arthur the truth – that Melwas never laid a hand on me.

But it wasn't just that. Could I still love him, knowing that Medraut might be his son as well? More to the point, did he still love me?

"It looks bad," I said, aware how hollow this argument sounded, even to my ears. "People will talk."

He gave a bark of bitter laughter. "That's all that bothers you? Well, I can remedy that. Tonight I'll spend in your bed, as requested. After the feast."

And turning his back on me, he proceeded to get on with dressing.

Chapter Two

T HE INSISTENT CRYING of the baby woke me. For a moment I lay listening to him in the chill darkness of our bedchamber, then I pushed back the heavy covers and slipped out of bed. The furs that covered the floor's cold flagstones felt soft beneath my bare feet as my fingers groped for my candle on the clothes chest beside the bed. Finding it, I picked it up, along with the spill that lay beside it.

The faint orange glow given off by the brazier in the center of the chamber guided me to it. As I waited for the spill to catch light, my feet grew cold on the slabs surrounding the fire, left bare as a nod to safety, and the baby's crying rose to a crescendo of hungry displeasure.

The spill caught, and I held it to the candle's wick. A flame flared, throwing light in a warm circle around me and just reaching the crib over by the bed. Arthur didn't stir. He'd come to bed long after me, much the worse for the drink he'd imbibed at the Samhain feast, and now lay gently snoring.

I set the candle back on the clothes chest and picked up the baby, cradling him against my shoulder. His cries immediately lessened as he smelled his mother and the prospect of milk. Holding him carefully, I climbed back into bed and drew the bedclothes up to keep us both warm.

Loosening the drawstring of an undershirt already wet with leaking milk, I held him to my breast and let him root for the nipple. All crying ceased as he latched on firmly, a tiny clenched fist resting against my skin as though he wanted to be sure I wouldn't escape his grasp. I leaned back against my pillows and relaxed as he fed.

If I'd been in my old world, fifteen hundred years into the future, I would have glanced at my phone to find out what the time was, read on my Kindle as the baby fed, or watched some late-night television. But I wasn't, and none of these things were available to me.

Instead, I studied my sleeping husband by the dim light of the candle.

It was odd how quickly he could be awake and ready to fight in any emergency. Yet the cry of his son left him undisturbed and me wide-awake and responsive to the child's every need. I suspected this was how it must be with most men. Perhaps only women possessed that sixth sense that woke them to their child's cry within moments.

Arthur lay on his back, one bare arm thrown up onto the pillow above his head, his dark wavy hair framing his sleeping face. A strong face, the brows determined and intense, the mouth, which I knew could be sensuous and sensitive, firm. Sleep had bestowed on him a boyishness I'd not seen of late, the perpetual frown gone, the lines of worry softened, his whole visage now washed clean of responsibility and above all, of doubt.

I liked to look on him while he slept. That he'd returned to my bed at all felt like a minor miracle. When he'd come tiptoeing to bed, evidently trying to avoid wakening the baby, I'd pretend- ed to be asleep myself, curled as close to the edge of my side as I could get. It was a big bed, and he'd made no contact with me at all as he got in. Until four days ago, our nights together had been when Arthur had felt like mine and mine alone, whereas by day I was forced to accept the tiny share of him left over after all his kingly duties were done with. Now, it seemed, all that remained for me was that tiny share.

The baby finished one breast and I swapped him to the other, his hungry little mouth searching out my nipple and latching on with gusto as though he weren't already half-full. He was a strong child already, at not yet four weeks old, and growing well despite the fact that he lived in the dangerous fifth century where so many children died in infancy. A fact I had to keep shoving to the back of my mind or else it would have eaten at my heart and kept me worrying every day for his safety.

Which brought Bretta's curse shouldering its way to the forefront of my thoughts. *I curse you, Queen of Dumnonia, and I curse your husband and your son. You and yours shall know the loss I feel.* She blamed me, and Arthur too, for the death of her orphaned siblings at Melwas's hands, after Arthur had ordered Melwas to deal with the problem of child beggars in Caer Baddan. The words of her desperate, venomous curse had ingrained themselves in my brain. Automatically, my hold on Amhar tightened as I swallowed down the fear that had risen in a surge of bile. Curses held no power. If I refused to think about what she'd said, it couldn't come true.

Beside me, Arthur stirred and turned onto his side, presenting me with his naked back. A little shiver passed through my body, making me tighten my hold on my son even further, as though he were in need of protection. I had more to fear than just a distraught woman's curse.

With my free hand, I stroked Amhar's dark baby-hair, already curling like his father's and Llacheu's. Too much like the hair of Morgawse's infant son Medraut.

The baby's eyes closed, thick lashes dark against his soft cheeks, still suckling, but with less vigor, as though sleep pressed hard upon him. My mind turned to Medraut yet again, as it had so often in the dark reaches of the night when all I had to do while Amhar fed was think.

I'd been brought up by my Arthurian scholar father, with my twin brother Artie, on the stories of King Arthur and the Knights of the Round Table, as well as the older Celtic myths and legends. So I knew that in many stories, Arthur was the father, through unwitting incest with his sister, of Medraut. But as with all these stories, I couldn't be sure which were true and which just medieval nonsense.

A year ago, before I'd stopped to think about it, I'd inadvertently turned the legend of the sword in the stone into reality when I told Merlin about it, and he'd seized upon the idea. Right now, outside the huge wooden hall in the old forum at Viroconium, a sword stood waiting, thrust deep into an enormous rock, for the right man at the right moment to draw it out and claim the title of High King. So always in my mind lurked the fact that I might make other things happen that never should have been. I feared the stories I knew might not be true, and worst of all, that some of them actually were.

Much thought, during the long nights since Amhar's birth, had brought me to the conclusion that perhaps Morgana, Arthur's other sister, when she'd been our prisoner, had put the thought into my head that Arthur might be the father of their sister's child. Morgana possessed the Sight, inherited from their mother, and could boast something even I, with my twenty-first-century upbringing, might classify as very like magic.

The more this thought banged about in my head, the more I'd become convinced she'd used her power to play with my mind. In fact, I wanted to believe she had, and I hung onto this like a beacon of hope. Because if she hadn't somehow read my mind, how had she come upon this very aspect of the legend by herself unless it were true? Surely, she must have plucked it from the recesses of my thoughts? Could it have been there, festering at the back of my mind, ever since I'd met Arthur?

Unwilling to keep her prisoner, Arthur had returned Morgana to their half-brother Cadwy in faraway Viroconium. I'd never been so glad to see the back of someone. If I never saw her again, I'd be well pleased. Not that I was in any hurry to see her much pleasanter younger sister either. She was Medraut's mother, a boy who, if the legends could be believed, was destined to bring Arthur to his death at Camlann.

I looked back at my husband, at the muscles beneath his pale skin, at the curls of his hair on the pillow, at his naked back. So much lay between us now, unspoken, but ever present. Whatever he'd said when first he'd told me Melwas's dying words, and however I'd refuted it, the doubt still lurked within him that Melwas had spoken the truth.

In a brief four days, the gap between us had widened to a chasm.

The baby let the nipple slip out of his mouth, his lips a perfect milky rosebud. He was asleep. Gingerly, I edged out of bed again, fearful lest I woke him, and laid him back in his crib. His tiny thumb went to his mouth as I tucked the warm blankets around him. Still quietly, I tiptoed back to bed, blew out the candle, and slipped back between the warm covers.

I WOKE BEFORE Arthur in the early hours of the morning. In his sleep he'd moved closer to me, and on waking I found he'd thrown an arm across my body, his slack fingers resting on my still flabby stomach. For a few minutes I lay there relishing the contact he'd been at such pains to deprive me of the night before. Then the baby began to snuffle himself awake. With reluctance, I slithered out of bed.

I was sitting in the high-backed chair Arthur usually occupied, feeding the baby, when I became aware of being watched. I withstood the temptation to look up, and kept my gaze fixed on Amhar's determinedly working cheeks as he filled his little belly. It was early, as yet, and only the glowing embers of the brazier lit the room.

The minutes slid past. All my senses flamed with the knowledge that Arthur's eyes rested on me. In the quiet of the room, my sharp ears caught the sound of his breathing above the gentle sucking made by the baby. From the body of the hall came the noise of snarling as two hounds disputed a bone and the curse of the nearest sleepy warrior. Far off, a hopeful cockerel crowed.

"You make a pretty picture," Arthur said, an unexpected gentleness in his voice.

I raised my eyes and looked across at him.

He lay propped up on one elbow, dark hair tousled from sleep. Something stirred within me that I'd not felt for months, and with a start I recognized it as desire. How could this man, who suspected me of deceit, and whom I suspected of incest, hold such a spell over me still?

"He's hungry." It was all I could think of to say.

He pushed himself upright in bed, the covers falling to his waist. "I...I've missed seeing you like this."

Was it an apology? Did he think it would be so easy to wipe away the fact that he hadn't trusted me? That he didn't trust me still? That he'd been in Tangwyn's bed?

I stayed silent. I'd used this tactic before, and it had stood me in good stead.

He swung his long legs out of bed. "I don't want us to be like this."

I had to answer. "Neither do I."

Amhar had dozed off on the breast, and now I slid my nipple gently out of his slack mouth. He pursed his lips, eyes closed, lashes dark against his soft cheeks. For a long moment I sat cradling him in my arms before getting slowly to my feet and carrying him to his crib. This brought me close to Arthur. I bent and laid the baby in his blankets.

As I straightened up, Arthur put out a hand and caught my arm. "Talk to me, Gwen."

I turned to face him. "What about? You and Tangwyn? Or you and Medraut?" I couldn't help myself. The words just came blurting out as though I wanted to hurt him as much as he'd hurt me.

In the dim light of the brazier, I saw his eyes widen in surprise. Whether it was at one of these claims or both, I had no idea.

He bit his lip. "I haven't been with Tangwyn."

He expected me to believe that? I'd seen her strutting around the fortress, hanging about in the kitchen courtyard with Cottia's daughters, with a smug smile on her face. I resisted the gentle pressure on my arm, pulling back against him, but he didn't release me.

"You don't believe me." He sounded affronted.

How dare he accuse me of not believing him when he so plainly hadn't believed my assurances about what had happened when I'd been in Melwas's clutches at Dinas Brent?

I snapped back at him, before I could stop myself. "Just as you didn't believe me when I told you Melwas never laid a hand on me."

His hold on me tightened. He wasn't good at putting himself in the place of others. Would he realize this was tit for tat? If he didn't believe me, I wouldn't believe him.

"I did...I do." Was that contrition in his voice? If so, I'd heard it all before.

"Then where've you been these four days? All I've had for company's been Maia. Granted, she's better than you'd be at changing a wet nappy and bringing wind up, but she's no substitute for a loving husband." I paused, unable to resist a closing jibe. "That is, if you love me still."

He got to his feet. The fact that he was quite naked didn't escape me, nor the fact that he was already partially aroused. "Of course I still love you. And no, I've not been with Tangwyn these last four days. I've not been with her since before I met you. I loved her once, but it was a boy's love. It's with a man's love that I love you."

"I can see that." I indicated his arousal with a nod.

The tiniest smile slid across his face. "Look what you do to me."

"You're just a man." I could feel my resistance weakening. "All men wake up like that, and any woman can provoke such a reaction. It's not me you want, it's sex. Pure and simple."

He shook his head. "If I wanted sex I could have it where I choose. But that's not all I want. I want you." He put up the hand that didn't have hold of my arm and cupped my chin, his fingers gentle. I could smell his masculinity, a curiously heady mix of sweat and pheromones. We hadn't made love since weeks before Amhar was born. I'd been too uncomfortable. Had he really been celibate for all that time? I wanted to think he was telling me the truth.

I was softening when he spoke again, forestalling me. "What about me and Medraut?"

I stiffened. "Nothing."

"You wanted to talk to me about him. What was it?" His hand under my chin was firm, forcing me to look up into his eyes.

I bit my lip. "Nothing." I was searching for an excuse because now that he was here, in our chamber, in my bed, voicing my suspicions might ruin everything. I was afraid of what I'd do if he admitted Morgawse's baby was his, afraid of how I'd feel. If it was just a suspicion it was somehow easier to tolerate, because there was still a chance it was untrue. I'd rather it stayed that way.

"I was just worried he wouldn't be safe in Caer Legeion gwar Uisc." I took a breath. "Where were you sleeping if you weren't with Tangwyn?" Anything to change the subject.

He regarded me for a moment longer, as though he wasn't sure I'd told him the truth, and then gave me a little lopsided smile. "Where else would I be but with my brother and his wife. I was with Cei and Coventina."

Relief washed over me. He couldn't be telling me a lie, because he knew I could ask Coventina if it were true, and, because we were close friends, she wouldn't lie for him. For the first time I felt a smile trying to break through.

"Why would you think I was with Tangwyn anyway?"

I shook my head. Honesty was required here. "Because I'm stupid. Stupid and jealous. Because I saw her giving me looks of triumph. Because I don't like her being here." My words were running away with themselves. "Because you used to love her. Because I can see she thinks I've only borrowed you, and one day she's going to get you back. Because I'm fat and unattractive." I prodded my flaccid baby belly with one hand. "Because I thought you believed that madman."

I didn't know whether a woman from the fifth century would have had such insight into how she felt, but I came from the touchy-feely twenty-first century and was used to analyzing my feelings.

He took me in his arms, holding me close against his body, my face pressed against his neck, his long hair tickling my cheeks.

I breathed him in. "When you came to bed last night I thought you couldn't bear to touch me."

He had one hand in my hair, cradling my head, the feeling of his body pressed up against mine with only my thin undershirt between us intoxicating. His breath felt warm in my hair as he spoke. "I was afraid to touch you. Afraid you'd turn me away because I'd doubted you."

Feeling guilty, that's what he'd been doing. Guilty that he'd not believed me. Had those four days with his brother and the sensible Coventina made him realize I was telling the truth?

I opened my mouth. It was on the tip of my tongue to have everything out in the open and ask him about his sister and Medraut, but the coward in me beat that question back down again and I pressed my lips together to keep them under control.

He spoke, close to my ear. "Can you still love me after I doubted you like that?"

I turned my head to stare into his eyes. "I never stopped loving you. How could I? I knew it was a lie, and I never stopped hoping that at last you'd realize it. Amhar is just like Llacheu, and you." I refrained from saying he also resembled Medraut, but it was there, in my head, a little nagging thought, jumping up and down like the child at the back of the class trying to get the teacher's attention.

"I love you, Gwen." He bent his head toward mine, our lips

less than an inch apart, his breath warm on my cheeks. "Can you forgive me for doubting you?"

Could I? For a brief moment I wondered if I actually could. Then common sense took over. I had to say I could. If I told him I couldn't, where would we be? I'd be sleeping alone and somehow Tangwyn would worm her way back into his affections. My life here would never be the same again. It wasn't an easy life, and now it was even harder, but it was the life I'd chosen that day on the Tor. I'd chosen Arthur, for better or worse, as the modern wedding vows go, so unlike the ones we'd taken. He'd made me his queen, and I had to behave like one.

Suddenly I felt sure of my answer. "Yes," I said, moving my hand up to the back of his head and pulling him toward me. Our lips met, I curved my body into his, luxuriating in the closeness and the warmth. He drew me down onto the bed with him, and I went willingly.

Chapter Three

"I'VE GOT SOME exciting news." Coventina, my friend and sister-in-law, was sitting on the cushion-covered wooden bench in my bedchamber. Outside, a November gale was blowing, and little draughts kept finding their way in under the eaves or through the cracks in the shutters and doors. The candlelight we were working by guttered unhelpfully, and with a sigh of resignation I set down the little bonnet I'd been painstakingly stitching for Amhar, my fingers sore from poking the needle through the linen.

"Have you?" I sucked my right thumb, by far the worst affected digit. "What is it then? Don't keep me waiting."

We'd been sewing together for the last hour, and I'd been aware from the start that some sort of secret bubbled in my friend's heart. From the expression on her homely face, it was a good one, so I'd kept quiet and waited for her to say something.

She also set down her work, a new shirt for Rhiwallon, her son, who was sprouting upwards like a weed, outgrowing his clothes as fast as she could make them. Her hazel eyes met mine, a shine in them – the twinkle of a secret she was longing to share.

"I'm with child."

A smile slid over my face. "That's wonderful news!" Rhiwallon was eleven now, and as far as I knew there'd been no other babies, not even ones who'd died. She'd been particularly attentive of Amhar when he was born, and kind to me in my pregnancy, so her news overjoyed me. "How far along are you?"

"Mother Donella did say I'd passed the danger time." She put her hands protectively over her still flat belly. "She reckons the babby'll be born about Beltane. I didn't want to tell anyone until I could be sure I'd not lose this one, like the rest. I didn't even tell Cei till last night."

She was my friend, and yet there was so much I didn't know about her. "You lost a baby? Babies?"

She nodded, the light in her eyes fading. "More than I'd like to say. All before this stage though. Nothing like babbies, they weren't. I've seen a still-born child at full term, and a babby born a few months too soon, and they all looked like babbies. But the mess that came out of me all those times was wrong – it didn't look like a babby at all. Like there were something not right about them." She had a lovely burr to her voice, where the accent of her birth and upbringing hadn't quite been erased by her years of marriage to a lord.

How to give her a human biology lesson?

Jumping straight in seemed a good idea. "They don't start to look like babbies – I mean babies – for quite a while. About now, your baby looks a bit like any baby animal does, but in another few weeks you'd really be able to see it was a tiny human."

She looked surprised. "How d'you know this, then?"

I patted her hand. "I learned about it in school – in Gaul." Gaul was my go-to for anything I knew or said that didn't match with the world I'd landed in a year ago. My bras and knickers were "Gaulish fashion", handstitched here by Cottia's daughters, my riding astride in boy's clothes, a Gaulish habit, the stirrups I'd introduced, a Gaulish invention. If I met anyone who knew Gaul well, I could amend it to somewhere further afield, like Rome, or maybe even Byzantium.

Coventina smiled. "My goodness, you're the cleverest person I know."

I shook my head. "Not where I come from." A particularly strong gust of wind rattled the shutters, and rain pattered against them like a hail of pebbles. Barely two weeks had passed since Samhain, and already winter had set in.

I fingered the little bonnet, with its tiny spots of blood from where I'd impaled my fingers. "I'm useless at sewing for a start."

She laughed. "That's because no one ever taught you when you was – *were* young. I think you must've been too busy with learning all about medicines and people's bodies." Her face grew wistful. "Where I grew up, I had to learn to do everything on the farm. I milked the cows, fed the pigs, drove the cows out to pasture, collected the eggs, cooked the meals with my mother, helped my father plough and weed, and harvest the wheat and barley. I learned to make bread and slaughter chickens, how to keep house, and..." she paused, "...sew clothes."

My turn to smile. Over in his crib, Amhar stirred. I froze, listening, but then he fell silent again, falling back into whatever dreams a baby so young might have.

"If you were a farmer's daughter so busy with all those chores, how did you meet Cei?" I kept my voice down low for fear of waking the baby.

Her hazel eyes glazed over dreamily. She very much loved her big, bluff, red-headed husband, and he doted on her. "My father farmed just to the north of Viroconium. One day, two boys came riding past our farmhouse, all done up in fine tunics, they was – *were* – on horses the like of which I'd never seen. I was working outside fixing the pig pen when I saw them. My hair was all of a mess, and I wasn't at my cleanest or my sweetest smelling." She gave a little chuckle at the memory. "I was only fourteen then, and Cei no older, but he saw himself as a fine warrior already. He asked me for refreshment, as is the due of any lord from the men who farm their lands, but with a friendly smile."

How feudal.

"I went and fetched my ma, and she came out with a jug of fine cider for both the boys, and we found they'd dismounted."

If Cei had been only fourteen, then Arthur could have been

no more than eleven. Hunger to learn more of Arthur's life before I met him, and her reminiscences of their childhood, held me rapt.

"Cei was so handsome, even then, with that fine head of red hair." She gave a little shrug. "I think I fell in love with him right then and there."

"What about Arthur? It was him with Cei, wasn't it? What was he like?" I knew very little of Arthur's childhood save that his mother had abandoned him when he'd been only seven years old.

She nodded. "It were – I mean it *was* Arthur." Sometimes she slipped back into the speech of her days as a farmer's daughter. "He was nothing but a little slip of a lad. Ten or eleven at most. But my goodness, he was polite. I had no idea he was the High King's son, a prince, nor that Cei was his brother. If I had, I'd've been tongue-tied, for sure. I wasn't used, back then, to mixing with royalty."

"How did you end up married to him?"

Leaning back, probably to ease her belly, she sighed. "After that, Cei came many times to our farm, sometimes with Arthur but often as not without. And I found every excuse I could to sneak away to meet him on my own. One thing did lead to another, of course. He was a lusty young warrior, and I just a girl in love with him. I knew all about what happens if you let a man have his way with you; I was a farmgirl, don't forget. But that didn't stop me."

A little chuckle bubbled up, probably at the memory of their illicit liaisons. "When I was too pregnant to hide it any longer, I went and told my ma. The next time Cei came a-calling my parents had a good talk to him. They knew he was a lord, so they didn't expect much. But they told him they wanted the best for me now I was carrying his child." A smile lit her face. "I think they thought he'd try and deny it, but he were thrilled."

She ran her hands over her belly, smiling to herself. "He said he'd stand by me and ask his stepfather for a house in the city for him and me to live in – together, like. That didn't happen, though. I ended up with him in the palace. It did shock me, for sure. I'd never seen the city before, never mind the palace. It was so big, with so many people everywhere, and so much noise. The High King was proper angry with Cei. He shouted at him a lot about not taking advantage of country girls. I was terrified. I just wanted to go home to my da's farm, but Cei stood his ground, young though he was. The old King finally gave in. He said I could share Cei's room in the palace with him. That's where Rhiwallon was born."

I'd always imagined she was a local girl from somewhere near Din Cadan. Why had I never thought to ask about her past?

"And did you come to Din Cadan with Cei when Arthur was sent here?"

She shook her head. "No, we came before that. Cei's three years older than Arthur, don't forget. The High King sent him here to serve Prince Geraint. He had charge of Din Cadan back then, afore Llongborth, of course. He was a son to the king's sister, I b'lieve. Some sort of relation, at any rate."

That name rang a bell. Hadn't Llacheu played at being Prince Geraint on the day I'd first met him? Hadn't one of the other boys pointed out that Geraint had died?

I had to ask. "What happened to Prince Geraint?"

Coventina pulled a wry face. "Rhiwallon were – was – but a year old when we came to Din Cadan. Cei was to join the warband what patrolled the south coast. We decided to wed, because if he fell in battle, there'd be care for me and his son. If we weren't wed, there'd be nothing."

A rudimentary welfare state. How forward thinking of this unknown Prince Geraint.

"The Prince got word of a huge landing of Saxons to the southeast, so he led out his army, and Cei went with him, and Arthur too. He'd marched his father's men south from Viroconium, though he were nothing but a boy. I think his father and Cadwy were off somewhere else, fighting. Geraint and Arthur met the Saxons at Llongborth. Cei did tell me as it was a sheltered harbor with an old Roman fort beside it."

Could she mean Portsmouth harbor and Portchester castle? That was the only Roman fort with a sheltered harbor I could think of to the southeast of Din Cadan. I'd visited its impressive waterside location as a child with Artie and my father.

Coventina continued. "It was a great battle. Cei told me about it after. But the Prince were – was – sore wounded. He kept fighting on, undaunted, but by nightfall when the battle was over, he was dead. He was a hero. Folk still tell tales of his bravery 'round their hearth fires at night. I'm surprised you've never heard one."

Arthur couldn't have been more than fourteen. A child in the eyes of the twenty-first century, but in this one, a man ready for blooding in battle. A sobering thought. My eyes slid sideways to where Amhar still slept. How short a time it would be before he, too, rode away from me to fight some distant battle. Maybe never to return.

With a little shake, as if to dispel the memory, Coventina picked up the shirt that lay discarded in her lap. "I don't know why I'm bothering with embroidering it – it'll be too small for him before spring comes. He do sprout like a weed in shit."

I nodded. "And I'm so slow at stitching, Amhar will be ready for his first wooden sword before I've done this pesky bonnet." We both laughed together about our sons, as women no doubt have done throughout history, stitching on in companiable silence for a while. Every so often I was forced to swear under my breath as I pricked yet another finger, which made Coventina chuckle. Perhaps it acted as a distraction for her, stopping her from wondering if this new child would make it through the crucial six months more that lay ahead of it.

She looked what she was – a hard-working farmer's daughter. Tall, and not classically beautiful, she possessed an air of deep calm and quiet that I found immensely soothing. The itch to unburden myself of the worries I had about Arthur grew stronger.

Eventually, my tongue loosened. "Do you think Arthur would ever go back to Tangwyn?" A reasonable place to start.

Coventina raised her eyes from the neat sewing job she was making of Rhiwallon's shirt, needle poised in hand, brows raised in surprise. "Would it bother you?"

My turn to be surprised. "Of course it would." Was I guilty of trying to impress my twenty-first-century viewpoint onto marriage in the fifth? Maybe they looked upon fidelity differently, for a man, of course. With more lenience. I licked lips that had suddenly gone dry, nervous at what her reply might be. "He was with her a long time. And they have Llacheu between them. He must have loved her since he wasn't much more than a boy. That's a big tie for any man."

She poked her needle haphazardly into the shirt so as not to lose it and set the garment down in her lap. "You're right. A child is a big tie. And the years do add another. But Arthur has always been a faithful man, I think. No, I'm sure. Not many men are so."

True. Even in the twenty-first century men had difficulty keeping it in their pants.

"But would he ever be drawn back to her, d'you think?"

Coventina shrugged. "Who can say? But I do know that when he was with her he was ever faithful."

"Really?" I thought about the brothel at Caer Luit Coyt run by a fat madam called Lucretia and was doubtful. "How do you know?"

"Because Cei told me so."

If I remembered correctly, Cei had gone off very willingly into that brothel, and so had Arthur. And Merlin. I'd been disappointed in their morals, one and all. "He never strayed? Not in all the time he was with her?"

She smiled. "I know that's most unusual in a man, but 'tis true. Cei swears it. He told me Tangwyn was his brother's first love. I do doubt very much if he's had any other women but you and her."

That was a surprise of monumental proportions. I'd never

27

asked him, of course, but I'd always thought he'd been like his brother Cei or his friend Theodoric, finding succor in any place with whatever women happened to be available. It was quite a shock to discover he had less experience than I had.

But what about Morgawse? Could I pose the questions I had about her and her son to my friend? Where would Coventina's loyalties lie in this? She'd only known me for a short year, but she'd been with Cei for more than twelve and known Arthur all that time. Best not to raise the subject.

Instead, I chose a topic that had been bubbling under the surface of my mind for several weeks. "Do you think it might be a good idea to get Tangwyn married off?"

Coventina narrowed her eyes in thought, her brow wrinkling as if she were weighing up her answer carefully. "That might be a good move." She gave me a wry smile. "Especially if you're concerned about her presence. The one to ask about that is Merlin. He has the king's ear, and if he suggests it rather than you, I think Arthur would see it as a sensible move rather than you acting out of jealousy."

"Hmmm." I mulled this over in my head for a few moments. "I see what you mean. So, if Merlin brings it up it would be better than me doing so. That's a really good idea."

I picked up the bonnet again, with reluctance, and turned the subject away from myself. "Cei must be very pleased he's to be a father again."

She nodded, but I could tell from her expression she was holding something back.

"What's wrong? Isn't he as pleased as you would have hoped?"

Her brow furrowed further. "Of course he's pleased, but he's upset as well. He knows how many babbies I've not been able to keep, that have slipped away from me. We both know that this time I've gone past the point where I lost the others, but he can't help but worry for me. He can't let himself be happy about this one, because he fears another child isn't meant for us."

Cei was a big softy with a heart of gold so I could see why he might worry for his wife now she was finally pregnant again. Men. What she really needed was support and someone to tell her everything would be all right. So that was what I did.

Chapter Four

T HE WINTER DREW out long and cold. Snow fell several times, once keeping everyone trapped within the fortress for ten long days. And when it didn't snow, it rained every day, or that was what it felt like. The warriors grew bored with inaction and many nights in the great hall the cider and wine loosened their inhibitions so much they became roaring drunk, often ending with a fight.

The blazing hearth fire made the hall cozy, but our chamber was less so thanks to the draughts which sneaked in through every crack. Maia hung tapestries over the window shutters, but when the gale howled even they weren't enough. Fearful for our baby, Arthur ordered a second brazier brought in to keep the cold at bay, and I began to seriously worry about carbon monoxide poisoning.

"How can what we breathe have body?" he asked, when I tried explaining to him the things that air was made of – and how dangerous it could be.

Unfortunately, I wasn't my brother, who'd studied physics, and trying to explain about invisible atoms to someone who steadfastly refused to believe what I was saying brought me to a grinding halt. "Because it is," I finished with. "We can't see them, like we can't see God. We just have to believe in them, like we do in God."

He raised a quizzical eyebrow at me and chuckled, shaking

his head as though I was some sort of madwoman to be humored.

Amhar, oblivious to the threats to his health, blossomed into a chubby, happy baby with a mop of dark curls just like his father's. His appearance gladdened my heart. Even though, twice now, Arthur had reassured me of his trust, instinct told me that had Amhar shown any tendency not to look like his father, the doubt would rise again. My own suspicions about Medraut stayed where I'd put them, hidden at the back of my mind, shut away in a locked compartment. For now.

Spring came early that year. Down on the plain, beneath the spreading oaks and ashes where the farmers grazed their pigs in autumn, bluebells carpeted the glades. The soft yellow of primroses and brighter hues of cowslips followed swiftly on, then pink campion, purple violets, small white stitchwort, and the deep blue of forget-me-nots. Every field bank burgeoned in a mass of spring flowers, and every tree branch blushed fresh green with the arrival of the leaf buds.

With the spring weather, a messenger arrived from Arthur's cousin Caninus in Caer Went, informing him that a Council of Kings would be called in Viroconium after the Beltane celebrations finished.

Understandably, Arthur wasn't keen to go. "I can't sit down at the round table and speak civilly with Cadwy. Not after what he did last year." He pounded the table with his fist, making the unlucky messenger cower. "I won't go."

It took the combined efforts of Cei and Merlin to calm him down and convince him it would be best to put aside his anger and accept the invitation.

Merlin had the best argument. "By not going, you play into Cadwy's hands. He wants your absence, and he'll use it against you." His was the voice of reason. Arthur listened, but with reluctance.

I had a suspicion, however, that wanting to see Morgana again might be partly behind Merlin's words. I'd not forgotten the looks of longing he'd given her on the few occasions I'd seen them together. That she didn't reciprocate his feelings had been fairly evident. Morgana was one of the most beautiful women I'd ever seen, with her pale, perfectly oval face, dark eyes and raven tresses that reached her waist.

But that didn't stop her being an out-and-out cold-hearted bitch, and probably a witch as well, with her rumored magical powers and gift of the Sight. If I was prepared to believe such things existed. I certainly wouldn't have been eighteen months ago.

Beltane came, with the ritual fires and the driving of the cattle between them to secure fertility for the coming year. A fair number of the newly married young women also ran between the fires to the ribald comments of their friends. In the greening fields all around the fortress, the sheep dropped their lambs, and out on the horse pastures, mares foaled. A feeling of fecundity hung about the land as it basked in unusually mild weather for this time of the year.

Despite Bretta's curse, Amhar continued to flourish, much to my relief. At eight months old he could already crawl across the furs in our chamber and pull himself up on the sparse furniture, much to Arthur's obvious delight. "Look at my son. Already as strong as a young bear," he said to anyone who'd listen.

"My son too," I muttered under my breath every time I heard him. After all, it was my milk making him grow like that.

By the time Beltane lay behind us, I'd almost succeeded in forgetting how I'd doubted my husband and he'd doubted me. The way he seemed to have bonded with our child gave me a warm feeling in my stomach and around my heart.

Arthur was often away from Din Cadan, though. Since early spring he'd been riding south or west to patrol the coast for days on end, taking with him his now highly trained warriors. This threw me together with the women of the fortress – amongst them Coventina, now proudly displaying her enormous baby bump and daily expecting to go into labor. No precise dates for deliveries in the Dark Ages – only rough guesses.

On a bright day just after Beltane, with the scorched rings left by the twin bonfires still evident in front of the hall, I finally approached Merlin on the subject of Tangwyn. She'd been flouncing around outside the hall again, presumably hoping to catch Arthur's eye, and looking annoyingly provocative in a low-cut gown, when she should have been attending to whatever work it was she had to do. There's only so much open rivalry a girl can take.

Merlin was sitting on the wall-walk in the sun, long legs dangling over the edge, heels kicking idly against the earthen bank as he whittled away on a piece of wood. Mustering my determination, I climbed the steps, approached along the wooden walkway and sat down beside him.

He looked up from his whittling, a knowing expression in his brown eyes and for a moment I suspected he knew why I'd sought him out.

That was just fanciful, though. How could he know? I pointed at the clean white wood exposed by his whittling. "What are you making?"

He held it up for me to see. "A whistle. Llacheu has a new hound pup. He asked me to make him a whistle like the one Rhiwallon has for his dog."

I kicked my booted feet against the earth bank below the wall-walk just as he was. "He'll be pleased." Now that I was here, it was hard to start a conversation that would take the route I wanted.

I twiddled my fingers in my lap, feeling awkward. "Do you like Tangwyn?"

He raised his brows. "I've not thought about it."

"Well, think about it now, please." The wind had snatched some strands of hair from my thick plait, and I had to push them out of my eyes.

He smiled. "Do *you* like her?" How typical of him to answer my question with another question.

Honesty would be the best policy. "No." There wasn't much else to say.

He nodded, as though he knew why and elaboration wasn't required. Putting the whistle down on the wall-walk's weathered boards, he looked away from me, over the jumbled buildings that made up the fortress, clustering over the rise toward the great bulk of the hall on the summit. "Does she bother you?"

I studied his profile. His young-old face had been tanned by wind and sun, with little lines around his eyes that might have been from laughter or from peering into the bright distance as he was doing right now. He had a long, straight nose and a thin mouth over a firm chin. His brown hair blew out behind him, the beads that someone had plaited into it rattling.

I nodded. "Yes, she does." I paused to consider my next words. "She's always around. Always in the corner of my eye. I can see she wants Arthur back in her bed. You should see what she had on yesterday before he rode off toward Caer Durnac." The picture of her rose in my mind – her auburn hair loose about her shoulders, her dress exposing more than half of her breasts, her cat's eyes smoldering as she paraded in front of the Great Hall where Arthur and his men were mounting up.

Merlin turned his head to look at me. "You're that insecure?"

I was taken aback. Was I insecure? Well, yes, I must be. The realization was painful. "I just don't like her always being there." My voice sounded petulant, even to me.

"He wouldn't go back to her." He sounded sure – as sure as Coventina had been.

I nodded. "But I'd like her married off, so she's got a man of her own to tend to and won't spend all her time mooning over mine."

He laughed. "Maybe you're right. Maybe it's about time she had a man of her own. She's been without one for going on a year and a half now. I'll speak to Arthur about it."

"Don't tell him it was me suggested it." I was anxious not to be associated with any of this, for fear she'd try and wreak revenge on me. From the looks she'd given me, I felt pretty sure she hated me. So, what with her and Bretta, that was two too many enemies to cope with.

I studied my boots for a while, spattered with dirt and scuffed as they were.

Merlin had picked up the whistle again, but it lay untouched in his hands still. "There's something else bothering you?"

Dared I ask him? My heart began to thump.

He smiled. "You can tell me."

"Can I though?"

He frowned. "You can tell me anything."

I pursed my lips and sighed. "You'll be shocked."

His eyebrows rose. "I don't think I will. Nothing much could shock me anymore. Whatever it is, I'll understand. Try me."

I licked my lips. So often I'd been on the verge of voicing my suspicions and shied away from doing so. But Merlin was right – he might understand. He might be the only person who could. "You know my father studied everything about the Arthurian legends?"

He nodded.

"Well, when I was a child, he read them to me. That was why I could tell you about the sword in the stone. Which you then made happen. I don't know if you doing that was something always meant to be, or if I changed history by telling you that story. I have no way of knowing if any of the stories I know are true, and I don't want to help them happen if they shouldn't." I hesitated. "And some of the stories aren't so...pleasant."

His eyes sharpened. "And there's one of these that has you stirred up?"

I nodded, slowly this time, the words clogging my throat. "There's one in particular...one that I don't want to believe can be true."

"Go on."

It felt as if I were betraying Arthur by putting my suspicions into words. "That Medraut is his son, not Theo's." There, I'd said it. I couldn't look Merlin in the eye after that, so fixed my gaze back on my boots.

A silence stretched between us. A lark called. Dogs barked over amongst the buildings. Children's laughter carried on a breeze that smelled faintly of the nearest rotting midden.

Merlin burst out laughing.

I forgot myself and raised my eyes to stare at him. What did he find so funny about this?

He put a firm hand on my arm. "That's a story that just can't be true." His eyes danced. "Physically impossible. Arthur's been here at Din Cadan since he was fifteen years old. When he left Viroconium, Morgawse was nothing but a child, with her mother in Din Tagel. She returned to Viroconium just before she married Theo. The first time Arthur saw her since their childhood was when you met her at the Council of Kings and helped deliver her son. If someone other than Theo's that boy's father, it's definitely not Arthur."

Heat shot up my cheeks. Why hadn't I thought of that? All this time I'd been fretting about a story that had probably been invented by some medieval pervert. I felt like slapping myself. It gave me hope that perhaps the story of Medraut one day rising in rebellion against his uncle might also be untrue.

BEFORE ANY WEDDING plans for Tangwyn could be made, something else occurred to take my mind off her behavior around my husband.

Only a couple of days after I'd spoken with Merlin, when Arthur and Cei were still absent in the direction of Caer Durnac, I walked down to the practice grounds to watch the boys fighting. I'd not been there long, sitting on the top rail of one of the horse pens, before Tulac, Llacheu's body slave, came barreling down the slope. His long arms and legs flailed like a windmill as he ran, and his face shone with the news he bore.

"Milady," he cried before he even reached me, his breath coming in pants. "Milady, the Lady Coventina's maid did send me for ye. She told me to say her lady's time is come."

The long-anticipated baby was coming at last. My heart did a little leap of excitement for Coventina, who'd been awaiting this day with growing anxiety for the last month, and staggering around the fortress looking as though she'd swallowed a hippopotamus. I glanced back toward where Rhiwallon and Llacheu were engaged in battling with staves with the other boys, the crack of wood on wood loud in the stillness of the day. Then I hitched up my skirts and ran after Tulac.

He must have been all of fourteen now and taller than me, with longer legs and no skirts to slow him down. I found him difficult to keep up with.

I reached Cei's house, gasping for breath, just as Donella, the midwife, arrived. Arthur had procured her for the fortress before Amhar was born, after I'd complained about the disreputable and uninspiring state of the incumbent. Her haste had flushed her face to a glowing pink that probably matched my own.

A small woman, she'd scraped her greying hair so severely back from her face it gave her features a slightly stretched appearance. A poor woman's face lift. But she was clean, the most important thing, and we'd had far fewer complications following on from births she'd assisted at.

"Milady." She bobbed a little bow, and I nodded back to her, as was the custom. "Ye've come to aid with the lying in?"

"I have indeed." I pushed open the door of Cei's house, and we went inside together.

As the king's brother, Cei owned one of the largest houses in the fortress. Oblong in shape, with a low thatched roof, inside, a latticed wall divided it into two. The daily living space, where Rhiwallon and the servants slept, took up roughly two thirds of the space, the other third being Cei and Coventina's chamber.

We found Coventina in the living area, wearing only her thin linen shift and leaning heavily on the table. Her maid, Keelia, an older woman accustomed to bearing children, was engaged in rubbing her back sympathetically. Her own latest baby, still only a month old, lay sleeping peacefully in a wicker basket beside the hearth.

"How goes it?" Donella asked, setting her basket down on the table and turning to the mother-to-be.

"Not well." Coventina spoke between clenched teeth. "'Tis not like I remember with Rhiwallon. I woke up this morning with a pain in my back and thought nothing of it. I've had back pains these last four months. I thought this were nothing more than the same again. But after breakfast, the pain grew worse, and Keelia said we should send for you. We'd just got hold of Tulac when my waters broke." She fell silent, her hands gripping the tabletop, knuckles whitening, as a pain washed over her. Fluid spattered onto the paving slabs beneath her feet.

Keelia spoke instead. "'Tis too much too soon." She rubbed her mistress's back in consternation. "And I think my mistress have grown too large." With her spare hand she indicated the mound of Coventina's belly, scarcely disguised by the drapes of her linen shift.

Donella took charge. "That's as may be. Into her chamber and let me have a feel of her belly."

When Coventina's contraction had passed, we all escorted her into the bedchamber, and, with difficulty, she lowered herself onto the bed. Donella raised the shift to feel her belly with strong but gentle hands. I remembered her doing this for me before Amhar was born, and the confident way she'd assured me everything would be all right. Surely it would be the same this time.

However, there was none of this now. Instead, she fixed her gaze on Keelia. "Fetch my basket and set water to boil. I fear we'll have to help this babby into the world. He feels a large one and I don't believe his head be where it should be."

"What can I do?" I asked, anxious to help.

Donella looked me up and down for a moment, as though searching in her head for something I would not damage. "Hold her hand, Milady."

Thus relegated to support staff, an undeniable relief, I did as I was told, pulling a low stool up to the head of the bed and taking Coventina's hand in mine. I was good at this. I'd done it before.

A pain came upon her again, and her grip on my hand increased, but she didn't utter a single sound, her face reddening, her eyes squeezed tight shut. I searched for something supportive to say. But, "It'll soon be over" sounded feeble when it came out of my mouth, and I rather wished it unsaid.

Coventina gave me a weak smile. "We both know it won't be," she whispered. "But I do think as how I've forgotten how bad it was. Or I might have thought twice before I let Cei anywhere near me."

I smiled encouragement. "I felt exactly the same when I was giving birth to Amhar. I even asked Donella to go and tell Arthur if he wanted sex again he'd have to get it elsewhere. She didn't. I think she's probably used to women saying these things when they're in labor."

Donella gave me a conspiratorial smile.

"Here it comes again." Coventina's face screwed up tightly and her grip on my hand became almost unbearable.

I stood it bravely, knowing how much worse the pain must be for her. Although a lot of the suffering of giving birth had faded in my mind, seeing her face contort like that brought it all back with a vengeance. "Squeeze as tight as you like."

"No need to keep silent," Donella said, running a soothing hand over Coventina's furrowed brow. "Let it all out if ye want to, my fine girl."

The pain passed, her grip on my hand lessened, and I settled onto the stool more comfortably. If her labor was anything like mine had been, this would be a long day.

I was right. It was a very long day.

Coventina went on getting pains that I estimated were only

about two minutes apart all morning. After a bit, Donella and Keelia got her up off the bed and made her walk up and down the bedchamber, supported on either side as she could barely stand. All I could do was watch in mute sympathy as every couple of minutes she bent double with pain and had to stand still while it was upon her. Yet, agonizing as it must have been, she still uttered no sound.

Donella's face grew more and more worried as the day progressed. Every so often she had a feel of Coventina's stomach, her brow furrowed with concern. While she let Coventina sit for a while on the wooden stool they'd brought in expressly for the birthing, she and Keelia went off toward the door and spoke together in hushed whispers that I couldn't catch and didn't like.

It must have been late afternoon when Coventina finally collapsed to the floor, too exhausted by the pains and the walking to take another step.

Donella went down on her knees beside her. "'Tis walking that'll bring this babby." She took Coventina's hand. "'Tis a big one, and it'll not come without it."

Coventina raised her head, her eyes shadowed with pain and suffering. "I can't." Her voice was scarcely above a strained whisper. "I'm too tired."

Donella's and Keelia's eyes met above her head, and for the first time I saw fear in them.

"Let her lie on the bed," I said in a hurry. "If she's tired let her rest a minute or two. You've been walking her for hours."

It took all three of us to get her onto the bed. When we'd done it, I took Donella's arm and drew her toward the door, leaving Keelia soothing her mistress's brow with a damp cloth.

"What is it?" I kept my voice low. "Why isn't the baby coming? I can see something's wrong by the look on your face. Tell me."

Donella's lips made a thin line before she spoke. "The baby's not down ready to be birthed. I can feel his head but 'tis overly large, I suspicion. The head needs to come down into the birth canal and it's not done that. I do think as it's too big to do that."

All the episodes of *Call the Midwife* that I'd seen crowded into my head, but I didn't think there'd been one where this had happened to the mother.

"If it can't be born, then she'll die, won't she?" It was a stupid question, but I needed to ask it.

Donella nodded. "If a babby can't be born, the mother do always die. Oft times the babby as well."

The cold hand of fate ran down my backbone. This was one of the outcomes I'd feared with my own pregnancy. Luck had favored me. I'd assumed that with a second baby Coventina would be safe from danger. She'd already done this once. Her pelvis had allowed a baby through before, but this time, by some cruel quirk of nature, her baby's head had grown too big to pass through. It seemed it hadn't even been able to engage.

"Is there nothing you can do?"

She gave the smallest shake of her head. "She's weakening fast now. It won't be long. This babby's going to kill 'er."

If only I'd become a nurse or doctor instead of a librarian. I might have been able to do a Caesarean section for her and save both her and her baby. If only.

"You're just going to let them both die? Without doing anything?" My voice came out as a hiss.

She shrugged her shoulders. What was there she could do? I glanced back at the bed where my friend lay, ashen faced, her breathing shallow, the great mound of her belly rising up like some horrible monster that was killing her from the inside. Surely there must be something we could do to save her?

Suddenly in dire need of fresh air, I opened the door and stepped out into the living area of the house. The fire smoldered in the hearth, and smoke curled about the rafters. I hurried to the outer door and opening it, stood there breathing in the fresh clean air.

I must have stood for some time, because eventually Donella came to find me.

"Ye'd best come in an' sit with her. It might bring her some comfort."

Determination gripped me. "Do you know what a Caesarean Section is?"

Donella's brow furrowed, and she shook her head.

I took a deep breath, acutely aware of my total lack of knowledge. "It's when you cut into the mother's belly and take the baby out." I swallowed. "We could save the baby, and if we're lucky, we might just save Coventina too."

Donella's eyes widened. "I've taken a baby like that afore, but never saved the mother. D'ye think we could do it? Do they do it in Gaul?"

I nodded. "Yes, they do it in Gaul." How hard could it be? The baby's location was pretty obvious. We'd have to be careful cutting, and keep everything clean if we meant to sew the wound up afterwards. We had no alternative. "We have to try."

We went back inside together.

A sheen of sweat covered Coventina's face and her hair stuck to her brow in damp tendrils. "Gwen!" she raised her hand, and I came and sat beside the bed and took her hand in mine. She was my friend. Tears stung my eyes.

"Where is Cei? Where is my husband?"

"With Arthur." If only he were here. Without him to make a decision, responsibility for this fell to me. "Don't you remember? They went south toward Caer Durnac because there were reports of Saxon pirates raiding along the coast. He'll be back soon. You'll see. Everything will be all right when they get back. Donella and I are going to try to help you." I bit my lip. "This baby's too big to be born naturally. We're going to cut into your belly and take him out that way." Her eyes flew wide in consternation, and I gripped her hand tighter. "Don't worry – they do this all the time...in Gaul."

Another pain racked her body, and a tiny whimper of suffering escaped her lips. She'd been so brave for so long. This was unfair.

The pain passed and her eyes focused on me again. "If I'm not here when my husband returns, tell him for me that I love him. Please."

My breath caught in my throat. "Nonsense. You'll be here. I won't let anything happen to you. I promise." I raised my eyes to meet Donella's on the far side of the bed.

The midwife turned to Keelia. "Fetch spirits. The lady'll need to feel as little as possible, and we'll need them to cleanse the wound to keep infection out."

Keelia hurried into the living area of the house. A few moments later she returned with a large earthenware bottle and a bowl. Donella took the bung out of it, sniffed the contents and nodded, her jaw set determinedly. "Get your mistress to drink a good deal of that if you can." She turned back to me.

She lowered her voice. "Cutting her may well finish her off, but you're right. We have to try something, or we'll lose them both. Come along. Get those clean sheets to lie her on."

I'd once read a historical novel in which someone did an emergency Caesarean, and I'd watched all the episodes of *Call the Midwife*, but that was as far as my knowledge extended. With my heart beating wildly in my throat, I helped Donella prepare a clean area to perform the operation.

"I 'ave me knives," she said, taking them from the roll of tools she'd brought in her basket and dunking them in the bowl of spirits Keelia had poured. "They're good 'n' sharp." Needles and thread joined the knives in the bowl. At least she now knew more about how infection could get into a wound thanks to me.

Coventina reached out and caught Donella's hand with her free one. "I don't care if it kills me. Save my baby. Save my child for me. For my husband. Don't let me die in vain."

Donella patted her hand. "We'll do our best not to kill ye or the babby, Milady. Be assured o' that."

Standing by the door, Keelia wrung her bony hands, tears streaming down her puffy cheeks. But this was not the moment for histrionics. I squeezed Coventina's hand. "Don't worry. We'll save your child." Hard to keep the tremble out of my voice.

But of course, I was terrified. We were about to carry out an operation on a woman who was wide awake. A woman who would die if we didn't try this, yes, but one who would feel every excruciating cut. A woman who was my dearest friend here in Din Cadan.

Doubt at what we were doing washed over me. I'd only done a first aid course, and Donella was barely one step better than a village wise woman. A severe case of the blind leading the blind. My insides knotted themselves in fear and trepidation.

But I didn't move. I held Coventina's hand in mine, her long fingers clasped tightly within my own. She'd closed her eyes and I hoped she might have lost consciousness, but as Donella approached with the knife, they came open again and for a moment went wide with fear.

"Look at me." I spoke automatically, and her gaze flicked to meet mine. "Don't look at Donella. Look at me."

She gave the ghost of a smile. "Will you sing to me?"

This was something strictly between the two of us. She liked my songs. And I liked teaching them to her. She didn't know, but they were the songs that linked me back to my own time. The music I'd liked to listen to as a child and teenager. The songs I remembered my mother listening to. I nodded, blinking back tears.

"Sing to me about the Chevy." Her voice had thickened as the alcohol took hold.

I bit back the tears and cleared my throat, never taking my eyes from Coventina's. I began to sing her favorite song, my voice wavering with sorrow. The words of "American Pie" grew stronger as I gained confidence. I sang louder, staring down at my best friend, willing her to be able to bear this.

Out of the corner of my eye I saw Donella making the cuts, her quick hands grasping, pulling, wrenching the baby out. Coventina's eyes had closed, perhaps mercifully. I went on singing. The song came to its end.

As it referred to a day of death, perhaps not such a good choice, but it was Coventina's favorite, even though she had no idea what either a levée or a Chevy were. She thought it came from Gaul.

Her hand slackened in mine. She'd lost consciousness. Her chest barely rose and fell. For a long moment silence filled the room, then the baby cried, loud and lusty, announcing its presence with vigor.

I turned my head. Donella was wrapping the baby in a blanket. "A fine daughter for Milord Cei," she said and passed the baby into Keelia's waiting hands.

Now able to let go of Coventina's slack grip, I rinsed my own hands in the alcohol and helped Donella as she carefully stitched up first Coventina's womb, after she'd removed the afterbirth, and then the layers of muscle on her abdomen. All we could do after that was wait and see if she woke up or not.

Chapter Five

ARTHUR, CEI AND their warband returned to the fortress three days later. Coventina had not died in the aftermath of her non-anaesthetized operation, nor even, by a miracle, had much of a fever, and was able to sit up in bed and feed her baby herself by then, although her belly was very sore. However, she was by no means out of the woods yet.

Llacheu came running to find me as soon as the lookout spotted his father's warriors breasting the southern hills, and I passed Amhar into Maia's capable hands. With Llacheu, who was well aware of what had happened to his aunt, I emerged to stand in front of the hall.

The day was warm, the sky dotted with white clouds, and larks sang high above our heads. A faint whiff of rotting rubbish from the fortress middens tickled my nostrils, mixed with the almost sweet smell of horse dung in the stables. The smell of home.

The main double gates of the fortress swung open beneath the wall-walk, and Arthur rode through on his grey mare, Llamrei. A moment passed and Cei was beside him, helmetless, his mane of red hair standing out like a fiery beacon. Behind them, the rest of the warriors entered the fortress, sunlight glimmering on their chainmail and the bosses on their wooden shields, as they rode up the slope toward the stables.

I walked down to meet them, Llacheu still by my side, stuck

as if by glue.

I had no trouble spotting Arthur, with his almost white horse, amongst the milling warriors. He swung down from the saddle and turned, his eyes scanning the crowd as though searching. Spotting me, his dirty, unshaven face broke into a wide grin. But the smile died as he saw the serious look in my eyes.

"Amhar?" It must have been his first thought. I kicked myself for not having realized he'd assume our child had sickened or died, as so many children did in his time.

I shook my head. "No, not Amhar." My gaze went past him to Cei, sliding down from his horse with a relieved groan. No doubt they'd been in the saddle a long time.

Cei turned toward me, a smile on his lips as well. And then he, too, saw my expression.

I'd better get it out quickly. "She's had the baby, but it was very big, and Donella had to cut it out of her." Cei's eyes widened in horror. Most likely he knew what these ominous words meant. I hurried on, gabbling in my haste to get my news out. "She's not dead. We sterilized everything, and Donella stitched her up afterwards. So far, she's only had a slight fever, which has passed, but there's still a danger of infection."

Arthur held out his hand for Cei's reins. "Better go to her."

His brother bolted in the direction of his house.

Arthur watched his rear view for a moment then turned to look at me. "You and Donella cut the child from her belly and yet she *lives*?" Astonishment colored his words.

"They do it all the time in my world. I've never seen it done, of course, but I knew it was possible." I licked my lips. "We had to try. She'd have died for sure if we hadn't. The baby was too large to be born naturally." I gave him a tight smile. "It's been three days, but signs are good. And the baby's thriving. Keelia is sharing the breastfeeding with Coventina, who doesn't have much milk while her body's recovering."

Arthur's face broke into a grin. "Another son?"

I shook my head. "No, a little girl. Well, a pretty big girl, to be exact, or we wouldn't have had to try that. It's called a Caesarean section where I come from."

All around us, the other warriors were dismounting, their voices and laughter rising skyward. Servants came out of the stables to help, and a man took the reins of Arthur's and Cei's horses, leaving him standing facing me, that silly grin on his face still. "He's always wanted a daughter."

I smiled. "Well, he's got one now. Rhiwallon is disgusted though – he wanted a brother he could teach to fight one day. He didn't believe me when I told him girls could learn to fight too."

Arthur looked up toward the Great Hall, and his shoulders rose and fell in a deep sigh. "These things happen. The priests would have us believe it was God's will. I'm not sure he has anything to do with it." He peered at me from beneath his dark brows. "She's lucky you were here. I doubt Donella would have tried this if you hadn't suggested it."

"Donella did all the hard work," I said, taking his hand. "Now, tell me how your patrolling went."

ARTHUR SET PREPARATIONS in motion to leave for the Council in Viroconium in three days' time, just over a week after Beltane.

Cei spent most of that time in attendance on his wife, which, she confided in me when I visited, had rapidly become a bit tedious. She couldn't move without him asking if there was anything he could do, and what she really wanted was to get back to normal. Or at least, what was to be her normal for the next couple of months whilst she recovered from her operation. For someone who'd been operated on in less than antiseptic conditions and without an anesthetic, she was making a remarkable recovery. They'd named the baby Reaghan.

With Amhar still so young and being breastfed, I was not to go to the Council. This bothered me more than I wanted to let on. Arthur would be meeting once again with his hated older half-brother, Cadwy, the man who'd brought about the deaths of their father's old seneschal, Euddolen, and indirectly of all his family. The man who'd tried his treacherous ways on Arthur more than once.

First, with poison that would most likely have killed me as well, and then by offering to relinquish Euddolen's family, his captives, to Arthur at a meeting where he intended an ambush. Luckily, Arthur knew what to expect of his brother, and went prepared. A bloody battle had taken place. No love lost there at all, and someone, ideally me, needed to be beside Arthur to curb the rage Cadwy so deserved.

The night before they were due to set out, I plucked up the courage to approach Arthur about going with them. We'd just retired to bed, and I was nestled within the curve of his arm, my cheek against his chest. In my left ear, his heart beat steadily, and the gentle rise and fall of his breathing soothed me. With my free hand, I fiddled with the hairs on his chest while inwardly composing what I wanted to say.

Perhaps openness was the best option. "I'd like to come." I waited for his reaction.

He stroked my arm. "We'll be bivouacking on the journey because I'm taking a considerable force. Sleeping on the ground. I can't have you doing that."

I kept on fiddling. "I've done that before, and you didn't object."

The stroking stopped. "It's different now."

"How?"

"You're the mother of my heir."

The thought curved my mouth into a smile, but I wasn't to be put off. "I'm still the same person who slept beside you on the ground at Caerwysg last year – and I was pregnant then. I don't mind sleeping rough. You know I don't."

His lips brushed against the top of my head. "I know. But you've Amhar to take care of. You're needed here."

I had every argument ready. "Maia is as good with him as I am, and he loves her dearly. I can leave him with her."

He was silent for a moment. I waited.

"Why is it you want to come?"

For a lot of reasons. "Cei's not going because he doesn't want to leave Coventina while she's recovering still. You'll be on your own. I don't trust Cadwy. You need all the support you can get."

His chest shook with a laugh. "Did Merlin put you up to this?"

I pushed myself up so I could look him in the eye. "No, he didn't. I don't do what he says. I do what I want." Inside my head, I added *"and what you say I can do"*, which, rather annoyingly, was true to a certain extent. It frequently irked me that he had the final say as to whether I could do something. The twenty-first century independent me still lurked beneath my skin.

"And if I say no, are you going to disguise yourself as a warrior and ride with us anyway, as you did before the Battle of Bassas?"

Touché. I'd been discovered before the battle and sent back, under escort and in disgrace, to the villa that was serving as Arthur's HQ. But Arthur had been very angry.

Two could play at this one-up-manship game though. "If I hadn't been there, Drustans wouldn't have been able to rescue Morgawse, and Euddolen's womenfolk."

He narrowed his dark eyes at me, but I could tell he wasn't angry. In fact, the corner of his mouth twitched as though he were trying not to laugh. "True."

I smiled in what I fondly imagined was a winning way. "I could be useful. I am the Ring Maiden after all. That counts for something, surely?"

My fingers automatically curled around the dragon-headed ring sitting on the forefinger of my left hand. It was touching the ring that had transported me here from the twenty-first century in the first place, although when I'd once tried rubbing it like Aladdin's lamp, it had resolutely refused to return me to my world. And now the fifth century was my home, and I no longer wanted to return to my old life as a librarian.

"I don't want you exposed to Cadwy and Morgana. They're too dangerous." He was trying to put me off, I could tell.

He rolled onto his side so that our faces were only inches apart. "I'd love to take you with me, but common sense tells me it wouldn't be a wise move. There'll be dangers for me, and I can't risk exposing you to them. Besides which, you're still feeding Amhar, and I'm definitely not taking him. Far too risky with Cadwy's inclination toward poison as a weapon."

"I could wean Amhar, get him a wet nurse like Keelia. She's helping Coventina feed Reaghan. It's the danger to you I'm worried about – not me. I don't like it when I'm not with you. I hate it when you go campaigning. My imagination runs riot, and I think all sorts of awful things."

Arthur's fingers made a hurried sign against the evil eye, and too late, I remembered the superstitions of this age, and how talking about the things I imagined wasn't such a good idea.

I put my hand on his. "That's not foresight – that's a woman's natural instincts."

He planted a kiss on the top of my head. "That doesn't make me any more inclined to take you, I'm afraid. You'll have to stay here with Amhar. Cei will be here, but I'll take Merlin with me. He can keep me safe and act as your guard dog."

Up against his intractability, I had to be content with that.

He pulled me closer. "Now come here and kiss me again."

I SPOTTED MERLIN strapping down his saddlebags the next morning in the great hall and hurried over. "I'm so relieved you're going." All around us other warriors milled, busy with similar preparations. I ignored them. "Without Cei, Arthur needs all the friends he can get at the Council. I asked him to let me come, but he refused. I'm relying on you to keep him safe…and prevent any fighting between him and Cadwy."

Merlin fastened the last strap on his bags. "I'll do my best, but he's my king as well as my friend, and I can't tell him what to do."

Very true.

"But you can advise him and keep him away from trouble." I paused. "Can't you?"

Merlin's thin face creased in a frown. "After what happened last year between him and Cadwy that might be hard. But I'll try."

The memory turned my stomach cold. The two half-brothers had tried to kill one another. More than once. Then, when Drustans and I had rescued the womenfolk of Euddolen, one of Arthur's staunchest supporters, we'd discovered how Cadwy had allowed his Saxon foederati to rape them. Ummidia had killed her two teenage daughters and herself after their ordeal, and Arthur rightly considered this all Cadwy's fault. As did I.

I pulled a rueful face. "I hate Cadwy as much as Arthur does. I'll never forgive him for allowing his men to use Albina and Cloelia the way he did." The image of those two girls danced before my eyes – not as I'd first seen them, as lively teenagers with a crush on my handsome new husband, but as the hollow-eyed, traumatized creatures their terrible experience had turned them into. Just before their mother slit their wrists in the bathhouse of the villa we'd been sheltering in. I shivered as though someone had walked over my grave. There was an awful lot about the fifth century I didn't like.

Merlin shouldered his baggage, and I followed him out into the brightness of the late spring morning. Arthur was clearly taking no risks this time and instead of the fifty men we'd taken to Viroconium when we'd gone to his father Uthyr's deathbed, he'd assembled a force of two hundred – enough to fight off any attack.

The hall doors banged shut behind me as I searched the as-sembled warriors for my husband's figure. Over by the stables

Tulac stood holding Llamrei's reins, Arthur's bear-emblazoned shield hooked on one of her saddle horns. My stomach, always a betrayer, did an unwelcome lurch as my eyes scanned the many faces I now knew so well. Unwelcome tears stung my eyes.

Llacheu came running from the direction of his mother's house, tall and sturdy and every day more like his father. Behind him, Arthur and Cei emerged from Cei's house, Cei's arm around his brother's shoulders, the dark head and the red close together in conversation. Arthur wore his mail shirt and carried his helmet, Cei only his tunic and braccae.

"Gwen!" Llacheu reached me and grabbed my hand. "Next time there's a Council of Kings, Father says he'll take me! That's so exciting. I wish I was going now."

In a hurry, I wiped my tears away with the back of my sleeve. "That's wonderful. By then you'll nearly be a warrior yourself."

The little boy beamed up at me, wise to my flattery, blind to my tears. "Not qui-ite." He puffed out his chest. "But nearly."

Arthur elbowed his way to where I stood in front of the hall. He dropped his lean, sunburnt hand on top of Llacheu's curls. "D'you want to fetch me my horse? Tulac has her."

Llacheu raced away, glowing with the importance of having been sent to fetch his father's horse.

Arthur turned to me, eyes alight with excitement. The only ornamentation on his dark clothing was the buckle on his sword belt and the fibula that fastened his cloak, yet he looked every inch a king. I gazed up at him for a moment, as though seeing him for the first time, struck anew by the wonder of being married to the man who would be known down the ages as the most famous of all British kings. Even after a year and a half, it was hard to comprehend the reality of what was now my life.

He gathered me into his arms with a chuckle and kissed me soundly on the lips. I put my own arms around his neck as my body responded, a warm glow spreading through me as I held him pressed tight against me, never wanting to let him go.

Just as quickly as he'd kissed me, he released me. Llacheu

emerged from the crowd of warriors leading Llamrei, his mouth fixed in a wide grin. Behind them trailed Tulac. The white mare had recovered well from the wound she'd taken last summer, but an ugly, raised scar ran across her left shoulder to match the one her master wore on his cheek.

Arthur took Llamrei's reins from his son, and with a last smile for me, mounted up. The two boys stepped back to join me in front of the hall, sensibly out of the way of being trampled as Llamrei pranced in excitement. Arthur's strong hands checked her, and her neat black hooves marked time in the dirt. He leaned toward me. "Come here for a last kiss."

I stepped up to the big horse and stood on tiptoes, one hand on Arthur's knee, conscious of the warmth of his body beneath my touch. His lips briefly met mine. "I've left Cei in charge, but if anything goes wrong and he can't do it, then you will have command here. But I've also left Gwalchmei to help you."

I clung onto his leg for a moment longer. "Take care." My voice held urgency. "Keep away from Cadwy. Return to me as soon as you can." The words felt hollow and meaningless. He was a man riding into the lion's den, but at least he knew the lion and was prepared.

All around me our warriors milled, laden with not only their weapons and shields but also with their bedrolls and enough supplies for the journey. Further down the hill toward the stables, half a dozen wagons waited, already laden with the tents and equipment necessary for the camp Arthur intended to set up outside Viroconium's walls. He was not about to make the mistake of staying within his brother's city this time.

Llamrei, her white coat a beacon amidst the sea of browns and chestnuts, wheeled around, and Merlin, on his sturdy bay, fell in beside Arthur. The train that was his army started out along the road to Viroconium.

Chapter Six

FIVE DAYS RIDE to Viroconium, up to seven days waiting around there for other kings who might not be on time and for the Council, five days to ride back. By my reckoning Arthur should have been back within seventeen days. He wasn't. The seventeenth day came and went, ticked off by Llacheu and me on a thin wooden writing tablet in the privacy of my bedchamber, where Cei wouldn't be able to see how I was fretting.

The eighteenth day came and went as well, followed slowly by the nineteenth. What could be keeping Arthur? From past experience, I knew the Council was a one-day affair, and surely if some of the kings hadn't arrived within a week, then they could be assumed not to be coming at all, so the Council could begin. Someone had once told me that the kings didn't all turn up for these meetings. Probably those from the furthest flung corners of Britain would only see the point in attending if it was for something important, like the election of a new High King, or if they themselves had a grudge to raise, or needed something.

Not that they had a High King now. Arthur had been elected Dux nearly two years ago, much to Cadwy's fury. The Council had decreed having a High King as well as a dux unnecessary. Then the sword had appeared, stuck in that stone in the middle of the forum, with its enigmatic message. Cadwy had tried his hand at yanking it out, along with most of the other red-blooded males present, and all had failed. That, and the fact that Uthyr had

---

divided his kingdom, leaving Dumnonia to Arthur and only Powys to Cadwy, had led to much of the animosity between brothers who had ever been rivals.

I tried to hide my worries from Llacheu. He was only eight, and as it was his father I was stressing over, imagining all manner of awful things happening to, I didn't want to frighten him.

Llacheu wasn't stupid though, and picked up on it. "Don't worry about Father." He laid a reassuring hand on my arm as we ticked off day twenty. "He's probably taken a detour to go and visit Uncle Theo in Caer Legeion."

And that detour would include Morgawse and baby Medraut, now eighteen months old. When he'd been born, and Morgawse had declared his name, I'd horrified myself with the guilty wish that he'd died at birth, and that thought wasn't far from my mind right now.

Shoving it aside, I forced a smile. "You're most likely right. That would be just like him." Not for the first time my mind strayed back to my old world where a simple call on a cellphone would have told me he was fine and where he was. Never had the Britain of the fifth century felt so large.

Satisfied he'd done his duty in caring for me, Llacheu's attention turned to little Amhar. "Can we take him outside? I want to show him my new pony." He'd recently graduated to a small cob, leaving his old pony, the little gray Seren, "for Amhar to ride".

I nodded and picked my son up off the floor where he was crawling round after the tabby cat who frequented our chamber, trying to catch her by the tail. She was an amiable creature who didn't seem to mind such treatment and was cannily keeping just out of his reach. I scooped Amhar up. As with all babies, he wore a loose shirt and nothing else, his chubby bottom naked during his waking hours. Nappies were a non-existent luxury here, and every mother or nurse held her baby regularly over the toilet bucket from an early age, to minimize accidents. I did so now, waiting, and he obligingly did a little pee. My old university friend Sian would have been impressed.

I sat him on my hip, and we went outside.

Despite it being day twenty and Arthur and his men three days overdue – by my reckoning – the daily life of Din Cadan was going on as normal. No one but me seemed in any way disquieted by the non-arrival of their lord.

Llacheu wound his way between the crowded, thatched buildings to the horse pens, and I followed more slowly, Amhar babbling to himself in baby-speak. Seren grazed contentedly in one of the pens, alongside a much bigger black pony. Llacheu put his fingers in his mouth and whistled. Both ponies' heads shot up. With a toss of their manes, they came cantering up the field toward us, keeping close together.

"Isn't Saeth a fine beast?" Pride colored Llacheu's voice. "Father chose him for me specially. He said he has hair like mine."

That was true. Saeth's ebony mane and tail fell in a shining wave not unlike Llacheu's own curly mop, which in turn wasn't unlike Arthur's.

The little boy fished some crusts of bread out of the front of his tunic where they must have deposited uncomfortable crumbs, and held one out to each of the two ponies. In my arms, Amhar held his chubby hands out too – for the bread rather than the ponies.

"You can't be hungry," I chided him. "I only just fed you."

Llacheu grinned up at me. "I'm *always* hungry." He chewed a piece off the bread himself and passed it to Amhar who took it in his fat little fist and tried stuffing it into his mouth all at once. As he had no teeth yet, it was going to get gummed to death.

Llacheu returned to the real reason he'd wanted to bring me out here, which I'd already guessed. "Can we sit Amhar on Seren?"

He was always trying to get me to let Amhar ride, even though I patiently explained a thousand times that nine months was too young to straddle a horse properly, even one as small as Seren.

I sighed. "Go on then, slip a halter on her."

Grinning all over his rather grubby face, he quickly retrieved Seren's rope halter from where it hung by the gate and slipped it onto her. Standing beside her now I was struck by how tall he'd grown – a much bigger child than the one who'd been eager to show me how well he could ride when I'd first arrived here all that time ago. Then, he'd been too small to put the saddle on by himself, and to put her halter on he'd had to stand on tiptoe.

I wriggled through the slip rail gate, and, while he held Seren, I sat Amhar on her back. Saeth watched with interest. Amhar, on the other hand, was unmoved by the experience, being keener on the piece of soggy bread he still clutched in his fist.

"When will he be able to learn to ride properly?" Llacheu asked, rubbing Saeth's black nose. "I can't wait to teach him."

I smiled. "Give him a chance. He can't walk yet. Don't you know that saying – don't run before you can walk? Well, in this case it's don't ride before you can walk."

Llacheu frowned. "If you couldn't walk, riding would be most useful."

I shook my head and lifted Amhar off. He generously wiped his wet bread across my cheek. There'd been a time when I'd have thought that was gross, but motherhood had changed me.

A horn blast resonated through the air.

Llacheu's eyes met mine. "Riders sighted."

My heart soared. He was back.

Together we hurried away from the horse pens, back through the web of buildings to the main thoroughfare of the fortress. People hurried toward the gates or stood about, watching, expectant looks on their faces. The horn sounded again, twice this time. Twice for friends approaching. Three for enemies. It had to be Arthur returning.

Llacheu looked up at me. "Can I run down to the gates?" He hopped from one foot to the other impatiently.

I nodded, my heart pounding with excitement. The three weeks Arthur had been gone felt like forever. "Of course you can. I'll wait here with Amhar."

He was off, long legs pelting down the cobbled road. I moved to stand on the low wooden platform in front of the great hall, shifting Amhar, who was growing heavy, to my other hip. The warm glow of excitement that I would be seeing my husband again at last coursed through me.

Now I was a queen and the mother of Arthur's heir, custom dictated that I should behave like one. Much as I'd have liked to run down to the gates with Amhar to be the first to welcome the king, dignity insisted that I should stand waiting by his great hall. And for once, I followed protocol.

From where I stood, I had a clear view down the cobbled road to the tall, double-towered gates, standing open to welcome home the returning warriors. I shifted Amhar again, who still clutched the remains of the soggy bread, setting him on my other hip, and pushed back the strands of chestnut hair that had escaped my plaits to blow in my eyes.

Cei emerged from his house supporting Coventina with one hand under her elbow. Nearly a month after her operation, she'd much recovered and could nurse the baby herself, although she still allowed Keelia to do the nighttime feeds. Donella had decreed she should rest as much as possible. The midwife's standing had sky-rocketed since news of her success with Coventina had become more widely known, not just here within the fortress but amongst the farms as well.

A rider appeared from under the look-out platform that spanned the gates. The summer sunshine sparkled on his mail shirt and the helmet hanging from one of his saddle horns. The shield that hung beside his helmet was yellow, with a blue falcon swooping across it.

Merlin.

Behind him came a group of warriors. But where was Arthur?

Half a dozen riders took the road up toward the stables, but no others appeared.

I waited, fidgeting as badly as Llacheu. No more emerged and the guards swung the gates shut behind them.

My heart, which had been thudding through my veins with such force I'd heard it pounding in my ears, did a sick leap then sank into my boots, making my stomach do an accompanying flip as it passed. Where was my husband? Why was Merlin back alone, with just a few men as his escort?

Maia had emerged from the hall to stand behind me in the shadow cast by the wide overhang of the roof. I thrust Amhar into her arms and on hurrying feet set off down the cobbles to meet Merlin at the stables.

He was dismounting when I reached them.

"Where is he?" The words tumbled out of me before Merlin even had the chance to turn to greet me.

He swung around. "Good day to you, Gwen." Even though I was the queen, when we were alone, he always addressed me by my name.

A servant came and took his horse, and I pulled Merlin to one side. "Where's Arthur? What's happened?" I kept my voice low, not wanting to be overheard, fearful that he brought bad news.

He must have seen the fear in my eyes, known the conclusion I'd jumped to. "Stop panicking. He's fine. Just not here. He sent me back on my own for a reason." His turn to pull me, away from the stables and up toward the great hall. "Come, walk with me. I badly need a drink and something to eat. Then I'll tell you everything."

A little relieved by his words, but still anxious to find out where Arthur had got to, I allowed myself to be hurried back up the road to the hall.

Inside, I sent a servant to fetch food and drink for Merlin, and he divested himself of his heavy mail shirt with a sigh of relief. "That's better. Too hot today for armor." He dumped the shirt down on one of the tables and proceeded to wriggle out of the padded tunic all the warriors wore beneath their armor. Underneath that was only his linen undershirt, sticking wetly to his hot body. The smell of sweat on him was strong.

He wrinkled his nose. "I'm sorry. I stink. I've been riding for five days, camping out at nights. No chance for even a wash or shave." He ran his hand over five days' growth of beard on his chin.

The servant returned with a tray holding a jug of small ale and a platter of cold meat and bread. I stopped him before he could leave. "Can you go and get the bath house ready for Lord Merlin, please?"

The man hurried away. Having servants to do my bidding felt more natural after all this time as queen of Dumnonia, although every time I did it, the feeling that perhaps I ought to be doing the requested thing myself lurked never far from the surface.

Merlin sat down at the table and poured himself a horn beaker of the ale. He downed it in one go then refilled it.

I sank with reluctance onto the bench on the opposite side of the table. "Where is Arthur, and why's he sent you back here on your own?"

He had a mouth full of food, so I kept going. "And what happened at the Council?" I watched him swallow. "I need you to tell me everything."

He eyed the food hungrily, but wiped his mouth on his sleeve and pushed it to one side, keeping the cup of ale close. "We made good time and set up camp outside the city walls. We weren't the only ones. Several of the more powerful kings had brought small armies with them. It seems no one quite trusts Cadwy. Or maybe it's that they don't trust one another."

I nodded. "Probably a bit of both."

He took another generous swig of ale. "Hot work riding. We've ridden down today from north of Caer Baddan without stopping. Arthur asked me to make haste."

I fidgeted impatiently. "What for? You haven't told me where he is yet."

Merlin set the horn cup down. "Heading north."

I swallowed. "North?" That could mean anywhere. Presumably somewhere north of Viroconium, though. "How far north?"

"The Wall."

For a few moments I didn't quite take this in. The Wall. Did he mean *Hadrian's* Wall? I stared at Merlin in consternation. How much further from me could Arthur go? The gap between comparatively safe southern Dumnonia and far off, dangerous Hadrian's Wall yawned like a chasm between us.

"What for?" If my voice held dismay, I couldn't help it. One of the things I'd failed to take into account when I'd decided to stay here in the fifth century with Arthur was the degree to which he wouldn't be with me. My heart twisted with an ache of desperation to see him, to hold him, for him to be safe in my arms.

Merlin picked up a slice of meat and chewed. For a moment we sat in silence. Then he swallowed. "I'm sorry. I'm starving. I haven't eaten since last night." He refilled the horn cup again. "He's gone to Caer Ligualid at the request of Meirchion the Lean and Lot of Lleuddiniawn."

I'd seen Meirchion at the previous Council of Kings, but Lot of Lleuddiniawn's name was one I only knew from my reading of Arthurian legend, back in my old world.

"Lot of Lleuddiniawn? Is that Lothian? Isn't he Gwalchmei's father?"

Merlin nodded. "He rarely comes to the Council, but he did this time. It seems their neighbor, Caw of Alt Clut, has been expanding his territory – east into Lot's lands and south into Meirchion's. He's been doing so with the help of Pictish foederati he's allowed to settle in his territories. There've been skirmishes, but Caw has twelve sons and he's a powerful warlord. And the Picts he's been using are wild barbarians. Lot asked for the Dux's help. Meirchion, who has the Wall between his lands and Caw's, backed him up."

In my head, I tried to populate the map I knew of the British Isles with these kingdoms whose all too fluid boundaries I was unfamiliar with. Real maps would be a useful thing to have. How much help would it be to Arthur if I could create one? A thought occurred to me. "But he has less than half his force with him."

Merlin nodded, picking up a piece of dark bread. "I know. That's why he sent me back. He marched north straightaway, along with Meirchion and Lot and their men. He asked me to come back here and bring more men to him. I'm here to muster the rest of his army."

The door of the hall banged open and Cei came hurrying in. "Merlin. What are you doing back with only half a dozen men? Where's Arthur?"

The tale had to be retold. This time, as Merlin ate and spoke and drank alternately, I sat brooding on my bench, mulling over what he'd told me, while Cei listened, his face growing more excited as the tale unrolled.

I'd been to Hadrian's Wall on more than one occasion with my father, in its tumbledown, robbed out, twenty-first-century state. And one thing that had just come leaping into my head was a particular fort along the Wall called Camboglanna. My father had taken me there especially, although the remains were virtually non-existent compared with some of the Wall's fortresses.

Some time in the eighteenth century a thoughtless landowner had built a mansion on the grounds of the abbey that had replaced the fortress – wiping out what little remained of the Roman-era buildings. My father had taken me there because a theory existed that this was the site of Camlann, Arthur's final battle. The battle in which he died.

"Many scholars are coming round to the idea that Arthur's battles took place up here in the North of England and the Scottish Borders," my father had said, standing on a rainy day looking down into the valley below the site of the fort. "And this place, Camboglanna, means the twisted glen. Look at the valley below us and how it twists. They think the name could easily have been changed over the years from Camboglanna to Camlann. And I'm not sure they're wrong."

And now Arthur was heading up there.

The worst thing about knowing all the hundreds of legends

and theories about Arthur that I'd learned at my father's knee was that I didn't know which of them were true. Yes, some stories said that he had to fall in battle against his nephew Medraut, but how was I to know if this was true? Medraut was scarcely more than a baby. Maybe Arthur was headed right now toward his Camlann, a battle against a king called Caw, not a rebellious nephew.

When Merlin finished, Cei banged his fist on the table, disturbing my disquieting reverie. "I'll come with you. Coventina's well enough now for me to leave her in Keelia's care. And Gwen's. When do you leave? Today?"

Merlin shook his head. "Tomorrow. It's late now, and I need to pick which men to take with me. Arthur said not all. No need to leave Din Cadan lacking in protection. That would be foolish."

My gaze flicked from one set face to the other. "I'm coming too."

Two sets of surprised eyes swiveled in my direction.

Merlin shook his head. "You can't. You have your baby to take care of."

I set my jaw. "Amhar needs a woman. Any woman will do. I'm a queen, and my husband needs me."

Cei shook his head. "I don't think he does. What good can a woman do in battle?"

How very male chauvinist of him. If only I could have shown him female soldiers in my old world.

Unable to do so, I bristled. "I'm the luck of Arthur. The men all know it. And I've been to the Wall before. I know it well. I can draw maps for him."

Merlin frowned, but his eyes showed a glint of interest. "Maps?" Clearly I'd hit on something he thought might be useful, and he was wavering.

Cei scowled. "She's a woman. She'll slow us down. She's got a baby to feed." He hesitated. "And she's the queen."

I pounced. "Exactly. Don't you know the story of Boudicca? She led a huge army against the Romans. She very nearly beat them."

Cei's gingery eyebrows shot into his hairline. Was it with shock?

I hammered home my advantage. "And as I'm the queen, you can't tell me what to do. Only Arthur can." I paused and fixed a stony stare on Merlin, daring him to lie. "Did he specifically tell you I couldn't come?"

In his eyes, honesty warred with the urge to judicially lie. Honesty won, as I'd guessed it would. "No, he didn't."

"Then I'm coming. I'll go and pack my saddle bags and organize a wet nurse for Amhar."

Before either of them could present me with further argument, I pushed the bench back across the flagstone floor with a clatter and marched into my chamber, keeping my back ramrod straight.

➤➤➤◄◄◄

ONE THING I'D neglected to take into account was how hard it was going to be to stop breast feeding suddenly like that. How hard, and how uncomfortable. I had the sense to speak to Donella about it before I left.

She tutted her tongue against her teeth. "'Tain't natural fer a lady to go off to war. You should be stayin' here with your babby."

I pursed my lips. "Thank you for your opinion. You won't change my mind. But what do I need to do about the milk I'm producing?"

She recommended binding my breasts and applying cabbage leaves to them, weird as that sounded. I packed a couple of winter cabbages in my saddle bags, feeling like an idiot.

"How long will it take for the milk to dry up?"

She made the sort of face that told me she was doing calculations in her head. "Could be quick, just a few days. Could take a while longer. Depends."

That wasn't the hugest amount of help, and she neglected to tell me how very painful a milk engorged breast was going to be. Then she went off and fetched Keelia, who was now only feeding Coventina's baby at nights, and had enough milk for another child. Maia was to be in charge of Amhar's care, and Keelia would come to breast feed him from time to time during the day. He'd have to have water at night. I emphasized to Maia a good twenty times that she had to see the water boil and then keep it boiling for a good five minutes before she cooled it down for him to drink. Under pain of severe punishment.

Cottia, Arthur's old nursemaid, frowned in disapproval when she came into the Hall on the morning of my departure and found me, dressed in braccae and tunic, telling Maia yet again that the water had to be boiled and cooled.

"Water? Fer a babby? What's wrong with mother's milk?" She tutted the same way Donella had. Had they been conferring behind my back? "Only this one's mother's off on a jaunt, not thinkin' of her child."

The bindings round my breasts were already uncomfortable, making me snap my retort. And I was sweating under the mail shirt Merlin had insisted I wear. "Any woman's milk will be fine for him. It's just at night, and only if he wakes, that he'll get water. And I can assure you that boiling it makes it safe."

The look she gave me told me she was not convinced.

I turned back to Maia, who held a beaming Amhar in her arms. He waved his chubby fists at me, blowing bubbles from his rosebud, toothless mouth. I smiled. "He loves you as much as he loves me, Maia. I trust you, so don't let me down. I hope I won't be away too long."

She bobbed a small bow as best she could for a slight girl with a hefty baby in her arms. "You tek care, Milady. Come back safe to us. I won't forget to boil his water, doan you worry."

I forced a smile. Right now, bringing my baby's father back safely most concerned me, and keeping him well away from

Camboglanna.

Outside, in the courtyard in front of the great hall, Llacheu stood holding Alezan, surrounded by our already mounted warriors. Merlin sat waiting, resting his hands on the horns of his saddle, Cei by his side. The warrior to be left in charge in our absence, Gwalchmei, stood to one side, a glum expression on his face. After all, we were heading for his homeland. Understandable that he should want to accompany us. But someone had to remain to guard Din Cadan.

Slinging the saddle bags over Alezan's back, I then did up the straps attaching them to the saddle horns. "I'm nearly ready."

"I wish I was coming." Llacheu's lower lip jutted rebelliously. "It's not fair that you get to go, and I don't. I do at least know how to fight. You don't."

I fastened the last strap. "Well, that's one of the problems of being a child. I'm a grownup, so I can do what I want. One day, you'll be able to as well. But don't wish away your childhood."

He scowled at me, looking more than ever like his father. "I don't *want* to be a child. I don't like it. I want to be a warrior. I'm nearly big enough." He stood on tiptoes next to me, the top of his head level with my chin. Too big and too dignified for me to pat on the head any longer.

Instead, I held out my hand, and he took it. I shook his hand as formally as I would have done the hand of a king. "Take care of your little brother, and help Maia keep him happy for me. Please. I'm relying on you." I paused. "But no riding for him. We'll do that when I get back. D'you promise?"

He pulled a wry face. "I promise."

"Good." I took Alezan's reins and swung myself up into the saddle. She fidgeted under me as I found my other stirrup and gathered my reins.

Over by the stable block Merlin gave Cei a nod and turned his horse downhill, raising his right hand in the air. "Onward." With our army behind us, we rode out of the courtyard toward the open gates of the fortress.

Chapter Seven

A HEAVY RELENTLESS rain fell, draping the land in a grey veil, leaching the color from the landscape and reducing visibility to less than a mile. We'd suffered miserable weather ever since we'd left Ebrauc, modern day York, to ride up into the highlands of Britain across bleak moors and under weeping skies.

My thick woolen cloak hung heavily about my shoulders, too wet to blow about but thankfully still keeping some warmth in. A fairly typical midsummer in the north of Britain. Not really a surprise. I seemed to remember it raining most of the time when my father brought me up here for our last trip, one chilly October half term. Artie'd shown no interest in visiting what remained of the ancient monuments and stayed in bed in the cottage we'd rented, playing on his iPad, texting his friends and listening to his music.

Unlike my twin brother, I'd already possessed a fascination for history and a keenness to please my father. Hanging on his words, I trailed in his wake around every soggy ruin, soaking up the history, oblivious to the miserable weather. We'd brought waterproofs, so what did it matter?

Here in the fifth century waterproofs didn't exist. And I felt as miserable as the weather.

From Ebrauc, where Coel Hen, the ruler of Bryneich, had welcomed us less than enthusiastically, we'd ridden on up the Roman road I would have called Dere Street, roughly following the course of the modern A1 trunk road. We spent an uncomfortable night in the crumbling fort at Catraeth.

For a while during my childhood, my somewhat inappropriate bedtime story had been the epic poem the bard Aneirin had written, The Gododdin, about a defeat of the Britons at Catraeth. My father had read each stanza aloud, first in the melodic original Brithonic, then the less satisfying English translation, his deep voice rising to the rafters. Not a tale guaranteed to encourage a child to sleep.

But this battle lay far into the future and didn't concern me and the people I cared about.

North of Catraeth the drizzle we'd experienced since leaving York grew heavier, and I'd been glad to reach the stone bridge over the Tyne, just south of the town of Coria. The bridge, constructed by clever Roman engineers centuries before, still stood, stalwart and weather-worn, allowing all comers to cross. It rose high and wide above the level of the water, and we had to tackle a sloping ramp that curved up from the road in order to use it. To our left, a huge retaining wall, bound together with rust-tinged metal clamps rather than mortar, protected the ramp and bridge from possible erosion caused by flood waters and the current.

On half a dozen sturdy stone piers, the bridge arched across the dark waters of the Tyne. It put to shame the tumbledown remains of the bridge over the River Exe I'd seen last year on my way to Din Tagel. I felt no nervous qualms as we rode over it.

On the north bank, the road rose steeply into Coria itself, an old Roman town nestling a mile or two south of the Wall. Here, surprisingly, we didn't find the level of decrepitude and poverty present in places like Caer Baddan and Catraeth. The population had diminished from Roman times, but in the spaces left by demolished houses, crops grew in abundance out of the dark, moist soil, flourishing in the warm wet. The town had reverted back to being a semi-prosperous farming village.

Here began the east-west Supply Road, built by the Romans

to service the string of forts south of the Wall as well as the frontier garrisons themselves. In my time it had gained the old Norse name of "the Stanegate" – simply meaning the stone road.

A night under shelter in a comfortable bed did wonders for my frame of mind, but the following day the rain continued with renewed enthusiasm as we set off westwards along the Supply Road toward Caer Ligualid. A good seven yards across, and made of cobbles covered in a thick layer of gravel that for the most part still remained, our way ran pretty much straight as a die across the undulating moors toward our destination.

But we weren't to reach Caer Ligualid.

Instead, here we were, approaching the still unseen valley in which the town of Vindolanda huddled, with the rain falling with even greater vigor. This morning, riders, who'd been on their way to Coria with a message for Merlin and Cei, had intercepted us.

A soggy Drustans, accompanied by three burly warriors, was very pleased to find us already on our way west. The son of King March of Caer Dore in Cornubia, Drustans must now have been about eighteen years old, tall, muscular and handsome, with his red-brown curls trimmed short for battle. A young man popular with girls wherever he went – as I'd learned to my cost when he and the Princess Essylt of Linnuis had fallen in love last year. Even though she was at the time betrothed to his father – to whom she was now safely married.

"Arthur asks you to meet him at Vindolanda," he informed Merlin and Cei, as the rain sleeted down on our heads. "He was at Caer Ligualid, but now he's moved to Vindolanda as it's more central." Something flashed in his eyes as he spoke, as though he knew more than he was telling. If either Merlin or Cei noticed, they didn't react.

His gaze moved past them and on to me where I stood just behind Merlin. With a sigh, his eyes rolled. He'd had personal experience of me trying to accompany my husband on campaign before. I gave him as cheery a smile as I could muster, given the awful weather and my aching legs from so many days in the saddle.

"Milady." He tipped a bow as best he could while mounted. Then he and his men turned their horses and fell into our ranks as we pressed on toward Vindolanda. Eventually he fell in beside me.

"Have you been learning to fight then?" he asked, then colored and hurriedly added, "My Lady." As a prince himself, perhaps deference to a queen came with difficulty. That or he still bore a grudge against me. Back in Din Cadan over the winter, he'd kept well out of my way after the hand I'd had in separating him from Essylt and dispatching her south to marry his father. Not that I could have done anything else. If anyone had found out he'd slept with the woman already promised to his father, execution would have been the best he could have hoped for. After castration.

"As it happens, I *have* been taking lessons." I nodded to Merlin. "He's been teaching me the rudiments of swordsmanship." Every evening on our way up here, no matter how uncomfortable I'd been, I'd persuaded a reluctant Merlin to spar with me and teach me the basics of how to handle a sword. Even he had seen it as a wise move. If I could look after myself, then I wouldn't need someone to do it for me.

Drustans' dark brows rose in something that might have been respect, or equally might have only been skepticism. Probably the latter.

My curiosity about the Council of Kings shouldered its way to the forefront of my mind. "Did you see your father at the Council?"

Drustans nodded. "I did." His voice was curt.

Unabashed, I pressed on. "And Princess Essylt? Did you have news of her?"

The boy's brows sunk low over his eyes, giving him a decided look of my husband when crossed. "She was there with him."

"Oh."

I hadn't counted on the old king bringing his new bride with him to the Council. But then, she was both young and very beautiful, so maybe he didn't trust her to be left alone in his fortress without him with lots of lusty young warriors. Wisely so, perhaps.

Drustans sighed. "She's with child."

I heaved a sigh too, but mine was with relief. If she was with child now, then the baby couldn't be Drustans', as a year had passed since I'd caught him in bed with Essylt and had to cover it up. She'd been dispatched off to marry her old betrothed straight after that.

"Do you still feel the same about her?"

His mouth twisted. "I do. I can't bear to think of her with him." He paused and his mouth formed a sneer of disgust. "With him...in bed. Making that child. Doing what she and I did. It's...disgusting. He's an old man and she...she's just a girl."

White haired King March must be in his fifties, and Essylt barely the same age as Drustans. I had to admit, it wasn't a nice picture to conjure. But neither of us could do anything about it. The time for action had long passed.

"Did you have chance to speak with her?" I asked, wiping strands of wet hair out of my eyes.

He shrugged. "A few words only."

How much must that have hurt for both of them. I looked forward again at where Merlin and Cei rode side by side at the head of our column, hoods drawn up to keep the rain off. Only Merlin knew what had happened at Caer Lind Colun last year, under the nose of Essylt's religion obsessed father. He'd been rightly shocked when I'd confided in him, but I'd persuaded him to say nothing to anyone.

Drustans went on. "She still loves me. I know it. She didn't say, but I could see it in her eyes. We weren't alone, so I couldn't ask her." His voice faltered. "She looked so...sad. And the worst thing was, I could do nothing about it. Nothing to help her." He swallowed with some difficulty as there must have been a big lump in his throat. "I wish he was dead. If he was, she could be mine." He spat the bitter words out, barely above a whisper.

This was a teenager in love talking, separated by fifteen hundred years from the teenagers I was more used to, but different in no other way where love was concerned. No use telling him that this was first love, that he'd get over it, that one day he'd find someone else to love. He wouldn't have believed me. And maybe he wasn't going to, if the stories about him were true.

However, this was the fifth century, and it wouldn't be unusual for a son to usurp his father's throne by bringing about his early demise, so I couldn't totally dismiss his anguished words. I sought for something to discourage any ideas he might have of patricide.

"I think that even when your father dies, whenever it is, you wouldn't be able to marry his widow." This was information I'd gleaned from reading about medieval monarchs – in particular Henry VIII. "Because Essylt's married to your father, the church now considers her your mother, even though there's no blood relationship. And you aren't allowed to marry your mother."

Drustans' jaw dropped. He'd clearly never considered how the church would view him taking his stepmother to wife, if his father conveniently died. "Are...are you sure?" Doubt filled his voice.

I pulled a wry face. "I'm afraid I am. It's in the Bible. I think, if I remember correctly, there's a pretty long list of who you're not allowed to marry in Leviticus." When I'd read a novel about Catherine of Aragon, I'd Googled where this was to be found in the Bible, which was lucky. Who'd have thought I'd one day be quoting it to the original Tristan from the Tristan and Iseult romance.

His shoulders sagged. "I'm going to ask someone other than you about this though. You might just be saying it." Now he sounded like a sulky seven-year-old.

My turn to shrug. "You do that. You'll find I'm right." I set my heels to Alezan's side and sent her bounding forward to catch up with Merlin. I'd had enough of sulky teens.

The supply road stretched wide and relatively well-maintained ahead of us, rising gently to the west. To the south, moorland rolled away toward distant hills, and to the north the high ridge of the Whin Sill rose, where the Wall, too far away for us to make out clearly, ran.

I reined Alezan to a walk beside Merlin and Cei, who looked as miserable as I did. "How long before we get there?"

Cei shrugged. "I've no idea. Never been here before. It's all new to me."

Merlin frowned. "I thought you were the one who could draw the maps. You should know better than we do."

Toward the west a chink of blue showed in the cloud, a promise of better weather to come, hopefully. I wiped my wet face with my equally wet gloved hand, squinting into the greyness of the day. I might have been a bit overly boastful when it came to map making. Although I'd been to the Wall a number of times, I'd never been the driver, always the passenger. I'd been an interested child and not paid the greatest heed to where we were going and the distances between places. The one thing I knew for certain, though, was that Camboglanna, with all its connotations, lay further west than this. I fell silent, in case Merlin pressed me more on my knowledge.

We breasted the rise, and the road began to head downhill into a valley, the moor to our south rising away from us. Distant smoke curled up from a hidden source to mingle with the mist that lay across the land. The rain, perhaps to encourage us, thinned and a few more bits of blue appeared, way to the west.

Vindolanda lay on a plateau just above the steep valley of a rushing burn, on the far side of which a stone and wood watch-tower rose like an accusing finger on the huge rise of moorland overlooking the town. Between the town and the watchtower, the burn ran through a small gorge that provided extra security for the inhabitants. Easy to see why the first Romans up here had chosen this site as a good spot on which to build their fort.

Someone must have been up in the tower, watching out for us, because light flashed in a signal from its upper levels as we approached.

We crossed the burn by a shallow ford in the valley bottom and rode up the hill toward the north gates of the fortress. The trees here had been cut back to an arrow shot's length from the road – something the Romans had done that clearly had continued into the post-Roman period. Did this mean dangers threatened even here, more than a mile south of the Wall?

Alezan must have been tired. I certainly was. Her step had lost its bounce, and she no longer fidgeted under me, eager to go faster. This had been a long journey of more than three-hundred-and-fifty miles.

The supply road continued on past the northern gates of the fortress. A short branch road ran up to the gates and into the walled town that stood where once a military fortress had thrived. The ruins of which I'd once stood in with my father.

Merlin and Cei led us through the massive gates, that still towered right to their crenellated upper level. To left and right, the sturdy town walls looked much as they must have done the day the legions abandoned them. The rain, after dogging us for days, chose that moment to cease, and a few more patches of blue appeared between scudding, higher clouds. Just as we reached shelter. Typical.

Our tired horses clattered up the main street toward the center of the town, past buildings that might once have been army barracks but now had been turned into houses, shops and workshops. Smoke drifted up from their mainly thatched rooftops as the sun peeped shyly from behind the clouds.

With the end of the rain, came the people, emerging from their houses to go about their business. In a blacksmith's shop a fire glowed white hot, the sound of metal on metal beating a steady rhythm. Aromas of baking bread, cooking meat, the sharp smell of urine from the communal latrines and the tannery, and the acrid stink of smoke filled the air. After the downpour, the town was surging back to life.

Little, barefoot boys ran through the puddles alongside our horses, staring up at us in open fascination. We must have seemed as foreign to them as African tribesmen would have done to children in my time.

Vindolanda had once been an army outpost supplying the forts along the Wall, but now a bustling frontier town lay within the military walls. Toward the east wall overlooking the gorge, the praetorium, the commanding officer's house, still stood. The tiled roof remained, somewhat the worse for wear, and rough stonework showed in patches through the flaking plaster. A low, thatched stable block had been squeezed in beside it around a square courtyard, and it was to there that we headed.

With relief, I slid down from Alezan's back and stretched my aching limbs, glad to have my feet back on the ground. All around me our warriors did the same. Concerned about my tired horse's welfare, I searched about me, looking for where I could find a lodging for her.

A gate that probably came from the praetorium swung open. Two men emerged, both heavily bearded, one dark, one fair. For a shocked moment I didn't recognize my own husband, or Theodoric, Morgawse's husband, a big blond Goth.

Arthur's gaze ran over the crowd of newly arrived warriors, a look of satisfaction on his face. Until he spotted me. His brows lowered, his eyes flashed fury, and he marched across the flagstones to meet me.

I stood my ground, gripping Alezan's reins until my knuckles whitened.

A quick sideways glance showed me Merlin and Cei making themselves conspicuous by their absence, hurrying their horses into the stalls.

"Gwen." Arthur's voice was surprisingly calm. "What are you doing here?"

I stood up straighter. "Helping."

A stony silence stretched between us.

He broke it. *"Helping?"*

I nodded. "I've been here before. I can draw you maps. I know this area."

He opened his mouth, shut it again and sighed. A resigned sigh. With his knowledge of where I came from, perhaps he believed me about the maps. I could hardly tell him the truth – that I feared he was drawing close to his fate – to Camlann and all that would happen there, and the maps were just an excuse.

"Merlin let you come because of *this*?"

I didn't want to drop Merlin in it. Well, not too much. Sometimes he deserved it. "He did. But I gave him no choice. I'm his queen. He had to do as I said."

Arthur snorted. "Sometimes I think he's no match for you." He put his hands on his hips. "I suppose you'd like a better welcome than this?"

I pressed my lips together in an effort not to smile. "I would."

"You think you deserve one after you abandoned our child and bullied my adviser into doing what you wanted?"

I couldn't hold the smile back. "I do."

He stepped forward and folded me into his arms, holding me close. "I've missed you, Gwen. There's no denying it. But I'd rather you'd stayed safe in Din Cadan."

My cheek pressed against the soft material of his tunic, the rhythm of his heart beating beneath my ear. A heart I was determined should keep on beating.

He cupped my chin, turning my face up to his. "Why I love you so much, I have no idea. You're a contrary woman, you know that, don't you?"

I nodded, feigning meekness, and he bent his head and kissed me on the lips, hard and hungrily. My body responded immediately, and I clung onto him, desire coursing through me.

After what felt like a long time he released me, his breath coming heavily to match my own. "You're soaking wet. Leave Alezan with a servant and come into the house. We'll find you some dry clothes." With deft fingers he undid the buckles on my saddle bags and slung them over his shoulder, then called a passing servant. Hardly a minute later, my hand in his, he pulled me through the door into the praetorium.

Like most Roman houses, the buildings clustered around a central courtyard, edged with a colonnaded walkway of tatty, cracked pillars. Faded paintwork decorated the walls, and underfoot the tiles undulated somewhat, as though the ground beneath them had subsided in places. In the center, a fountain played into a square pond, stone seating edging it.

The rooms Arthur had commandeered occupied a two story building that took up the whole of one side of the courtyard.

He pushed open the door and led me inside. From the table in the center, a man rose stiffly to his feet. Grey haired, portly, and with a heavily lined face, he came around the table and approached me, his expression full of intelligent curiosity.

"My wife." Irony edged Arthur's voice. "The Lady Guinevere. Gwen, this is Riacus, the magistrate here at Vindolanda. This is his house."

Riacus bowed to me, and I held out my hand. He took it in his own large paw, his eyes fixing on the dragon ring on my finger.

Arthur nodded. "Yes. The Ring Maiden."

"Milady." Riacus had a deep, melodic voice that matched his stature. "It's a pleasure to welcome you here to my humble abode." He released my hand. "And an honor to meet the Ring Maiden herself."

I smiled, liking him immediately. "My Lord Riacus." He had the air about him of a benevolent grandfather.

"My wife is soaked after her journey here, and exhausted." Arthur fidgeted, a little impatiently. "I'll take her up to my rooms and make sure she gets dry clothing and a rest before our evening meal. Can you see we're not disturbed?"

"Of course, my Lord Dux." Riacus bowed to both of us.

Arthur shot me a grin Riacus couldn't have seen. "Upstairs."

We climbed a wooden staircase to the upper floor, where

above our heads the roofbeams rose blackened and ancient to a high cathedral ceiling. A big bed stood at one end of a spacious room, and at the other a table and benches. On the table lay Arthur's sword and sword belt, his daggers and his mail shirt. His helmet sat on one of the chairs.

He threw my saddlebags down on the floor and turned back to me, in one fluid movement pulling me into his arms. I went willingly. I might have been tired after my journey, but it had been a long time since I'd seen my husband, and I was as hungry for him as he was for me.

His mouth found mine, his lips hot and demanding. I kissed him back, as demanding as he could be. Without releasing my mouth, he managed to undo the clasp on my wet cloak. It pooled at my feet in a soggy heap. Someone would have to hang that up to dry, but not now.

My fingers ran through his dark hair, pulling him closer, while his hands fumbled with my belt. Difficult to do when pressed together kissing with all the passion five weeks parting can bring.

We staggered apart, separated by our mutual need to undress each other.

"I'll do it myself," I managed. "I'll be quicker."

Arthur nodded, dragging his own tunic off over his head. I did the same, and in a matter of minutes we were both naked, locked together again in a passionate kiss. His hands ran over my skin, his touch electrifying. As he explored every curve, I pressed my body against his, his arousal hard against my belly, eager to be satisfied. My own arousal felt pretty much the same.

"Bed," Arthur muttered, sweeping me off my feet and carrying me to it. We fell onto it together, and I eagerly opened my legs as he slid between them. Intent on pressing him as deep as he could go, I locked my legs around his back to hold him to me. We'd both been desperate, eager, ready for this before we'd even got our clothes off.

Absence certainly makes the heart grow fonder. We galloped

to a mutual climax within a few hectic, sweaty minutes, faster than we ever had before. At last, spent and drenched in sweat, we collapsed back onto the bed.

After a minute or two, I regained my breath enough to speak. "I missed you too."

He rolled onto one side, propping his head on his hand. "A bit extreme to travel three hundred and fifty miles to slake your lust."

I grinned. "And yours."

His fingers ran across my right breast, and I felt that lust renew itself slightly. So much for getting a rest. He grinned back. "I can't say I approve of you leaving Amhar and riding into possible danger, but I have to admit, I'm glad you're here."

I slid my hand down his belly. "I thought you might be."

His eyes danced. "If you want more of that then you'll have to give me time to recover."

I smiled into his eyes. "I can wait."

Chapter Eight

T HAT NIGHT WE dined in Riacus's hall. Merlin and Cei joined us from across the courtyard where they'd been billeted, and Theodoric appeared from some place within the town. Knowing Theodoric, I could guess what sort of an establishment he'd been frequenting, despite having a pretty little wife at home.

Riacus didn't keep Roman dining practices, thank goodness. He was all British himself. "Local born and local bred," he proudly told me, his accent reminding me somewhat of the sort of accent I'd heard when I'd been up here with my father, far into the future that was now my past. Could accents hang on over the years and remain the same as they'd been in the past? It seemed perhaps they could.

His wife, Elen, a much younger woman, sat beside me at the table and engaged me in conversation while the men talked war. I'd have liked to have at least eavesdropped, at most to have joined them, but this was a period of time that liked to exclude women from men's talk.

"Are you from around here?" I asked Elen, scraping the bottom of the barrel for some small talk. She was a few years older than me, her honey-blonde hair piled in elaborate curls on top of her head, in sharp contrast to my own demure plait. With no one to help me dress except Arthur, I was lucky I even had that plait. The hands that had been supposed to be plaiting had kept straying where they weren't meant to go. And I was sure the laces on my dress were lopsided, the way he'd been distracted by my body while he was doing them up.

Elen nodded. "I was born here in the town. My father's a wool merchant. Our sheep graze right up to the Wall."

It seemed there was more to her than I'd thought. "Have you been to the Wall?"

She laughed, a girlish, tinkling sound. Anyone less like a sheep farmer's daughter would have been hard to find. She looked as though she'd have been more at home as a twenties ingenue in an Agatha Christie novel. "Of course I have. When I was a girl my father used to take me up there when we gathered the sheep for shearing. I've ridden most of the length of the Wall."

Again, she surprised me. "Astride?" Not many women rode, due to their long dresses, and I much preferred to ride astride like a man.

She nodded. "Of course. How else? I'd make slow progress if I rode behind a man on one of those pathetic pads they like us women to sit on. Far too easy to slide off." She giggled. "Splat in sheep poo. There's plenty of that lying around."

I joined in her laughter. Maybe she wasn't the airhead I'd assumed her to be. Maybe I'd been guilty of making assumptions based on what she looked like.

"I saw you ride in," she said. "In your mail shirt." Her brows furrowed. "And yet now you look as much a woman as I do."

Well, maybe not quite. As well as the elaborately piled curls she'd tinted her cheeks and darkened around her eyes. And she reeked of perfume. I smiled. "I wear the mail shirt for safety – in case we're attacked while we're on the road."

She smiled back, showing me uneven front teeth that could have done with some orthodontistry when she was a child. "Maybe if you stay here for a while we could ride out together. I scarcely ever get the chance to ride with another woman. That is, if you don't mind, my lady." A hint of worry edged her voice – perhaps she'd just remembered she was talking to a queen.

"I'd love to. If we stay here. I've no idea what my husband

has planned."

As one, we turned to regard our menfolk, heads together at the other end of the table, deep in discussion of who knew what. At this rate I wasn't likely to find out.

Elen got to her feet. "Shall we leave them to it? I have some wine in my parlor that my husband acquired from the Mediterranean a few years ago. It's still good. He's been saving it for a special occasion. I think entertaining the Ring Maiden counts as one."

With a final glance back at the men, and a feeling of lasting annoyance that I wasn't a part of their discussion, I followed Elen out of the dining room and into a room equipped with several wide seats and a low table. Sure enough, on the table stood a jug of wine and a couple of beautiful green glass goblets.

"Where was this wine brought in to?" I asked, as we sat down on one of the seats. The bottom had a sort of basket weave made from bands of leather. The pleasing give they created made the seat very comfortable, helped by the back being piled with cushions.

Elen poured the wine, a rich gold, into the goblets. "Segedunum, on the east coast. But we've not had any now for several years. Riacus says luck brought that ship this far north. Luck and a storm. He says he doubts we'll see another in our lifetime. Too many Saxon pirates in the German Ocean."

She meant the North Sea, and she was most likely right. I picked up my goblet and tasted the wine. It had been watered, but was still rich and heady. Hopefully she'd either had the water boiled or taken it from a clean spring.

She must have read my thoughts, or seen my dubious expression. "We have an aqueduct that brings in water from a spring – you needn't worry about its cleanliness."

I took another sip, and she picked up her own goblet. For a moment or two we drank in silence.

The room was not large. Underfoot a mosaic of some sea monster adorned the slightly uneven floor, within each corner a small ship tossing on stone waves. The walls had been painted terracotta to waist height, and above that, fake alcoves painted on with pictures of statues adorning them.

Elen finally broke the silence. "My husband thinks a woman's place is at the hearth, with babies on her knee, I'm afraid. But we've been wed these ten years and not a baby for me to dandle. So, I do other things instead." For a moment sadness clouded her wide blue eyes. "He thinks I'm too much of a woman to understand his office, but gradually, over time, I've come to exercise a certain influence on him. It irks me that he's excluded us this night from their discussion. If it were just him and me, with visitors, he'd have let me listen."

I set my goblet down. Stronger than the wine we'd drunk at dinner, it wouldn't do to gulp it. "You're right. My husband's the same. He didn't want me to come with him. We have a small son, and he thought I should be staying with him. Men." The thought of Amhar brought an unwelcome lump to my throat. I couldn't dwell on that, or I'd break down and cry. Instead, I concentrated hard on Elen.

She giggled very girlishly. Easy to see why her husband thought her an airhead. I'd made the same mistake myself. "One day, perhaps, men will come to see that our ideas have value," she said.

I nodded. "One day." Little did she know how long women would have to wait.

She leant back against her cushions. "But I do know what's going on. I'm particularly good at listening at doors. Hard to keep things secret in this house. And my servants are faithful to me. Men so often forget that servants have ears."

I sat up straighter. "Can you tell me? All I know is that there's trouble up here between the neighboring kingdoms and they asked for help at the Council of Kings. What d'you know about it?"

She finished her goblet of wine and set it down on the table. "What d'you want to know?"

I set my own unfinished wine down beside her empty goblet. "Everything. The background. The history. The politics between the kingdoms."

She nodded. "Very well. Up to the Wall, this side of it, is the kingdom of Rheged. Our overlord here is King Meirchion Gul, the Lean. That skinny old bastard. His oldest son – Cynfarch – rules the south of the kingdom. He's a miserable beggar with not an ounce of humor in him. His nickname's Cynfarch the Dismal. I had a lucky escape there – my father had him in his sights as a possible husband." She chuckled. "I foiled him there, by running off and marrying Riacus. Father was shocked, but by then there was nothing he could do. And I wasn't cut out to be a princess."

It seemed Elen was a woman who knew her own mind.

She went on. "North of the Wall there are two large kingdoms. In the east there's Guotodin, running up the coast toward the old earth wall. Lot's king there. He's a strong king and a good defense against the Saxon raiders who sometimes sail up the coast."

I nodded. "His son, Gwalchmei, is one of our warriors. A fine young man and a skilled musician. He's back at Din Cadan."

"A good place to be. To the west lies Alt Clut, the lands of Caw. He's a different bowl of eels. Slippery as one of them too. He has twelve sons at last count, and each one of them greedy for his own place to rule. His territory stretches far to the north, and *that's* where the troubles started. His northern holdings are hard to farm and he's allowed the Painted People, the Picts, from the lands beyond his border, to come south and settle. They scratch a poor living from the moors, but they're fearsome warriors and, with him backing them, they're craning their necks over the Wall now, their eyes on the fat south."

"Have they managed to breach the Wall?" In my time only ten per cent of the original wall remained, most of it just a few blocks high, but when Hadrian first had it built it had stood fully nine feet high along most of its length. The historian in me longed to see it for myself, in all its original splendor.

She nodded. "A few raids south that our king repelled, a few farmsteads burnt, women carried off. Riacus says there've been more raids to the east into King Lot's lands. He thinks Caw wants to rule everything north of the Wall. Lot's furious, of course. It was his idea to call on the army of the Dux at the Council of Kings, and he persuaded Meirchion to join in his demand. That was probably all the help he could expect from that old fart." She sniggered at the name she'd called him. "Riacus says Caw encourages these raids because he sees he can ride in on their cloak tails and increase his own holdings. With twelve sons he needs to expand."

I nodded. "So Caw needs putting in his place and the Picts need driving back beyond the old earth wall? Back to their homelands?"

She poured herself more wine. "You have it. That's what they'll have been talking about tonight while we were left to ourselves to talk about boring women's matters. They don't think women could ever possibly be any help in men's business."

I smiled. "You're so right. But what our husbands don't know yet is that I know this area quite well."

Her eyebrows shot up.

"I came here as a child, many times." Her eyebrows rose even higher. "Probably you never noticed me. You'd have been a child yourself." I couldn't possibly explain how I came to know her homeland, now could I? "And I can draw a map for them."

"A map?" The concept seemed alien to her. Probably her husband, too, would never have seen one. They must be few and far between in the Dark Ages, although clearly Merlin knew what a map was.

My heart beat a little faster. "A picture of the land with the towns and fortresses marked on, and the Wall, and the coastline." I paused to consider what I could remember. "And the high hills and the rivers." This was asking a lot of my memories, but surely I could manage an approximation of northern England where it met southern Scotland? "Do you have paper and pen?"

She fetched me a roll of parchment, and a pen and inkpot from her husband's office, and we weighted down the corners of the parchment with stones from the garden. I dipped the pen into the ink, knocked it off against the side of the pot, and began to draw. Luckily maps had always fascinated me. I had a whole shelf full of ordnance survey maps of everywhere I'd been in a bookcase in my old house. As a child I'd passed the time drawing my own maps of my fantasy lands.

Sketching out the shape of the coastline of northern Britain wasn't so difficult. But putting in the areas of high land came harder. I racked my brains. A large part of the land north of the Wall lay under forest, even in my time, and much of the rest was high moorland, unsuited for most agriculture. If I could recall where the modern roads went, that would help me pick out the areas suitable for travel now. Maybe the Roman roads that had once run north of the Wall, heading all the way to the Antonine Wall, Elen's 'old earth wall', might still be useable.

I put a crenellated line in to show the Wall running between Caer Ligualid in the west and Segedunum in the east and marked crosses for the forts and towns I knew. I drew a little wiggly line for the north-facing cliffs of the Whin Sill where it lay, due north of Vindolanda. A formidable barrier for any would-be invader before ever they reached the Wall itself.

Elen leant over my shoulder, entranced by my drawing. "Is this what our land looks like...from above? Like a bird would see it?"

"Yes. Only the bird would have to be very high up. Higher than a bird can go." I wrote Caer Ligualid at one end, and marked Vindolanda roughly where I thought it might lie. Then added in the Stanegate running between Coria and Caer Ligualid.

"This is magic." Elen's voice brimmed with awe.

"Where are the seats of the kings of Alt Clut and Guotodin?" I might be able to put them on.

Elen frowned. "I think I heard Riacus say that Lot has his court at Din Eidyn. I'm not sure about Caw – would it be Dun

FIL REID

Breattann?" She paused. "Do you *know* these places?"

I shrugged. "I can hazard a guess." Din Eidyn had to be Edinburgh. Probably on the site of the present castle, which sat on the plug of an extinct volcano. That would be an excellently well defended spot to hold your court from. But Dun Breattann? Could that be Dumbarton, and if so, where was that? I struggled to mark it on the map inside my head. Wasn't it on the River Clyde? Near Glasgow? And if so, not that far from Caw's rival's court. I marked these two on the map as best I could, more certain of Din Eidyn than I was of Dun Breattann.

But a map's not a lot of use without a scale. How long was the Wall? Eighty miles? No, a little less. About seventy-five. That would have to do. I drew a line to one side, the same length as the Wall, and beside it wrote '75 miles'. I divided it into five and marked each as fifteen, then one of them into three and labelled them as five miles each.

"You can read and write?" Clearly impressed, Elen ran her fingers over the words I'd just written and smudged them a little.

"You need to let the ink dry." I rewrote the fives. "And yes, I can read, write and reckon."

"Oh, I can reckon," she retorted. "In my head and on my fingers. But no one I know except my husband can read and write. It's magic."

The paneled wooden doors from the dining room opened, and the men came out, Arthur by Riacus's side, Merlin, Cei and Theodoric behind them. Riacus, seeing Elen and me on our knees at the low table, approached.

Elen leapt to her feet, eyes shining. "Come and see what the Queen has done, my love. What she's made."

All of them came over. For a long moment they stood staring down at the crude map held down by the stones on the table.

Merlin spoke first. "A map." Most likely at least Riacus needed telling what this was. Might Theodoric, as a sailor, have seen one before?

Arthur moved closer, bending over the map.

I got to my feet and took a step back. As maps went, it wasn't the best by a long way. "I can do better," I said, apologetic that they'd come upon it in its infancy. "It's just a sketch as yet."

Arthur was quick on the uptake, as usual. "This here, this is the coast? The land is this shape?" His finger jabbed at the line of the Wall and where I'd marked Vindolanda. "And we are here?"

Elen nodded, eyes alight with excitement. "It's as though we were birds, flying high in the sky, looking down on our world." I couldn't have put it better myself.

Cei frowned. "How can you know what a bird would see? How can this be right? Is our land so strange a shape? What's this and this and this?" He pointed to the amorphous blobs I'd scattered around the lowlands of Scotland.

"Higher ground. Big hills, deep valleys, where it would be difficult for an army to pass. Not impossible, but not ground you could make fast progress over. Probably some bogs, ravines, cliffs. I can't be sure." What I wouldn't have given for Google Earth.

Arthur's finger landed on Dun Breattann. "This is Caw's stronghold? Here? So far north? So close to Lot's own fortress?"

I nodded. "On this river. I think it's called the Clyde."

"It is." Riacus traced the river's course. "This is a wondrous thing to behold." He turned to Arthur. "The Ring Maiden is worth her weight in gold."

Kind of him to say so.

Merlin turned to me. "You say you can do better? If we find you more parchment, can you put more detail on?"

If I'd had Google Earth to look at, I could have done better still, but I didn't. All I had was my memory, which, good as it was, might well be fallible. "I can try. I came here long ago with my father. We visited many of these places. But I was only a child, at best fifteen or so, and that's a long time ago now." Longer than all but Merlin and Arthur knew.

"A proper map would be most useful," Arthur said. "For in two days time I'm marching north."

I gazed down at my crude map, wondering how I was going to persuade him to take me with him.

Chapter Nine

A S IT HAPPENED, at first it didn't look like I'd need to persuade Arthur to take me with him, as he'd already been planning to do just that. We were to ride north of the Wall up what remained of Roman Dere Street to King Lot's fortress at Din Eidyn. However, the evening before our planned departure, everything changed. Messengers arrived from Lot. They'd ridden straight down Dere Street to Coria, hoping to find Arthur there, and after a change of horses continued to Vindolanda.

They came upon us in the stable courtyard, where, in watery evening sunshine, Barden, the town farrier, was paring our horses' hooves. None of them wore shoes, which had once surprised me, but their hooves were rock hard from constant use. However, a cavalry unit is only as strong as its horses' feet, and they needed reshaping every so often to keep them in tip-top condition. Barden, a short-legged, bull-bodied man of indeterminate middle age, with a shiny bald head and the bushiest eyebrows I'd ever seen, had one of Alezan's front feet clasped between his knees when Riacus hurried into the courtyard. Following him, trailed three travel-weary warriors, leading horses white with sweat.

They approached Arthur where he stood grooming Llamrei. Straightening, he let the hand holding his brush fall to his side, brows lowering in a frown. The three dust-covered young men dropped as one to their knees on the cobbles in front of him, heads bent, long hair stuck to their heads by sweat.

My heart pitter-pattered with sudden anxiety.

Arthur waved them to their feet. "You have the look of bearers of bad news."

Their leader, probably the oldest of the three, spoke first. "My Lord. I am Elffin ap Gwyddno, warrior of King Lot. He sent us south five days since bearing messages for you and his ally, King Meirchion. We are besieged. Our farmsteads are burning. Not from the Pictish settlers already in Alt Clut. These are new invaders. Wild Dogmen from the far north. We're attacked on all sides – from the north over the earth wall, and from the sea. They've taken to their boats and are heading south. My king told me to tell you they'll be breaching the Wall itself if we can't halt them."

Cei and Merlin had downed tools and moved closer to listen to the message. Theodoric was nowhere to be seen. Off whoring most likely. I'd long since learned that every town or fortress possessed a street of whorehouses.

Cei narrowed his eyes. "If we ride north now, we'll leave south of the Wall vulnerable."

Arthur shook his head. "No. We'll send word back to old King Coel in Ebrauc. He can put his men on alert for Pictish boats along the coast. The Wall's a formidable barrier, and the frontier forts are still manned. We have to go north – we have a job to do. Lot's asked for our help and we can't deny it to him."

Merlin's eyes narrowed. "D'you think it possible the Dogmen and Caw could have formed an alliance with the Saxon settlers south of the Wall, to our east? If that's where they're heading in their boats?"

Who were these Dogmen? I controlled the urge to butt in and ask, instead listening attentively.

Arthur chewed his lip. "They could have. On their own, the Saxons of the north are not numerous enough to trouble us. They're farmers now, not invaders. But if they *have* formed an alliance of some kind, and more ships have come, then they'll be an added problem."

Cei leaned on Llamrei's gleaming quarters. "Good thing you gave those Pictish settlers in Alt Clut a warning beating. I doubt they'll be keen to engage with us again."

Arthur pulled a skeptical face. "I wouldn't count on that. Caw of Alt Clut is a greedy man. Don't forget he has twelve sons to provide for. He held back when we crossed the Wall into his territory to fire a few Pictish settlements and kill some of their warriors. But if he thinks he can profit, he'll stir up the Picts he's already got and add new ones from north of the Clyde to rise against Lot and Coel – and us. Against Meirchion too, although *he* thinks himself safe in Caer Ligualid. Mark my words. Caw'll do that in the blink of an eye."

Elffin put a dirty hand up to wipe the sweat from his brow. "My Lords, should I ride on to beg King Meirchion to supply us with extra men? When my king sent me there once before, Meirchion sent me off without so much as a flask of ale, telling me that it wasn't his job to repel the Picts for Lot of Lleuddiniawn if Lot couldn't do it himself. He refused to pledge any of his warriors to our cause. I fear he'll be the same this time and my journey will be wasted."

Cei snorted. "That's because he thinks he's secure behind the double protection of the Wall itself and the fortifications of Caer Ligualid. It's always the same. If people think they're safe, they don't want to help those that aren't. It's only when they're threatened themselves that they start thinking about organized help."

All this time I'd been listening in silence, Alezan's warm head pressed against my chest as she half dozed. Barden had finished paring her feet and moved on to the next horse, uninterested in our talk of war. Like Meirchion, he probably thought himself safe from harm here in Vindolanda. The Wall made a tangible yet psychological barrier between everyone south of it and the barbarian north.

Now, I straightened and stepped forward. "Shouldn't you stay to defend the Wall?" The last thing I wanted was Arthur leaving me here, now he thought danger threatened. Not because I was afraid for myself, but from the fear I had for him of Camboglanna.

Arthur cast a fleeting glance in my direction, but his mind was clearly elsewhere, no doubt planning for his departure. "We'll march north at first light, as we'd planned. Cei, can you send messengers south to Ebrauc. Two men will do. It's not through dangerous territory. Elffin – I suppose you and your men had better ride on to Meirchion, but I fear you're right. He won't be offering us support."

I opened my mouth to protest, but Merlin put a hand on my arm. "His mind's made up. He's going north. That's where the biggest threat lies. The Picts are not great sailors – unlike the Saxons. Their boats are small – nothing more than large coracles. There'll not be huge numbers of them sailing south. And," he jerked his head upward into the rapidly clouding sky, "a storm's coming. That'll stop them in their tracks for a while."

He was right. The darkening sky held the promise of rain to come. As a child, up here with my father, the rain had never mattered to me. My memories of coming here with him seemed populated by sunny days, although they couldn't have all been like that. As I led Alezan into her stall, I hugged the thought to myself that at least if Arthur were riding north, he'd be moving away from Camboglanna.

Outside, Riacus beckoned the messengers. "Put your horses in the stables, and then come inside and my servants will see you fed and watered before you ride on."

THAT NIGHT IN bed, Arthur told me he'd changed his mind, and he wasn't taking me north with him. I'd been expecting that. When he'd said I could come, it had been to a well-defended fortress not under attack. The only threat had been the Picts already occupying Alt Clut, and he'd thought he'd dealt with those before I got here. Now, with the incursion of fresh barbarian warriors from the wild north, the situation had changed.

He chuckled. "And no disguising yourself as a man so you can join my army."

I was lying in the crook of his arm, our naked bodies pressed together after another round of feverish lovemaking. Absence had definitely made our hearts grow fonder.

"As if I would." Repeating that stunt had been far from my mind, as apart from anything else, it would probably never have worked a second time.

"Don't play the innocent with me. I can tell you're plotting."

"Am not." I let my fingers play with the hairs on his chest. "And I do understand that now it's going to be dangerous. But you can't blame me for worrying about you. I'm sure all your men's wives do the same."

He sniggered. "Worry about me?"

I tapped his nose. "No, silly. Worry about their husbands."

Silence fell between us, but neither of us slept. After a bit, I slid my hand across his belly. "You will take care, won't you?"

He sighed, partly with resignation and partly because I'd slid my hand lower. "Of course I will. I always do."

That made me snort with derision. "Oh really? Then why is it I can trace your battle history by the scars on your body? Like this one here…" I gave his side a prod. "And this one." Another prod on his upper arm. "And this one-"

He caught my hand and imprisoned it in his own. "All right. I take your point. But all warriors suffer wounds in battle. It's the way of the world. I'm a warrior king. I have to fight." He paused. "And I love to fight. You're a woman. You wouldn't understand."

One thing you could say about Arthur was that he was completely unreconstructed. No feminine side to get in touch with, and not all that good at putting himself in the place of others. Especially not women.

"I'll have you know I've been learning swordsmanship – swords*womanship* – on my way up here. Just in case." I wriggled my hand in his. "And if you insist on holding my hand I can't continue what I was just doing. And which you seemed to like…"

He released my hand and I slid it provocatively down his chest and belly, then lower, but stopped just short of where he clearly wanted me to touch him.

He lay silent for a moment or two. "Are you cross with me?"

I chuckled. "Maybe. Do you want me to do it again?"

"Of course." His voice was hoarse.

"And you promise that when you ride north you'll be more careful than usual?" For all I knew, Camboglanna was a red herring. His last battle might be in its very general vicinity. Letting him go off like this tore at my heart.

"Yes."

I resumed what I'd been doing before. Nothing like leaving him with the best possible memory of the fun he could be having with me, to make him keep himself safe and get back to more of it.

HE RODE NORTH with his army at first light, leaving behind half a dozen men, under command of a seasoned warrior named Anwyll, as my personal guards. I got up and pulled on my tunic, braccae and boots to walk down to the stables with him in the pre-dawn twilight. The stable courtyard milled with warriors, their horses hung with saddle bags, supplies and weapons. Riacus joined us there, and to my surprise, Elen came with him, dressed in a pale blue, almost diaphanous gown that made her look like a beautiful orchid amongst a field of wild dandelions.

Arthur finished fastening his saddle bags to his satisfaction and turned back to me. His expression told me he'd not forgotten last night. Good.

Taking me in his arms, he held me close against his mail shirt, the rough links rubbing my skin. With one hand, he tipped my chin upwards so I could gaze into his eyes. For a long moment he studied my face as though searching for something, and then, with the smallest of shrugs, he bent his head and kissed me.

I put my arms around his neck and held him tight, wanting the kiss to go on forever. But it couldn't. Gently, he prised himself free of my grasp, eyes still locked on mine, and stepped back to where Merlin held Llamrei.

I swallowed down the lump that had formed in my throat. Every time I watched him ride away with his men, the feeling that this might be the last time I saw him rose to the surface. This time it was worse.

He set his foot in his stirrup and swung up into the saddle, settling himself between the saddle horns and gathering his reins. Llamrei, fresh after several days' inactivity, danced under him, skittering across the cobbles, her newly pared hooves neat.

Merlin mounted his sturdy bay gelding. Castrated horses made far better warhorses than stallions did – quieter and easier to keep in a group, altogether calmer mounts, and not likely to be distracted by a mare in season. He gave me a nod, his set jaw and worried frown telling me I was right to be concerned.

As the army rode out of the courtyard and onto the main street of the town, I moved closer to Elen and Riacus. We stood watching until the last rider vanished from sight.

Elen turned to me, a bright smile on her face. "Time to break our fast I think." She took my hand and led me back into the praetorium. Relief that I had the company of another woman swept over me. Perhaps her companionship would lighten the burden of waiting for news.

TWO DAYS AFTER the departure of the army, with the storm

passed to the east, Elen suggested we should go riding together. Eager to do something other than sit badly sewing a shirt for little Amhar with my poor, needle-pricked fingers, and that by the time I returned to Din Cadan probably wouldn't fit him, I agreed with pleasure.

"Of course," she said, as we saddled our horses. "We can't possibly go alone. Riacus would never allow it, and nor, I think, would your husband. We're to take four of my husband's warriors."

That he had any was news to me. This town, despite its proximity to the Wall, had seemed, in the short time I'd been here, to consist of shopkeepers and farmers, not soldiers. But it seemed the male inhabitants doubled as warriors in their spare time, and four of them proved eager to escape the confines of the town and accompany us. I did wonder about taking Anwyll and a couple of my own guards, but Elen seemed proud to provide our escort so I didn't quibble. We should be safe enough close to Vindolanda.

The sun had risen high in the sky by the time we rode out, a party of six. I hadn't worn my mail shirt, but I did carry both the short sword Merlin had given me after our lessons, and the dagger I'd had from Arthur long ago. Elen also carried a sword, and had a dagger tucked in an ornate sheath on her belt.

We cantered north toward the Wall, across open moorland, purple with heather and dotted with small farms. Despite the differences in geography, this could just as easily have been the lands about Din Cadan. Small, sturdy sheep grazed everywhere, and far to the east a herd of ponies emerged from a patch of scrubby woodland.

"I don't see any wheat fields," I said, as we passed a farmstead where a woman and two young girls were weeding a small patch of leafy vegetables. "What do the people here do for bread?"

Elen smiled. "Trade. We have our wool up here, and your rich lands of the south, and to the east from here, have wheat for bread. You take our wool, and we eat your wheat. Simple."

Of course. I was being dense. Sheep were a great commodity.

No wonder her father was a wool merchant.

Alezan picked her way across uneven ground dotted with rocky outcrops and smaller stones. She was agile, but nothing like the sturdy pony Elen rode, shaggy maned and tailed, with long hair that I'd have called 'feathers' on its lower legs. The four young men who made our escort rode similar animals, and Alezan with her long legs and fine head and neck stood out as much as Elen had earlier in the stable yard – a bird of paradise on a garden bird table.

From overhead in the grey sky came the mewling cry of a red kite, soaring on the thermals, searching the ground for its prey. I squinted up, thinking of my map, which I'd redrawn with as many details as I could remember. Arthur had ridden off with it safely packed in his saddlebags.

We left the Supply Road behind us, and the ground before us dipped before rising slowly up toward the Whin Sill, that mighty row of towering, north-facing cliffs. With a brisk breeze blowing from the west, we crossed the impressive ditch and banks of the vallum. Half a mile ahead of us, the Wall, nearly twice the height of a man, ran along the clifftop, a formidable barrier against any Pict who might try to stage an attack. No wonder the people of Vindolanda felt comparatively safe.

Elen pointed eastward. "We can ride to Vercovicium and see my sister. It's not far."

Housesteads. That had been its modern name when I'd visited the hilltop ruin with my father on a wet and windblown, long-ago November day. I couldn't deny my eagerness to see it in the days of its habitation.

A rough road led us northeast, cutting across boggy terrain and heading at an oblique angle toward the Wall. On the brow of the hill the high stone fortifications of the Roman fortress rose up intact and impressive, backing onto the Wall itself. On the steep slope below the fortress, the tumbled ruins of long-abandoned houses seemed to be slipping downhill into the valley. Sheep grazed between all that remained of their walls, amongst purple heather and stunted hawthorns.

Nothing had prepared me for what greeted us in Vercovicium. The dirty blond hair of the guards manning the massive stone-towered gates hung to their shoulders, and they had long drooping moustaches not unlike Theodoric's. And he was a Goth, cousin to the Saxons who were our enemies.

Who were these strange, fair-haired warriors on duty in what had once been a Roman fort and now served to keep out the enemies of the British? Enemies who might look just like they did.

The guards, whoever they were, clearly recognized Elen and her warriors. They flung open the gates and allowed us to ride beneath the arch and up the steep, paved road toward the center of the town. We passed cheery women carrying baskets of goods, men chatting together while their women worked, and children ran about, dangerously close to our horses' legs. Like every Roman town I'd been to, the smells of animals, woodsmoke, and middens filled the air.

To either side, the formal grid layout of the roads betrayed the fact that this had once been a Roman fortress, even though as at Vindolanda the buildings had changed a lot since the Romans had left. Elen took a right turn before we reached the center, down a busy side road, where houses crowded close, and shop fronts and workshops jammed in cheek by jowl.

The women going about their daily business were a mixed bunch – many as fair as the guards, but a good many dark or red-headed. Here and there, armed warriors stood about eating street food from the shops, almost all of them blond. Could this be a Saxon fortress?

The thought that Elen had brought me into enemy territory rose unbidden. What had I walked into? Might she, despite all other indications, be my enemy? She was blonde, after all.

Outside one of the houses, a shop selling freshly baked bread, where the delicious smell made my hungry stomach growl, she slid down from her pony and handed the reins to one of our guards.

She glanced back up at me, a smile on her face. "This is my sister's house. Jump down, and we'll go in and surprise her."

Not having much choice, I slid down from Alezan and handed her reins to another of our escort. They sat resting their hands on the pommels of their saddles, an air of resignation about them. Did Elen perhaps come here often? The fact that the guards weren't afraid calmed my worries a little.

Several women of varying ages occupied the small shop front, haggling over the price of the loaves the baker had just taken out of an oven behind his counter. His homely, red face dripped with sweat as he peered over their heads at us. "Elen. Go on through," he called.

Elen led me through a small door and into the house beyond. As it must have been part of the army barracks once, it in no way resembled the sort of ex-Roman house I was used to. A long, narrow hall ran away from the shop with a hearth fire in the center. The smoke from the fire rose to the rafters of the thatched roof, where it should filter its way out eventually. Right now, unfortunately, a smoky fug filled the room.

Three small children played on the floor near the fire, and a woman sat to one side in front of a loom. As soon as she saw Elen, she jumped to her feet, eyes alight with excitement.

"Elen!"

"Rhiannon!"

The two women embraced. Rhiannon was an older, more careworn version of her sister, her blonde hair confined in a long braid that hung down her back to her waist. The three children, none of whom could have been more than five years old, were even blonder than their mother. Their long hair and loose tunics prevented me from telling whether they were boys or girls.

Elen released her sister. "You'll never guess who I've brought to meet you," she said, with the air of a conjuror about to produce a rabbit from his hat. "Queen Guinevere of Dumnonia, the Ring Maiden."

Rhiannon's eyes widened. "Oh my, and I've not tidied." Her

eyes darted around her sparsely furnished house. "I'm so sorry, Milady. If I'd known…"

Poor Rhiannon. I'd have rather Elen had just introduced me as her friend, but it was too late now. I stepped forward and took Rhiannon's hands in mine. "Please don't worry. Your house is lovely and your children remind me how much I miss my own little boy. Don't treat me as a queen. Today I'm just Gwen, Elen's friend."

Rhiannon's eyes opened all the wider.

Elen bent to the children. "Teyrnon, Pwyll, Idris, come and say hello to your Aunt Elen." The children ran to her. Judging from their names, they must be boys.

Rhiannon smoothed the skirts of her dress down then clasped her hands, shifting her weight uneasily from one foot to the other.

How to make her feel at ease entertaining a queen? I stepped over to the loom. A half-finished plaid filled it. "This is beautiful. You're a gifted weaver, I see." I smiled. "I've no idea myself of how to do this. Maybe you could show me?"

By the time she'd explained how to weave and let me have a clumsy go, which I was certain she'd have to redo after I'd gone, she was at ease with me as much as her younger sister. The children fetched the kittens their cat had recently produced and set them on my lap as we drank a beaker of cider together. I fussed over the kittens and told the children how beautiful each of them was, and before much longer we were all laughing together about our husbands, as women do the world over, immaterial of the time period.

I stroked the fourth kitten which had been left for me while the children went off to play with the ones they'd claimed as their own. "Do you mind if I ask you a question?"

Rhiannon smiled. "Of course not."

"Is this place…? Are the men here *Saxons*?"

A slightly awkward silence.

Elen broke it. "Once they were. Now they're as British as you and I. We're all British up here." Her voice had taken on a slight defensiveness.

I frowned. "I don't understand."

Rhiannon set down the horn beaker she'd been drinking from. "You're right that we have Saxon blood running in our veins up here. Look at me and Elen. Both our parents have Saxon blood. Our grandfathers, or was it our great grandfathers, came here to fight for the legions. As foederati."

Elen joined in. "It might even have been our great-great-grandfathers. Who knows. They came over here as Roman auxiliaries and when the legions left, they stayed. They married local women so our blood is mingled, but we're all British now. No one here likes the German Sea pirates who sail up the coast to pillage and rape. We're soldiers and settlers here. We belong."

Of course. These young women were probably fourth or fifth generation immigrants, and like those in my old world, from more far-flung countries, they'd made this land their own. They were British now. How fascinating to find the exact same thing had happened in Britain down the ages, repeating itself over and over again. The fact that I was more likely to be descended myself from Saxon immigrants than the native British who were now my people was not lost on me. And really, no one could have been more of an immigrant than I was, could they?

Chapter Ten

T HE DAYS IN Vindolanda ticked by all too slowly. I rode out with Elen almost every day, despite the weather, but we rarely went as far as Vercovicium again. Instead, she showed me the moors around the fortress or we rode up to inspect the Wall and the ruined turrets.

The Wall had fortresses every six to nine miles, and in between them, mile-castles, like mini-forts, situated at every Roman mile, which was a little less than a modern mile. In between these mile-castles sat the simple turrets, a third of a mile apart. Keeping the forts and mile-castles manned must have been work enough – the turrets had been mostly left to rot.

Their roofs lay in the long grass that grew both inside and out, just discarded piles of broken slates and rotting roofbeams. However, most of their walls still reached their eaves, save a few which had been robbed out to make sheep pens sheltering up against the Wall. Ever practical farmers had utilized whatever materials came to hand. The mile-castles clung on, occupied by a motley collection of elderly warriors, and sporting sparse thatch, like old men losing their hair.

Overall, the state of the Wall impressed me. In my old world, ninety percent of it had been robbed away for building houses or roads or just field walls, but here the Wall still stood to its original height – and I wished not for the first time that I had a camera to record it. Not that I'd have had anyone to show the pictures to.

Merlin might have been impressed, but I had a sneaking suspicion Arthur might view them as witchcraft.

"All the fortresses are manned," Elen said, as we rode along the rough track that skirted the Wall. "All the local towns and farms have to supply soldiers – for these forts and for the ones beyond the wall, like Bremenium. Riacus has to send a conscript of men to Vercovicium to our east, and Aesica to our west, more in times of trouble." She put a hand up to shade her eyes – the sun was out for once. "Not to mention the mile-castles between the two. I'm afraid they tend to be manned by the oldest warriors – men without young wives. Our young men can take their wives to the fortresses, but no woman would want to spend time in a mile-castle."

Most of the Wall fortresses had become small towns. As at Vercovicium, the civilian population, that in Roman times had occupied the vicus outside the fortress walls, had moved inside the walls and set up shop. Aesica was smaller, but exactly the same.

It seemed the northern frontier was still comparatively well-guarded.

Elen seemed to know a lot about the politics of the area. With a knowing smile she told me how men were happy to talk in front of a woman, never thinking she might understand and remember what they'd said. Riacus rarely excluded her from his meetings. Her sharp brain held a very useful source of information. I began to form a picture in my mind of the machinations of the Hen Ogledd – the Old North.

Every morning, Riacus held meetings with his councilors – those of the town and often those from outlying farms and villages. On more than one occasion, Elen and I stood in the shadows of the council chamber's doorway, listening to what went on.

So it was that ten days after Arthur had left, we overheard something that set my heart pounding and the hairs on the back of my neck prickling upright.

Riacus had a desk at one end of his council chamber with a stout, high backed chair behind it. Not a throne, for his unostentatious personality would never have allowed that. But the placing of the chair behind the large desk imbued his presence with a sense of gravity, and those who came to him always looked in awe.

On this particular day it was raining again. Not the fine drizzle I'd grown so used to, that wouldn't have put Elen and me off riding out, but a heavy, leaden downpour that rattled on what remained of the tiled roofs of the praetorium. After breaking our fast together, Elen and I slipped into the corner of the council chamber and sat ourselves on the stone bench tucked into the alcove beside the door. Its placing almost felt as though Riacus had ordered it installed just so his wife could hear his judgements. And now his wife's friend and guest.

We settled ourselves comfortably on cushions we'd brought, today both wearing plain day-dresses instead of our riding tunics and braccae. On the roof, the rain rumbled like distant thunder.

Riacus was listening to a dispute between two shopkeepers, one of whom had accused the other of sabotaging his shop front. The middle-aged, rotund accuser had an angry bulldog face with heavy jowls and a belly that hung low over the belt of his tunic.

"All my wares – my beautifully baked breads – went rolling into the gutter," he complained, in a high, whiney voice. "And when I looked, I found the wooden leg o' my stand 'ad been near cut through. Soon as I put weight on it, it collapsed." He had a similar accent to Riacus, rich with the tones of the north.

The other man, a tall, skinny fellow with a narrow, rat-like face and a missing front tooth, glowered back at his accuser. He possessed thin cheeks spotted unattractively with the purplish-red lines of broken veins, a dead giveaway that he was a drinker. "He lies. Why would I need to do that when my bread's so superior to his? It's he who's been putting salt into my flour to make my bread taste bad."

The accuser spluttered his disagreement with that statement.

"Who's he think he's foolin'? I don't need to do nothin' to make his bread taste bad. If his bread is half as good as mine, I'll eat my bread peel."

"His what?" I whispered to Elen.

She peered around the corner of the alcove at her husband's back, where he sat ramrod straight in his big chair. "The long wooden paddle he uses to slide the bread in and out of the oven."

Of course, she'd know that with her older sister married to a baker. I stored the new word away in case I ever needed to use it again. Unlikely, but you never knew.

The dispute carried on, each man increasing his accusations, and would have continued even longer had there not been a sudden disturbance by the door into the courtyard. Riacus's two men standing guard there, to regulate the arrival of the people seeking his judgement, clashed their spears together to prevent a young man from breaking in upon the audience.

The young man, his long, wet hair plastered to his head and his cloak hanging heavy with rainwater, pressed against the crossed spears, desperation written on his face.

"My Lord Riacus," he shouted across his two detainers. "I have need of audience with you. Now. I bring news from the north."

From the north? My unruly heart fluttered, and my hands clenched into fists in my lap.

Riacus nodded to his men. "Let him in." The two rival bakers had enough sense to step back out of the way.

The young man strode up the hall toward the table. Halting in front of it, he hurriedly bowed his head. "My name is Dewain. I'm part of the squad posted at the fortress of Bremenium." He rubbed his wet sleeve across his face, swiping the hair out of his eyes. "Although 'tis hardly more than a farm nowadays. I've rid here as fast as I could. My commander sent me to warn Coria. There they gave me a fresh horse, but I'm done in. I've been in the saddle for two days. Can you send on my message to the west, to Caer Ligualid?"

Riacus nodded. "I can. Hurry, tell me your news so I can set my men upon the road."

Elen reached out and took my hand. Had she sensed my sudden fear?

"It's the Dogmen. They dint use the road. They came swarming down from the forest west of Bremenium. We saw the farms burnin' afore ever we saw their warriors. Painted men, naked, covered in blue dye, eyes like madmen." He hesitated, clearly remembering. "No, not men at all. Beasts. We got the gates barred and manned the walls, but they had no fear of us and there was too many of them. They mocked us as they passed. We couldn't stop them going south."

I looked a frown at Elen. "Dogmen?" I'd heard that term before.

She nodded. "The Picts. They wear dogs' heads and pelts and not much else. I've never seen one, but I've heard the tales." She shivered. "They say they eat their victims' hearts. Many think they really are half dog, half man..."

And they were heading this way. To the Wall.

"How is it you got through?" Riacus asked Dewain.

The exhausted young man pulled himself up straighter. "I dint want to leave. My place is with my fellow warriors. My commander chose me because I've lived man and boy on the farm and know the lands thereabouts right well." His eyes took on a faraway expression. Perhaps wondering if his fellow warriors had survived.

He shook himself. "I went over the wall and sneaked away. But I needn't ha' feared. The Dogmen scarce bothered to attack our fortress – they're more interested in the rich lands to the south. We're not important to them. I took me a horse from a farm a bit to the south, and warned the farmer and his family to flee. Then I rid here as fast as I could, through the night. It's been two whole days since I left, and I fear those creatures'll be at the Wall soon, even though they're marchin' afoot."

Riacus asked the question I'd been dying to pose. "And the

FIL REID

army of the Dux? Do you know where it is?"

Dewain shook his head. "We saw them march north along the old road. They made camp outside our walls. I didn't see the Dux myself as I'd drawn guard duty. That was nine days ago."

Of course, he couldn't know what had happened when Arthur had reached Din Eidyn. But the fact that these Dogmen had been brave enough to infiltrate the southern regions suggested Arthur was either otherwise engaged, or somehow out of the picture. My stomach did a roll, and I tasted bile.

"Arthur probably doesn't know they've come south," Elen said, reading my mind. "If they've come from the west, it's mountains and forests. No one would know what they were doing. Riacus says you'd need spies in every valley to keep track of someone there, and no one has that many spies. Not us, for certain."

Riacus got to his feet and motioned to one of his guards to approach. "Quickly, send for Murtaugh. We need to get this news to every fort and milecastle along the Wall."

The guard hurried away, and Riacus poured a generous goblet of wine and handed it to Dewain. "You've done well, young Dewain, to bring us advance warning."

The young man took a long swig of the wine, runnels streaking his scanty beard.

Riacus moved around the table. "No one else could have done that. Only a native-born warrior. If you go to the kitchens, my servants will see you well fed."

Setting the empty goblet down, Dewain departed.

Elen jumped to her feet and hurried to her husband. I followed more slowly.

Riacus enfolded her in his arms, clearly very fond of her. "My little sparrow." He planted a kiss on the top of her head. "I thought you might be here." His words were loving but the eyes that met mine over Elen's blonde curls brimmed with anxiety.

Elen extricated herself from his embrace, and he bobbed a small bow to me. We'd grown less formal over the previous ten days, but he was more aware of my status than his wife was. "Milady the Queen. I'm afraid danger threatens us. But have no fear. I'm sending messengers to King Meirchion to ask for his help. He has a good-sized army of warriors ready to do his bidding."

The king who'd already refused to help my husband. Was he going to want to help us now? I didn't have Riacus's faith.

"What can we do?" I asked.

His eyes widened. Evidently he was unused to being offered help by a woman. "Keep yourselves out of the way of my men. Stay safe here within the praetorium. No riding out." His eyes slid to his wife. She smiled at him demurely as though nothing had gone wrong with the day, her expression that of the little woman being kept safe by her big strong husband.

He patted her on the head. "I have to go." And with that, he hurried out through the doors into the courtyard.

Elen rubbed the top of her head. "Oof. I love him dearly, but sometimes he can be so condescending."

This was so close to how I often felt about Arthur that I had to smile, despite the fear gnawing at my heart.

"Can you fight?" I asked. "We may need to."

Elen grinned. "Is wine wet? My brother taught me from childhood. He often had no one else to practice with, so it was me or nothing. Rhiannon was older than us and more demure. She'd no more have picked up a sword than a dog turd." She paused. "Can you?"

"I've been learning."

She nodded. "Good move. But we may be getting ahead of ourselves. The Wall and all her defenses lie between us and the Dogmen."

I nodded. "But it can't hurt to be ready. Care to practice with me? I won't be as good as you, I should think, and I could do with some tips."

We changed into tunics, and in the confines of my chamber, unsheathed our swords. Elen had found us two light shields to wear. "Riacus has no idea I have this," Elen said, weighing the sword in her hand. "It was a present from my brother on the day of my wedding. He told me not to let my skills rust."

I drew my own sword. "Where is he now?"

Her face darkened. "Dead. The Dogmen. Five years ago." She swung her sword through an arc. "I'd like very much to settle that score one day." She grinned. "Maybe eat a heart or two myself."

She was a better swordswoman than I was, and good at teaching. On our journey up from Din Cadan, Merlin had been an unwilling tutor, disagreeing with my assertion that I needed to be able to defend myself. Now, with a better teacher, improvement came in leaps and bounds.

At last, sweaty and tired, we lowered our swords. My right arm ached from its weight, and I had a bruise coming across my ribs where Elen had smacked me with the flat of her weapon.

She grinned. "If I'd been a Dogman, you'd be dead. Learn to use your shield as a weapon too."

My breath came hard and fast. "The shield gets heavier and heavier, I swear. Both my arms ache really badly."

She sat down on the bench seat. "You've only been playing at it so far. You need to get serious. When I practice, I think of my brother. It helps me focus. Think of something like that yourself. Someone you want to avenge."

I didn't know anyone who'd been killed by the Dogmen. The memory of Ummidia and her two teenage daughters, dead at their mother's hand because Cadwy's Saxon foederati had raped them again and again leapt into my head. The Dogmen were like the Saxons – enemies of us British. Us British. The thought brought a smile.

"What is it?" Elen sheathed her sword. "What's made you smile?"

"Nothing." I couldn't tell her. Even though she carried Saxon blood herself, yet thought of herself as British, I couldn't tell her what made that thought so alien to me. The only person I'd ever told was Arthur. Merlin knew, of course, as he'd brought me here using my dragon ring. I turned it on my finger, remembering that day.

>>>><<<<

A FULL DAY passed with no further news. The fortress remained on high alert, with no one allowed out of the gates. The farmers and villagers from the surrounding area arrived with cartloads of their most treasured belongings and somehow squeezed themselves into the narrow streets.

Elen and I practiced our swordswomanship several times a day. Her idea, not mine. In between whiles, we listened in to Riacus's councils with the headmen of the town and those from the villages, as he sorted out disputes between the new arrivals and the townspeople and organized their help with manning the walls.

On the morning of the second day, we awoke to smoke rising in the west from the direction of Aesica. Thick, dark smoke, billowing up into a cloudless blue sky – for once it wasn't raining and visibility was excellent. It didn't look like hearth fire smoke.

Elen and I met on the verandah outside my room, which overlooked the courtyard. The small fountain played in the center as though nothing had happened, but the feverish activity going on around it gave the lie to that. Men tramped in and out of the gates, servants carried trays of food out toward the walls, dogs ran about excitedly barking at each other as well as the newcomers, and Riacus stood in the center, surveying the activity in yesterday's dirty tunic, his scant grey hair standing on end.

Directly north, over a mile distant, the hills where the Wall ran seemed quiet and undisturbed. Outside the praetorium chaos reigned, the sounds of panicked townspeople rising to greet us.

Down in the courtyard, Riacus ordered his captains out to reinforce the guards along the walls and make sure every gate had been secured. Vindolanda was large, and the run of the walls long, but they were tall and stout, and if well-defended should surely withstand even an attack by the mad Dogmen. Hopefully he was also sending out scouts to bring back news of what was going on.

The day passed all too slowly. Elen and I remained inside the praetorium as we'd been told to, mainly because the town was so crowded and there'd have been nothing for us to do outside the house. Riacus left with his captains and didn't return until nightfall, his face drawn and haggard. I'd given him the six men Arthur had left to guard me to use on the town walls, and every man from the beardless boys to the old greybeards had been co-opted into the defense force. All the male servants had gone, leaving only a bunch of frightened women in the house with us.

As the day wore on, more smoke rose into the for-once hot blue sky, and the unaccustomed sun beat down without mercy on the helmeted heads of our warriors where they waited, ranged along the city walls.

Elen and I, dressed in our riding clothes, went down to the kitchens and helped the nervous servants prepare food and drink to be taken to the walls. An air of expectant fear hung over everything.

Where was Arthur? Had he reached Din Eidyn and King Lot, or was he right now campaigning somewhere in the vast reaches of the Scottish Lowlands, unaware of our imminent danger?

Helping with the food gave me more than enough time to worry about him. I was glad when Elen distracted me with random chatter about the people, most of whom she knew, who kept coming to the praetorium to transport the food. She must have been as frightened as me, worrying about her sister and her little boys in Vercovicium, although that fortress had seemed better defended than we were here.

By nightfall, smoke was rising from farms much nearer to the town, black clouds billowing up into the evening sky, the stink of it carrying to us on the light breeze that had sprung up.

The Dogmen were drawing ever closer.

Chapter Eleven

E VENTUALLY, I HAD to go to my bed. But sleep didn't come. I lay tossing restlessly in the cool dark of my chamber, my mind darting between worrying about where Arthur was and fear of what the next day would bring. I must have slept a bit, because the next thing I knew someone was shaking me awake.

I came alert with a start. Candlelight flickered over a face distorted by shadow.

Elen gave me another urgent shake. "Get up. They're outside the walls. One of our captains came to wake my husband."

I sat up in bed, heart thumping. I'd been reassuring myself that they wouldn't attack so large and well defended a town. I'd been wrong.

Elen set the candle on the table, its light throwing huge leaping shadows up the walls. Fear hastening me, I scrambled out of bed and pulled on my riding clothes. I didn't stop to redo my plait. It hardly seemed necessary. "Are we surrounded?"

She shrugged. "I don't know. Probably not. Don't forget that on the south and east we've the steep gorge, making it harder for them to attack from there. They'd have to get up close to the walls and our men could pick them off. We have skilled archers amongst our troops."

I pulled on my boots, careless of how hot they'd make me later. In the chill of early morning I was glad of them. "What do we need to do?"

"Arm ourselves, just in case."

Her sword hung on her belt. I buckled on my own, glad of the practicing we'd been doing. Who knew if I'd need to use it this day?

Together, we ran down the stairs into the courtyard, where in the dim light of dawn Riacus was organizing his men. Despite being a civilian magistrate, he'd crammed his rather portly self into a mail shirt, and a helmet sat askew on his head, straps dangling. He spotted us at the bottom of the stairs and his already furrowed brow furrowed even further. "My Lady. Elen. What are you doing here? Get back inside. It's not safe."

"We're here to help," I said. "Tell us what to do."

Indecision clouded his eyes. Necessity won. "Hand out the weapons from the arms store. Then I can get to the wall."

We ran to the arms store, and Elen flung open the doors. Inside, racks of spears and shields lined the walls, with swords and bows heaped in untidy piles. It seemed Riacus was a man who thought of every eventuality. I hurried to take the spears down and pass them out to the townspeople who'd come crowding into the courtyard, pressing up to the doors of the storeroom. Women too. All too quickly the racks began to look alarmingly empty.

A young boy hardly older than Llacheu reached out a grubby hand as I passed over the bows and arrows, making me hesitate. Surely he was too young to fight?

The boy thrust his hand out more determinedly for the bow I held. "I'm a good shot. Lemme have it."

"How old are you?" I had to ask. He had straight dark hair to his shoulders, his grubby face streetwise and sharp, but he was just a child.

His lip curled. "Old enough. I c'n fight with a bow better'n you can with that sword, I'll bet."

More than likely true. I handed him the bow, and he disappeared into the crowd.

We kept on going until the arms store was bare.

The courtyard emptied of people like water down a drain,

leaving Elen and me alone by the gently splashing fountain. The double doors onto the street stood open. Men, women and boys ran past, some only armed with pitchforks or lumps of wood, headed for the walls and gates.

I couldn't stand there, not knowing what was happening. I grabbed Elen's hand. "Come on. We have to see for ourselves."

In the street, people seemed to be running in every direction. Some with purpose, many in a blind panic to find somewhere safe to hide their families. Keeping to the side, close up against the walls, we headed for the main west gates. That would surely be where the Dogmen would be massing.

The massive oaken gates between the twin towers stood closed and heavily barred. Between the crenellations on the tower, helmeted heads showed, and a forest of spears pointed their tips skyward. We ran to the right, along the wide street that followed the inside of the wall, until we came to a set of wooden steps in the huge earthen bank. Above our heads, and all along the wall-walk, warriors, shopkeepers, blacksmiths and merchants alike, with women and boys amongst them, stood ready to fight, and more had massed at the foot of the steps.

The little boy who'd taken the bow and arrows climbed the steps to the wall-walk a few people ahead of us. He must have gone home first, because now he wore an ancient, rusty mail shirt that reached below his knees. Perhaps it had been his father's.

My turn came, and I climbed the steps with Elen following at my heels.

The stone wall-walk ran wide and flat in both directions. Forty yards to our left the double towers of the gatehouse rose. To the right the wall curved away toward the corner and a smaller, single tower. In the distance, the twin towers of the north gate rose up above the thatched rooftops of the houses.

People crowded at the crenellations, peering through at what must lie beyond. I tapped a tatty youth on the shoulder. "Can I see?"

He glanced round, eyes wide with something between fear

and excitement, before reluctantly stepping back to give Elen and me our first look at the Dogmen.

Where the vicus, the old civilian settlement of the fort had once stood, its ruins lay: long-abandoned tumbled stone walls around rough street outlines, on a slope rising to distant trees that hid the westbound supply road. Near the top of the slope, the distinctive square shape of a Roman temple, still with its tiled roof, huddled beside a stand of stunted willows.

What looked like hundreds of Dogmen packed the plain between the ruins of the vicus and the temple, not in ranks, but randomly scattered, just out of accurate bowshot for our archers. Beyond them, was that the shadow of more men partly hidden by the scattering of trees on the brow of the hill? I couldn't be sure.

From where I stood, crammed into the crenellation with Elen, it was hard to make out the Dogmen's exact appearance. None of them looked like the sort of warriors I was used to. Most were almost naked, their skin festooned with bright blue decorative swirls and shapes from head to foot. They wore fur headdresses, that could have been dog or wolf heads, in place of helmets, and ragged fur cloaks hung down their backs. But it was their eerie silence that struck me most.

They stood almost motionless, staring at us across the expanse of the ruins, without making a sound. Somehow, I'd expected barbarian hordes to shout and howl and shriek, especially ones called Dogmen. But not these.

"Oh my." Elen's voice in my ear broke into my thoughts. "They look fierce."

Jammed as we were, my sword was digging into my hip, so I wriggled out of the crenellation. Elen joined me. The youth grabbed his place back again before someone else stole it.

"What'll they do?" I asked. "Stand there staring at us all day? Scare us into submission?"

Elen bit her lip. "I don't know. I believe St. Germanus did that once. Well, not with silence, with noise. It was called the Alleluia Victory. The barbarians just ran away." She paused. "We've never been attacked like this before. Never been attacked at all, in fact. The forts on the Wall have been, but not us. We thought we were safe here behind the Wall."

A man pushed past me, tall and sturdily built, smartly dressed in mail shirt and a helmet that did nothing to hide his scarred face. He stopped to stare. "Milady." His eyes ran over Elen as well. "What are you doing here? This is no place for women."

Anwyll. One of the warriors Arthur had left to guard me.

I gestured around myself. "Do you not see other women here, ready to fight?"

He frowned. "They're not queens. They are not the Ring Maiden, and I've not been charged with keeping them safe."

I frowned back. "More reason then for me to be here than them. For as the Ring Maiden, I bring you luck." Not that I believed that myself, but the knowledge that Arthur's men did had me half convinced of its efficacy. "You should tell the men of Vindolanda that. Inspire them with the knowledge that my presence will ensure victory. I'm going nowhere."

Anwyll's broad, scarred face momentarily softened with understanding. "But not here, Milady. It's too dangerous. They'll have archers themselves. If you're to remain, you'd best both get into the towers on the gate. There's protection behind those thick walls." His eyes travelled to our swords. "Let's hope your luck holds, and you won't need to use those."

He ushered Elen and me along the wall-walk, past the watchful people's army, and into the tower through a wide-open, weathered wooden door.

We found ourselves in a square chamber with a wooden staircase in one corner rising to the floor above – the roof. Riacus stood with several of his captains, staring out of the single narrow slit window in the wall facing the slope. He didn't even turn his head when we came in.

His duty done, Anwyll returned to the wall-walk, and I pulled Elen toward the stairs. We ran up them before Riacus could notice us.

Archers crowded the roof, a man at every crenellation, poised and ready for the onslaught. If I stood on tiptoe, I was tall enough to just see over the top of the wall at its highest point. The Dogmen had not moved. But up on the brow of the hill that dark shadow of further warriors showed more clearly from here – a solid mass of men in ranks, armor glittering, unlike the undisciplined, unarmored Dogmen.

Running footsteps sounded on the stairs. Riacus appeared, fastening his helmet straps, followed by his fellows. "What are you doing up here?" His voice rose in consternation. "Haven't I enough to do without having to worry about two women?" His face clouded as he realized he'd been rude to me. "I'm sorry, Milady, but this is no place for a queen." He glared at Elen. "Nor my wife."

I held out my hand, fisted, to show the dragon ring. "I'll bring you luck. I need to stay. I'm the Ring Maiden."

Indecision furrowed his face.

"And if she's staying, so am I," Elen said, jaw jutting in rebellion. "I'd rather be here and know what was happening and help defend the town than hide in our house, waiting for the Dogmen to arrive to rape and kill me."

"It's not just the Dogmen, is it, though?" I asked. "There're other warriors hiding in the trees."

Riacus shot me a look. "You're right. Those aren't Picts up on the brow. Those are men of Alt Clut."

Confusion washed over me. "But aren't they British? Are they going to attack the Dogmen from the rear?" If so, why hadn't they done it yet and come to our rescue?

Elen, shorter than me, stood on tiptoe to try and peer over the wall and failed.

Riacus nodded, eyes somber. "You're right again. They're British. And no, they're not going to come to our aid. They marched here with the Dogmen and, with them as allies, fired the farms along the way. Caw of Alt Clut has ranged himself alongside the Picts for his own gain. One of my scouts returned in the middle of the night with news that it wasn't just the Dogmen we have to contend with. The other scouts haven't returned at all."

A battle horn sounded, then another, raucous in the silence of the early morning. One of the archers turned to interrupt the magistrate. "They're on the move, sir."

A howling filled the air, raw and vicious, like a thousand wild dogs. Riacus turned away from us. "Be ready to shoot," he called to his men, then glanced over his shoulder. "Elen, Milady, get inside. Now. They have archers just as we do and neither of you is wearing armor."

I quickly stood on tiptoe once more for a last peek over the wall. The horde of blue painted Dogmen was running through the ruins of the old town toward us, silent mode forgotten, mouths open in screams of battle lust.

"When they reach the old forge, open fire," Riacus ordered.

Elen grabbed my hand, and we ran down the steps. We didn't see the archers draw their bows, take aim, and fire, although the hiss of their arrows taking flight followed us down into the gloom of the tower room.

No one remained below, so we ran to the slit window and peered out at the limited view it gave us.

My heart fluttered with primal fear. "They've got scaling ladders."

They must have had them hidden, lying flat on the ground, behind the low stone walls. Now, two men to every ladder, they came charging at our walls. Arrows swished through the air, but where a semi-naked, blue-painted ladder-carrier fell, another swiftly took his place. How many were there? A bigger army than Arthur's cavalry, that was for sure. Had Arthur already met them? Could they be here because they'd beaten him? I pushed the terrible thought that he might even now be lying dead on some far-off battlefield out of my head.

Elen pointed up the hill. A line of foot soldiers came marching out of the trees behind the Dogmen, a banner billowing in the breeze, proclaiming their allegiance.

"That's not Caw's banner," Elen said. "That's his son, Heuil."

So where was King Caw? Hope for Arthur sprang in my heart. Could he be somewhere else fighting Caw?

The men of Alt Clut numbered less than the Dogmen, but had better discipline. They kept together in ranks behind their leader, jogging down the slope toward the vicus ruins, shields held up to protect their torsos. Arrows took flight again. Dogmen fell to left and right, skewered by feathered shafts. On the paved roadway that ran down through the vicus to the town gates, a Dogman yanked a broken arrow from his shoulder and kept running, blood mingling with the blue paint. They were brave, I'd give them that.

The first ranks of the Dogmen dropped behind the nearest stone walls, out of sight of our marksmen. What were they doing? I couldn't tear myself away from the narrow window.

A moment later one of them stood up, an arrow fitted to his short bow. An arrow with a flaming tip. He released the arrow, and it took flight, soaring over our walls and into the streets behind. The streets of thatch-roofed houses.

An arrow from one of our own marksmen slammed into the blue archer full in the chest, and he toppled backwards out of sight. But that didn't deter his fellows. They popped up all along the walls, and a stream of deadly fire-arrows arced over our walls and into the town.

I ran to the door onto the wall-walk. In the street behind, several arrows had lodged themselves in the thatched roofs of the nearest houses, the damp straw smoldering blackly. Thank goodness for all the rain we'd had – the thatch must be water-logged. Perhaps it wouldn't burn.

Right beside the gate towers the top of a rough ladder ap-peared against one of the crenellations. Then more, all along the walls. Our warriors, our bakers, our blacksmiths and our merchants pushed away the tops of the ladders as best they could. Some fell back, but further along, on the corner by the tower, a blue painted warrior surged over the wall, teeth bared in a wild grin, a vicious sword in his hand. He struck out at the lad who'd been guarding that crenellation, blood spurted and the boy fell off the wall into the street below, rolling down the grassy bank. But the Dogman was alone, and another of our men, lacking either mail or a helmet, his bald head shining in the early morning sunlight, ran him through with a pitchfork, pinning him against the stone wall.

Elen came to the door beside me, her sword in her hand. Remembering mine, I drew it as well.

More painted men surged over the wall. Some of our men fought them hand to hand, others threw back the scaling ladders as fast as the Dogmen got them up there. Down in the street bloodied bodies sprawled on the cobbles, one or two crawling away into the shelter the houses offered. Was that blue paint and a fur cloak on the one staggering down an alleyway?

"That's a Dogman escaping into our town," Elen said through gritted teeth. "We have to stop him. Come on."

I clattered down the stone stairs behind Elen to the lowest level of the gatehouse. Turning sharply left into the road, we raced toward where we'd seen the escaping Pict. Smoke curled up from a rooftop to my right, thick and dark, and an alleyway ran between that house and the next. I turned down it, hard on Elen's heels.

The Dogman stood leaning on the rickety fence at the back of the house, his way blocked, unable to flee further. Blood ran freely down his chest from a gaping wound below his neck, but that had done nothing to diminish the grip he had on his short sword. From beneath his dog headdress, mad eyes flashed, and his lips curled back in a ferocious snarl. Sliding to a halt, I took a deep steadying breath. The smell of smoldering damp thatch settled into the alleyway in a pall, stinging my nostrils.

Blue paint scrolled across the man's entire body in an intricate lacework that must have meant something to him. His long hair, beneath the hood he'd made from a dog or wolf's head, hung, plastered with a chalky paste, in rat tails to his shoulders. Mad with battle lust, he glared back from under similarly plastered brows.

Elen pushed me to one side. "This is for my brother." Before I could stop her, she leapt to the attack.

The man was injured, probably badly to judge from the white of bone showing where the wound gaped across his breastbone, and the blood sluggishly pumping from it to run down his body and mingle with the blue paint. But he blazed with the fanaticism of the blood lust of battle. He leapt to meet Elen, their swords clashing together.

For a moment, all I could do was watch in horror as the two unequal warriors fought. If he hadn't been so wounded, she'd have had no chance. Despite all her training, she was still a woman with a woman's body and weaknesses. Hand to hand sword combat to the death was not something at which women could claim equality.

But he was weakened by his wound. Showing no mercy, she beat him back against the yard wall, hammering blows at him with the same almost mad vigor he possessed. She must have dearly loved her brother.

I shifted the grip on my sword, unsure what to do. Plainly she wanted to kill this man herself and wouldn't thank me for interfering, but I desperately wanted to help.

Their swords clashed again and again. Sweat stood out on Elen's brow and blood oozed, less freely now, down her foe's chest. He was weakening fast, and he must have known it. Suddenly, he made a mad lunge for Elen's stomach, throwing caution to the winds. The blade slashed through her clothing, and she sidestepped away from it, agile as a cat. But she'd forgotten the pool of his blood on the ground, and her foot slipped. For an instant, it looked as though she'd keep her balance. Her free arm flailed. Then she crashed to the ground.

The Dogman lunged at her, and she rolled sideways. She needed me now.

I swung my sword in an arc and sliced it across the dogman's back, cutting through his fur cloak to leave it hanging in bloody tatters. My blade grated on bone, making my treacherous stomach heave, but I refused to let it overcome me.

Elen scrambled to her feet, propelling herself up with a hand on the rickety fence, her sword held out in front of her. With all the power she could muster, she punched it into the Dogman's unprotected belly, the blade sinking in up to her fist. He fell, wrenching her sword out of her hands, mad eyes staring up in impotent fury.

"Yes," she panted, standing over him. "Killed by two women. We breed them strong and tough here on the Wall."

Those mad eyes began to glaze.

His sword slipped from his bloody hands. I kicked it away as Elen put a foot on his chest and yanked her own sword out of his belly. Not much blood came. He must have been nearly out of it.

Blood covered her from head to toe, from where she'd slipped in his, and across her stomach where he'd sliced her clothing.

"You're hurt," I gasped.

In the dirt, the dogman's feet kicked in the dance of death.

She shook her head. "Just a scratch."

I'd heard that before.

"Let me look."

She raised her tunic. Sure enough, the cut across her belly was shallow and short. He must have just caught her skin. The bleeding lessened even as I examined her.

She pulled her tunic back down, shaking her head. "Now I've killed one for myself, somehow I don't feel as good as I thought I would. My brother's still just as dead, and I'm no less sad."

"Not going to eat his heart then?" The only way I'd cope with this was by treating it light-heartedly. A man lay dead by our hands, sprawled there in the dirt in a mess of his own blood and ordure. Out there beyond the walls, a thousand more wanted to get in here and do the same to us. Flippancy had its place.

She shook her head a bit more. "No…it was perhaps better to imagine what I'd do if I met a Dogman than it was to actually do it." She gave the inert body a kick. "But good to help the cause of battle. If we'd left him living he might have threatened any of the families sheltering in their homes."

I nodded, sobered. The maniacal laughter that had felt dangerously near the surface died away. "I killed a man once. It's a terrible thing to do. The only thing you can do now is forget it. Otherwise you'll dream of it forever. Bad dreams."

She nodded. "Wise words." But her jaw trembled.

We trudged back to the road.

Up on the wall-walk no sign remained of blue painted warriors fighting with ours. Had they fallen back? We ran to the steps and scrambled up them. From there, the burning rooftops of the town became clearer, a veil of smoke settling over them, infiltrating the streets and alleys, black and acrid, as their damp thatch smoldered. No breeze to shift the smoke.

"Fire!" shouted a man. A shower of arrows arced into the sky to rain down on the enemy below. "Bows down now. Let them retreat. Don't waste your arrows when they're out of range."

The men standing at the crenellations stepped back from them, bows hanging by their sides, arrows still nocked in readiness.

Cautiously, I peered through the nearest crenellation. Our attackers were retreating fast. At the foot of the walls lay their discarded ladders and piles of bodies, not all of them dead yet. The still living moaned and moved restlessly, as they waited for death to snatch them. Already the stink of evacuated bowels had risen like a miasma to fester in the hot air.

An idea formed in my head. Leaving Elen peering at our retreating enemy, I ran along the wall-walk into the gate tower and up the stairs to the roof. Riacus leant against the rail at the top of the stairs, while a man bandaged his upper arm.

He met my eyes. "It's nothing. An arrow is all."

I nodded. No time to sympathize. "They're in retreat."

He nodded. "But they'll be back."

My turn to nod. "They've left their ladders. Send men out to collect them when they're too far away to run back and attack. That'll stop them in their tracks if they have no way to climb our walls."

His face lit up. The man tied a quick knot in the bandage and Riacus pulled away. "You're right. Good idea." He turned to one of his captains. "Bevan. Wait until they reach the brow, if that's how far they're going. Then take a squad of the youngest, fastest men out of the gates, and get out there and grab those ladders as fast as you can. Speed is of the essence. Send word to the north gate and tell them to do the same."

Bevan ran to carry out the order.

I went to the crenellations and looked over. The retreating enemy were almost at the old temple. Below me, the gates swung open, and thirty men raced out, keeping close to the town walls. Not even stopping to finish off the enemy wounded, they made for the ladders and, picking them up, ran back toward the gates.

Up on the hill a howl of fury rose.

But they were too late.

A glow of triumph surfaced in me. Perhaps I was truly the luck of Arthur. But where was he?

Chapter Twelve

I N THE STREETS, people raced to put out the fires started by the fire arrows, but in some cases it was too late and a few houses here and there blazed determinedly, despite precious water being thrown over them. Wood and thatch were not ideal building materials.

The enemy did not return that day. "They'll be off making new scaling ladders," Riacus said. "At least your idea has bought us time."

While they were gone, he ordered the enemy dead who'd fallen within the fortress collected up and thrown back over the walls, where swarms of flies were already massing, their audible hum a steady background noise. It wouldn't be long before those broken bodies began to stink worse than they already did. Riacus had our own dead carried into the center of the town and laid out. Wailing ululated through the hot afternoon air as women arrived to retrieve their menfolk's bodies.

Elen and I went back to the praetorium to help her servants prepare food and drink for the defenders. Bread was brought in from the ovens set for safety in the earthen banks beneath the town wall. At my suggestion we packed slabs of the bread with cold meat and cheese to make rudimentary sandwiches. Elen watered down the wine and beer and we sent that off in earthenware jugs with volunteers.

As we worked, I kept expecting to hear news of the attack

being renewed, but as the long day progressed, nothing happened. "Let's hope they've had to go a long way to find wood to make more scaling ladders," I remarked to Elen as we sliced up more meat. The almost unbearable heat in the kitchens from the fires laden with roasting meat had me sweating so much I'd discarded my tunic and was working in my undershirt. But even that was too hot, the material clinging to my sweaty skin. Oh, for lightweight cotton tops. And shorts. And open-toed sandals. My feet and lower legs felt as though they were being roasted alongside the skewered meat.

Elen must have been as hot as me, her face flushed an unattractive red, her hair hanging in lank curls she had to keep swiping out of her eyes. "Hopefully miles."

Toward evening, Elen and I, at Riacus's suggestion, walked the entire run of the wall-walk, stopping to talk to the defenders as we went. News of my identity, and how my husband's men regarded me, had gone before us. Everyone knew I was the Ring Maiden and the luck of Arthur.

The heat of the day had faded and although we were both exhausted, it was good to leave the boiling kitchen behind and walk in the comparatively fresh air. All the fires had been put out, leaving a few smoking ruins, and the air was redolent with the sour smell of wet soot. The men, faces grimy with sweat and dust, and leaning tiredly on their spears, smiled gladly at the sight of us.

"C'n ye touch my spear for me, Milady? Gi' me luck for the mornin'."

"God's blessing on ye, Milady."

"Let me touch your hand. I know it'll bring me luck ter-morrer."

"'Tis an honor to meet the Ring Maiden 'erself."

It was an honor to see their touching faith in me, stirring my soul to such pride in their fortitude, tears sprung in my eyes that I had to wipe away with my dirty sleeve.

By nightfall, no attack had come and, exhausted, I retired to bed, fully dressed but for my boots, ready to be up in a moment if any attack came overnight. But sleep wasn't my friend, and my dreams were full of Arthur lying covered in blood on a far-off battlefield, the men I knew and loved scattered around him – Merlin, Cei and even Theodoric, whom I didn't much care for.

I awoke with tears on my cheeks to the half dark of early morning and couldn't recapture sleep. After lying restless for a few minutes with unwelcome images dashing through my head, I got up and slipped my boots on. Outside, the praetorium lay quiet under a moonless sky, thick dark shadows coagulated around the walls. I padded down the outside steps into the courtyard and rinsed my face at the fountain, the cool water restoring a little of my humanity.

On weary feet, I plodded out into the street, heading in the direction of the west gates. Against the blue-black night sky, the silhouettes of the vigilant rose beside the black outline of the crenellations. The town was not sleeping any more than I had been.

I let myself into the ground floor of the right-hand gate tower and climbed the stone steps to the room above. A single smoky torch burned in a wall bracket, and Riacus sat in a rickety chair someone had found him, slumped to one side in awkward sleep. On a table lay the remains of a rough meal – empty goblets, breadcrumbs, a few rinds of cheese.

He started awake at my arrival.

"Milady." He moved as though to get to his feet.

I waved him back. "You're tired. I'm sorry I disturbed you. I couldn't sleep."

He sank back into his chair and rubbed a hand over red-rimmed eyes. "Not many of us can. I've done my best to ring the changes of the guards on the walls, but we've not a huge number to call on. Our best men are – were – stationed along the Wall. I sent messengers to call them back at the same time I sent the scouts out westwards, but I don't know how many will have got through, nor if help is on its way." He sighed. "And even if they come, I don't know how they'll get through the enemy lines to join us."

I perched on the edge of the wobbly table. "Why would Caw and Heuil do this? Ally themselves with the traditional enemies of their own people? With men who should be their own enemies, surely?"

Riacus snorted. "Greed. What other reason might he have? Caw's a man with twelve sons he needs to provide for. A man whose lands are not of the most productive. He sees the richer lands south of the Wall and he wants them for himself."

He rubbed a hand through his sparse hair. "And his mother was half Pict herself, so I hear. They are his natural allies. Fearless fighters, afraid of nothing. I doubt it's pure greed that motivates them. More likely their love of killing." He pulled a face. "And up here the people see themselves as different from the men of the soft lands to the south. Caw won't see himself as British. He's a man of Alt Clut, and that's all. Everyone else is his enemy."

"And King Lot? Why would Caw attack him? For the same reasons?"

Riacus managed a wry smile that did nothing to light up his grey face. "That and their ancestral blood feud. It goes back generations. Caw's not a man to forget a wrong once done, even if it was on his grandfather's grandfather. And nor would he let his sons forget it. Memories last a long time up here."

"Why now, though?"

"It's not really a question of why now. More that the two of them are always raiding one another's lands. Their border's a bit fluid, if you know what I mean. Depends on who has the upper hand. Caw must think he has right now, with the help of his Picts, or he'd never be as openly aggressive as this. I wonder if there's something we don't know."

I did too.

The door from the wall-walk swung open, and Anwyll came in, his helmet tucked under his arm. On the threshold he hesitated. "Milady. I didn't know you were here." His gaze went to where I was seated. "I'll fetch up a chair for you."

I held up a hand to tell him not to, but he was gone.

Riacus sighed. "I should give you my chair."

I shook my head. "Nonsense. You're exhausted. Stay seated. Please."

Anwyll came puffing up the stairs with another chair. He set it down beside the table and I slipped into it.

He stepped back. "I'll get one of my men to fetch you both breakfast." And he was gone again.

Riacus and I sat in a silence that might have been companionable had it not been for our circumstances. Through the narrow window to the east, the sky began to lighten, the blue-black fading to a pale shimmer. Breakfast came – dark bread, onions, watered wine and cold meat. The smell of it brought the hunger I'd forgotten racing back. Had I eaten at all the day before, despite having been in the middle of all that food? I couldn't remember.

I tucked in with gusto to the simple repast.

By the time I'd finished, the sun was rising over the hills behind the town.

THE SECOND ATTACK didn't come until late in the afternoon. Riacus was right, they'd been off trying to build new scaling ladders. Thanks to the lack of decent forest here on the moors, they'd clearly been hard pressed to find the wood they needed, and they didn't have nearly as many scaling ladders as now resided in the pile of firewood inside our gates. But, undaunted, they made a second charge.

Elen and I were in the kitchens of the praetorium, sorting supplies for the defenders, when it came. Even from inside, we heard the battle cries, and raced out into the courtyard.

"Have they broken through?" The panicked question came from one of the younger maids, a doe-eyed, skinny girl barely into her teens.

I listened. Had they? My heart hammered.

"No." Elen let out the breath she must have been holding. "That noise is coming from outside the walls. We're safe yet. Back to work. Our men need sustenance if they're to fight."

Before long, fire arrows came raining down again. Several bounced off the tiles of the praetorium's main building to land sizzling on the paving slabs in the courtyard. One embedded itself in the dark thatch on the one side of the praetorium that no longer boasted a tiled roof. Dark smoke billowed upward, the acrid stink mingling with the smoke already lying over the town.

"Fetch water from the fountain," I shouted to the staring servants. With every utensil we could find in the kitchens we hurled water onto the thatch. Luckily, it was single storied, and hit only by the one fire arrow that we'd caught quickly. Being toward the eastern, back wall of the town, not many arrows came this far. Eventually, the smoke died to nothing, leaving a black scar on the dark thatch. In the courtyard, however, the fountain sat nearly empty of water, the fish floundering in the shallows.

Just as we had the fire out, the wounded arrived. They'd been going to the grain store up until then, but now the overflow was to be brought to us in the praetorium. Men with arrows embedded in their bodies, wide sword slashes, even bite marks. We had nowhere to lie them but outside in the hot, sun-drenched courtyard, the rooms being too small.

"Put them down here, in a row. We'll get to them as fast as we can."

Elen ran to the kitchens and came back with two servants carrying piles of clean bedlinen to tear into bandages. We worked feverishly to stem the blood, but we weren't doctors or surgeons.

"How do we get these arrows out?" I asked, faced with a man with an arrow deeply embedded in his chest, unconscious yet miraculously still living.

Elen picked up a long, thin knife. "We have no choice. If we don't take it out, he'll die from an infection."

I stared at the knife, the cruel blade flashing in the sunlight. "We have to cut it out?" My voice shook. "We could kill him."

She nodded. "We have to. There's no other way. An arrow has a barb – it goes in far more easily than it'll come out. Pulling won't work."

The man's eyes were closed, the lids blue-veined, the lashes long and dark on cheeks pale beneath his tan. Hopefully he would remain unconscious.

Elen bent over him. "You'll have to help me. Hold him steady while I cut."

I put my hands on the man's shoulders, holding him flat. He made no move to stop me, his mouth hanging slackly open. She began to dig.

He was young, fair skinned with the scarring that comes from teenage acne, a fluff of beard on his chin. Not much more than a boy. Why were the men who died always so young? Where were the old men?

Blood poured out of the wound. Elen swore. "I can't see what I'm doing."

Blood drenched the young man's clothes.

"I've got it." She picked up what looked like a pair of long tweezers and dug further into the wound. With a grunt of triumph, she pulled hard. For a moment nothing happened and then the arrowhead came free. More thick red blood welled up from the wound. Had she hit an artery? I had a vague idea from Human Biology at school where the arteries ran, but that was all, and Elen had none.

"I'll put pressure on it." I slapped a wad of linen over the wound, but the blood soaked it no matter how hard I leaned on it. The man's face, pale and sweaty, slackened further as his life blood drained away.

Elen shook her head. "Too late. We'll have to leave him. There are others we can better help."

Blood covered both of us. His and that of the others we hadn't yet killed.

I squared my shoulders and turned to our next victim.

As the hot summer's evening dragged on, and the battle for the walls continued to rage out of our sight but always in our ears, stretcher bearers brought in the boy to whom I'd given the bow and arrows. He no longer had them, and lay, white-faced and still, his right sleeve soaked in blood.

I motioned to his stretcher bearers to set him down beside the fountain where the low wall would give him a little shade. They slid him off their stretcher with scant attention for his well-being and hurried off, leaving him in a crumpled heap at my feet. Lying on the ground, he looked smaller and younger than I'd first thought him, his features soft with childhood. I knelt beside him.

His eyes flicked open. "'Ere, d'you know wot you're doin'?"

Still cocky.

I nodded, but that was a lie. I'd done a first aid course back in my old world, but that was all, and nothing I'd learned there had prepared me for the battle wounded. But I had, at least, seen battle before. "Yes, of course I do. Just keep still while I take a look at your arm."

With my dagger, I slit his ragged homespun sleeve to above the elbow and gazed down at the mess surely only a club could have made of it. Bones poked out, blood oozed. It was no longer what you could call an arm.

He needed amputation. But only a surgeon could do that, and we didn't have one. Not that I'd have trusted anyone in this world calling himself by that name. This was beyond me, but what I had to do was clear.

I gently covered up the mangled arm. "You'll need something to dull the pain, I think." My voice cracked. "I'll just go and find it."

I hurried to where Elen was tending to another man. "Do you have the poppy seed cordial?"

Her eyes widened. "Just a little left." Her eyes slid past me to the child. "What's happened to him?"

I bit my lip. "The blow of a club. His arm's shattered. There's nothing we can do. It won't mend. He'll die from gangrene – infection. A horrible death. I want enough poppy seed cordial to make him sleep...forever."

Elen glanced around the crowded courtyard at the bloody wounded. "What about all of them? Won't we need it for them?"

I glanced back at the boy. "He's a *child*, Elen. A child. I know you're not a mother, but think of your nephews. If this were to happen to one of them, would you not want someone to help them die a painless death?"

She chewed her lip, and I shifted my weight from one foot to another. Then she nodded. "I'll get it."

I knelt beside the boy again. Tears had made clean runnels down his dirty face. "It's all right. I'm back. I'm going to help you."

Elen handed me the leather bottle of the poppy seed cordial and a small beaker. "You'll need to give him a full beaker."

I poured the dose then put my hand under his head and raised him slightly. He grimaced in pain but made no sound. Why hadn't I studied medicine at university instead of English Literature. Whatever use was that to me now?

Holding him close, I put the horn beaker to his lips. He sipped and pulled a face at the bitterness.

"Drink." I kept my voice as gentle as I could. "You'll feel better if you swallow it all down quickly. The pain will go away."

Brave as an adult warrior, the boy gulped the bitter poppy cordial down. "Ugh." His voice was scarcely a whisper. "It don't taste like good med'cine. You sure you knows what you's up to?"

I smiled at him, still holding him close. Around me new casualties arrived, but I remained kneeling with him in my arms. "Of course I do. You close your eyes and think of wonderful things. Think of your mother."

"Ent got no mother." His eyes closed.

"D'you not remember her?"

"Nope. She died birthin' me." His words became a mumble.

"Then think of the nicest thing you've ever done."

"Fishin' in the burn. Nice fat tasty trout..." His voice trailed away.

I sat with him as his breathing grew more and more shallow, cradling him in my arms. Night fell before it ceased. I got stiffly to my feet. All around me lay the wounded, some of them crying out or stretching out a hand for help, exhausted women moving between them like ghosts.

I'd just killed a child. Sat with him as his life ebbed away. My stomach twisted, and I had to lean against the wall and retch, bringing up only bitter bile. This was war.

Chapter Thirteen

I SLEPT SLUMPED against the fountain wall, too tired to climb the stairs to my bed, waking as the sunlight crept into the quiet of the courtyard on the morning of the third day. Elen was already up, moving between the wounded men with a jug of watered wine and encouraging words.

I pushed myself upright off the hard ground using the fountain wall and rubbed the sleep out of my eyes. What I'd taken for silence was nothing like it. Small groans and moans filled the morning air, the heavy breathing of the injured, the rustle as they moved restlessly on their makeshift beds, the drone of flies. I sank down to perch my bottom on the fountain's wall.

Elen came over and held out the horn beaker filled with wine. My mouth felt bone dry, my tongue sticking uncomfortably to its roof and tasting the sourness of morning breath. I took the beaker and drained it, then held it out for more.

"Have you been up all night?" My voice came out croaky despite the wine.

Elen shook her head. "A short while before you woke. I slept here beside you. No more wounded came in after dark."

I wiped a weary hand, dark with dried blood, across my face. Once that would have made me retch, but now I didn't have the energy or the time for that.

Elen took my elbow. "Come into the kitchens, and we'll get some food. You'll feel better with a full stomach."

We sat at the long kitchen table and ate stale bread dipped in wine to soften it, the leftovers from a wheel of cheese and a handful of raisins each. It tasted like the food of the gods.

When we'd finished, Elen pushed her lank, dirty hair back from her eyes. "I'm going to the gates to see my husband now. And find out the situation. Before another attack comes, and we're stuck in the praetorium tending the wounded again."

"I'll come too." I got to my feet. "I need to see for myself."

We threaded our way through the streets to the west gates. The defenders, less numerous than before, sat slumped against the walls, as tired as we were. The street below had been cleared of bodies.

The stairs to the first floor of the gate tower seemed steeper than before. We found Riacus slumped in sleep across the table, his head on his arms and his helmet by his side. Dark blood crusted the bandage on his arm.

Elen ran to him.

"Riacus, my beloved." She went down on her knees beside him, and he lifted his head to gaze into her eyes. His own were red-rimmed from lack of sleep.

Shy of intruding on their intimate moment, I turned away and climbed the next set of stairs to the roof. Half a dozen warriors, bowmen, all of them, remained up here. All but one of them sat on the floor, leaning against the cool stonework, their helmets and bows tossed aside. The one man still standing turned toward me, and I recognized Anwyll, dirty bandages around his head and hand.

"Milady." He made a little bow.

I nodded at his bandages. "What happened?"

His mouth made a grim line. "They didn't have as many scaling ladders this time, but that didn't stop them. No matter how many we killed, there didn't seem to be any less of 'em. We threw back their ladders time and again, but they swarmed like ants on honey. When they managed to get onto the walls it was hand to hand fighting. That's how I got these. But we drove them back." He straightened his sagging shoulders. "They're the fiercest warriors I've ever met. Not a stick of armor to protect them. Next to naked but for breech clouts. I think they believe all that blue paint's as good as proper armor. We showed a lot of 'em it wasn't." He shook his head in disbelief.

Stepping to a crenellation, I surveyed the battlefield the slope had turned into. Bodies, mostly covered in blue paint, lay everywhere, but the warriors of the enemy were not in sight. "Where are they? Have they given up?" A faint hope.

He shook his head. "Retreated back over the brow. Don't want us to know what they're about, I'll wager."

I leant against the crenellations. "How much longer can we hold out for?"

He sucked his lips, perhaps weighing up whether to tell the truth or not.

"You can tell me. I need to know."

His brows lowered. "Perhaps for today. If we're lucky. The gods alone know where they're getting all their men from. We keep on killing them, and more seem to appear. If I didn't know better, I'd say magic had a hand in this."

A shiver ran down my spine.

He grimaced. "But we're more desperate than they are. We've more to lose. Our people won't give up." He gestured round at the slumped forms of his men. "They're brave as lions, every one of them."

I nodded, thinking of the boy archer. "The women and children too."

A deep sigh escaped me. Might today bring defeat and all the devastation that would follow? I harbored no hopes that the victors would be magnanimous in victory – we'd all be dead or taken prisoner. We women raped, most likely. I fingered the hilt of my dagger. Could I kill myself if they broke in? If rape and danger threatened? Would desperation drive me to it? The memory of Ummidia's daughters leapt into my head, the happy teenagers I'd first met and then the dull, catatonic rape victims their mother had killed from shame and pity and love. I didn't want to end the way they had.

I pushed myself off the wall. "Is there anything I can get you? I'm going back to the praetorium to help Riacus's wife again. The wounded have been brought there."

Anwyll pulled a wry face. "Only if you have more men hidden somewhere, and more arrows."

I started down the stairs to find Elen and Riacus, but before I'd gone three steps, a howl echoed round the valley. War horns blew, and a great shrieking began, like wild animals in pain. I raced back up to the roof.

Anwyll's men had all leapt to their feet and now crowded the crenellations, but they were few and there was still room for me.

The horde of dogmen and men of Alt Clut came storming over the brow of the hill scarcely three hundred yards from us, war horns blowing, screaming as they ran. But this time it wasn't just them. Running with them came reinforcements – tall, armored men with long yellow hair, tawny beards and horned helmets. Saxons.

I couldn't help but gasp in horror. "They were hiding from us so we wouldn't know they had reinforcements."

Anwyll, standing close beside me, nodded tersely. "Best get below, Milady. This is going to be bad."

He turned away from me as his men notched arrows to their bows. "Let each one count. Aim carefully." Anwyll's words rose above the din of the attack.

I descended a few steps down, partly out of harm's way, but something held me here, telling me to stay.

"Don't fire until I say." Anwyll's orders came, barked sharply above the howling outside the town. "Wait. Wait. Pick your man and aim for his heart."

Elen ran up the steps to stand beside me, her hand slipping into mine. "Saxons. They've got Saxons to fight with them. We'd best get back to the praetorium where we can be of use."

"Fire!" Anwyll shouted. The arrows soared, and the air sang

with their flight.

"I know. I saw." I squeezed her hand. "You go. I have to stay."

She squeezed my hand back, unwilling to let go. "I can't leave you here. It's not safe."

I put my other hand on my sword. "I have this."

Her eyes slid past me to the men on the roof. "It pains me to admit this, but we're women, and swordsmanship is not our strongest point. You have to come with me."

I shook my head. "I don't know why, but I have to stay. I'm certain I'll be all right. Believe me."

Reluctantly she released my hand. "I'll be in the praetorium with the wounded. Be careful." Then she was gone.

I turned back to the roof, keeping half inside the stairwell.

"Fire!" A second flight of arrows shot skyward.

More war horns sounded. Was that more Saxons arriving? If it was, we were doomed, but I wouldn't go down without a fight.

Fire arrows arced through the sky into the town. Some found their targets, but many fell into the roads and fizzled out. Women and children rushed out into the streets to throw water over the roofs of their houses.

A fire arrow struck the wall above my head and fell down into the tower below me. The sound of feverish stamping arose.

The war horns sounded again, louder this time, closer. I had to know if more Saxons were arriving. I had to look.

I scrambled up the few steps to the roof and edged my way to the crenellations, keeping my head low. Anwyll didn't even notice my presence. The war horns blasted out again, and a ragged cheer rose from the walls below us. What was happening? I needed to see.

Pressing my face against one of the archers' sides, I peered out at the battlefield below us. It took me a moment to get my bearings. The slope seethed with our attackers, naked, blue-painted Dogmen shoulder to shoulder with tall Saxons and the men of Alt Clut. But they weren't looking at us. Instead, their heads were turned toward the north.

From the Supply Road, a mass of mounted warriors, lined up in wedge formation, galloped toward the hoard of allied enemies. A banner flew in the breeze caused by their speed – a white banner with a black bear rearing up across it.

Arthur had come.

I couldn't help the cheer that rose in my throat. At the same time, the archers on the tower with me let out shouts of mixed relief and encouragement. Down below on the walls, the cheers grew louder.

The Dogmen, Saxons and men of Alt Clut were forced to turn to face the cavalry onslaught on their left flank, hurriedly forming themselves into some kind of disorganized ranks. They'd probably never expected an attack to come from the side. They abandoned their scaling ladders, the fire arrows ceased to fly, and more cheers echoed from the defenders on our walls. I joined my voice to them.

At the head of the charge rode a man on a snow-white horse – Arthur on Llamrei. In his left hand he held his white shield with the black bear emblazoned on it. Sunlight glittered on his mail shirt and the metal plates on his helmet. Close beside him I spotted the yellow shield of Merlin with its blue falcon in flight, and Cei, with his fish emblem, silver in the morning sun.

Anxiety quickly replaced relief in my heart. The force Arthur faced outnumbered his army, and the Dogmen were mad creatures, careless of death.

The charging cavalry met the men on foot with a crash that reverberated around the valley, their wedge formation scattering the ranks of the enemy. Weapons clashed, men howled, horses screamed. The noise that rose skyward was worse than our enemy's morning charge had been. Where was Arthur? Llamrei's white coat had vanished in the mêlée before me.

Anwyll pushed me to one side and ran to the steps. "With me." His men raced after him.

The gates swung open, and our brave town warriors charged

out to join Arthur and his army, to attack what was now the right flank of the enemy.

Standing pressed into the crenellation, my knuckles white on the stone edging, and careless of my own safety, I had a perfect view of the battlefield. Our courageous townsmen, our merchants, our beardless boys, our craftsmen, hurtled at the flanks of the Dogmen, shouting their own bloodcurdling war cries. I couldn't make out any of the men I knew, but Anwyll and perhaps Riacus were amongst them.

A patch of white caught my attention right in the center of the mêlée. Llamrei reared up and struck out with her hooves, with Arthur crouched forward on her back. His sword flashed, blood spurted as the head of a Dogman went spinning away like a badly thrown football. Llamrei's white flanks darkened with the man's spurting blood.

Was that Merlin's shield toward the side, battling an enormous Saxon wielding a long two headed axe? My heart leapt into my throat for my friend. The Saxon swung the axe and Merlin's horse went down. For a moment, Merlin disappeared from sight. I grasped the edge of the crenellation tighter still, my knuckles whitened to the bone. Then Merlin was up and fighting, his sword sending sparks as he drove the Saxon back. The Saxon made a mistake, the sword sliced savagely, and the Saxon fell.

Where had Arthur gone? My anxious eyes searched the mass of seething humanity. Toward the temple the now not-so-white of Llamrei appeared, riderless. My world swayed about me, and only my grip on the parapet kept me upright. This wasn't Camlann. It couldn't be. We were miles from Camboglanna, if that really was the place. Where was he? The beat of my heart drummed loud in my ears and my breath came fast and furious.

My love, where are you?

I scanned the battlefield, finding nothing. Time ticked past. Then I saw him, fighting in a patch of clear ground, close to the temple, hand to hand with an enormous warrior – a man of Alt Clut. The man must have had four inches on Arthur height-wise, his massive plumed Roman helmet giving him still more height. His reach was longer, but he was the lesser swordsman. Their weapons clashed again and again, with Arthur steadily gaining ground.

Men ran up the hill. They weren't ours. Was it the Saxons? Or could it have been the men of Alt Clut? Blue painted bodies littered the battlefield amongst larger, helmeted men in mail shirts. By the temple, Arthur and his huge foe fought on with grim determination. More men fled. Cries of the dying filled the air. Some of our men galloped their horses after the fleeing enemy. They weren't going to get far.

We were winning. The enemy, numerous or not, were broken.

The few defenders left on our ramparts, mainly women and boys, set up a ragged cheer. From down in the town, doors flew open, and people came tumbling out of their houses. With faces bearing disbelief and hope in equal measure, they ran to climb the flights of steps to the wall-walk.

I couldn't take my eyes from Arthur. His foe was tiring, that was obvious, but so was Arthur. The huge warrior must have seen his fellows fleeing, must have known they'd abandoned him. The battle thinned all around the two furious fighters. Suddenly, only Arthur's own men remained, circling the two fighting men. Arthur stepped back away from his foe, and the big warrior lowered his sword, yielding.

FROM MY VANTAGE point on top of the gate tower, I watched the slow aftermath of the battle. Plaintive cries rose from the dying, cut short by a quick knife cut to the throat as our men walked among them. Women too, eager to avenge our fallen – their menfolk. The riders who'd given chase to the fleeing enemy eventually returned, some with severed heads hanging from their saddle horns and blood encrusted on the shoulders of their horses. How near the surface barbarism lurked. Scratch and you'll find it, even in men you think you know.

Stretcher bearers searched out our own wounded and carried them with care into the town. The stink of the rotting dead lying at the foot of our walls mingled with the stench of blood and shit rising from the battlefield.

Someone caught Llamrei for Arthur. He swung himself back into the saddle, stiffly as though every bone ached, his helmet straps undone, shield arm hanging down in what must have been exhaustion. Merlin, on foot, and Cei, still mounted, recognizable by their shields, joined him. Without hurrying, they made their way down the slope, picking a route through the dead toward the tumbled ruins of the vicus.

They took the paved road toward the open town gates, and I abandoned my post on the tower and ran helter-skelter down the steps. As Arthur rode through the gates, Merlin walking by his side, and Cei just behind them, I burst out of the bottom door.

"Arthur."

He turned his head. A moment passed before recognition dawned. I must have looked very different from how he'd left me.

He did too. Sweat plastered his dark hair to his head and a thick growth of beard covered his chin. If it hadn't been for his shield, I'd have had a similarly hard job recognizing him.

"Gwen!" His voice held relief and shock, mixed. Kicking his feet out of his stirrups, he slid down from Llamrei and flung her reins to Merlin.

In two long strides he had me in his arms, filthy as I was. As we both were. His beard tickled my chin, softer than it looked, and his mouth found mine in a heartfelt kiss. I melted into his body, exhaustion loosening my limbs, and for a moment the world spun giddily about me. Lack of food, the aftereffects of the siege and the tension of witnessing the battle, combined with sheer tiredness to undermine me.

His strong arms held me up, pressed against the hard links of his mail shirt, his breath on my hair, warm and vital and alive. If I smelled as bad as he did, that was terrible. But I didn't care. He was back, and just in the nick of time. And he was alive. That was all that mattered. I put my arms up around his neck and pulled him back into another kiss.

Chapter Fourteen

ARTHUR AND I walked hand-in-hand back to the praetorium, with Merlin and Cei following with the exhausted horses. I clung onto his callused hand with a fervor born of the fear I'd had of losing him. And he hung onto me, perhaps for the same reason.

The wounded still occupied the courtyard of the praetorium, although some had already been moved back to their homes. Elen was busying herself tending to them, although now that was mostly making sure they had something to drink, as the unaccustomedly hot summer sun beat down on all our heads.

She looked up as Arthur and I entered through the gate from the town, her drawn and dirty face full of anxiety. "My husband?" Her voice shook.

Arthur put her out of her misery. "He's back at the gates. Alive. Wounded, but not badly. Have no fear."

She gave a little sob. "Thank the gods." Then, as if she suddenly remembered she was meant to be a Christian, crossed herself. "And thank God Almighty in his infinite mercy."

Arthur snorted. "This has nothing to do with any god. This is man's doing."

I pulled his hand. "Come into the kitchen, all of you, and I'll find you food."

Arthur, Merlin and Cei followed me into the chaotic kitchen. Dry heels of bread lay uneaten on a table covered in crumbs and morsels of meat, flies crawling over everything. Fetching one of the earthenware jugs from the counter at the side, I poured three horn cups of watered wine. Arthur picked his up and turned to Cei and Merlin.

"To you and all my brotherhood of warriors – to my *combro-gi*."

They raised their cups and downed their wine, each with one gulp.

I took a better look at them. All three sported beards, Arthur's and Merlin's dark, but Cei's a bushy red, a few grey hairs amongst the ginger. And all of them smelled very bad indeed, of sweat and horses, dirt and death. Blood, and other bodily fluids I didn't want a closer acquaintance with, flecked their faces, mingled with the dirt of long hours on the road.

I must have looked much like that myself. Thank goodness I didn't have a mirror. I'd come a long way since being a librarian, or even since I'd watched the Battle of the River Glein.

Scurrying round, I found cold meat under a cover and free of flies, and a wheel of as yet untouched cheese. The men made short work of it, and thirstily downed more of the watered wine until the jug emptied.

I watched Arthur, drinking in his presence, content to do so in silence. And they were too hungry to speak. Before long the food had disappeared.

Arthur stretched, rolling his shoulders. "And now to deal with our prisoners."

THE PRAETORIUM'S COURTYARD had been cleared of the wounded. The prisoners stood there surrounded by a crowd many deep – of warriors and townspeople, still more of them massed in the streets outside the praetorium's gates. Not many of the enemy had been taken alive. A couple of blue painted and tightly bound

Dogmen. Three Saxons. Two men of Alt Clut. And King Caw's heir – his oldest son, Heuil.

If it hadn't been for Heuil, my attention would have been taken by the Dogmen, standing snarling like the rabid dogs they were named after. As it was, the giant whom I'd watched Arthur fight drew my gaze and held it. Close up, even though he'd lost his helmet, he was a monster of a man. Well over six feet tall, and with the build of an over-muscled bull that the armor he'd worn had exaggerated, he dominated the courtyard.

Long sandy-brown hair hung down his back in tangled dreadlocks, and heavy, almost Neanderthal brows overhung furious dark eyes. Dried blood encrusted the high cheekbones on the right side of his face and had run into a gingery beard streaked with grey, not thick enough to hide his full, sneering lips. Sensibly, someone had tied his hands behind his back. Even so, he emanated threat and danger from every pore. Could his eleven brothers be anything like him?

Arthur stood beside the nearly empty fountain, still in battle-dress, flanked by Cei, Merlin and Theodoric, who'd come swaggering in late, a couple of severed heads attached to his saddle by their long hair. I watched from a little further back, beside Elen and Riacus. She had her arm linked through his, from time to time glancing up at him as though to reassure herself he was still there.

When Cei stepped onto the low wall around the fountain and held up his hand for silence, the hum of voices rising from the watching crowd died away. I studied their hostile faces as they glared at our prisoners, every one of them brim full of hatred. There'd be no mercy shown here.

Arthur stepped up onto the low wall beside his brother, every inch a warrior king and very much a man of the people. Dirty, unkempt, blood spattered, like every battle-weary man and boy in the crowd.

The hush was tangible, so thick I could have cut it with the dagger in my belt. Only the distant raucous shrieks of the crows settling on the corpses outside the walls broke the silence.

Arthur's gaze ran over the crowd, gathering them in. He knew how to play an audience as well as any actor from my old world.

Elen's hand crept into mine. I shot her a quick smile, my heart bursting with pride in my husband.

Arthur cleared his throat. "Warriors of Vindolanda," he began, his deep voice resonating around the courtyard. He meant everyone in the crowd, from the youngest boy who'd taken part in the defense of their town to the oldest greybeard, as well as the seasoned warriors. "You make me proud to be British." He turned on the spot to make sure the whole crowd knew they were included. Clever of him to ally himself with them by claiming not just his, but *their* Britishness. No petty kingdoms here. We were all one people.

A murmur ran through the crowd. A few small cheers.

Arthur paused a moment, waiting for silence to fall once again, then turned back toward the prisoners, his eyes still sweeping the crowd. "You defended your town with great bravery. You held out against the massed forces of the wild Dogmen, beasts who are less than human, and the traitors from Alt Clut. You stood firm even against the arrival of the Yellow Hairs. You fought bravely side by side – *your* warriors, *your* guards, *your* tradesmen and *your* merchants. Your women *and* your children. All of you are worthy of the title British warriors. I salute you."

Bedlam broke out. Men, women and children cheered, waved their arms in the air, threw helmets up. Feet stamped, and some banged the shields they still carried with their spears.

Arthur stood silent, listening, until the cheering finally died away. When at last complete silence fell once more, he turned his attention to the prisoners. "This is all that remains of your treacherous attackers, save those that ran like the cowards they are and evaded my warriors' pursuit."

He waved his hand to encompass the eight bound men before

us. Unlikely that the Dogmen could understand a word of what he was saying. "The scum who have burnt your farms and stolen your livestock, killed your menfolk, raped your women and enslaved your children."

A growl of anger rumbled through the crowd, and they surged forward a step, threateningly close to the prisoners. Heuil glowered at them as though he thought a look from him would quail them. It didn't.

Arthur rested his hand on his sword hilt. "These men have offended the word of God. They stand before you as Godless creatures. The Dogmen are no better than the beasts they name themselves for. The men of Alt Clut are traitors, to a man. The Yellow Hairs our sworn enemies. Together, they thought to burn a swath across the north. But *you* stopped them. Here, in Vindolanda, against *your* fortitude, they met their match."

How wise to let the crowd know he saw it as their doing that the prisoners stood here, taking no credit for himself. As one, every man, woman and child had grown in stature since he'd begun his speech, their sense of accomplishment magnified by the acknowledgement of a man like Arthur. Their Dux.

Arthur fingered his sword hilt as though he'd like to draw it. "They deserve to die for their crimes. And I, as your Dux Britanniarum, pass sentence of death on them. All, save one."

Did Heuil's surly gaze grow sharper? Did he think Arthur meant him?

Arthur's roving eyes came to rest on the Dogmen. "They shall hang, like the dogs they are, from the walls of this town." No reaction. They didn't understand our language. He moved on to the Saxons. "Hanging for them too." Still no reaction. They'd find out soon enough.

A small part of me recoiled at my own reaction to this. No protest welled in my heart, no desire for leniency. These men who stood before us would have done the same to us, or worse. Showing them mercy had never been in the cards, and my willingness to accept their sentences of death shocked me to my core.

The two men of Alt Clut shifted nervously. Facing death in battle must be one thing, but facing death by hanging quite another. One was an older man in a blood-stained undershirt and braccae, his bare feet raw and bleeding from where he'd been dragged through the streets and stoned. The other was younger, bullish and angry.

Arthur pointed at the younger warrior. "Hanging also." For a moment fear showed in the young man's eyes, then angry resignation settled over them. Arthur looked at the older man. "Not you. You're old, and your fighting days nearly over. You can take a message for me, to Caw."

Heuil strained against his bonds. He must have just realized that Arthur hadn't meant him when he'd said one wouldn't die. He'd meant this older man. But four men held him, and it was pointless.

Arthur fixed Heuil with a cold stare, before his gaze returned to the older warrior. "You, old man, may tell your king how Arthur the Dux deals with traitors." He drew his sword. "Bring Prince Heuil forward."

My hand tightened on Elen's, my mouth suddenly dry.

His four captors dragged Heuil toward the fountain. Arthur and Cei stepped down, and Arthur's gaze ran over the crowd. "My father taught me young that if I had to decree a man's execution, then it was for me to carry it out." He turned to the four men restraining Heuil. "Hold him down."

The men forced Heuil to his knees. Not an easy job. He fought them all the way, but in the end they had him kneeling with his neck exposed.

He glared up at Arthur. "My father will see you rot in hell for this," he spat. "And my brothers. We're not a family that forgets a wrong done to us."

Arthur didn't pause. His sword arced upwards in the hot afternoon sun, then swung back down, light bouncing off it, straight and true. The force of it sliced through Heuil's neck almost all the way. Blood spurted upwards, Heuil's bare feet drummed the flagstones, the head hung suspended by a morsel of flesh.

A great cheer went up. This was how to treat traitors.

I swallowed down the bile that threatened to rise. No way was I staying here to watch the other prisoners hang. Slipping away from Elen, I ran up the outside stairs to my chamber, closing the door firmly behind me to shut out the blood lust in the voices of the crowd.

The stuffy air made me itch and sweat. Without a pause, I wrenched off my bloodstained boots and wriggled out of my filthy clothes, leaving them puddled at my feet. Oh for a bath, but there was zero chance of that. Instead, all I had was a jug of water standing on the small table beside the bowl I'd washed myself in three days ago.

Doing my best to ignore the shouts from outside, I tipped the water into the bowl, then sloshed it over my face, tasting dirt as the water ran into my mouth. With a rag, I feverishly washed my body all over until the water was cloudy and grey, then stood there, naked, letting my body cool. Outside comparative silence had fallen. No doubt the hangings from the walls were taking place.

I wouldn't think about that. They weren't people – they were the enemy. An enemy who would have done worse than hanging to me. I must never let myself think of them as people. With resolution I shoved thoughts of them to one side, concentrating hard on getting myself clean.

Nothing much I could do about my hair apart from unbraid, brush it and braid it up again. My scalp itched with the need and longing to be washed.

Footsteps sounded outside the door. I snatched up a blanket from the bed and drew it round my nakedness.

The door swung open.

Arthur stood on the threshold. Somewhere he'd discarded his mail shirt, helmet and quilted tunic. His once cream undershirt was as dirty as mine, his boots covered in dust and blood. He looked me up and down.

I managed a hesitant smile. This wasn't a day for merriment.

He came in and shut the door behind him, going to the table. His nose wrinkled at the dirty water still filling the bowl. Without a word he returned to the door and shouted. "Bring water to my chamber."

It came quickly. The thin, frightened girl servant brought two heavy buckets to our door. Arthur took them from her and carried them to the table, setting them down with a thud that made them splash all over the wooden surface.

I sat down on the bed, still wrapped in my blanket.

Arthur pulled his boots off and threw them across the room with the air of someone who never wanted to see them again. His filthy shirt followed them, and then his braccae. Standing naked he picked up my washrag and began to clean himself, starting by dunking his head in one of the buckets. Clean water ran down his face and neck, trickling in rivulets over his skin, passing over the bruises of battle.

I watched him in silence, taking in his long, lean body, the muscles rippling under his skin, the concave hollow above his buttocks, the lines of his thighs, the movement of his shoulder blades as he bent and straightened.

At last, he turned to face me, wet hair plastered to his scalp. "Soap would have been good."

I nodded. "I thought that too."

He approached the bed and held out his hands to me. Taking them and standing, I let the blanket fall away. He dropped his hands.

For a long minute he surveyed my body, then, with a gentle forefinger, he traced my nose and lips, down my chin, neck, right breast and stomach. "I thought I'd never see you again," he whispered, his voice husky with emotion.

"I thought the same." My own voice echoed the huskiness.

I reached out and touched one of the bruises, purpling on his chest. More festooned his arms, a large one on his thigh. "You haven't been taking care of yourself."

A smile ghosted his lips. "Have you?"

I let myself return his smile. "Probably not."

He removed his finger from my belly and wagged it at me. "A little bird told me it was your idea to gather up their scaling ladders. If you hadn't thought of that, we'd have been returning to the burnt ruins of Vindolanda. You gained us time."

That hadn't occurred to me. My cheeks warmed under his praise. Maybe I could think a little like a warrior as well.

He put that finger back under my chin, tilting my face toward his. "When we received news of what was happening here, from Riacus's messengers, we came as fast as we could. But I feared we'd be too late." The finger grazed my lips, his touch tender. "Because of you, we weren't."

I kissed his finger. I wanted to kiss him all over. By the look of him he wanted to do the same to me. I smiled. "I could hardly bear to watch you fight. I thought you were down when I saw Llamrei riderless. And then when I saw the size of Heuil…"

He grinned, irrepressible as ever, all semblance of seriousness suddenly vanished. "Big bugger wasn't he? I must admit, he had me worried for a bit. There was a moment when I thought he might beat me. But then his men fled, and he was left behind and gave up. The luck of the battle. The luck of the Ring Maiden."

I smiled more widely. "I thought you didn't believe in that stuff?"

He winked. "Don't I?" His hands went to my hips, warm and gentle, caressing my skin. "I've missed you more than I ever thought I could. My little warrior queen."

I put my own hand on his chest. "Not so much of the little, thank you."

His hands slid up my body toward my breasts. "And you know what warriors do after a battle, don't you?"

I couldn't help but smile. "I do."

His hands roamed across my breasts, exploring.

Every part of me tingled with anticipation, a hot feeling in my groin, my head almost spinning again with love for him. I was more than ready for this.

He bent his head and kissed me, featherlight, gentle. This wasn't enough. I put a hand behind his head and pulled him to me, my lips locked on his, tongues meeting, almost devouring him.

He got the message. Almost roughly, he pulled me closer, his own mouth hot and hungry.

An aeon passed before we parted, both panting slightly. The gold flecks in his dark eyes twinkled at me. "You want this badly, don't you?"

We were by the bed. I pushed him. He sat down on it and it took nothing to push him flat. I straddled him. "Yes, I do."

Chapter Fifteen

S UNLIGHT FILTERED IN through the closed shutters of our
chamber, dancing across my eyelids and wakening me. I
rolled over sleepily, reaching out a hand for Arthur. Empty space
met my touch, and rumpled bedclothes. I opened my eyes.

By the amount of light around the shutters, it must be full on
morning. I rolled onto my back, luxuriating in the possibility of
staying in bed and not getting up. The last few days were a
nightmare I never wanted to relive. This was a new day.

I curled into a ball, hugging last night to myself. After our first
somewhat frenzied love making, we'd found clean clothes and
descended to join Riacus, Elen, Cei, Merlin and Theodoric for a
less than opulent celebratory meal in their dining room. Elen was
looking as smug and self-satisfied as I must have been, so maybe
she and Riacus had participated in their own reunion much as we
had.

Then we'd retired to bed, and a more self-indulgent, relaxed
lovemaking before falling asleep tangled in each others' limbs. No
wonder I'd slept in so late.

The sounds of the house carried to me. Someone was working in the courtyard. The swish of a broom on flagstones joined a
blackbird's joyful song. Impossible to believe that only yesterday
we'd all been staring death in the face. Laughter echoed.
Something I'd never thought to hear again. A girl's voice rose, her
words inaudible. More laughter. The young are ever resilient.

What was I thinking? I was young too. Lying in bed in the mornings was for the staid and elderly. I pushed the covers back and jumped out of bed. How good it felt to be alive and to know my husband was as well. Naked, I stretched my arms above my head, glad of my slender body and youth. My stomach had bounced back easily after Amhar's birth, and my breasts were small again, if not quite so pert as they'd once been. A body to be proud of.

Where were my clothes? In a pile of dirty material on the floor where I'd left them yesterday. I wasn't wearing them ever again. I'd ask Elen to have them burned. I wanted no reminder of the terrible three days we'd all endured. Instead, I found a simple pale blue gown in my saddle bags, sleeveless, gathered on the shoulders in the Roman style, and only a little crumpled. How good it was to wear women's clothes again. The thought made me smile – I'd always been a jeans and T-shirt girl in my old world. Odd that today I should prefer a gown. The fifth century had changed me in more than one way.

On bare feet I padded to the door and opened it. Bright sunlight filled the covered verandah at the top of the outside stairs. The faded, patched walls of the praetorium gleamed white as though newly plastered, and down below me the fountain played. Somehow they'd refilled it with water overnight. Or maybe this morning. The day had a feeling of being late on. I must have slept for hours.

Elen emerged from the shade of the colonnaded walkway on the opposite side of the courtyard, dressed like me, in a girlish gown, her blonde hair braided neatly.

I lifted a hand. "Elen."

She looked up, and her face split into a wide smile.

Hitching up my skirts, I ran down the stairs into the courtyard and we embraced. As we pulled apart, she smiled up at me. "Arthur told us not to disturb you. That you needed your sleep. None of us were early risers today."

I glanced around. "Where is he?"

She waved a hand toward where the gates onto the street stood with one side open. "Gone to help with the work of rebuilding, preparing to bury the dead, burning the enemy bodies. There's a lot to do. Riacus has gone with him. All the warriors have."

Of course. Stupid of me not to have thought of that. No one else was going to do it. This was an age where if something needed doing, you did it yourself. "What can I do?"

She took my hand. "Eat. I woke up starving, so I'm sure you are too. Come into the kitchen."

After a plain breakfast made delicious by my hunger, I found a pair of sandals in my saddlebags, and Elen and I walked through the strangely quiet streets to the west entrance. The wooden gates stood wide open onto the plain, with no guards on duty. Every able-bodied man was outside working, and many of the women too. The acrid stink of smoke mingled with the sickly-sweet stench of decaying bodies.

Beyond the low walls of the old vicus, they'd lit fires. Some men were dragging more firewood to feed them. Others, less lucky, and with makeshift masks tied across their mouths and noses, disentangled the stinking, mangled dead from the shallow ditch surrounding the town walls. The air buzzed with the drone of a million flies. The fetid miasma of death caught me in the throat, making me cough and retch and have to steady myself by putting a hand out for the support the nearest wall could give me.

Elen slapped her hand over her mouth, eyes wide with shock. Some of these bodies had been lying here four days in the hot sun and were so bloated and misshapen they no longer resembled people. Brindled dogs from within the town had been at them, and not all the corpses were still whole. Perhaps foxes, or even wolves, had been here for a nighttime feast.

With my hand over my own mouth and nose, I surveyed the scene, searching for men I knew. I found Merlin first, stripped to the waist and helping separate the bodies and load them onto carts. Theodoric was with him, dressed in only his undershirt and braccae, already filthy from the job.

I didn't go rushing over to greet them.

Instead, I scanned further afield. Was that Arthur beside the nearest bonfire, unloading a cart? He was going to need disinfecting before I let him anywhere near me again. Best to leave him to his work.

I glanced at Elen. "We can't help with this. Let's go and see if we can help with the wounded. There must still be work to do there."

Elen and I retreated back inside the gates, but the stench followed us, clinging to our clothes and tunnelling up our noses. Impossible to escape it as it hung like a pall over the whole town, mingled with the oily black smoke of the funeral fires that left a fine layer of smut on every surface.

WE BURIED OUR own dead outside the town walls as was the custom, with due ceremony and some haste, as rotting was not confined to the enemy corpses. Some of the worst wounded joined their number, despite the best efforts of we women. Without proper doctors and sanitary conditions, it was a foregone conclusion that a good proportion of even the more lightly wounded wouldn't recover.

Clearing up began in the town: removing the burned remains of the houses that had caught alight, repairing the roofs of those that had only been damaged, clearing the roads of the debris a collapsing house had caused. Slowly, day by day, life began to return to something resembling normality.

The farmers and villagers who'd taken shelter within the walls returned to the burned ruins of their homes, and Arthur and Riacus sent out squads of warriors and townsmen to help them with the rebuilding to be ready before winter set in. Arthur labored every day from dawn until dusk on any task his men undertook, returning to me at nightfall dirty and exhausted.

Elen and I took it upon ourselves to make sure the families who had suffered the most had help in the form of clothing, food and seed for their damaged fields. It may have been barely past midsummer, but the fear of a bleak northern winter lying ahead occupied everyone's minds. No handouts here, no social services. If your crops failed or your house burned, who was there to help you? Only your overlord. Riacus was a good one.

Gradually, I wormed out of Arthur what had happened when he'd marched away north toward Din Eidyn. I had to do this bit by bit because as soon as we retired to bed each night and his head hit the pillow, he was half asleep with weariness.

They'd travelled across country from Vindolanda to join Dere Street, the road to Din Eidyn, close to Dewain's outpost fort of Bremenium. But before they arrived at Din Eidyn, they came upon the forces of Caw of Alt Clut. Where the reaches of the dense Caledonian forest crowded close to the old Roman road, three huge mountains overlooked the battle site Caw had chosen. Arthur called the old Roman fort they'd found there Trimontium, a name that rang a bell for me but, try as I might, I couldn't place.

The fighting was fierce. Caw of Alt Clut was as strong and brave a man as his late son. His men, half as wild as the Dogmen who peppered their ranks, fought with ferocious determination. With a grimace, Arthur recalled the battle. "The leader of the Dogmen was a mad thing called Gwrgi Garlwyd. Never mind calling himself a Dogman – he fought like a mountain wild cat...or a she-wolf guarding her cubs. And so did his men. They believe their blue paint works like armor. We showed them it didn't. Him in particular."

The battle lasted a full day, from early morning until darkness forced the warriors apart, exhausted, starving, parched by the unaccustomed summer heat. Caw's men retreated back into the forest like ghosts, Arthur's to the old, riverside fortress to use the ruined walls as shelter and protection.

The next morning, with no sign of the enemy, Arthur led his

men north along the Roman road, only to be attacked again by
Caw's men, who knew the forest like their own home fields and
had circled around to cut Arthur off. More frenzied fighting
ensued, but Arthur had the advantage because his men were on
horseback and Caw's were not.

Arthur grinned mirthlessly at the memory. "They thought
they could move faster through the dense forest on foot. They
could, but once they were out of it, we had the advantage of our
horses." He paused. "And our stirrups."

Caw had chosen to attack on a river crossing, where the
forest thinned and mounted men had the advantage.

By the evening, Arthur's men had won the day. Caw and the
wild men of Alt Clut with their blue-painted allies beat a retreat,
not quite with their tails between their legs, but this time for
good.

Arthur had kept on going to Din Eidyn.

"It's on a great rock," he told me, lying in my arms one night.
"Like a cliff, rising up above the land around. Impregnable, I'd
say, unless you had skilled climbers amongst your men."

I stroked a lock of hair off his forehead. "I wish I'd seen it."

He kissed my wrist. "I'm glad you didn't. If you'd come with
me, you'd have faced Caw on the way, and I don't know if I could
have kept you safe."

Good point. Not that staying here had been a walk in the
park. But I didn't say that.

At Din Eidyn he'd met with Lot of Lleuddiniawn, king of
Guotodin.

He yawned. "Lot's my blood relation. Direct descendant of
Cunedda, just as I am. We got on well."

Lot had proved to have plenty to say for himself. The men of
Alt Clut had been pushing hard on the border lands and Lot was
furious. Caw had allowed the Dogmen to settle some of his land,
but they hadn't been happy with that, and more of them had
poured over the old earth banks – the Antonine Wall – into both
Alt Clut and Guotodin. While Lot had an army of his own, he'd

had to stretch it thin to protect his borders to north and west. He wanted Arthur to help him do this and drive back the Dogmen for good.

Which was what Arthur had been doing when a messenger arrived from Bremenium. Riacus's messengers recalling his troops to help defend Vindolanda had arrived there, and the commander had immediately sent off his lightest rider on his fastest horse, northward up the road to Din Eidyn, to find Arthur. When Arthur received the news, he abandoned Lot and headed south as fast as he could.

"All I could think of was you." He tightened his arms around me. "I'd left you here because I thought it would be safe. And it turned out that was probably the worst thing I could have done."

I clung onto him, my face against the soft hairs on his chest. "But you came. I knew you would."

He yawned again. "Merlin told me you weren't dead, but that we had to hurry. He said time was running out."

How had Merlin known this, yet not known in time to warn Arthur it would happen? He'd told me once that he had no control over his magic, that sometimes he was gifted with insight, and at others could see nothing at all. But he'd also told me that he'd seen me "with Arthur to the end, if there is one", a statement that had greatly puzzled me at the time, and still did now. Had he told Arthur this as well? Or was Arthur blissfully unaware of the hand his adviser had in his future?

The days became weeks. Grass began to peek through the burned patches on the far side of the vicus where the dead had been cremated. Inside the town walls, houses rose out of the ashes again, and in the wider area surrounding the town, new farm buildings sprouted on the ruins of the old, the crops that had been trampled underfoot by the invading horde springing back to life. After the violence of the summer, my heart soared to see the way both town and countryside could flourish.

Deprived of their commander and harried by our forces, what remained of the Dogmen, Saxons and men of Alt Clut retreated to lick their multiple wounds well behind the Wall. Arthur sent out local scouts, Riacus's men, who found their trail heading back north through the Caledonian forest in the general direction of Dun Breattann on the River Clyde.

The scouts, who knew the lands beyond the Wall nearly as well as they knew their own, reported that the men of Alt Clut had limped back to Caw. The Dogmen, tails between their legs like beaten curs, had fled north of the earth wall, and the Saxons had headed to their ships, sneaking east across Guotodin by night. Hopefully, Lot's patrolling warriors would have prevented a fair number of them from reaching their ships on the coast.

West of Vindolanda, a few of the milecastles had been attacked and burnt, their charred beams now black skeletons above the devastated walls. The raiders had burnt Aesica and slaughtered any survivors of the garrison – the smoke of their demise had been what we'd first seen, rising thick and black into the summer sky.

Rebuilding was underway all along the Wall.

SUMMER WAS WEARING on, and the days shortening, when Arthur told me we were to ride to Caer Ligualid, where Euddolen, Uthyr Pendragon's old seneschal, had come from. Meirchion the Lean, helped by his dismal son, Cynfarch, ruled there. I'd not much liked the look of Meirchion when I'd first seen him at the Council of Kings, and paying him a visit didn't sound an attractive proposition. Plus, he'd already refused to send men to help defend the Wall. Although perhaps now he didn't see his position tucked away at one end of it as quite such a secure one.

One windy grey day in early autumn, we rode away from Vindolanda along the Supply Road heading west. Leaving Elen was hard. Our experience during the siege and battle had bound us together like sisters. In my own world we'd have exchanged email addresses and kept in touch, perhaps promised to meet up again in a few months. But this was the fifth century, and in all likelihood we'd never meet again.

Standing in the courtyard of the praetorium as our husbands bade each other farewell with handshakes and serious words, Elen and I flung our arms around each other. Her tears mingled with mine as I held her tight.

"My nose is running," Elen said with a sniff as we parted. My own nose had joined in, and tears streaked my cheeks.

I wiped my hand across my eyes. "Take care, won't you?" It was difficult to find the words. Apart from Coventina, she was the woman I'd bonded with the most in this difficult world.

She nodded, sniffing again. "If you will, I will."

I managed a watery smile. "And keep your husband safe. He's a good man."

She clasped her hands together. "As is yours. A brave man and a great leader."

More than once I'd been almost overcome with the longing to confide in Elen about my past, and why I was here. I'd never felt like that with Coventina. Perhaps the fact that I'd be leaving Elen behind, that any secrets I confided in her would stay with her, here in the far north of Britain, made my tongue want to loosen. But so far, I hadn't said a thing. Right now, standing in the courtyard of her house, the desire rose again.

On an impulse I pulled her close in a second hug. "He is," I whispered in her ear. "He's going to be the greatest king that ever lived. I know it for a fact. In times to come, his name will live on. People will never forget King Arthur."

As we parted I met her gaze. Her eyes had widened, and her mouth hung slightly open. Had the intensity of my whisper given something away? She closed her mouth in a small smile that told me she'd believed me. She was a Dark Age woman, and foresight and magic far more believable to her than if I'd tried to get her to believe cars or planes could ever exist.

I smiled back, knowingly, and turned to where a servant held

Alezan for me. I swung myself up into the saddle, found my stirrups and settled comfortably.

Elen moved to Riacus's side, her hand slipping into his.

Arthur turned toward the gates into the road, and I followed. As I passed through the arch, I twisted in my saddle. Elen was watching me, an expression of wonder on her face. That of a woman who's just had a revelation. I lifted my hand and waved.

Chapter Sixteen

W E FOLLOWED THE Supply Road all the way to Caer Ligualid, a substantial walled town one day to be called Carlisle, a name not too far distant from the fifth century one. The good condition of both the road and the autumn weather, combined with the fitness of our horses and men, enabled us to make the march in one long day. Well aware of Camboglanna's close proximity to the road, just to the north of the River Irthing, I was glad we hadn't stopped anywhere, my biggest fear having been that Arthur might suggest we spend the night there.

But we didn't break our journey even for food, and arrived at Caer Ligualid's gates as the sun disappeared beyond them.

The well-maintained city walls stood practically unchanged by the years that had passed since the Romans quit Britain's shores – a sign of the need for extreme protection up here, no doubt. Within the walls an air of gentle prosperity hung over the buildings, even though many of their tiled roofs had given way to thatch. As with all ex-Roman cities – and I'd seen a few by now – a strong smell of cooking food, drains, and smoke draped streets that even now, as darkness fell, thronged with people.

Our horses clattered up the main street – the Via Principia – toward the forum, guided by two young warriors who'd ridden out to meet us. Arthur had sent scouts ahead to warn King Meirchion of our arrival. We were a large host to have to house.

Meirchion occupied the biggest house in the city, a collage of different building styles cobbled together to make a sprawling palace fit for a northern king. A vast range of thatched stables lay beside it, the familiar smell of fresh horse manure and ammonia filling the evening air.

To my relief, once inside the wide stable yard, I could at last dismount.

I halted Alezan and kicked my feet out of my stirrups, stretching my aching legs. Riding everywhere was something I'd always imagined as idyllic, but today had drummed into me that long distances like this were better taken in motorized vehicles. I shifted my shoulders under the heavy mail shirt, and slid down to the flagstones. I'd end up bandy legged at this rate.

Alezan rubbed her sweaty head against my stomach, as tired as I was, most likely. At least I hadn't had to walk the entire distance.

Beside me, Merlin swung himself down from his horse, thin face drawn and eyes shadowed. "Well, here we are. King Meirchion's palace. The man who refused to help us." Did I detect a hint of irony in his voice?

I glanced around. The stables seemed less than half full, the rear ends of horses, tails swishing at the evening flies, visible in only some of the doorways. Could his cavalry be this small, or were they stationed elsewhere?

In no hurry to meet this unhelpful king, I led Alezan into the nearest stall, and started to untack her. Merlin took the stall next to mine. On the far side of him, a stranger led in Llamrei. My ears pricked. Where had Arthur gone? Leaving Alezan snatching at the hay in her manger, I went back to the door, but my husband was nowhere to be seen. Had he gone on his own to meet the king? A dangerous thing to do even in a friendly kingdom.

I turned to Merlin. "Where is he?"

In the act of unfastening his horse's girth, he turned to face me, shadowed in the gloomy stable. "Gone straight to see the king."

"Is that safe?"

"He took Cei with him."

At least he hadn't charged off on his own. A little reassured, I squeezed myself back in beside Alezan and undid her bridle so she could eat her rations more easily when I tipped them into her manger. Then I twisted up some hay into a wisp to rub down her sweaty sides.

All along the rows of stalls our warriors did much the same. Unless circumstances were exceptional, it was my job to care for Alezan. Sovereignty in the fifth century was not a bed of roses. Not that I cared. I loved Alezan with her finely bred head, her speed and endurance, and her sweet nature. Arthur had given her to me the first Christmas we'd spent together, and she was by far the best horse I'd seen here, perhaps not counting Llamrei.

I worked in silence, pounding at her muscles, in a horsey massage. When at last she'd eaten her grain and started on the hay, I turned to her tack. And Merlin.

"What exactly are we doing here?" I asked, as I rubbed oil into my saddle where it sat on the low wall between our stalls. On the other side of the wall, he was attending to his own tack. A cavalry is dependent on the condition of their horses and their equipment, and every man in Arthur's army put their horses before anything else.

Merlin looked up from his work. "God knows." He went on rubbing. "To try and persuade that old goat to help, I should think."

"D'you think he'll be able to?" On our ride here Arthur had been deep in his own thoughts, and I'd left him to them, riding instead with Cei or Merlin, who'd both been much chattier.

Merlin shrugged. "He'll try. And we both know he can be very persuasive when he wants to be."

I wiped the bit clean, scraping off the lumps of dried grass with my thumbnail. It was a jointed snaffle. Odd to think that in my old world, bits like this were still being used. The design had hardly changed in fifteen hundred years. "If Meirchion chooses not to help, won't Caw just renew his attacks after he's licked his wounds? If he thinks there's no opposition. He does have eleven other sons to fight for him, after all."

Merlin stopped rubbing. "Yes, he will." He paused. "But getting Meirchion to believe that will be the problem. He's a stubborn man, and once he's made his mind up, it's hard to make him change it." Aside from being drawn and tired, his face was grubby with sweat and dust from the road. No doubt mine was too.

"Will Caw come this far south again and attack this city, d'you think? The fear of that might sway Meirchion's decision."

Merlin rubbed his forehead with an oily hand, pushing the hair out of his eyes. "Possibly...but probably not. This town is extremely well defended. The run of the walls is long, but they're high and pretty impregnable. If Caw has any sense, he'll just bypass this city and head south into the fatter lands he craves."

"But would Meirchion just sit back and let Caw pillage his lands? Kill his people?"

He sighed. "That's the important question, isn't it?"

I hooked my clean bridle over one of my saddle horns. Alezan swished her tail at the few flies that had dared to come inside the stables. Tack clean and horses fed and watered, it was time, as night closed in, to head to our allotted accommodation.

I'D RATHER HOPED to find Arthur in the chamber I was shown to by a servant girl, but the room was empty. It opened off a small, colonnaded courtyard that looked as though it had once been part of the house next door to Meirchion's and had been annexed some time in the past. A small fountain played in the center, the music of the water lending an air of cool refreshment to the close night air. A room opened off each of the four sides. Merlin, Cei and Theodoric had also been billeted here.

Someone had lit wall torches on the central pillar down each side, but their light threw only meagre yellow circles onto the flagstones of the colonnade and courtyard. The corners still lay in dark shadow.

Inside my dingy room, the only light came from a smelly oil lamp sitting on the wooden chest at the foot of the bed. Its feeble light revealed someone had left me bread, cheese and wine on a wooden platter on the small table. The bread was stale, the cheese dry, and the wine sour, but I was hungry. I polished it off.

Then I stripped off my clothes and washed in the bowl of cold water that had been left. Having dealt with my tooth hygiene, I slipped into a clean undershirt and, heaving a sigh of relief, climbed into the bed.

It was not the most comfortable bed I'd ever slept in. For a start, instead of ropes across the base, it had solid wooden slats. Ropes acted like springs and made the wool stuffed mattresses more comfortable. And this mattress could have done with that. Having slept on many patches of bare ground in my travels, some festooned with hidden rocks and roots, I'd never expected to find a bed nearly as uncomfortable as they were. But this one was. It must have been ancient, the wool stuffing balled into lumps in places and in others so thin I could feel the hard boards beneath it.

But I was tired, and after tossing and turning for what felt like hours, I finally fell asleep.

Arthur's arrival woke me. I couldn't have been deeply asleep. The door creaked open, and his booted feet padded toward the bed. The dim oil lamp, still guttering on the chest and still smelly, threw his face into startling planes of dark and light that could have been frightening. I sat up in bed.

He jumped. "I didn't mean to wake you."

"I've hardly been asleep. You'll see why when you get in yourself. This bed must have been on Noah's Ark." I chuckled. "And even then, I bet it was old."

He sat down on the end of the bed and pulled his boots off. "Oof, yes. Hard boards. I hate this kind of bed." His boots slid across the undulating mosaic floor.

"You wait till you feel the lumps in the mattress."

His turn to chuckle. "I'd heard Meirchion was a parsimonious old bastard." He tugged off his tunic and shirt. "Did they at least leave water for washing?"

Guilt washed over me. "They did, but it's not very clean now." Luckily I hadn't chucked it away, but only because I hadn't been sure where to do that. "Over there on that table."

He got up and took off his braccae. The gloom over by the table would hide how I'd left the water, never stopping to consider that he'd need to use it too. We'd both endured a long, dirty day in the saddle. His figure as he sponged himself clean was scarcely visible. The sounds of him doing his teeth with powdered charcoal came to me. He spat a few times into the water.

"No mint leaves," he muttered, half to himself. I'd noticed that. Charcoal on its own was not a pleasant tooth cleaner.

After a bit he returned and got into bed beside me. Lying down, he shifted uncomfortably. "You're right about this bed."

"I know. I hope there're no bugs. I don't think I've been bitten yet, so there's hope."

The oil lamp finally gave up on life and fizzled out, plunging us into warm and smoke scented darkness.

I rolled to face him. "Were you with Meirchion?"

"I was."

"What happened?"

The darkness hid his face, but his sigh was audible. "He's of much the same opinion as before. He wants to keep his men under his own control. Here, around Caer Ligualid, defending rather than taking battle into enemy territory. He begrudges me the six men he had to send after I was elected Dux and doesn't think I need any more. He thinks if Caw dares to come south again, he'll do it further east and leave this city untouched."

"That's very selfish."

"Yes."

"And you couldn't persuade him?"

"No."

I put my hand out to touch his arm, still damp from his make-shift wash. "Does this place make you think of Euddolen?"

Silence.

I rubbed his arm. "I'm sorry, I didn't mean to upset you."

"I'm not upset. Not really." He paused. "And yes, I have been thinking of Euddolen and his family. I daresay some of his kin live here still. But I'll not be asking."

Euddolen's face popped into my head, grey haired, clean shaven, sharply intelligent. I pushed him away. I didn't want to think about his dead wife and daughters.

Instead, I moved closer to Arthur. Despite his wash, he smelled of stables and horses and sweat, but I was used to that by now. Probably I smelled a bit like that myself. "Will we stay here long?"

His breath warmed my cheek. "I'll try once more to get him to change his mind and join the fight against Caw, I suppose. Much good that will do me. But after that I'll need to ride north again."

My heart sank. "And me? What about me?"

He put an arm around my shoulders, drawing us closer still, our faces so close together we shared the air we breathed. "I don't want to leave you here with him, that's certain."

I put my hand to his cheek, bristly with his short beard. "When will you shave this off? I prefer to be able to see your face." The feeling that I needed to make him realize he had to take me with him grew. "Much nicer to kiss." To illustrate my point, I leaned forward and kissed him, savoring the moment. He kissed me back, his tongue on mine. The kiss deepened, as our bodies pressed together.

A little breathless, our mouths parted, and he chuckled. "Don't worry. I'd already decided not to leave you here. This bed just reinforced my decision." He paused. "And your kiss."

"Awful, isn't it?" I wriggled to get off a particularly hard lump. "The bed, I mean, not my kiss. We'd be better off on the floor."

He caught my hand in his and kissed the palm. "I'm not shaving this off until Caw makes a peace settlement…or lies dead."

I snuggled in closer, breathing in his masculinity, thanking my luck that he wasn't going to leave me "safe" here in Caer Ligualid. Although the fear of our proximity to the fortress of Camboglanna remained beneath the surface, pushed away, but not forgotten.

His breathing deepened as sleep took him. I lay awake in his arms, reflecting on my dilemma. One of many. My father's lifelong study of all things Arthurian had peppered my childhood equally with tales of knights in medieval armor living in many towered castles, and visits to archaeological sites with Arthurian connections. My bedtime stories had been of the romantic tales of Arthur's court, of the gods and goddesses of the pre-Christian Celtic world, and of magic. So, most of the stories and legends had imprinted on my brain indelibly.

My biggest problem was that I had no way of knowing which were based on history and which had been made up by later writers, or stolen from other heroes, or embellished out of all recognition.

From reading what the obscure English monk Nennius, who might or might not have really existed, had written in the ninth century, or maybe not written, depending on whose opinion you read, I knew the list of Arthur's supposed twelve battles that would culminate in the Battle of Badon. So far, the list had been correct, and now, perhaps, we were in the region where the Battle of Coit Celidon, the Battle of the Caledonian Forest, would take place. Or maybe it already had when Arthur had defeated Caw on the edge of the forest at Trimontium. Again, I had no way of knowing this.

Nennius had been the earliest writer to list Arthur's battles in full – and he had most likely gleaned his information from older, now lost, documents. The Welsh Annals mentioned Badon, known as the last of the twelve main battles, as well as Camlann, the battle in which "Arthur and Medraut fell". But no one even knew if these were not just later additions to the chronology, put in by monks eager to associate Arthur with their cause.

Some scholars thought Camlann the only historically accurate battle – and the one most associated with Arthur – which wasn't at all comforting to me. However, I now knew for certain that some of Nennius's list was correct, wherever he'd got it from, so there was nothing to indicate Camlann was not real and would not also take place.

Even Gildas, that rather moany cleric writing in the middle of the sixth century, the closest any writer came to being contemporary with Arthur, had mentioned one of the battles – Badon. But frustratingly, no one had ever indicated where it, or any of the others, took place. The suggestion that Camlann might have been at Camboglanna on the Wall was one of many theories ranging from as far south as Camelford in Cornwall right up into Scotland. Which meant I had to be constantly on the alert for danger.

Arthur slept on, seemingly immune to the discomforts of the bed. Probably years of campaigning had hardened him to lumpy sleeping places. His arm around me slackened.

I caressed his face, brushing the hair back from his forehead. How long would he be mine? How limited was our time together? His mother had looked into her scrying glass and seen his bloody end on a battlefield that could well be Camlann. Were she and the writers of the Welsh Annals correct? Or could I, a woman from his future with all the knowledge I had in my possession, change the course of history forever?

I was certainly going to try.

Chapter Seventeen

TWO DAYS LATER we left Caer Ligualid, following the still useable old Roman road north toward the forested wastes of Caledonia. A stone and wood bridge, maintained by the men of Caer Ligualid, took us across the nearby River Itouna. Beyond that lay the lowlands of Alt Clut, and as we advanced ever deeper into enemy territory, we left the Wall and civilization behind us.

At first, the appearance of the farms and small villages we passed showed a hint of Roman influence. Although rough and simple, houses were rectangular, and the fields, where wheat stood stooked and drying, square and neat, and edged with stone and earth banks to keep off the wandering livestock. Half decent sheds and barns clustered around square courtyards where scrawny chickens scratched in the mud.

However, before long the settlements underwent a meta-morphosis, turning rapidly into subsistence farms with small, thatched roundhouses, their uneven enclosures fenced in by tumbledown stone walls. Pied sheep and small, hairy cattle grazed between rocky outcrops on the rough moorland. Purple heather, stands of bracken turning red-gold under the autumn skies, and stunted gorse bushes replaced the fields of stubble. Pigs snuffled in isolated clumps of woodland in valley bottoms, searching for tasty acorns with their long snouts. As the land grew ever wilder, so did it become less and less populated.

Before long, we left the moorland behind and entered the

thick Caledonian Forest.

I rode beside Arthur at the head of our men, the banners stowed away. He'd sent on scouts ahead of us, very aware that as we drove deeper into the woodland, the chances of attack grew ever greater. Despite the clammy heat and having to wear my mail shirt, I didn't complain, just glad I hadn't been left behind in Caer Ligualid to sleep on that bed for God knew how long. I even had a helmet hooked on my saddle horn. Quite the soldier.

"If we're attacked," Arthur said, knee to knee with me, "you're to flee with Merlin. They'll be on foot if they stage an ambush, so you should be safe. They won't catch you on Alezan."

I glanced over my shoulder at where Merlin rode next to Cei, deep in conversation. At least he was close. But would I want to run and leave Arthur? Common sense told me it was the thing to do, but my heart said something else entirely.

Arthur must have seen it in my face. "You'll be helping me if you do. I won't have my attention taken by having to make sure you're safe. I need to know you'll do as I say and go with Merlin."

I pursed my lips and sighed. "Very well. I'll do it. But we won't go far."

"You won't need to. A mile at most. It's unlikely any ambush would have men further from the attack than that."

"And how will we know when to come back?"

He grinned. "I'll send a man to fetch you."

And with that I had to be content.

That first night we pitched camp in a forest clearing close to where a gurgling stream crossed the road, shallow enough to ford. The men strung ropes between the pine trees to tether the horses, who stood there, tails swishing at the flies and midges, stamping their hooves restlessly. Ever vigilant, Arthur posted guards out in the forest, as well as up and down the road, and refused the men permission to light a fire.

"Don't want to advertise our presence more than we have to," he told me as he tethered Llamrei beside Alezan after watering her at the stream. "These woods will be full of Caw's eyes. No doubt he already knows we're in his lands."

Not a comforting thought.

And nor were the midges comforting, swarming in their millions around us as well as the horses. At least the smoke of a fire might have kept them a little at bay.

By the time the horses were cared for and the first watch of guards dispatched to their positions, night had almost fallen, made darker still by the towering trees surrounding our camp. My chainmail shirt discarded, I sat beside Arthur on the hard, pine-needle strewn ground, leaning against my saddle, as the men passed the food around. The hard black bread, cold meat, and skins of cider, warm from being carried by our horses, tasted like the best meal I'd ever eaten. I'd had a few of them lately.

"I doubt they'd attack at night," Cei said, through a mouthful of bread, spraying crumbs. "It's too damn dark up here for that."

"Maybe they can see in the dark," Bedwyr, sitting opposite us, suggested.

Cei shook his head. "That's cats, not dogs."

Arthur hooked his arm around my shoulders, drawing me closer, swatting at the clouds of midges with a hand holding a skin of cider, and nearly slopping it out. "Let's hope you're right about that."

Theodoric, on his other side, took the cider, probably to save it from being spilled. "I don't much like the silence up here. Makes me think something's brewing. It's too quiet." He put the skin's spout to his lips and swallowed several long gulps.

As if to prove him wrong, an owl hooted somewhere not far off, and Cei chuckled.

I snuggled closer to Arthur, swatting at midges. A lot of ugly red weals had risen on my exposed skin already, itching like mad. The night felt warm and muggy, but no way was I taking any clothing off and letting those little beasts feast on my tenderer bits.

Theodoric swiped at the clouds of midges and passed the cider on to Merlin. "I can see why the Romans withdrew back to the Wall and abandoned the earth wall at Din Eidyn. Bloody midges."

Despite the attacks of the insects, sleepiness came creeping over my weary limbs as I leant against Arthur, my head on his solid shoulder. Concentrating on the conversation grew harder, and my eyelids drooped.

"They lost a legion up here once," Cei said. "I heard the tale at my mother's knee."

"Really?" Theodoric's voice held curiosity.

I struggled to stay awake to listen to this story, but my rebellious eyelids had other ideas. Matchsticks would have been good.

Cei nodded, his figure dim in the darkness. "Marched north never to be seen again."

Theodoric grunted. "Not surprised. There's something about this forest I don't like. It's not just the silence – there's a feel to it that's not right. Like it's brooding and biding its time." He paused. "Watching us. As if the trees might move when we're not looking."

Poetic thoughts – for him.

Arthur, who'd been resting his head on the top of mine, chuckled, and my eyes opened. He tightened the arm about my shoulders.

Cei made the sign against the evil eye. "Do you feel it, Merlin? Is there evil in these woods?"

Merlin had been sitting a little to my left, silently polishing his dagger with a rag. Turning my head, I could just make out the pale shape of his face. "I don't know…There's something. You may be right. It does feel as though the trees themselves are watching us."

"Devils," Cei muttered. "Pagan devils. Spirits in the trees."

Arthur snorted. "No such thing. It's the darkness that's got to you. And the silence. This is nothing but a quiet forest. Nothing evil about it at all. You should be ashamed of yourself, Merlin, encouraging them."

Merlin shook his head. "The evil in these woods comes from

men, not devils. We're in the territory of Alt Clut, don't forget."

I scratched my itchy scalp and wished for insect repellent – jungle strength.

The owl hooted again, further off now.

Arthur removed his arm. "Let's sleep. We need to be up at first light tomorrow."

I struggled sleepily to my feet and let him spread our blankets side by side. The hard ground felt no worse than Meirchion's guest bed had, as I lay down fully dressed beside Arthur. He put his arms around me, holding me close, his bearded cheek against mine.

I pulled my blanket up over our heads as those bloody midges swarmed.

WE SPENT OUR second night in the ruins of a small Roman fort, only a few acres in size, but still with a lot of the stone walls intact.

Like the old road we were following, this fort had certainly seen better days. Weeds pushed up between the cobbles, creeping across the gravel. Probably no one had ridden this way in a long time. Had the lost Roman legion Cei had mentioned come this way? Were its ghosts still walking these old roads, patrolling the ruined walls? The thought that we might be riding deeper and deeper into the territory of an enemy who had seen off an entire Roman legion festered under the surface of my mind.

However, with guards stationed along the run of the walls as well as further out, I felt well protected enough to sleep more soundly than I had the night before, after all that talk of demons in the forest. Although the midges were just as bad.

Late in the afternoon of the third day, the road plunged into much thicker forest. Towering trees crowded close to the road, and the air stifled sound and any breeze there might have been.

High in the treetops a few lighter branches stirred, but down here on the road, not even the slightest breath of fresh air reached us.

Riding beside Arthur, with Merlin just behind chatting quietly to Cei and Theodoric, I kept my eyes on the dark recesses of the forest where anything could be lurking, mindful of a film I'd once seen about werewolves in probably just this sort of spot.

An arrow came swishing through the air and struck Llamrei's saddle, embedding itself in the leather, inches from Arthur's leg. It must have penetrated to her skin, because, with a squeal of pain, she reared up, almost unseating Arthur who'd been looking over his shoulder to make a remark to his brother.

More arrows rained down. Several men near me toppled from their saddles before Llamrei's front feet touched the ground again. Arthur whipped his sword from its scabbard as Llamrei snorted and curvetted under him, nostrils reddened, eyes rolling wildly. More swords glinted in the dim sunlight, as out of the dense undergrowth twenty paces from the road a horde of blue painted Dogmen surged, howling like mad things.

For a brief instant, I stared at them in horror, seeing them close up for the first time since Elen and I had killed that one in the alleyway. Eyes wilder than Llamrei's, red-rimmed and staring, blue paint in intricate patterns over their totally naked bodies, dirty furs on their heads and backs. The smell of them hit me – rank and foul, like the hunt kennels I'd once gone to as an anti-hunt protester. Sweat, shit, dirt and their rancid breath.

"Get her away!" Arthur shouted at Merlin. Blood ran black down Llamrei's white shoulder.

Merlin drummed his heels into his horse's sides, and it leapt forward beside Alezan. I did the same, as a wild Pict hurled himself at me, reaching to grasp my tunic, a long dagger in his other hand. Merlin's sword swung down, the savage fell back, clutching the stump of an arm severed above the elbow, blood spouting. Alezan shot forward, me crouched over her neck. I didn't even have time to check Merlin was with me. Straight into a gallop, she bolted up the road, arrows whizzing over my head.

The road curved to the left between tall trees, rising gently uphill. My heels hammered Alezan's sides. As if she sensed the urgency of her mission, she stretched out her neck and thundered up the road as though she'd sprouted wings. Panic had seized her as well as me, and it was a while before I even tried to slow her down. Her sides heaving, coat white with sweat, she dropped down to a canter, then a trot and, almost immediately, fell into a walk.

I looked over my shoulder. No one was there.

Alezan ground to an exhausted halt, head hanging to her knees. Only the sound of her breathing – and of mine – broke the silence all around. Where was Merlin, my champion?

I sat for a few minutes, listening to the quiet of the forest as it grew ever quieter and more ominous, while Alezan regained her breath. Clouds of steam rose from her heaving flanks. The flies, that I'd thought we'd left behind, massed around us. How far had I come? No sounds of battle carried to me on the still forest air. Only the soughing of a gentle breeze in the gloomy treetops that didn't reach to the sultry forest floor.

Should I go back? No. Arthur had said he'd send someone to find me after the battle. But what if he lost? What if he lay dead right now? Only luck had prevented that first arrow from finding its home in his leg. Bitter experience had shown me what taking out an arrow could do. The damage caused by such an operation was worse than a deep sword cut.

Alezan's breathing began to quieten. So did mine, but my heart and stomach remained knotted with anxiety. If I'd had my feet on the road, I'd have been hopping from one leg to the other in indecision. Alezan fidgeted, picking up on my nervous tension. She tossed her head up and down to rid herself of the flies that kept settling on her head and neck. I swiped at them myself as they buzzed around my face.

How far had we galloped? I tried a mental calculation. Thirty miles per hour or more, for how many minutes? Two minutes would be one mile. Had I ridden at that speed for more than five minutes? Two and a half miles along the road? Enough to ensure I wouldn't hear the sounds of battle, that was certain. Or could we have gone further? How far could a horse gallop before exhaustion brought them to a halt? Wasn't the Grand National horse race over four miles? Could I have ridden that far?

Loneliness pressed in on me. Lost in a hostile world of dark forests with unseen eyes watching my every movement, a shiver ran down my sweaty back. Separated from everyone I loved and cared for. Vulnerable. Fear bubbled in my chest, and I tightened my grip on my reins.

No, I mustn't think like this. I wasn't vulnerable. That was the old Gwen. My hand went to my sword hilt. I'd killed a man before, hadn't I? I could do it again if I had to. I thought of the driver of the cart carrying Ummidia and her poor raped daughters, and how I'd stabbed him in the back when he'd tried beating her to a pulp. The image of the Dogman Elen and I had killed followed quickly on that thought's heels. I wasn't a librarian anymore, I was a queen – a warrior queen. Arthur's warrior queen.

I put my helmet on and did up the straps, my mind made up. I'd go back.

Turning Alezan back the way we'd come, I started down the road in a walk. Her exhaustion, and my own trepidation, prevented me from going any faster. Two and a half miles would take at least forty minutes, if not longer. And if I'd ridden further, maybe as much as an hour. Not that I had any way of telling the time other than by estimation.

Alezan's unshod feet made next to no sound on the graveled road. In her flight, her hooves had left deep imprints in the gravel. The only ones. No other signs of human presence appeared. I kept on walking. Time crept slowly by.

The road followed the contours of a thickly wooded hillside, its curve preventing me from seeing far ahead. To my right, the hill rose steeply, the trees crowding close and dark – the perfect place for werewolves... No, I wasn't caught in a horror film. I was me, the Queen of Dumnonia, in real, war-torn Dark Age Britain. I resisted an impulse to look over my shoulder and urged Alezan into a slow jogtrot.

We hadn't gone much further when from up ahead came the sound of approaching hooves, the drum of a fast canter on the gravel. For a moment, my first impulse was to hide, but then I remembered the Dogmen had been on foot. This had to be someone sent to find me.

I drew my sword, nevertheless. No point not being prepared.

Merlin came into view, astride a strange horse. As soon as he saw me, he drew rein, relief written all over his face. He pulled the horse to a halt. "Thank God. You're safe. You did what you were told." A frown hovered. "Just about. Why are you on your way back? We told you to wait until someone came to get you."

I bristled. "You told me you'd be with me."

He had the grace to look contrite. "I'm sorry. My horse was shot out from under me before I had chance to follow you. It fell, trapping my leg." He rubbed his dirty right knee. "I was stuck. I'm lucky to be alive. Theodoric managed to pull me clear, but it was too late to get away. I had to stay and fight."

"Arthur? Is he all right? Did you fight them off?"

His face clouded. "We fought them off all right. But Arthur..." He paused. "He's wounded. You'd better come and see."

"Wounded?" The thought of having to dig an arrow out of my husband sent an ice-cold chill drenching over me. "Where? How?"

"His leg."

I kicked Alezan into a trot. "Then hurry."

Merlin spun his horse, kicking up gravel, and we both pushed our mounts into a fast canter.

In five minutes, we were back at the battle site. The bodies of a number of blue-painted Dogmen lay scattered in the shallow ditch at the side of the road, along with a few dead horses, Merlin's amongst them. A little group of warriors stood clustered to one side. One of them held Llamrei's reins.

Oh God no.

I flung myself from Alezan's saddle and ran the last few yards to push my way through the crowd.

Arthur was standing upright, but leaning heavily on Cei, a bloody bandage encircling his thigh. Cei had a supporting arm around his brother's waist. Bent over, Bedwyr was putting pressure on the wound.

My eyes went to Arthur's face. Ashy pale. He flashed me a rueful grin. "Sorry." The apology came through gritted teeth.

"Sword or arrow?" I asked, my voice steadier than I'd ever imagined it could have been in a situation such as this.

"Dagger." He pointed. A Dogman lay nearby, his cruel, jagged-edged dagger slack in his dead fingers, his intestines spilling from a huge gash across his belly.

"Deep?"

He nodded. "The bleeding's slowing down."

He pulled himself away from Cei, standing up straighter. "I'm all right. I can't say it's just a flesh wound, because it's not. But I'll live."

Bedwyr looked up with a frown. "Keep still. Let me get this bleeding stopped. If you'd sit down, it'd be easier."

He shook his head. "I'm the king. The dux. I stay standing."

Men and their machismo. Not that he'd ever have heard of that. I took his hand. "You should do what Bedwyr says – he's the healer here."

He squeezed my fingers. "And so are you. If I sit down, I might not want to get up again. I stay standing."

He kept his voice low, but Bedwyr heard. "I've got some poppy syrup. I can give you a dose."

Arthur shook his head. "Not yet. I need to stay in command. That'll make me sleep. I don't want to...yet." Still gripping my hand, a little too tightly for comfort, he motioned to Theodoric to come closer. "We'll have to make camp here. I don't think they'll be back after the number we killed. You'd think by now they'd have realized that blue paint isn't as protective as armor." He chuckled, but it rang false. "Organize the camp for me...and the guard rotas."

The blood had stopped oozing out from under the pad Bedwyr was still holding tight to Arthur's leg, and now he wrapped another bandage tightly round it, securing it in place over Arthur's braccae.

Arthur glanced down. "All this fuss about a little scratch. How many men have we lost?"

"Not so much a little scratch," Bedwyr muttered, fastening the bandage.

"Half a dozen dead," Cei said, shaking his head. "The same amount wounded. None fatally, I think."

Arthur put his hand on Bedwyr's shoulder. "You'd best go and tend to the others then. Gwen will stay with me." The pallor under his tan deepened. "And someone check my horse – she's got blood down her shoulder from where that arrow struck her."

Somewhat reluctantly, the crowd of warriors dispersed, and I heard Theodoric's raised voice as he shouted orders to some of the men to head off in all directions as sentries. Bedwyr slipped a little leather bottle of the poppy syrup into my hand. "See if you can get him to just have a mouthful. It'll help."

Arthur followed Theodoric with his eyes for a moment, before returning his gaze to me. Only Merlin remained, hovering close by, holding Llamrei's reins.

Arthur grunted. "Can you take her saddle off. I need to know she's not badly hurt."

The arrow, its shaft now broken, still stuck out of his saddle, inches from where he'd been sitting. Merlin undid her girth and carefully lifted the saddle off. Just the tip of the arrow had penetrated the thick leather pad, making a small cut in her shoulder. She'd bled a lot, but she'd been luckier than Arthur.

Merlin set the saddle against his hip, and ran his hand down Llamrei's shoulder. Already, flies were swarming the drying blood. "I'd better wash this off her." He glanced at Arthur. "I don't know how our scouts missed spotting this ambush."

I stared. "Scouts?" The sudden thought that my flight should have caught me up to them rose its ugly head. "I didn't see any."

Arthur shrugged. "Most likely dead then. Dogmen move like stealthy animals through these woods." He shifted his weight and grimaced.

I slid my arm around his waist. "Better come and sit down. You need to rest your leg."

With Merlin's help, I got him to where they'd laid out some blankets. Merlin set Llamrei's saddle down, and together we lowered Arthur to a sitting position, leaning against it with his leg stretched out straight in front of him. Sweat beaded his brow from the exertion and pain.

A little more blood oozed out of the wound, soaking his bandage afresh. It didn't look at all clean, and the flies were finding the blood very attractive. Really, I wanted to get his braccae off him and clean the wound with spirits. Honey would have to do for an antiseptic, but it wasn't a bad alternative and aided healing. That and a clean dressing and bandage as soon as possible.

But I'd have to wait. "I'm not shifting that bandage in case I set the wound bleeding again," I said, laying a blanket gently over his legs to keep the flies off. "But I think you'd better have that poppy syrup now."

Arthur pulled a face. "I don't need it."

I frowned down at him. "I think you do. Take it and stop being so brave." I pushed the bottle into his hands. "One swig, that's all. It'll help you sleep, and sleep will help you heal. In the morning I'll change the bandage."

With a wry grin, Arthur took a swig from the bottle, pulling a disgusted face as I put the stopper back in. "Revolting." He leaned back and closed his eyes.

I sat down beside him, wishing there were something more I could do. The fact that he'd stopped bleeding was good, but now the biggest danger was infection. Neither his braccae nor the bandages around his thigh looked clean.

He shifted a little on the pile of blankets. Never mind the poppy seed syrup – a shot of morphine was what he needed. He might well be in shock. What did I know about that? Keep the patient warm? I put another blanket over him, and he opened his eyes.

I managed to smile. "I thought you might be cold."

"Don't worry. I'll be all right."

I covered his hand with mine. "Too right you will. Amhar's too young to become king of Dumnonia." Hard to keep the emotion out of my voice.

He chuckled. That was good to hear. "I've had worse."

Had he? This looked pretty bad to me, and by now I'd seen a lot of battle wounds.

He pulled my hand. "Stay with me."

Like I'd been going to leave him.

Taking great care not to nudge his leg, I squeezed myself onto his blankets, still holding his hand. He turned his head to look at me. That bloody beard. There was far too much of it hiding his face. "I'll be glad when this is gone," I whispered low enough that no one else could hear, and kissed him lightly on the mouth.

He sighed and his eyes shut again. "Feeling sleepy. Be better in the morning."

Chapter Eighteen

T HE SMELL OF woodsmoke and bacon frying woke me. For a moment I had no idea where I was, then I opened my eyes to a clear blue sky above a ring of dark pine trees, and felt the knobbly ground beneath my back. The events of the day before came rushing back, helter-skelter into my mind.

Arthur.

Somehow while sleeping, I'd slipped down from my propped-up position of the night before. Someone had spread a blanket over me – a blanket now wet with dew. I pushed it off and sat up.

A fire burnt in the center of the camp, and a couple of the men were frying bacon in a cast iron pan. The aroma drifted skyward on the still air, making my mouth water.

Arthur was sitting up beside me, eating a chunk of bread and some slices of bacon, some color back in his cheeks. No sign of fever. Not yet, anyway.

He grinned at me through a mouthful of food.

I wrinkled my nose. "Ew. Keep that to yourself." My eyes went to his leg, still covered by the blanket. "How's your leg this morning?"

He swallowed. "So long as I don't move, not so bad."

Merlin came over with a plate of food which he held out to me. "Here, eat."

What I really wanted was a strong cup of coffee and an electric toothbrush, but I wasn't about to get either of them. I settled for the best alternative and took the plate of bread and bacon.

Merlin sat on the ground in front of us, cross-legged, and watched me eat. Messy, with just fingers, and the bread was hard and stale, but the bacon tasted excellent.

"That Dogman who went for you," Merlin said to Arthur, as I was licking my rather grubby fingers clean of bacon fat. "He knew who you were. They all did. There were half a dozen of them after you when they could have been fighting us."

Arthur shrugged. "Perhaps." He finished up the last morsel of his bread and picked up a wineskin to take a swig.

Merlin frowned. "I've told you time and again that riding the only white horse isn't a good idea."

That thought had more than once occurred to me as well.

Arthur shrugged again and took a second swig at the skin. "My men need to be able to see me."

"So they might, but the enemy don't need to."

Arthur's turn to frown. "I beg to differ. I like my enemy to know I'm there. I *want* them to see me."

I sighed. If Merlin thought he was going to change Arthur's mind with this old argument, he didn't know him very well.

"Didn't work yesterday, did it?" Merlin muttered.

Arthur grinned, white teeth flashing in his dark beard. "I'm not dead."

Merlin passed the skin into my outstretched hand and I, too, took a swig. Watered wine. I took a second pull, beginning to feel more human. As a coffee substitute it wasn't so bad. I handed the skin back to Arthur again. "If you're feeling better and the bleeding's stopped, I'd like to look at your leg and put a clean dressing on it."

Arthur bridled. "It feels fine. No need for that."

My turn to frown. "You know you can't leave it like this. You need clean braccae as well. Otherwise all that blood's going to attract every fly in the forest today. Let Merlin pull your boots off, and we'll get you on your feet and take your braccae off. I've clean bandages and honey in my saddle bags."

In his condition, there wasn't much he could do to stop us. Merlin pulled his boots off, which clearly hurt Arthur although he made no sound, then we levered him into a standing position as carefully as we could, beside a tree he could lean on for support. From the drawn expression on his face, this hurt even more, but he didn't make a sound.

As he'd been bandaged over his braccae the day before, I had to unpick the blood encrusted mess before we could even try to get his braccae off. The blood had formed a solid hard pad of the bandages, and they didn't want to budge. I ended up slitting them with my knife, taking great care not to cut him. Fresh blood ran sluggishly down his leg once I'd prised the bandages off. I undid the lacings of his braccae and slid them down as gently as I could. Where they'd stuck to the wound, I had to peel them off. His breathing quickened, but he still didn't make a sound, even though the pain must have been excruciating.

I flung the offending, blood soaked braccae as far away from us as I could, hoping the flies would follow. Then, with clean cloths and a bowl of strong spirit, I washed the wound. This did provoke a reaction – a muffled groan at the sting of the alcohol in the open wound. He pressed his forehead against the trunk of the tree, breathing heavily and holding tight to it.

He'd been stabbed halfway down his thigh, on the outside, the mouth of the wound not wide, but jagged where the knife had been pulled out. He'd been lucky it hadn't severed an artery. Ruthlessly, I tried to get the cleansing alcohol as deep into the wound as I could, as the only thing standing between him and serious infection, hating every moment of how this was hurting him. Fresh blood seeped out which I wiped away. Probably best not to try stitching so deep a wound – I didn't want to shut in infection that might otherwise ooze out.

Once it was clean, and the blood had stopped trickling down his leg, I covered the wound thickly in honey from an earthenware pot, making sure I packed as much into the wound as possible. Then put a clean, thick pad over it all, and bound it firmly, but not too tightly, with a couple of rolls of bandage Bedwyr provided.

To try to keep the wound from rubbing, I asked Cei for a spare pair of his own, much larger braccae, although Theodoric's would have done just as well. Both of them were only a little taller than Arthur, but more heavily built. Then, with Cei's help, and Merlin supporting Arthur, we managed to get him into his clean braccae and boots by the time we needed to break camp.

We didn't have any wagons though.

"If we did, I wouldn't ride in one," Arthur scoffed, sounding offended I'd even considered the possibility. "If you can get me on a horse, I can ride."

Cei and Theodoric's strength came in very handy for that, but it was a white-faced Arthur, his breath coming fast and hard, who finally sat astride a bay horse whose rider had been killed in the skirmish. I lifted his foot for him and slipped it into the stirrup – they should make him a little more comfortable.

"Do we head back to Caer Ligualid?" Cei asked when at last we were all ready to ride, the remaining embers of our fire kicked into the dirt.

Merlin, leading Llamrei whose shoulder was now washed clean of blood and dosed with honey, but couldn't have a saddle on top of the wound, rode up beside Arthur and me. "Back?"

Jaw set, Arthur shook his head. "We came this way to beard Caw in his den and nothing is going to stop me doing that. Amongst those Dogmen were men of Alt Clut, painted blue, but men of Alt Clut, nevertheless. He's got them hiding amongst the Picts to do his dirty work."

Merlin's eyes strayed to Arthur's leg. "How far can you ride?"

Arthur glared. "Stop worrying. I'll be fine." He reached out and rubbed Llamrei's forehead. "But I'd rather be back on her."

Merlin's expression told me he didn't share that sentiment.

We set off, riding at a walk along the road I'd fled up yesterday, the scouts ahead and behind us doubled. We didn't come upon the bodies of the ones the Dogmen must have killed, nor their horses. And we didn't come upon the Dogmen or their Alt Clut fellows again, either. Thank goodness.

The sun climbed into the sky, beating down mercilessly on the back of my head, making me sweat inside my helmet and mail shirt. I kept close to Arthur, watching him like a hawk, but surprisingly, he seemed to weather the ride well. Either that or he didn't show the pain he was in, which on the whole was more likely. We rode in comparative silence as he seemed disinclined to talk.

When we stopped for some food at midday, still within the forest, he refused to dismount and ate his stale bread and sweaty cheese on horseback, leaning his weight heavily on the horns of his saddle as though to ease his leg. I caught Merlin watching him covertly, clearly as bothered as I was that his friend no longer looked as comfortable as he had first thing.

"A short ride this afternoon," Merlin muttered to me. "We'll make camp as soon as I spot a suitable place. I'll tell Cei and Theo."

As good as his word, as soon as the forest thinned and the land sloped down into a wide valley with a river running through it, Merlin and Cei called a halt. A small farm squatted on the riverbank, just a thatched, wattle and daub round house and some lean-to sheds. On the rough ground of the valley sides sheep grazed – fewer sheep by the time we left.

With lookouts posted, the men threw caution to the wind and utilized the farm's substantial woodstore to light several cookfires. The dispossessed farmer and his family came to stand in the door of their hut, silent and surly as we pillaged their livelihood, too afraid to stop us. But this was war, and we needed the food they had. Their chickens went into sacks, the two pigs rooting in a small orchard were butchered and cooked. Cold pork would be our fare for the next couple of days.

I wanted to feel compassion for the farmer, but something stopped me. Once, I'd have been on his side, all indignation at the cheek of stealing his livelihood. But I'd lived too long in the Dark

Ages not to know that it was a dog-eat-dog world, where the strongest would be the victors and the weak would perish. Self-preservation had reared its ugly head, and all I could think of was not going hungry myself in the days to come.

Merlin pitched a shelter against the rough stone wall encircling the farm, and, not without some relief, Arthur lay down there at last, his face beneath the tan as white as the fleeces on the sheep we'd stolen. But his skin felt cool to my touch, and he had no temperature. I sniffed the dressing on his wound. "There's no sign of infection, so I'll leave changing it until tomorrow morning." I put my hand on his forehead again, just to reassure myself. "Rest is what you need."

He pulled a wry face. "A king can never rest."

I frowned. "D'you want to end up like your father? With a wound that would never heal? Unable to straddle a horse." I leant a little closer so only he would hear. "Or me."

For a moment the pain in his eyes receded to be replaced with the twinkle I was more accustomed to. He touched my leg with his fingertips, featherlight, suggestive. "You know I don't."

I bent forward and kissed him on the lips. "Then do as you're told."

When the food was ready to eat, Merlin and I helped Arthur up, and he hobbled the short distance to a row of round logs Cei and Theodoric had set out as seats. Gingerly, he eased himself down onto the tallest log and stretched his leg out straight in front of him. The freshly cooked pork was passed round, and we feasted on succulent ribs, sucking the meat off the bones.

Afterwards, I sat and picked out bits of meat that had got themselves stuck between my teeth with a sharpened twig as a toothpick, wishing for my twenty-first-century interdental brushes.

Skins of cider and watered wine did the rounds as the sky darkened from the west, the sun now vanished behind the forested hills. One of the men sang a song about some long-ago hero, but, tired from the events of the last two days, I barely listened. Beside me, Arthur shifted in discomfort, and it wasn't long before we all took to our beds.

We made the same slow progress for the following five days as Arthur's, and the other men's, wounds gradually began to heal. Behind us, we left a trail of pillaged farms where the inhabitants would go hungrier than normal, but we burnt none of them. "We aren't barbarians," Arthur said, when Theodoric asked him why we'd left them unharmed.

I changed the dressing on Arthur's wound every day. The flesh around it remained red and swollen, with a little discharge at first, but as he still didn't get a fever of any sort, I guessed the healing process was taking place as it should. By the fifth day, the swelling had begun to go down, and I wormed out of him that it hurt him less. Being a man, he didn't want to admit to noticing the pain at all. Jolly good thing he'd never had to give birth. He'd have noticed that for sure.

We reached the banks of the River Clyde three days after that, with Arthur claiming he was now fit for anything. Which of course was a lie, although he hid it well.

The tide was on the ebb, and an expanse of mudflats met our eyes as we gathered on the shore, Arthur's banner rippling in the breeze as Anwyll held it high. On the far bank of a river that had to be three quarters of a mile wide, the twin peaks of Dumbarton Rock rose up like a pair of blunted, too-close-together pyramids. On their summits, a fortress sat: wooden houses, palisade fences, smoke rising. Beyond the Rock the misty shapes of the mountain range where Loch Lomond was located shimmered in the grey distance.

"Dun Breattann," Arthur said, pointing unnecessarily. "Fortress of the Britons. How like Caw to claim that name for his own capital."

"Wow."

His eyebrows shot up. That just might have come out in English.

"I mean – it's huge. And so steep. No one could ever get in

there."

Arthur grinned. "You'd have said that about Din Tagel, but my father got in there all right. And I'm the proof."

Very true. But we were on one side of the mighty river Clyde, and Caw was on the other. Probably.

"There's a ford a mile or so upriver," Merlin said. "A causeway built by the legions long ago. But it's still used, or it was when I was last up here. It's only uncovered at low tide, so if we get a move on, we'll be able to get across it today."

I shot him a curious look, but Arthur had taken this statement in his stride. "Lead on."

We followed the riverbank eastward through willows and banks of reeds, the far shore drawing slowly nearer with every step we took. By the time we reached the place Merlin said held the causeway, the river could only have been a few hundred yards wide. The causeway, made of stone slabs and gravel, rose up above the level of the water not very invitingly. How fast might the tide come in here? Although if the Romans had been in the habit of using this crossing, surely it must be relatively safe?

Arthur wasted no time. He kicked his horse into the shallows and onto the causeway, leaving me no choice but to follow. The column, strung out across the twenty-foot-wide causeway, crowded in our wake.

How weird to be riding a horse across as mighty a river as the Clyde. Behind us lay the farmed lowlands of Caw's kingdom with the forest just a dark shadow on the far horizon. In front stretched the towering mountains of the northern regions of Alt Clut. Beyond that, Pictland.

Before we reached the north shore of the river, we found the channel divided, and we were crossing a sandy island. On the far side the causeway appeared again, taking us across a much narrower stretch of water. Marshy ground made up the northern bank, but the Romans had built this causeway to last. Thank goodness. However, I was never more pleased to find Alezan's feet on solid ground. Perhaps apart from the time I'd crossed the

River Severn in what looked a less than seaworthy ferry.

We turned our horses back toward the west once again, following a substantial track out of the wetlands and into rich farmlands dotted with small stone farmhouses. The frightened people in every fortified settlement we passed ran inside as they saw us coming, dragging what animals they could out of our way. A wise move. We were a large and hungry army.

Ahead of us the rock of Din Breattann drew ever nearer, rocky and impregnable, more smoke rising from the summit fortress. Half a mile off, Arthur called a halt. Here, in good view of Caw and his retinue, he ordered his men to make camp. Curt commands sent men off to raid the local farms. Fires blossomed like golden flowers, and men strung out our horse lines, well out of bowshot of the fortress.

Were we settling in for a siege?

Chapter Nineteen

"WELL, IF HE didn't know we were here before, he knows it now," Merlin said, as we sat around one of the campfires in the warm darkness of the first night. All around us, the dancing flames of more fires sent motes of glowing ash skyward as our warriors feasted on roasted mutton and new bread. The land here was fat and prosperous, the farms, although well defended, full of food. It hadn't taken much to round up enough to supply the army.

We'd taken over one of the farms. The largest. Its stone walled fields now held flocks of local sheep and pigs, and we had their chickens shut in one of the barns. Their sheds bulged with the sacks of flour and vegetables, barrels of beer and earthenware jars of cider the men had collected. We'd arrived when some of the autumn harvest was still going on. Our hungry horses filled their bellies with this year's hay from the myriad of stacks scattered around each farm. If this was to be a siege, we weren't going to go short.

Arthur laughed. "I think he might have got the message."

We were seated on large rocks looted from the nearest wall, me between Arthur and Merlin. The meat Cei had roasted over our fire had been reduced to a pile of well-gnawed bones. A skin of cider was doing the rounds.

"It's an impressive spot for his fortress," Cei remarked. "Sitting on top of cliffs on almost all sides. More impressive even than

Din Eidyn."

Arthur nodded. "Not quite all sides. No fortress is fully impregnable. How do you think they get in and out themselves? That's their weak point." He glanced past me at Merlin. "Where's the entrance?"

"Facing the river and their dock."

"No ships in port at the moment," Cei remarked. "We'd've seen them otherwise."

"There's a town a little up the River Leven," Merlin said. "On this bank. They have docks there as well. Probably a lot of their ships go straight there."

"So, are you going to attack them or sit out here and starve them out?" I asked.

Arthur, who had his arm around my shoulders, tightened his hold. "I'd like to show them we mean business. But if we attack their main entrance, that's what they'll be expecting." He rubbed his beard. "I think we'll move a squad around to sit outside their gates first thing in the morning. That should prevent any supplies getting in either by land or water. Just to sit there, though. Let it look as though we intend to starve them out."

I nestled in close. This sounded like my kind of quiet warfare, not putting my husband in direct danger. His leg still had a lot of mending to do.

As if he read my thoughts, Arthur shifted his leg, rubbing the wound. He still wore a pair of Cei's braccae for comfort. He looked over my head again at Merlin. "There has to be another way in, though."

Uh oh.

"You've seen the cliffs," Cei grumbled. "Sheer. I doubt there is another way."

"Climbing," Arthur said. "We need to scale the cliffs. They won't be expecting us to do that."

A vague memory came to me of a school history lesson about General Wolfe seizing Quebec from the French by having some of his men scale the cliffs around it. Was this what Arthur was planning, nearly thirteen hundred years before Wolfe would do the same?

"Well, you won't be doing that," Cei said. "Not with that leg."

Arthur's body stiffened, but he stayed silent. Probably he could see Cei was right. But being a man, and a king at that, he wouldn't like being told he couldn't do something. After a long pause, he finally spoke. "I can't send men to do what I would not do."

Cei, sitting on the other side of him, touched his arm. "You can't lead in everything, little brother."

Arthur shook his head. "A good general leads his men from the front."

"Not on a bad leg," Merlin muttered. "And not up a sheer cliff face."

Cei nodded. "We have men amongst our ranks who are climbers, many from coastal regions where they scaled their cliffs for birds' eggs as boys. I can form a squad to send up the cliffs." He patted Arthur's arm. "I'll do it in the morning."

THE MORNING BROUGHT a light rain, the mountains to our backs swathed in mist that rendered them invisible. Cei and Arthur between them selected a troop of twenty of the best climbers. Then, under cover of moving half his troops around to blockade Dun Breattann's main entrance, the climbers surveyed the rocky outcrop for a possible route up it.

I studied it as well. On the side nearest to us it rose in rocky splendor to the wooden walls of Caw's stronghold a good two hundred feet above our heads, the steep slopes covered in gorse, heather and spindly shrubs, where they might find footholds. Not insurmountable for modern day climbers with ropes and spikes and proper climbing boots, but for armed warriors wearing chain mail and helmets, not such an easy matter.

Arthur and I rode around toward the main gates along with Theodoric and his men, and saw them settled on the flat ground between the gates and the shoreline, where an empty wooden dock stuck out like a dark finger into the waters of the Clyde. The tide was out, and a few small fishing boats lay drawn up on the mud flats, with no sign of any fishermen. We left Theodoric organizing his camp while, with our climbers for escort, we returned to our base camp. A few arrows rained impotently down from the fortress, but we kept well out of range.

Once back at our main camp, Arthur and I met with the leader of his climbers, Morfran of Linnuis, one of the young men King Manogan had given to us the year before. He'd been a friend of Manogan's youngest son, Prince Anwar. Morfran, a wiry youth with a shock of dark hair and a beard more unkempt than Arthur's, swept a low bow to me and Arthur. The dark eyes in his sallow face danced with enthusiasm. The prospect of leading the attack on Dun Breattann must have been an exciting one.

"Can you climb at night?" Arthur asked, staring across the farmlands at the rise of the rock.

Morfran nodded. "I can indeed, Milord. And so can my men." His voice rose in barely suppressed excitement. "When do you want us to do it?"

Arthur grinned. "Not yet. They'll have been expecting us to attack almost as soon as we got here. I've made it look as though we're settling in for a siege. Let them get used to that. Then we'll go. Meanwhile, you and your men train together, eat together, sleep side by side. I want you ready to climb at a moment's notice."

Morfran put his hand to his heart. "We will do you proud, Milord Dux."

WE SAT FOR seven days on the plain below Dun Breattann, living off the fat farmlands that belonged to Caw. Theodoric kept any small boats that tried to land on the wooden jetty at bay. Not that there were many. Those that tried it had to sail back, still full, to the town, which so far, we'd left alone. The inhabitants retreated behind their wooden palisade walls and did their best to make themselves look unimportant.

Arthur's leg healed well. I was able to remove the dressings and let the air get to it. He still walked with a limp as though it pained him, but he refused to admit that even to me. Every day he rode to Theodoric's camp and moved amongst the men with words of encouragement and support. Sometimes he sparred with them as they occupied their days with training.

Up on the walls of the topmost fortress, the outlines of watching warriors could be seen, spear tips pointing skyward. Sometimes a few arrows rained down in our direction, but Theodoric had set up his camp just out of their reach, and they fell harmlessly to the ground between the camp and the rock.

In the deep cleft between the twin peaks, a high palisade wall stretched across, with double gates and twin towers, barely three hundred feet from the riverside camp. The wall there bristled thickly with Caw's warriors, glaring out at us across the divide. How hungry would they be getting? How much food did Caw have stored in his stronghold? It being late summer now, and harvest time, when stores would be replenished, perhaps not much. And as for water...did they even have a water source up there on top of a volcanic plug?

On the seventh day we roasted a slaughtered pig over a huge fire, the mouthwatering scents wafting toward the fortress – I hoped. Probably not many pigs up there. It was all day cooking, tended by a couple of our best cooks. The skin crisped and crackled, and the fat dripped into the fire and made it spit.

Come nightfall everyone in the base camp gathered to eat, our fires stacked high and the flames blazing up toward the moonless night sky, sending red hot ash blowing across the fields.

We made a fair bit of noise. Not enough to sound unnatural, but sufficient to indicate we were celebrating, out there in the dark below the fortress.

And under cover of this, Arthur sent his climbers out, armed with ropes, swords and vicious daggers. Silently, they padded across the plain to the foot of the rock, and began their climb, out of our sight and hopefully out of the minds of the hungry inhabitants of the rock.

Then we waited. The fires died down, and, led by Arthur and Cei, our men crept through the darkness on foot toward the riverside camp to join Theodoric and his men.

As usual, I was left behind. With Merlin as my jailer.

However much I knew that in battle a woman would be a liability, I couldn't help but rage against my impotence. I wanted to be there with Arthur, saving him from harm. That he was not invulnerable had become frighteningly obvious after that nasty stab wound. But no, I had to stay at the farmstead with Merlin and three other warriors, watched by the wary farmer and his family, whose livelihood we'd wrecked.

We sat around the glowing embers of our fire in silence, every ear straining for sounds of battle. But nothing came. No battle horns, no shouts, no screams.

Merlin took a long gulp of cider and passed me the skin. I pushed it away. I wanted a clear head, and this northern cider was strong.

The farm dog came crawling on its belly, tail wagging hopefully. A small, brindled terrier type with one upright ear and one flopped forward over its left eye. I threw it one of the pork bones and it ran off into the darkness, intent on not sharing its booty.

The silence stretched on, so tense an almost unbearable urge to scream came over me, and I had to dig my nails into my palms to stop myself. Merlin's fingers beat a drum tattoo on his knees. The man opposite me chewed his nails. The fire died to glowing ashes.

At last, the unmistakable sound of a battle horn rang out,

long and clear. I sat up straight, ears straining. It came again, and then again. Shouts, whooping, the battle horn again.

Merlin and my guards jumped to their feet, and so did I, our heads all turned toward the sound. My fingers made fists in the front of my tunic, and my breath came fast and hard. Having seen so many battles now, I had a good idea of what was happening. In the dark. Would they even be able to see what they were doing?

All we could do was stand and listen as the din of battle rose to the star-speckled blue-black sky. It went on and on, rising and falling, filling the silence of the night. A glow rose from behind the hump of the rock – was part of the fortress on fire? Maybe the main gates? I wanted to go and look, but Merlin firmly refused, a look of horror on his face.

"He wanted you safe here. There'll be time tomorrow to see what damage our men are doing. Arthur will win. Mark my words."

The night grew longer. The sounds of battle diminished, faded, vanished. The glow also died down, almost invisible now behind the shoulder of the hill. Listening to the eerie quiet frightened me more than listening to the din had. I copied the warrior and chewed my nails along with him.

I couldn't rest. I couldn't sit down again by the red embers of the fire. In the east the sky began to lighten, and little by little, the land edged out of the shadows of the night. Heavy cloud hid the rising sun from us, and distant rain misted the horizon.

In the dim, early morning light, a dozen warriors came galloping across the fields toward us.

I ran to the gates of the farm, Merlin and my three guards hot on my heels. The warriors slowed to a canter then a trot. In a moment they were walking. Cei rode at their head, a grin of triumph painted across his bearded face. Thrusting his reins into one hand, he punched the air. "We did it!"

Relief flooded over me, weakening my knees to the point where I had to grab hold of the stone gatepost for support.

Merlin slipped a supporting hand under my elbow. "And

Caw?"

Cei's grin widened. "A prisoner."

"H-his sons?" I couldn't keep the tremor out of my voice.

"All eleven of them. Some dead, some living." Cei swung himself down from the saddle and strode over to me. "Arthur is fine. Stop worrying." He enfolded me in a bear-like hug, the bristles of his ginger beard tickling my cheek.

I clung onto him, a tangible link to the man I loved, tears squeezing themselves out of my eyes and running down my cheeks to soak into his beard. "Thank God," I murmured.

He released me. "Arthur sent me to fetch you all. He's in the fortress and wants you there. Fetch your horses."

Our horses had stood, tethered ready to be ridden at a moment's notice, all night long. I tightened Alezan's girth and mounted. Cei spun his horse around to join his men and, leaving our three guards to watch over our horse lines, we jog-trotted back through the small square fields to the far side of the Rock.

The gatehouse lay a blackened, smoking ruin, the riverside camp empty of all but the horse lines with a few men to guard them. Arthur must have his men inside the fortress.

We left our own horses with the guards and walked the short distance to what was left of the gates. The wooden towers still partly held their shape, but the upper floors were gone and only the charred lower floors remained. To either side of them the palisade fence had burnt to the earth banks it stood on.

Half a dozen of our men stood guard with not a man of Alt Clut in sight – not a living one, that was. Bodies strewed the hillside where it rose behind the gatehouse. We had to pick our way between them as we climbed the steep and narrow gully toward the fortress on the summit.

More buildings had been burnt in the cleft between the twin peaks of the rock, and more men lay dead. The narrow path wound up toward the eastern peak, where the palisade walls still stood intact, the gates open wide.

The climb was difficult even on this path, so how Morfran

and his climbers had done it in darkness and on the steeper side I had no idea.

We passed through the gates. The palace enclosure was not large, confined as it was by the geography of the site. A medium sized hall sat in the center of a cluster of buildings, heavily guarded by our men. The doors stood as wide open as the gates had. Cei led us through them.

King Caw of Alt Clut had his hall laid out much as ours at Din Cadan, but on a smaller scale. At one end on a raised dais sat the high table. In the center a fire pit smoldered.

Arthur, still in his armor and helmet, stood on the dais in front of the high table on which sat something lumpy in a sack. Facing him stood an older man, held between two of our heftiest warriors. Long sandy hair generously streaked with grey hung down over shoulders so massive he looked almost triangular in shape. As we entered, the man swung around, and I looked into the eyes of King Caw of Alt Clut.

I must have seen him at the Council of Kings I'd attended, but the memory eluded me. His lined face and grizzled hair suggested he might be around fifty years old, but his musculature and upright bearing was that of a much younger man. Recognition dawned in his pale blue eyes. Even if I couldn't recall him, it appeared he remembered me.

The two warriors on either side of him grabbed his arms, perhaps suspecting he might do something untoward, but he made no other move.

Ignoring him, Arthur stepped down off the dais and came up to me, arms outstretched. "Gwen." He took my hands and led me back to the dais. A strong stench of something rotting came from the sack on the tabletop.

Merlin perched himself on the edge of a trestle table, one leg swinging, eyes watchful and alert.

Standing beside my husband on the raised platform, I took a better look around the hall. It was not empty. Down the sides, most of the benches had been pushed back, and a row of prisoners with hunched shoulders and angry faces stood between our men, their hands bound, armor removed. Nine men and boys, all sandy haired and heavy browed. Of course – they had to be Caw's sons, but only nine of them. Had two more perished?

Arthur unfastened the strap on his helmet and set it behind him on the table, next to the stinky sack. His dark hair, almost to his shoulders now, hung damp with sweat. He cleared his throat. All eyes rested on him. "Caw of Alt Clut, you stand here accused of the crime of allying yourself with the painted people of the north. And of using them to attack your neighbors." His voice, clear and deep, carried around the hall, rising to the rafters. The nine sons shifted restlessly, their booted feet scuffing the dirty reeds underfoot. Dust rose from the beaten earth floor.

Caw glowered from under thick sandy eyebrows. He was not a tall man like his son Heuil, but his presence filled the room. A pit bull facing a hunting hound. "And who gave you leave to judge me, you upstart boy?" His voice rumbled like the deep growl of the dog I'd thought him.

Arthur seemed unfazed. "You attacked the lands of Lot of Lleuddiniawn, your nearest neighbor. You sent your men south of the Wall to attack and burn the fortresses there. The very fortresses that guard Britain from the Picts. This is a time of danger for all the kingdoms of Britain. *We* are not your enemy, yet you attacked us. The common enemies of the British are the Picts to the north, the Saxons from the east and the Irish in the west. If we do not join together to fight for the common cause, then Britain will be lost." He surveyed the nine sandy haired sons. "And *you* will all have had a hand in causing this."

Caw glowered at him some more. "'Tis every man for himself here, in the wild north."

Arthur turned and picked up the sack. "Your heir is already dead, executed for his hand in attacking Vindolanda." He tipped the sack out. Heuil's head rolled across the reed covered floor like a badly-shapen football, scarcely recognizable any longer as being human. It finished at his father's feet. Someone had tarred it in an effort at preservation, but the features had gone, and maggots crawled in the empty eye sockets.

My stomach roiled. I dug my fingernails into the palms of my hands in an effort not to disgrace myself and embarrass Arthur by vomiting at the sight. Caw had no such reservations. He doubled over to retch onto the reeds, and when he straightened, his eyes flashed venomous hatred at Arthur. Only the restraining hold of his captors prevented him from lunging forward. "You bastard."

I swallowed down the bile that had risen, glad of the table behind me to lean against. I hadn't been expecting this.

Unmoved, Arthur gestured at Caw's remaining sons. "Your heir is already dead. These are your sons who still live. If you want one of them to succeed you, then cease your strife with your neighbors. Stop coveting their lands. Build your own kingdom on trade and defense, not attack and theft." He nodded to Theodoric, who shoved forward the youngest, a boy of eleven or twelve.

"This boy will be my hostage. I hear he is your favorite. He will ride south with us when we leave, and if you rise again, with or without the help of the heathen Dogmen, he will die." He paused. "And I will send you back his head in a sack. Just like his brother's."

The boy's sandy eyebrows glowered at Arthur, his square jaw jutting. A smaller version of his brother Heuil, that was for certain. Their mother couldn't have been a looker.

Theodoric shoved the boy past his father and up to the foot of the dais.

Arthur studied the furious face. "What is your name, boy?"

A series of emotions flashed across the boy's face – anger, rebellion, suspicion, a touch of fear. He hesitated, maybe considering refusing to answer and then dismissing the thought as it might make him appear childish. This was a boy who thought himself a man already. "Gildas," he replied.

I stared. Gildas was the name of the man whose sixth century account of the Dark Ages was the nearest thing to a contemporary document available in my own time. A man who never once mentioned Arthur. Could this surly boy be him?

Chapter Twenty

TWO DAYS LATER, leaving Caw of Alt Clut to repair his damaged fortress and replenish his pillaged farms as best he could, we rode south. Arthur had refused to allow his men to burn the food stores and barns. "If we leave them starving, we've made enemies of them, not allies."

There'd also been muttering when he'd refused them permission to loot more than the food we needed, but he was a good leader, and his men, albeit somewhat begrudgingly in a few cases, did as they were told. We had enough food for the march south toward Bremenium and from there, on to Coria.

Young Gildas made an unpleasant travelling companion at first. Surly, bad tempered, rude and haughty, and seemingly very conscious he was a prince, he rebuffed all my efforts to talk to him. He rode under heavy guard, as Arthur strongly suspected that at the slightest opportunity, he'd make a run for it. A warrior sandwiched him on either side, deep within the column of riders, each with a lead rope to his horse's bit. He had his hands tied in front of him to help him balance, and so he could hold the reins, but the guards watched him closely all the time.

We didn't hurry. Although Arthur didn't want to admit it, his leg still troubled him a lot. More than once I caught him rubbing it when he thought no one was looking, but held my tongue, not wanting to draw attention to it. He wouldn't want his men to think him weak. Cei must have noticed too, because he set a slow and steady pace as we left the mountains behind to ride south through the Caledonian Forest. Once out of the forest, and onto Dere Street, we made better time as we headed toward the Wall.

Our road traversed a purple, heather-covered vastness, dotted with gorse and bracken, stunted hawthorns, and small, scrawny sheep. The moorland rolled away into the distance in a vast bare ocean, here and there dipping down to treacherous peat bogs that lurked in the hollows. To the west, the dark shadow that marked the edge of the forest hugged the distant hills, and to the east, nothing but moorland as far as the eye could see.

The weather, that had remained sultry since we left Dun Breattann behind, took a turn for the worse, the air redolent with the damp scent of autumn. Mist swathed the hills every morning, often creeping down onto the land around the old Roman road and making me glad we had a proper road to follow. Sometimes it seeped down into the valleys and hollows, giving them the appearance of strangely ethereal white lakes. When it wasn't misty, bouts of scudding rain chased us down the road as though hurrying us out of the northern territories where we were no longer wanted.

Bremenium lay on a rise in the moorland a scant twenty-five miles north of Coria. A small fort, now half fortified farm, it was home to a hardy garrison of men mostly from Vindolanda and Coria, or, like Dewain, locally born and bred. They must have seen us coming a long way off, with their unbroken view up the road to the north, because the narrow gates stood open to welcome us inside.

We tethered our horses under the lean-to stabling along the run of the wall and saw them comfortable and fed. Then Arthur and I, along with Cei and Theodoric escorting Gildas, headed for the commanding officer's residence, a building that had seen better days in what was probably a chequered history. Arthur walked stiffly in an effort to disguise the limp that always worsened after a long day in the saddle. He wasn't fooling anyone. Being forced to ride every day was not doing his leg any good.

Arminius, a grizzled soldier wearing what appeared to be the tarnished leftover armor of a legionary, greeted us at the door. His short-cropped hair and clean-shaven jaw on top of the armor reminded me sharply of Roman reenactors back in my world – the Ermine Street Guard. "My Lord Dux." He used Arthur's military title rather than his royal one as he made a short, welcoming bow.

"Commander." Arthur clasped hands with the old officer, and we followed him into a small courtyard surrounded on all four sides by low, thatched buildings. The late afternoon sun, watery and weak, cast long shadows across the rough grass in the center, where a few herbs grew haphazardly. Gildas looked around himself with a sneer on his broad face. He was not a good-looking boy, and his expression did nothing to enhance his looks.

"I'd be honored if you would dine with me this evening," Arminius said to Arthur, his voice gruff and slightly accented, but pleasant to the ear. "I've put you in the best bedchambers we have, but this is a barracks, so please don't expect too much."

Arthur smiled. "We've been sleeping rough for days – a bed of any sort'll be a nice change. Is there any chance of hot water?"

Arminius straightened his back and saluted. "Sir, there is indeed. I'll have it sent to you immediately." His eyes slid sideways to look at the surly, hand-bound boy we'd brought him. "Do you require a locked room for your prisoner?"

Arthur eyed Gildas. So did I. He was far from home now, in lands that should be strange to him, but the glint in his pale eyes showed that he'd probably not given up on escape. Arthur nodded. "Your most secure room. He's our hostage and the ticket to keep his father peaceful. I don't want him anywhere he could escape from."

Arminius snapped his fingers, and a soldier came running. "Take the boy to our lock-up, and see he's fed."

Gildas glowered around at everyone, generous with his disgust.

Arthur's mouth twitched but he didn't let himself smile. "But take care – he's a slippery customer."

The chamber Arminius had put at mine and Arthur's disposal was small and square, with a bed hardly wide enough to be classed as double. We'd certainly be cozy in it. The floor was some sort of bare cement, unadorned by rugs or decoration. A single unglazed window high up in the wall let in a small amount of light, as well as the misty dampness, and an oil lamp sat unlit on a well-worn wooden chest.

I unbuckled my sword belt, and Arthur helped me out of my mail shirt. There being nowhere else to put it, I laid it on the floor, then helped him out of his.

He sat down on the bed, stretching his bad leg out in front of him. "That's better. So long in the saddle's made my leg stiffen."

"I've noticed." I pulled off my padded outer tunic, that prevented the mail shirt rubbing me. Its quilted layers tended to broil its wearer alive in the summer heat, so I'd been glad of the cooling in the weather. Fewer midges as well.

Arthur reached up and, catching my undershirt, tugged me closer. His hands went to my waist. "A proper bed to sleep in."

I let a smile play around my lips. "There is."

His hands slid up inside my undershirt, warm on my bare skin, and a stirring of desire kindled in me. I ran my hands through his hair, loosening the curls where they'd been stuck damply flat by his helmet, and leant closer.

He laid his head against my belly in an oddly gentle gesture, cheek turned toward me, the hairs of his beard tickling.

I stroked the top of his head. "You said you'd shave that beard off once we'd sorted Caw out."

He didn't look up. "I'll do that now. I've grown fed up with it myself."

Twisting a lock of his hair around my fingers, I whispered in his ear. "You'll be a new man."

I felt his grin rather than saw it. "What will your husband say if you have a new man in your bed tonight then?"

That made me chuckle. "He's a very jealous man. He won't like it one bit. I think he might come after you."

He turned his head and kissed my belly through my shirt. "But what if this new man pleases you more than the old?"

"He just might, if he's beardless."

He chuckled. "Better go and hurry that hot water along then."

Searching for the hot water proved unnecessary, as when Arthur opened the door to our chamber, a soldier already stood there, carrying two large buckets of steaming water.

Real hot water. The bliss of it. Who'd have thought the presence of two wooden buckets of water would provoke such pleasure? I stripped off as fast as I could and had a stand-up wash before the water had a chance to cool, using the soap Arminius had kindly supplied. Real soap. What a luxury. Then with Arthur's help, I washed my hair.

Arthur did the same. The floor ended up pretty much as wet as we were, and what remained of the water in the buckets turned murky grey with dirt. But we felt more human – well, I did at any rate. Arthur was probably much more used to being dirty on campaign than I was.

We stood drying ourselves on the rough towels Arminius had thoughtfully provided. As I rubbed down my own body, my eyes were drawn to Arthur's. He'd lost some muscle in his wounded leg and the scar looked angry and prominent, but otherwise his body had hardly changed since the day I'd first seen it. A little more patchworked with scars, perhaps, but as long and lean and attractive as it had ever been. Dark hair curled across his chest and down his belly, and muscles slid beneath his skin, so pale where it hadn't seen the sun.

His eyes met mine. "Like what you see?" A parody of what I'd once asked him, the first time we met.

I grinned. "Of course. All the better that it's whole and healthy." I chuckled. "And beardless." He'd begun his ablutions by carefully shaving off the beard, and now stood before me smooth chinned and handsome.

I touched the side of his face with a finger. "I can see you properly again."

His dark eyes danced. "You don't like the barbarian me then?"

I pulled a face of mock indecision. "I might. But with a beard you have an unsettling look of your brother. Cadwy, not Cei."

With a frown, he put out a hand and pulled me to him, pressing our naked bodies together. "Be thankful I'm not him. But you've made me think I'll never let that beard grow again." He paused. "But you? You prefer the Roman dux to the savage bear?"

I pressed closer, standing on tiptoes to swiftly plant a light kiss on his lips. "I prefer you, my love, however you are."

His hand slid up to the back of my wet head, and his mouth came down on mine, eager, demanding, hungry. My lips parted under his questing tongue, and I melted into his embrace, the core of my body molten fire. In a few steps we were on the bed, his hands roaming over my body. I lay back, pulling him down on top of me, and willingly gave in to my desires.

⟫⟫⟪⟪

OUR ARRIVAL AT Arminius's dinner table some time later raised Cei's brows into his ginger hairline. A slow grin of understanding slid over his face, and he winked at Arthur.

Were we so obvious? I glanced sideways at my husband. His tanned face certainly held a telltale flush, so presumably mine must as well. I patted my hair, now confined in a damp braid and hanging down my back, and the reason for our lateness at the table. Wet and tousled from sex, the ultimate in bed-hair, it had been extremely hard to tease apart. Luckily, I'd had two combs in my bag and Arthur had done one side whilst I did the other. But it had still taken forever. Short hair had never been so tempting.

Despite clinging on so strongly to the old Roman ways of soldiering, Arminius didn't have couches to recline on while we ate, but a proper table and wooden chairs. Perhaps all Roman soldiers had used tables and the couches had only been for the rich townspeople. Thank goodness. I'd had experience of eating while lying down and felt relieved I wasn't expected to here.

The food was plain but good, and plenty of it. As we ate, I spared a thought for the sullen boy in the lockup, and whether he'd been fed adequately. He'd taken very badly to being a prisoner. But then, I had too, when I'd been locked up by Melwas. I couldn't help a certain fellow feeling for him, so young and snatched away from the only life he'd known.

Tired from the journey, not to mention the sex, I didn't pay too much attention to Arminius's conversation with my menfolk. Every so often I caught a few words – "he had a lump on his head the size of a ballista stone…", "the spring in the valley never runs dry…", "my grandfather served under yours…", "couldn't ever leave the Wall…". And on and on. I'd had enough talk of war, fighting and defensive measures to last me a lifetime.

My attention wandered back to the days of my imprisonment, so distant now but in reality only eighteen months ago. And that brought little Amhar back into my head, and an ache into my heart that I'd been trying to ignore. We'd been gone now for nearly four months. He'd be nearing one year old, maybe walking. Would he even remember me? A few tears trickled unhindered down my cheeks, salty on my lips. I pushed my plate away, half eaten, the lump in my throat so large I couldn't bring myself to swallow.

Merlin, sitting beside me, must have seen. "Gwen?" He kept his voice down low. "What's wrong?"

Arthur hadn't noticed. Arminius was telling him all about how he'd withstood an attack by the Dogmen a year ago – in great and gory detail.

I bit my lip to stop the sob rising in my throat. "Amhar," I whispered.

His eyes widened. "What about him? Did you have a vision?"

A vision? What was he talking about? He was the one with

the Sight, not me. I shook my head. "I just miss him. I've been refusing to think about him all this time, but now, when we're on our way home, I couldn't hold it back any longer. I need to see him."

Merlin's brow furrowed. He was a man, after all, and a childless one at that. Most likely he had no idea about a mother's love. Cei might have been the more sympathetic a one to confide in, but he was hanging on every word Arminius was saying.

Licking his lips, and clearly searching for some platitude, Merlin shifted uncomfortably in his seat. "Not long now." He glanced across at Arthur. "We'll have to take it steadily though."

I studied his lean face. "You've seen it too?"

He nodded. "He hides it well, but no one can hide something like that completely. It's in his eyes."

He was right. Dark shadows circled Arthur's eyes and his face had grown thinner. Not just from the strain of a long summer's campaigning. I fingered my knife. "He isn't sleeping well."

Merlin frowned. "I thought as much. Has he said anything to you?"

I shook my head. "Only that his leg is stiff after he's been riding all day."

Merlin glanced toward where Cei was laughing at something Arminius had said. "We've done our best to keep the stages short, shorter each day in fact, but ploughing on down the Ebrauc road and beyond will be a hard slog for a man with a bad leg." He rubbed his chin. He, too, had taken the opportunity for a shave, unlike Cei, who still resembled some wild man of the woods.

"What can we do?"

"Short of insisting on ten-mile stages, not much. He won't listen to me."

"Have you tried?"

He shrugged. "Not in so many words. But to ride nearly four hundred miles in ten mile stages at the start of winter isn't a good idea either. And the longer we take the more supplies we need."

I wasn't an idiot. I could see where he was heading with this.

But what about Amhar? Reluctantly I pushed thoughts of him aside. Arthur had to come first. If anything were to happen to Arthur, where would Amhar and I be?

And Merlin was right. We either had to head south as fast as we could or stay here in the north for the winter. Remaining seemed the obvious answer. Vindolanda. Why not there? The town was big enough to support our army over winter. Enough accommodation existed, and it would give Arthur months for his wound to heal properly – a chance he'd not given it yet. But Amhar? The longing to see my son burgeoned in my aching heart until I thought it might overwhelm me.

That night, as we settled down in the cozy intimacy of our narrow bed, I nestled against Arthur's chest, his heartbeat loud in my right ear. He shifted slightly, as though easing his leg. The time was right to broach my suggestion, much as I didn't want to make it.

I'd thought long and hard about how I'd phrase the matter. "Do you think Caw will keep his part of the bargain you made with him?"

Arthur shifted again, very slightly, but enough to tell me how uncomfortable he must be. "I don't know. Hard to tell with a man such as he."

I peeped up at him. "I suppose as he has eight other sons he won't miss just the one." Arthur's profile was toward me, outlined against the faint light from the high single window. Outside, a full moon shone down across the moors. I played with the curling hairs on his chest. "A man – or a boy – can fall from favor when he's no longer under the eye of his father. How long do you think it will take Caw to fix on one of his other sons as a new favorite? He'll have forgotten the boy by Christmas."

"That's quite likely true."

"So is it a wise move to retreat back to the south and leave the Wall unguarded?"

His head turned toward me. "Not unguarded. The frontier forts remain garrisoned, as does this one. And Lot is the stronger now for Caw having been weakened."

"Do you think Caw cares if we kill his son? He has eight more of them." I'd struggled to put myself inside the head of the gruff warrior king we'd met. A difficult task, and one I wasn't sure I'd succeeded in. "Why do you think the boy looks so surly all the time? Because he knows his father will forget him. That's why. He hasn't grown up in his father's court without noticing how his brothers, and his father's warriors, fall in and out of favor. It happens in all courts. Kings are fickle creatures."

Arthur chuckled softly. "You're a wise woman now, are you? Wise in the ways of barbarian kings. Where did you get such knowledge of a world you weren't born into?"

I tapped my forehead. "Up here. I'm guessing how that boy's been brought up. Guessing how his father feels about him. Maybe I see it more clearly just because this isn't my world. Maybe being an outsider helps."

He chuckled again. "My wise counselor. Maybe you should join me on the Council of Kings and give me your insights on the other members."

I poked him. "Don't mock me. Think about this. If we sit here, just below the Wall, for the winter, Caw will soon find out we're still here. That, and the boy, will keep him locked up in his fortress instead of out pillaging to make up for what we took from him."

For a long minute Arthur stayed silent, the sound of his heart beating a steady rhythm in my ear. Then, "You mean you think we should winter here instead of heading home?" He shifted his leg again, his breath catching as if a shaft of pain had caught him.

"Yes. I do." *Oh, Amhar. I'm sorry.*

More silence. "You may well be right. I'm not mocking you. For a woman, you have some good ideas."

I bristled and gave him a mock smack on the chest. "For a woman? Do I not have a brain the same as yours?" I couldn't resist the temptation to let him know how I felt.

A low chuckle rose in his throat. "All right, all right. You have a brain. I just forget it sometimes. I'm not used to discussing my every move with a woman...yet."

I tapped him again. "Well, you should be by now. Where should we make our base?"

"Vindolanda. Meirchion won't welcome us with open arms at Caer Ligualid, although it's bigger and better provisioned to support an over-wintering army. I've a feeling Riacus would be glad of our presence, though."

Vindolanda. I'd see Elen again, which would be a comfort. But although I lay silently in Arthur's arms, long after he'd fallen asleep, my heart was breaking for my son, left alone with Maia in far off Din Cadan.

Chapter Twenty-One

THE ONLY THING good about a winter spent in Vindolanda was that I got to spend time with Elen, whom I'd thought never to see again. But that was all. Rations were sparse, as the town struggled to support our army, and the weather worsened rapidly as autumn progressed. We had deep snow before Christmas and very spartan celebrations.

Not that I wanted to celebrate. With the inaction the snow brought, I had more time to dwell on Amhar, so far away, growing up without either of his parents. My only comfort was the knowledge that Maia loved him every bit as much as I did. Perhaps because I was missing my child so much, I determined to make a friend of young Gildas.

He was confined to the courtyard of the praetorium, much to his annoyance. Guards stood watch on every door – both the main ones and the lesser, and the windows in the outer walls were too small for even a boy his age to wriggle through.

I started by making a point of greeting him every time I met him, smiling in my friendliest librarian fashion. I'd always been a hit with children who came to the library, but Gildas proved a hard nut to crack. Only after weeks of me grinning at him like an idiot did he at last design to talk to me.

He finally succumbed just after Christmas. "Why do you keep greeting me? And smiling?" We were in the snowy courtyard where I was scattering corn for the hens. They ran about after it, clucking excitedly, small feet scraping at the snow to dig up the best morsels. He'd been passing through, head down, arms tightly folded across his chest, but this time, when I called out a cheery 'good day', he stopped.

He'd grown some since he'd come to us, and his bony wrists stuck out of the ends of his tunic. An awkward, gawky boy, not quite the man he longed to be, but no longer a child.

I smiled a bit more. "Because I'm a friendly person." I'd have liked to have pointed out that he clearly wasn't, but that probably wouldn't have helped.

"Oh." He stood in the snow, staring at me out of his pale expressionless eyes, brows jutting. Not a looker, nor any promise of turning into one.

I felt like a grinning idiot. "My name's Gwen." The bowl of scraps for the chickens hung empty in my hand.

He nodded. "I know. You're *his* wife."

Of course he did. Now he was talking to me it was hard to find something to say to keep the conversation going. What sort of small talk could one use with someone who was to write the only surviving account of the era we were living in? Despite his age, I felt a certain awe.

"Would you like something to eat?" Boys were always hungry. I knew that from growing up with a brother, and this particular boy looked on the skinny side.

He nodded. Perhaps he wasn't getting full rations as he was one of the enemy.

"Come on then."

He followed me into the kitchen. Brangaine, the praetorium cook, was taking loaves out of the oven that occupied one side of the room. The smell of hot bread wafted to us as we entered, and the boy swallowed convulsively. Probably drooling.

Really, I shouldn't have been offering him extra food, but I justified this to myself for several reasons: most likely he was getting smaller rations than everyone else, he was a growing boy, and I wanted him to like me.

Brangaine slid the loaves onto the table, Gildas's hungry eyes following every movement. One of the loaves looked smaller than the rest.

I could have just picked it up and walked away, but then Brangaine would have thought I was a thief – or worse, that Gildas was. So instead, I stepped up to the floury tabletop. "Brangaine?"

She looked up, a rotund, red-faced woman with small, too-close-together eyes and a perpetual drip on the end of her squat nose. "Milady?" She wiped her floury hands on her broad apron.

"I see you have a smaller loaf…just there." I put my fingertip on the hot bread. A suspicion that Brangaine had made this loaf for her own consumption crept over me. How else was she still so fat when everyone else grew thinner?

Brangaine sucked her lips in. She couldn't deny it.

I counted the other loaves out loud. Twelve. This one made the baker's dozen. Twelve was the number she was asked to bake every day. Now I knew I'd guessed right, and from the expression on her face, she knew I knew.

"From the look of you, you clearly don't need extra food," I said curtly. "And this poor boy does. You can see how thin he's got." I fixed her with a hard stare. "And how fat you are. I think I'll take this loaf for the boy." I picked it up, and before Brangaine could think of any retort, marched out of the kitchens with Gildas hurrying after me.

In the shelter of the colonnaded walkway, I handed the hot bread to Gildas. "Best eat it now before anyone else sees. She won't be telling. You probably guessed why."

He nodded. "She's been helping herself to the flour barrel." He bit into the bread with his large, off-white teeth and chewed with appreciation.

The smell made my mouth water. I was hungry too.

He'd eaten half the loaf before the thought that he ought to offer me some as well came to him. Sheepishly he held out the uneaten half, but I shook my head.

"Like I said, you're thin. And you're a growing boy."

He wolfed down the rest of it before I could change my mind. When he'd finished, he sat down on the stone bench under the shelter of the colonnade's tiled roof, and I perched beside him. He regarded me out of wary, curious eyes. "Why'd you do that?"

"Like I said, I'm friendly."

He scratched his matted thatch of sandy hair. Maybe he'd had a mother in Dun Breattann who'd made him brush it every day. Clearly, he hadn't done it since. Close up, he seemed a rather pathetic specimen – skinny, gawky, big bony hands and feet, clothes that didn't fit him and were too thin for this weather, a face that hadn't seen soap and water in some time. And he smelled.

"Then why're you being friendly to me?" Under the grime on his face the shadow of a bruise showed, the purple blotch half-hidden by his shaggy hair. I'd never seen anyone strike him, but it seemed at least one person had. The people of Vindolanda, our own warriors too, had no reason to be kind to him. His older brother and his father had caused a lot of death and destruction over this past year.

I shrugged. "Perhaps because no one else is. Everyone needs a friend."

He scratched his arm. Very likely he had lice. Although Arthur allowed him the run of the praetorium by day, at night he was still being shut in the lockup, which had probably housed all sorts of filthy criminals in its time.

"I don't."

I changed tack. "Do you miss your family?"

His eyes flew wide open. "No." Incredulity at my question edged his voice.

But would he have admitted to it? Most likely not.

I smiled. "I miss mine. I have a baby boy back home. He'll be learning to walk now." A hard-to-swallow lump rose in my throat.

Interest flickered in his eyes. "What's his name?"

"Amhar." I mustn't let my sadness show.

"Why're you here then? Why's a queen here with her husband's army? Queens should be with their children."

"Not this one. If I can, I march with my husband."

Disbelief flitted across his face. "Why? Why would a woman want to march to war?"

I marshalled my thoughts. No way could I tell him about my fears about Camboglanna, groundless as they'd so far proved to be. "Because I want to be near my husband. Because I love him, and want to help. And because I bring his men luck. Look." I held up my hand on which the dragon ring sat. "I'm the Ring Maiden, don't forget."

He studied the ring at closer quarters. If I'd been his mother, I'd have sent him off for a good all over wash and some clean clothes. And a de-lousing.

"That's the ring? The one in the prophecy?"

I nodded. "The one and only."

He grunted. "I s'pose you and it did bring luck to your husband. Or I wouldn't be here."

I nodded again. Arthur would have disputed that, for sure. "What about your mother – do you miss her?"

Another grunt, scornful this time. "My mother's dead."

Not unusual. If the poor woman had produced twelve sons she'd probably expired from exhaustion.

"Do you miss your brothers?"

He shook his head. "Not likely. Bastards, all of them. 'Cept Heuil, and he's dead."

As I had no idea whether this might be their actual legal state, I stayed quiet. Twelve sons was a lot for one woman to have produced – possibly some of them were from women other than the queen. Or Gildas could just have been expressing his honest opinion of them.

"I have a brother," I said. "He's far away and I don't think I'll ever see him again. We're twins."

He raised his brows. "Did you like him?"

I nodded. "Most of the time. As children we quarreled a lot, but that's what children do. I expect you quarreled with your brothers, didn't you?"

The scowl returned. "They picked on me."

Now we were getting somewhere. "Oh. That's not nice. Some of them looked a lot older than you."

His hands, now no longer occupied with food, had dropped to his grubby tunic front, twisting it up as he spoke. "My brother Heuil kept me safe." He looked down at his hands. "But *he* killed him." Resentment filled every word.

So, the only brother who'd cared for him had been the one Arthur had executed. The hatred in Gildas's voice when he spoke of Arthur sliced sharp enough to cut the cold winter air. I shivered involuntarily. Under my bottom the stone bench felt icy cold. We'd both get piles if we sat here much longer.

"Your brother broke the law."

Gildas shot a furious glance up at me. "He was carrying out my father's orders."

An age-old excuse. Sorrow for this poor confused and bereft child swept over me, but even if I could have changed what had happened, I wouldn't have tried. Arthur had been right to execute Heuil when he'd stood before him. Heuil would have done the same to him. But a child's logic would never see that.

"What about your other brothers? Were none of them kind to you? Not even the ones nearest you in age?"

His perpetual scowl deepened as he shook his head. "They were jealous of me."

"Because you were your father's favorite?"

A sly smile crept over his face. "Because I'm cleverer than them."

Interesting reply. His pale eyes did indeed hold sharp intelligence. I wasn't sure I liked what I saw. This was a boy who might not make a trustworthy man – or friend.

What I knew of his writings flashed into my head. I was twelve again, sitting with my father in his study while he explained that for some unknown reason Gildas had never mentioned Arthur in his writings, even though he praised Ambrosius. His words echoed to me down the years – more years than he could ever have guessed at. "It's been suggested that Gildas had a grudge to bear against Arthur, and that's why he never mentions his name, even though he names Badon as a battle. In fact, most of what he wrote was one long spiteful complaint against the rulers of his day." He pushed the spectacles, that had slipped to the tip of his nose, back up toward his eyes. "And some scholars think that as Gildas never names Arthur, that's proof he never existed."

I shook myself out of my reverie, back to a present where I was face to face with the boy who would write those spiteful words. "Were you the youngest?"

He nodded. "Really, I have – I mean I *had* – five brothers. The others're not my mother's children, so they're not princes. And that's another reason they didn't like me. Because I was a prince and they were not. Only two of us left now, though. *He* killed Heuil, and my other two proper brothers died defending Dun Breattann."

I latched on to the first part of his speech. "I suppose that makes sense. Boys can be cruel. Didn't your father stop them?"

The frown deepened. "He was too busy to notice. Too keen to be out raiding, or sending my brothers out to do it for him." A note of scorn tinged his voice. Somehow, I got the feeling he didn't quite agree with his father's and brothers' conduct.

"You'd have had to do that soon as well. You must be nearly old enough to become a warrior." Flattery might get me further than sympathy. From being around Llacheu, I knew how much boys longed to become warriors.

The sly little smile returned. "Never."

Now that surprised me a lot. "You don't want to be a warrior?" Didn't all small boys nurture dreams of fame and fortune with a sword in their hands? Like Llacheu and his friends.

The shake of his head couldn't have been firmer. "No, I don't.

I want to be educated." His lip formed a sneer. "Any man can wield a sword. I want to wield a pen. There's few who can do that. The name of a man who can write lives on. The names of warriors turn to dust and are forgotten." He grinned. "Unless the man who can write records their names."

Very true. And he was the one who one day would write my husband out of his history in just this way.

I shrugged. "My husband can wield a pen, and he's a warrior and a king. You don't have to be one or the other. You can be both." Though why I was arguing against his decision, I didn't know. Maybe I didn't want him to grow up to write that moaning diatribe against the kings who kept him safe.

His eyes narrowed. "He can? I didn't know." For a moment he considered his hands again, the twisted cloth of his tunic front tangled in his bony fingers. "But kings don't make old bones, do they? I intend to die an old man, with great works to my name. I'm not fool enough to want to take up arms and fight and die for another man." He paused. "Although being a king means you fight and die for yourself...I suppose... So it's not quite the same."

I smiled. "I think your decision is wise beyond your years. Perhaps you're right, and one day, hundreds of years from now, men will be reading your 'great works' long after they've forgotten the kings you so despise."

His hands relaxed and a satisfied smile spread across his face, illuminating it with an inner glow. "That's true. I'd like that. That would show my father. The men of the future would read my words and know the truth. About him and all the other kings." The sly look crept back. "And the truth would be what I wrote, not what kings would have me write. No one could tell me what to do."

Goosepimples prickled over my skin. Prophetic words from one so young.

"Good idea," I said. "Better not try to escape then, because I know a monastery that would take you in and educate you. I can ask my husband about it for you."

Abbot Jerome *would* be surprised.

Chapter Twenty-Two

O N A BRIGHT morning in late spring, our horses clattered down the cobbled road toward the huge hill of Din Cadan, where many columns of woodsmoke twisted up into a clear blue sky. My heart soared with elation at the sight of the imposing ramparts and palisade walls, and I could barely contain my excitement. I would be seeing Amhar at last after nearly a year away. What would he be like? Would he even remember me? Even though I'd prepared myself for him not to know me, I couldn't help the surge of anticipation in my stomach.

We'd spent a long, cold winter in Vindolanda, but it had been worth it. Arthur's leg barely troubled him now, Caw of Alt Clut had stayed sulking in Dun Breattann, well aware of our presence, and I'd made tentative friends with young Gildas. He rode unfettered now, a few rows back in our column of riders, chatting to Drustans, Prince of Caer Dore in Cornubia. Drustans was still young enough to remember his own boyhood, and the two had formed an easy friendship.

The farms that clustered the drier lands on the plain around the fortress buzzed with life. Men were out ploughing in their small square fields with yokes of sturdy oxen, women tended their garden patches where fresh shoots already showed hopeful and green, the first hints of blossom pricked out on fruit trees and hawthorn bushes between the houses and barns, and in the pasture lands, lambs gamboled after their wooly dams.

My heart glowed with the warm feeling of returning home, and I hugged it to myself in satisfaction. Home. This was indeed my home. Thoughts of my old world had receded further over this last winter as I entered my third year of living in the Dark Ages.

Glancing sideways at Arthur told me he shared my excitement. His eyes glowed much like my heart, flicking left and right as he took in the scenes of labor and plenty all about us. People out stone-picking the newly ploughed fields left their work and ran along next to the column as we passed. Children reached up their grubby hands to touch our legs as though that might bring them luck.

Arthur knew many of them by name. He'd either met them on our rides out or had them up before him in his court to sort out some dispute.

"Culain, how's that son of yours?"

"Lavena – your garden flourishes, I see."

He even knew the names of their children.

"Galvyn – how you've grown. Your father must be very proud of you."

I shook my head in amazement. "I don't know how you remember all their names – I struggle to sort out some of your warriors, never mind your farmers and their families."

He grinned back at me, half a boy today. "Easy. I like them. If you like someone, it's far easier to recall their names. When I talk with them, they tell me about their lives, their families. I love to hear their stories, and it makes it much easier for me to remember them all."

We reached the foot of the hill where the cobbled road wound up the side toward the huge, west-facing gateway. Where the track narrowed, even riding in pairs became more difficult. The long line of the army strung out behind us.

The men on gate duty shouted their welcome as we approached, clashing their spears against their shields as we rode under the gate towers and into the fortress's wide enclosure.

I gazed about myself, taking in every detail of the place I loved: the cobbled road climbing to the imposing bulk of the thatched great hall, the workshops, barns, store-sheds and houses, that seemed to fill almost every space on the hilltop. Dirt paths twisted through the narrow gaps between the buildings and wooden fences corralled the horses. The small fields squeezed into every spare space were being ploughed, ready for sowing vegetables. Cabbages, most likely. We seemed to eat a lot of cabbages.

From out of the houses poured the womenfolk of Din Cadan, the wives and daughters and mothers of the returning warriors, abandoning their spindles and their loom shuttles. From in the stables and workshops the men came hurrying out, Goff the blacksmith with a hammer in his hand. Elfydd the shoemaker hobbled out with his two lanky sons, both now his apprentices.

A ragged cheer went up that grew louder as the laborers from the small cabbage fields joined the ranks lining the road to the great hall. Their king was back.

"Arthur!"

"Dux!"

"The King!"

And amongst those shouts for him, some for me as well. "The Lady of the Ring!"

"The Ring Maiden!"

"The Luck of Arthur!"

Before we'd gone more than a few yards, Arthur threw a leg over the pommel of his saddle and slid to the ground, taking the proffered hands of all his people, one after another. They reached out eagerly to touch him, to shake his hand, to slap him on the back. Maybe they'd feared he wouldn't be coming back. A year was a long time to have been away.

Surrounded by the crowd, he led Llamrei up the road as far as the stables, where he handed her reins over to one of the waiting servants. Today wasn't a day for looking after her himself, even if he'd wanted to.

Turning to where I still sat astride Alezan, he held out his hands. With a smile I slid down into his arms and for a moment he held me tight.

"Go on," someone close by shouted. "Kiss 'er."

He bent his head and did as he was told, kissing me long and hard. A returning victorious warrior knows what his people want to see, and kissing the queen was clearly one of them. A loud cheer of encouragement rose into the afternoon sky.

Releasing my mouth but not my waist, he turned toward the great hall.

Which was when I saw them. Three figures stood on the wooden platform just outside the hall. A man and two women. Gwalchmei, whom Merlin and I had left in charge of Din Cadan. But who were the women?

Theodoric answered that for me. With a shout of delight, he threw his horse's reins haphazardly at a stable boy and ran past us up the slope toward the hall. Seizing the smaller woman, he swung her up into his arms in a huge bear hug. Morgawse.

My heart, which had been soaring, plummeted down into the toes of my boots. But who was the other, taller woman?

Drawing nearer answered that. Morgana.

What in God's name was *she* doing here?

Arthur had me by the waist, so there was no dodging meeting her face to face. He strode up the cobbles toward the hall, and I steadied my resolve not to be made to feel small and inadequate by his beautiful sister. Fat chance.

They were a good-looking family. Morgawse, now clasped firmly to her husband Theodoric's side, was much the smallest, being petite and fragile to look at. I, on the other hand, had witnessed the steely side of this young woman – a side I could bet she never showed her husband. Morgana, however, stood nearly as tall as Arthur. Long and slim but without his muscles – or not all of them anyway. I wouldn't have liked to have tackled her in a hand-to-hand fight. Both women had long hair as dark as Arthur's, even Morgana's confined in thick braids today.

Much to my annoyance, Morgana wore a beautiful, and spotlessly clean, pale cream gown, with a girdle made from gold links that accentuated her slender waist. Considering the last time we'd seen her and the plot she'd been party to, intending to betray Arthur to his death, she had a colossal cheek showing her face here in Din Cadan.

Arthur halted on the wooden platform facing his two sisters. The desire to watch for his reaction to Morgana's presence bubbled in me, but the desire to see Morgana's to him, won over. I fixed her with a hard stare.

She kept her lovely face virtually immobile, the slightest smile lifting the corners of her perfect mouth, but not travelling as far as her unreadable eyes. Behind me, I caught a movement out of the corner of my eye. Merlin had come to stand five paces off, no doubt making puppy-dog eyes at the object of his love. For a clever man, he was an idiot.

"Morgana. Morgawse." Arthur glanced sideways at his youngest sister, where she stood, clasped in his general's arms. "Welcome to Din Cadan."

Gwalchmei had the grace to look embarrassed. He must have known from the moment they arrived that Morgana wouldn't be welcome, but been unable to turn away the king's sisters. How clever of Morgana to have arrived with Morgawse and made it impossible for him to send her packing.

Morgawse, a possessive arm around Theodoric's waist, smiled sweetly back at her brother. "We've been here a week already. Morgana told me you were on your way back from the Wall. She said she knew Theo would be here."

Of course. Morgana had the Sight. Did she possess an obsidian scrying glass like her mother, into which she could gaze to discover the future? I wouldn't have been surprised. She was very like Eigr.

Arthur smiled. "Of course she did." His gaze travelled back to Morgana. Although I was watching her like a hawk, I kept half a wary eye on my husband.

"Morgana. What brings *you* here?"

The smile twitched a little. Why did she always look as though she knew a secret she wasn't going to tell you? Bloody smug woman.

"I spent some of the winter with my sister in Caer Legeion gwar Uisc. I saw she was lonely and needed company with her husband away fighting in the north...for you." Her eyes narrowed, cat-like, but still unreadable. "When I told her Theodoric would be returning, she wanted to come here to meet him. I couldn't let her travel all this way alone."

The cat-like eyes – so similar to those of another woman I disliked – slid sideways toward Merlin for a second, and the smile increased just a fraction, as though she were drawing him toward her landing net. I bristled with indignation for him. That she didn't love him back, I felt certain. That she had decided to enmesh him in her claws, I strongly suspected from that look. Over my dead body.

As if she read my thoughts – could she? Frightening possibility – she shifted her gaze to me. "Why Gwen, how nice and rustic you look."

I'd never been more conscious of how dirty I was after long days on the road: of my dusty boots and undoubtedly stinky clothes, of my untidy, greasy braids and my dirty face. However, I was also a queen, and she only a princess. I schooled my face into as condescending a return smile as I could manage. "And how nice to see you haven't changed a bit."

If I'd been Arthur, I'd have thrown her in that nasty smelly lockup he had over against the outer wall. A week in there'd have her not quite so smug and perfect, having to sleep in her own ordure. But she remained his sister, whatever she'd done or planned to do, and a princess as well. My thoughts of sweet revenge would have to stay that way – just thoughts.

Cei came stumping up the cobbles. "Morgawse!" He sounded overjoyed. "Morgana." Not quite so. But she was also his sister. Snatching Morgawse out of Theodoric's protective embrace he gave her one of his big-brother bear hugs. Almost, he tried the same with Morgana, but an icy stare from her cold eyes stopped him in his tracks, and instead he held out his hand. "Welcome to Din Cadan."

She put her slender hand into his great dirty paw with obvious disdain. Cei wasn't stupid. Gripping her hand tightly, he gave it a vigorous shaking, and didn't let go. She had to pull herself free. From the look on her face, she considered her hand defiled by his touch. They might be half-brother and sister, but she clearly thought herself way above him in the hierarchy. Not that Cei would have cared, or even noticed.

However, I'd underestimated him. He wiped his hand on his tunic as though trying to get the dirt of her touch off.

It didn't go unnoticed. Her eyes flashed angrily.

"Shall we go inside?" Arthur said. "My wife has ridden a long way and needs sustenance." He turned to Gwalchmei, who had wisely retreated into the shelter of the thatch out of harm's way. "Can you organize some food for us all?" He glanced skyward. "Nothing too much, as evening draws in. Just enough to tide us over until we dine. Wine, cheese, that sort of thing."

Gwalchmei, looking relieved not to have to explain why he'd welcomed Morgana into Din Cadan and let her stay for a week, hurried off.

Inside the hall, a fire burned in the central hearth, and over it the carcass of a deer turned, attended by the same blond slave boy I'd met the first time I'd ever come here. His face as sweaty-red as usual, he bobbed a bow at us as we passed him.

Arthur flung himself down into his throne – really a bigger, more ornate chair than the rest that stood there. Throwing Morgana a look of triumph, I took my place at his side and, leaning back, crossed my legs. That left Morgana standing awkwardly alone, as Theodoric pulled Morgawse aside and perched her beside him on the next table down, her legs swinging, and a huge grin on her face. She must have been well aware of the awkwardness of the situation. She looked as though she were enjoying it, the naughty girl.

Merlin and Cei had followed us inside but halted near Theodoric. Cei leant against the same table, but Merlin stayed standing in the central aisle, eyes fixed on the back of Morgana's beautiful head, eyes hungry for her. What a klutz.

A boy ran in with a tray of bread and cheese which he laid down hurriedly on the high table in front of Arthur. Another brought a flagon of wine and some horn cups. Arthur poured wine with exacting care into two of the cups, not spilling a single drop, then handed one to me. "Home at last." The edge in his voice betrayed his displeasure, but the smile on his face hid it. Though probably not from Morgana.

I drained my cup and cut myself a chunk of cheese. No way was I foregoing this much needed sustenance just because that awful woman was here.

"Where have you been sleeping?" Arthur asked, as he took a small sip of his wine. No mistaking the icy edge to his voice.

Morgana's lip curled. "Of course, we took the best chamber." She nodded to the back wall and the door to Arthur's and my chamber.

What? She'd been sleeping in our bed? The urge to give her a good hard slap burgeoned in my chest, and I had to clench my fists to prevent myself from leaping up and flooring her. It might not have been a wise move, fun though it would have been.

Arthur took another sip. "I'm sure we can find you more suitable accommodation now I'm back."

Yes, in the lock up. With the shit. But I didn't say so. Maybe I'd tell Arthur that later.

She looked decidedly unimpressed, so I gave her my sweetest, I-know-exactly-how-you're-feeling, smile. Ha bloody ha.

The cheese was good, so I cut some more and tore myself a hunk of bread. Cei got up from where he'd been leaning and came and perched on the edge of the high table so he could help himself to some food as well. I poured him a cup of wine. In the aisle, Merlin stood as though mesmerized. Sap.

"I'd say you could stay in my house," Cei said, deliberately offhanded, a twinkle in his blue eyes, "but my family's grown a bit lately. There wouldn't be any room. Not unless you don't mind sleeping by the fire with our maid."

Morgana's eyes flashed momentarily as her guard dropped. "I will need accommodation fit for a princess."

Good for Cei. He'd riled her. I resisted the impulse to give him a triumphant slap on the back and ate some more cheese instead.

Arthur set his cup down. "Have no fear. We won't make you sleep by the fireside with the servants. Not today." He glanced at Cei. "Our brother is teasing you. He'll find you somewhere comfortable. How many have you brought with you?"

Morgana drew herself up taller still. "Thank you. Brother. Just my maid, and a squad of twenty soldiers – some from Viroconium, some from Caer Legeion. They've been housed as befits their rank."

The door from our bedchamber swung open and Maia came in. Two small boys walked beside her – one on sturdy legs, the other toddling. Amhar. I was on my feet in a moment, pushing my chair back and rushing round the table to meet them.

So alike they might have been two ears of corn from the same stalk, the two little boys made a beeline for Morgawse, passing me by without a second glance. She swept the larger one up into her arms with a cry of delight. "Medraut, here is your father come home to you."

The other little boy hesitated for a second, and I made a move toward him. But Morgana was there first. With a sickly-sweet smile on her face, she held out her arms to him. "Amhar, come here to your Aunt Morgana."

Frozen to the spot, I watched my son turn toward my hated enemy and toddle into her arms. She lifted him easily and settled him on her hip, his dark eyes laughing up into her cold, cruel face. Or maybe I was demonizing her expression.

"Come," she cooed. "Give your aunt a kiss."

He put his little wet lips against her cold pale cheek.

Chapter Twenty-Three

"**M**AIA, BRING MY son." The words fought their way out of my mouth between my gritted teeth. Without waiting to see her do my bidding, I marched through the door into the royal bedchamber, slamming it behind me.

A moment later, Arthur followed me through, Maia close behind him, Amhar in her arms. His fretful grizzling at being snatched from "Aunt Morgana's" welcoming arms grated on my nerves immediately. How dared she? In front of me like that. Instead of taking Amhar, which would probably have set him wailing even louder – which Morgana would hear over the dividing wall – I paced up and down the room, my fists balled by my sides.

Maia halted, trying to distract Amhar to no avail, and his grizzling became a whingey cry. Could she not cheer him up and stop him making that noise? I needed to think.

Arthur had stopped just inside the door and was watching me as I paced back and forth. "She's been here a week. No doubt she's played with him and made him like her."

I halted in front of him. "*Made* him like her? Used her magic on him, that's what." I kept my voice low, lest anyone in the hall next door overheard me.

He shook his head. "I don't think so. I don't know why she's really here, but it won't be to steal our child." He plainly had the same worry at being overheard as me, because his voice stayed quiet.

"Won't it?" I couldn't keep the fury out of my voice as it rose in an indignant hiss. This was a woman I hated with a vengeance, a woman who I sensed would see me dead sooner than help me with anything.

"We can keep her away from him." Placatory words.

I glanced at Maia, who had sat on one of the seats by the table, cuddling Amhar close to her body. He'd stopped crying and his thumb sat firmly in his small pink mouth. The mouth that had kissed that woman.

I switched my fury and glared at her, the words spitting out of my mouth like hot coals. "What did you let her near him for? She's dangerous. There'll be a reason for her making him like her, you mark my words. You should have kept him away from her. She's a witch."

Maia's frightened eyes regarded me over Amhar's dark curly head. "I-I'm sorry, Milady. I dint know. Lady Morgawse, she did bring his little cousin to play with him the first day, and the little prince did like that. The next day she did come back with her sister, the Princess Morgana." She hesitated, biting her lip. "She did play right nice with both the babes." As though that were an excuse for having let a witch near my child.

I narrowed my eyes at her. "She's to come nowhere near him. She can see Medraut as much as she wants, but she's not coming anywhere near Amhar. That's an order. Now, take him to your own room and leave the king and me alone, please." Time for winning my child back when there was no one about to witness him not liking it.

Maia got to her feet and, still holding Amhar close, scurried out of the side door of the chamber. The door closed with a heavy clunk, and silence fell between Arthur and me. No sound came from over the partition wall, so perhaps Cei had taken Morgana off to find some suitable accommodation. Morgawse and Medraut would have gone with Theodoric to the house he used when he was in Din Cadan. Hopefully there'd be no trace lying about of any of the women he liked to invite back to it.

Arthur sat down on the bed and yanked his boots off. "Nothing we can do about it now. She's here. She's met Amhar. Unfortunately, he likes her."

I stayed where I was, my arms folded tightly across my chest. "But why's she here? There has to be a reason. I don't trust that woman one tiny bit."

Arthur undid his sword belt and threw it on the bed. "I don't know any more than you do. And yes, you're right. She never does anything without a reason."

"Could Cadwy have sent her?"

He pulled off his tunic and stretched. "No idea. I need a bath. It feels as if I haven't had one in forever."

I wasn't to be distracted. "Did you see how she looked at Merlin?"

Arthur was rummaging in his clothes chest. "I did."

His lack of reaction to his sister's arrival irked me. "Don't you *care?*"

He straightened up, holding a plain black tunic edged with simple gold embroidery. "Of course I care. Merlin is my friend. My counselor. But I've known for years how he feels about her. What do you expect me to do about it?"

"Stop her. Send her away."

He shook his head. "She's here with Morgawse. She's a royal princess. I can't just throw her out if she's done nothing wrong."

Inside, I seethed. Why was he being so obdurate? "Not done anything wrong? What about what she helped Cadwy plot? What about Ummidia and her daughters? And Euddolen? She's been party to everything Cadwy's done all along. And now she's here for a reason. Even though we don't know what it is, I want to stop her."

Arthur sighed. "I can have her watched. She won't get the chance to do anything I won't know about. But unless she puts a foot wrong, what do you expect me to do?"

Merlin's lovesick face jumped into the front of my mind, how it had looked when Morgana had smiled at him. How a woman can make a fool of a man with a single look. Not only did I have to save Amhar from her machinations, but Merlin too.

Arthur bent over the chest again. "Find yourself a beautiful gown and then come over to the bath house with me. You'll feel better when you're clean." He grinned. "We can bathe together if you like." His eyes twinkled with promise, but sex was so far from my mind right then it might well have been at the north pole. Not that he'd have heard of the north pole.

I was going to have to work on him. With a resigned huff, I gathered the first gown in my own clothes chest and followed him out of our chamber toward the bath house. Forewarned is forearmed, so the saying goes, and I considered myself very much forewarned.

Much good it was going to do me.

MORGANA DID NOT leave as I hoped, but took up residence with her maid in one of the houses nearest to the great hall, close to Theodoric's and Morgawse's. She showed no sign whatsoever of wanting to depart back to her beloved Cadwy in Viroconium.

Meanwhile, a messenger from the south coast arrived with news that fresh Saxon ships had landed near a place called Caer Peris and were looting the surrounding area.

"Will you go?" I asked Arthur, after the messenger had been taken off by Cei to be fed and watered.

We'd received him in the great hall, which was empty except for two guards by the doors, Arthur on his throne, and me beside him on my smaller chair. "He's one of my spies, not an emissary from a fellow king," Arthur said, meaning the messenger. "I have them posted all over the south coast to bring me news of any incursions by our enemies. If he'd come from Natanleod of Caer Guinntguic, asking for help, I wouldn't be sitting here now talking to you."

I took off the simple gold circlet I'd been wearing and set it on the table. With it on, I had to be careful not to move too quickly. Without it I had more freedom of movement. This being a superstitious age, a queen who sent her crown flying while in audience with her people would have been looked on as a bad omen. Merlin was a good teacher.

"So we sit and wait?"

He nodded. "Not so much of the 'we'. I'll be sitting and waiting. You won't be coming this time." He paused. "If they ask me for help that is."

I put my elbow on the table and leant my chin on my hand. "Oh? Really?"

He frowned, but more from exasperation than anger. "How many times do I have to tell you that women, and more especially queens, don't ride to battle?"

A smile sneaked over my face. "Probably a lot." I gave his arm a prod. "And how many times do I have to tell you that women from my world get to do whatever they want? To be in charge of men, to fight in wars, to be themselves and not just a vehicle for creating an heir."

A smile played about his mouth which I could see him trying to control. "You seem to keep forgetting that you're not in your world now. In this world you behave as other women do – as my queen should."

I pulled a face. "When I'm not with you I spend my entire time worrying."

He sighed. "The fate of all women. There's nothing I can do about that. Nor you."

Brooding, I fell silent. He was right, and it irked me. At least when I was being angry with him I could forget, slightly, to worry.

I changed the subject. "When are your sisters leaving?"

He glanced at me. "I don't know. I think Morgawse will stay until Theo returns to Caer Legeion and his fleet. He has work to do there after a year away – maintenance on his ships for a start. His second-in-command is good, but the fleet needs his guiding hand on the tiller."

"Hmmm."

"You're bothering about Morgana again, aren't you? She's not been near Amhar. I made sure of that."

True. Amhar and I were slowly rebuilding the mother and son relationship we'd had before I left, but the task was an uphill one. Likely he regarded Maia as his mother now. She understood, of course, that he had to be brought to realize she wasn't, but she'd had full care of him for nearly a year and she loved him as dearly as I did. Hard for her to relinquish his love. A year apart from my child had left me awkward as a stranger with him. How vexing that within a week he'd somehow taken so willingly to Morgana, yet a week after my return he still remained distrustful of me.

"Have you spoken to Merlin about her?" I asked. I hadn't seen much of Merlin since we arrived back and had an uneasy suspicion as to the reason.

"No." He frowned. "Why?"

Well, if he didn't know, he was very unobservant. But then again, he was a man and a warrior at that. Probably if what was going on with Merlin had to do with fighting, he'd have been the first to notice. Matters of love? No chance.

I pulled a face. "He's your friend. Where's he been?" Best to let him work this one out for himself.

He shrugged. "Busy teaching the boys?" His eyes took on a faraway look. "Have you seen how much Llacheu's grown? He'll be a warrior soon."

I frowned. "He's nine. Back to Merlin. Are you certain he's been teaching the boys?" I'd been deliberately seeking him out, but it had been hard. He'd been suspiciously elusive.

Arthur's turn to frown. "No. I'm not. Why? Do you think he's doing something I should know about?"

I bridled. "I don't know. Maybe. I just haven't seen much of him, and usually he's in and out of the great hall all the time."

"Oh. Perhaps I'll make a point of finding him, and we'll ride out together."

Hooray. "Good idea."

❯❯❯◀◀◀

INSPIRATION ABOUT HOW to track Merlin came over me the following day. I would follow Morgana. A good plan, as firstly, I didn't trust her one bit, and secondly, where she was, surely Merlin would follow. For my plan, I recruited Llacheu and Rhiwallon, Cei's son. They proved to be very keen to follow their aunt about as neither of them liked her.

"She turned up her nose at me," Llacheu said with disgust. "Like she had a bad smell under it. Said I was a bastard." He paused. "I know I am, and I don't care, but she'd no cause to say it the way she did."

Rhiwallon, a couple of years older than Llacheu and a full six inches taller, copied Llacheu's disgusted expression. "She doesn't like me either. Said I was 'that Cornish brat'. She didn't think I heard, but I did. Ugly fat cow."

I chuckled. Two better conspirators it would have been hard to find.

"You mustn't let her see you," I cautioned them. "It'd be hard for me to follow her about because I'm so noticeable, being the queen and in a dress. But two little boys – no problem. She's already proved she thinks you're below her notice." I paused. "Ugly fat cow."

The two boys giggled.

"Old witch," Llacheu said.

"Lump of dog shit," Rhiwallon improvised.

My turn to giggle. I was suddenly ten years old again and thinking of things to call a teacher I hated. "Moldy bag of bones."

When we'd finally stopped laughing at our amazing wit, I

packed the boys off to do their job and retreated to my chamber to try and play with Amhar.

For the first day they didn't bring back much news. She just sat with her sister and played with little Medraut.

"She thinks he shits gold," Rhiwallon announced. "You'd think he was a prince, the attention she gives him."

"Makes me want to puke," Llacheu added, nose wrinkled in scorn. "He's nothing special."

I heartily agreed, but wasn't about to tell them why. "Not so special as you two."

On the second day, they spotted her with Merlin. Their reaction to this was interesting.

"He was making cow's eyes at her," sneered Rhiwallon, too young as yet to find girls attractive. "And she was doing sort of creepy smiling back at him. They were by the horse pens, so I could sneak up close and watch."

"Glad I didn't see that," Llacheu said. "I would've puked for sure. Girls are revolting." He glanced sideways at his friend. "Not your little sister though. She's all right."

Rhiwallon grinned, showing his overly large teeth. "That's because she's so little. I bet she'll be awful when she's big. Like that fat girl, Ardena, Cottia's granddaughter."

Llacheu snorted with laughter. "She so fancies you."

Rhiwallon shuddered. "She won't leave me alone. Horrible."

Probably best not to tell them that one day they'd find girls irresistible. They most likely wouldn't have believed me.

It wasn't until the third day that they struck gold. Llacheu came running to find me, panting with excitement. He burst into my chamber, where Maia and I were playing with a slightly more tractable Amhar.

"I didn't puke!" he gasped. "You have to come and see."

Leaving a somewhat puzzled Maia with Amhar, I followed Llacheu out of the hall and down several side alleys between the buildings. A few lanky weeds grew up the walls, but a narrow dirt path had been beaten between the wooden walls by the passage of many feet. At the end of the alley, Rhiwallon stood, peering around a corner.

Llacheu put his finger to his lips, and we proceeded in stealth mode, walking on exaggerated tiptoes.

Rhiwallon turned to greet us, his face alight. "Take a look," he whispered, stepping back from his vantage point.

Warily, I peered around the corner of the building. An as yet empty open-fronted barn stood to my left, horse pens to the right. Just inside the barn, Merlin and Morgana were locked in a passionate embrace. I retreated back behind my cover.

"Yuck," Llacheu whispered. "See why I nearly puked?"

Rhiwallon nodded. "And I had to watch that while you were gone, to make sure they didn't leave without me seeing. I'm traumatized."

Oh dear. This was what I'd been fearing. The baited lure she'd been dragging around behind her ever since she got here had hooked the fish she wanted.

I peered around the corner again. Either they'd dived into a second clinch, or this was a very long one. The bitch. Poor Merlin. He'd waited such a long time for this he must be like a man lost in the desert who'd finally been given water. His hands were groping all over her curves as though he wanted to feel every inch of her body.

I turned back to the boys. This could very quickly get X-rated, and they were just children. "You can go and play now," I whispered. "I can do this bit of observation on my own from now on. Thank you for your help."

"Phew," Llacheu whispered back. "I like Merlin, but he's acting really weird."

"Too true," Rhiwallon added, grabbing his friend's arm. "Come on. Let's get our swords and have a fight." They ran off, their footsteps in the dirt made silent by their soft leather boots.

A short search found me a handy knothole in the wooden wall of the barn which sheltered me. I put my eye to the hole to see where Merlin and Morgana had got to.

Oops. Now I felt like a peeping tom. Her dress was rucked up by her hips and his hand had tight hold of the white curve of her buttocks. Should I watch? Should I intervene? That she was seducing him for some other reason than love screamed at me, but he was an adult, and she was willing. Who was I to stop him? One more peek.

Maybe not. That heap of last year's hay was coming in handy, her long pale legs wrapped around his back, pressing him closer to her.

I turned away, not wanting to watch her succeed in her seduction, which the sounds now coming from inside the barn told me she was.

Indignation, mingled with fury and something else, washed over me. Was I...could I be jealous? I scowled, my fingers entwining themselves in the dangling cords of my belt. The possibility that I was, once it had reared its ugly head, refused to go away. I liked Merlin a lot. He was my friend. But I didn't love him. Or maybe I did, but not as a lover, more as a brother. Would I be feeling like this if I'd caught my real brother, Artie, romping in the hay with a woman? Most probably not. I'd be running away embarrassed. I couldn't understand my feelings of impotent anger.

I huffed, and my shoulders rose and fell sharply. The real problem here was who Merlin was doing this with. Not to mention what her motivation for this was. The certainty filled me that Morgana was not a woman who could ever love anyone better than herself. That she was doing this for a reason. If only I could remember more of the legends about her and Merlin. Wasn't it Nimuë who'd ensnared Merlin and locked him away in a crystal cave for all eternity? Was that Morgana's aim? Was any of it even true?

Putting my hands over my ears to stifle the rising moans coming from inside the barn, I retreated back up the path between the buildings, not wanting to have to listen to a moment more of this.

Chapter Twenty-Four

Now THAT I'D found out what was going on between Merlin and Morgana, I was faced with a quandary. I couldn't tell Arthur, because she was his sister and she was having sex with someone she wasn't married to. My experience with Essylt and Drustans nearly two years ago had left me well aware this would be a big mistake. Arthur might – would – be bound to protect his sister's honor, and it would drive a wedge between him and Merlin. Which was no doubt what that awful woman wanted.

So what was I to do? I had no idea. Feeling fed up, annoyed, and yes, a bit jealous that my friend was being deliberately snatched away from me, I wandered back to the rear door of the hall and let myself in.

The sound of childish laughter carried from my bedchamber, and I pushed the door open. Medraut and Amhar were playing on the floor together with the pile of wooden bricks I'd had Devin the wood turner make for my son. Morgawse sat cross-legged on the fur rug, building towers for them to knock down. Maia had retreated to a stool where, head bent, she was industriously stitching a new shirt for Amhar.

Morgawse looked up, face alight with enjoyment.

Hurriedly, I schooled my own face into something resembling normality and pushed thoughts of Merlin and Morgana out of my head. "Morgawse."

She didn't get up, being in the middle of constructing a tower of huge proportions for the two little boys. "Gwen."

Amhar, dressed only in a knee length shirt, reached out a chubby hand and pushed the base, leaving her holding the topmost block as everything else crashed to the ground. He let out a squeal of baby excitement. "'Gain, 'gain." Now he was past eighteen months old his vocabulary was growing every day.

Medraut, in a tiny tunic and braccae as he'd reached the age of not being likely to have an accident in his clothes, grabbed a handful of bricks. "My bricks," he declared as Amhar reached for them. "Leggo of 'em."

He ran a few paces and set them down where no rugs covered the flagstones and it was easier to build. Amhar toddled after him, hands outstretched, so, to prevent a fight, I swept him up into my arms.

He was not amused and struggled manfully. Ignoring his protests, I sank down onto one of the chairs, beside where Morgawse sat on the floor. "Look, your Aunt Morgawse will build you a tower of your own." I set Amhar down, and she distracted his attention with the new tower. Over by the unlit brazier, Medraut continued with his own construction.

I watched my son playing with his aunt. Now he was more of a small boy than a baby, his resemblance to both Medraut and Llacheu had become even more striking. Morgawse had been right when she'd said the Pendragon bloodline ran strongly in their children.

Maybe Morgawse could help me with my dilemma over Merlin. This was the first time since our return that I'd been alone with her, as shunning Morgana had meant not seeing her sister. Now that Morgana had other fish to fry, I at last had her to myself.

I glanced over my shoulder at Maia, but she seemed totally preoccupied with keeping her stitches small. "Morgawse?" Nevertheless, I kept my voice low.

She looked up. "Yes?"

"Why did Morgana come to see you at Caer Legeion do you

think?"

Amhar knocked the tower down with a crow of delight.

Morgawse began to rebuild it, a frown on her pale brow. "She said she'd looked into her scrying glass and seen Theo on his way back to me. She said she came to tell me."

My eyes widened. So I'd been right in my suspicion. "She has a scrying glass?" Memories of looking into their mother Eigr's obsidian scrying glass flashed into my head, of seeing terrifying images I hadn't wanted to see.

Morgawse nodded. "Of course. She has the Sight. Why wouldn't she?"

"I didn't realize. I saw your mother's, and for some reason thought she was the only one who had one. Stupid, really." I paused, against my will consumed with curiosity. "What exactly did she say she'd seen?"

Morgawse's brow furrowed some more. "She said she'd seen a great battle and that Theo was unhurt....snow on a fortress, and a man humbled. Then an army marching south. I think that was all."

I nodded. "I still don't understand why she chose to come here with you. Why didn't she just send a messenger in the first place, to tell you what she'd seen? Why come herself? And more to the point, why come here after what she did two years ago?"

Morgawse pursed her lips. "Can we talk about this somewhere more private?" Her eyes slid sideways toward Maia, who still appeared to be concentrating on her sewing, but could well be listening.

I got up. "Maia, can you leave your sewing and come and play with the children, do you think? The Lady Morgawse and I are going outside for a walk."

Maia set her sewing down on the table – was that a look of disappointment on her face? – and dropped to her knees with the children. "Yes, Milady." She took over tower building duties with Amhar, which made him crow with delight. He still preferred Maia to me.

Morgawse and I let ourselves out by the side door into the hall courtyard. A few children played in the dirt with a couple of hound puppies. One of Cottia's daughters sat in her house doorway in front of her loom, her hands flashing back and forth with the shuttle as the cloth she was weaving grew. The tabby cat lay curled in a patch of hot sun, and someone was hanging out wet washing on a line.

Leaving them behind us, we threaded our way between the buildings, me steering well clear of where I'd spied on Merlin and Morgana, until we reached the steps up to the wall-walk. Without saying a word, I led the way up to the wooden path along the inside of the crenellated battlements. Warriors stood on watch at forty-yard distances. I stopped halfway between two of them. The wind that almost always blew up here would prevent any eavesdropping.

Down in the practice area, the boys of the fortress were engaged in sword practice, sporting shields and helmets that made it impossible to see if two of them were Llacheu and Rhiwallon. I turned to look outward, leaning on the top of the wall. Below me, the rooftops of the village peeked from amongst the leafy canopy of the surrounding trees, smoke curling upward in the warm air.

Morgawse leant beside me. "What is it?" she asked, after a moment's quiet contemplation. "There's something troubling you, I can tell."

I had to confide in someone. The knowledge, even though I'd discovered it so short a time since, had already burnt a hole in my heart. "Can you keep a secret?"

Her eyebrows shot up, and tendrils of her dark hair blew across her face. She swiped them away with her hand. "I can. Do I need to swear?" Her tone held a hint of mockery, as though she weren't taking this quite seriously enough.

I nodded. "I think you do."

"That bad?" The mockery vanished. "Well, I swear on the life of my husband and son that I won't tell anyone your secret." She laid her arm across her chest. "Will that do?"

It would have to. "Yes." I licked my lips. Where to start? "I don't trust Morgana."

Morgawse smiled. "Wisely so. Does anyone?"

"Cadwy might."

She chuckled. "You think so? My brother trusts no one at all. Still less my scheming sister. I'd be surprised if he even trusts himself."

Her attitude puzzled me. "Then why did you bring her here?"

She sighed. "I didn't so much bring her here as get dragged along in her wake. You don't think I'm stupid enough to fall for her charming wiles again, do you? I'm not the same girl I was back then. I was young, naïve, foolish. And of course, I was pregnant and without my husband. She was kind to me when I needed support, and I fell for her lies. I'm a woman and a mother now, not a girl."

"So *she* brought *you*? She suggested coming here so you could welcome Theo?"

"I suppose so…" Her voice rose a little as though realization were just dawning. "She did seem very keen to come here. Maybe I was her excuse. In fact, now I come to think of it, that's exactly what it was." She put her hand on my arm. "Probably she didn't dare to come here on her own, so she came and fetched me first. She knew I'd want to see Theo."

That made sense. "What do you think she wants here?"

Morgawse shrugged her slender shoulders. "No idea, but there must be something. She was very keen to meet your son. Arthur's child. Very keen. Could that be why she wanted to come?"

I shivered. "She won't be seeing *him* again. I've made sure of that. Arthur's made sure of it too."

She shook her head, puzzlement shadowing her face. "Yet that doesn't seem to have bothered her at all. She's quite happy, even though she's not seen Amhar for a week. Some of the time she's with me and Medraut, and some of the time she goes off on her own. I don't know where."

Now or never. "I do."

"You do?"

I nodded. "She's been with Merlin."

A heavy silence hung between us, punctuated by the mewling cry of a kite far above our heads. Morgawse shut her mouth, which had fallen open at my revelation. "With Merlin? I-I thought she hated him?"

"Clearly not."

Morgawse shook her head as though to clear it. "I can't believe it. I've heard her ranting about him so many times. She hates that he's more powerful than her. She hates that she had to learn her arts from him. She hates that he's helping Arthur. She – she just *hates* him."

"Well, she's not behaving like that anymore."

Her eyes widened. "Go on."

"I had Llacheu and Rhiwallon follow her. I pretended it was a game. She's been meeting Merlin. The boys found them...um, in a barn. Llacheu came and got me. By the time I arrived it was getting heated. I had to send the boys away...They were – they were having sex. Noisily. They *both* sounded like they were enjoying it."

Her mouth fell open. "No," she hissed. "Not Merlin and Morgana. No. I can't believe it."

"I wouldn't believe it myself if I hadn't seen it with my own eyes."

She ran her hand across her face. "And you say she gave herself to him willingly?"

The fact that she suspected Merlin, *my* Merlin, might have forced himself on her sister galled me. "More willing even than he was. It had the look of being her idea." That was a tiny lie, but Merlin was my friend and I didn't want Morgawse thinking of him in a bad light. And besides, I knew what I'd seen. I licked my lips. "You knew he was in love with her, didn't you?"

She nodded. "No one could have missed it. He's been in love with her for years. He was her teacher. He was *our* teacher – mine, Arthur's, Cei's...even Cadwy's."

The twenty-first-century part of me that still remained re-coiled at the fact that as her teacher he'd fallen in love with her. How old had she been? No, I didn't want to go there. And anyway, until now it had been a distant, unrequited love. And now she was definitely an adult, a scheming woman who knew her own mind. Only he was old, much older than he looked. Older than I could imagine, most likely.

I shoved the ethics of this quandary to one side. "I don't think she loves him back," I said. "No, I'm certain."

Morgawse nodded. "You're right. My sister loves no one but herself."

"Just what I thought. So why is she suddenly not just encour-aging him, but giving herself to him – like a...like a whore?" I couldn't resist that word. It fitted her so well.

"A whore?"

"That's right. A whore." The more I said the word, the more I relished it. "When I saw her, that was the first thing that leapt into my mind. That she was behaving just like a whore." My view might have been a tiny bit colored by the way I felt about her. Although probably any well-bred and still unmarried woman in this time would be considered a whore if she'd done what I'd seen Morgana doing.

"I suppose you're right. I hadn't thought of it like that."

"It's what Arthur will think." Not to mention what he'd think of Merlin for taking advantage of her, even though I felt certain it was the other way around.

Morgawse's hand flew to her mouth. "God, no. We can't tell him."

"You see why you had to swear?"

She nodded. "Actually, I definitely *didn't* need to swear. I could never tell anyone this – she's my sister don't forget, and it's her honor we're talking about here."

"Honor? You think a woman like her has honor? Have you forgotten how she was prepared to see Ummidia and her daughters executed on the battlefield at Bassas?" I swallowed. "I'd be surprised if it wasn't her idea in the first place."

Morgawse swung around and stared toward the great hall, as though she might pick her errant sister out amongst the small figures moving about between the buildings. "She's still my sister."

I bristled. "And Merlin's my friend. He's the reason I'm here. I can't let him get ensnared by her…magic. She's evil. His power is good, but hers is bad." I paused. "I need your help. I don't know what to do to save him."

A puzzled frown crept over her face. "Save him from what, though?"

How to explain the dreadful feeling that had been creeping over me since I'd seen them together this afternoon, without giving away where I came from and the knowledge it had given me. I sucked in my lips, thinking hard.

Finally, inspiration came. "Nobody knows, but I can see the future too. I have the Sight. I looked into your mother's scrying glass and saw terrible things."

Her eyes widened. "What terrible things?"

Your son killing my husband.

I shut my mouth firmly, gathering my thoughts, then drew a deep breath. "Things I can't repeat. Secret things. But there is one thing I can tell you. It's about Merlin and Morgana. She wants him in her power. She wants to steal his power for herself and take it away from him, so he's in her thrall. And she'll succeed if we don't stop her, and then Arthur will lose his most trusted adviser." I paused. "And I'll lose my friend."

"How do we prevent this?"

I swallowed. "I'm not at all sure we can, that's the problem. I don't know if it's written in stone or something we can change. But I do know that I don't want to lose Merlin. That I can't lose him. I don't think she plans to kill him – just lock him away somewhere he can't escape from. Away from Arthur." I paused. "I'm going to need your help in this."

She faced me. "You have it. But no harm must come to my sister. Do you promise?"

Behind my back I crossed my fingers. "I promise."

Chapter Twenty-Five

T HE ANTICIPATED MESSENGER from King Natanleod of Caer
Guinntguic arrived the very next day. Whether this was a
good thing or a bad thing, I couldn't decide. At least Arthur
wouldn't be here to stumble upon his friend in a compromising
clinch with his sister. But he'd be going into battle again, and
without me.

"Do you have to go?" I asked, conscious I sounded whiney
and pathetic.

The messenger had arrived late in the evening so Arthur had
declared the army would ride out at first light the following day.
Now we were in our chamber after the evening meal in the great
hall, and he was packing his saddle bags ready for the morning.

He didn't look up. "You know I have to. That's what being
the Dux is all about. When one of the kings has need of me, I go."

I sat down on our bed, watching him as he moved from his
clothes chest to the table where the saddle bags lay open.
"Suppose you're not back all summer. What then? You're leaving
me here with that awful sister of yours."

God, I sounded worse than whiney.

"Morgawse isn't that bad."

I huffed. "You know I don't mean her."

He chuckled. "You're more than a match for Morgana."

An idea formed. "Who're you taking with you?"

He rolled a spare pair of braccae up and stuffed them into his bag. "Theo will come, and Cei."

"What about Merlin? Aren't you taking him?" That would get him out of Morgana's clutches very nicely.

Arthur shook his head. "I thought he should stay here and take care of you. I know how well you get on with him, and he'll be an ally for you against my sister."

Damn it.

I kicked my boots off. "I think I'll be fine without him. You should take him with you."

He began fastening the buckles on his bags. "He said he'd rather stay here."

I bet he did.

I rolled my stockings down and off my feet, burying my toes in the fur rug by the bed. "But you're the king. If you say, he'll have to go with you."

He looked up, clearly puzzled. "Don't you want him to stay with you?"

Awkward. "I can manage on my own. I don't need a man to help me."

A chuckle escaped again. "You and your independence. Your world must be very strange if women are all like you. Do you even need men?"

My turn to chuckle. "Men have their uses. Could you come and undo the laces of my dress d'you think? I can't reach."

He came over to the bed. I turned my back to him as his fingers began the rather laborious process of unlacing my gown, while I pondered how to get him to take Merlin with him, preferably until Morgana gave up and returned to Viroconium.

As the gown loosened, he slid a hand inside, his touch warm on my bare skin. "I'll miss you." His voice lowered as he planted a soft kiss on my neck. "I promise not to be away too long. This time."

I twisted until I was half looking at him over my shoulder. "I'll miss you, too. I'm glad I went with you to the Wall. I couldn't have borne it if we'd been apart for a year."

With distinctly unsteady hands he went on undoing my laces, his face so close to mine I could feel the warmth of his breath on the back of my neck. "It's not so far this time. Caer Guinntguic is on the Test River, not far from the south coast." He planted another warm kiss on my exposed back. "The Saxons have had settlements around some of the river mouths for several generations, and they're usually no problem. But the new arrivals have nowhere to call their own. They think Caer Guinntguic should be theirs by right. Their upstart leader claims it was stolen, and he wants it back." He ran a line of kisses down my back where my dress had loosened, sending shivers of expectation coursing through my body.

My words caught in my throat. "How does a Saxon come to believe a British town should be his?"

"His mother was a Saxon – his father ruled in Caer Guinntguic." Arthur's voice sounded as hoarse as my own.

"Possession is nine tenths of the law," I quoted, leaning back toward him, my breath coming fast. "But you should take Merlin."

He pushed the gown off my shoulders, and his hands slid round to cup my breasts. "I think I feel a need for possession right now." His mouth came down on my shoulder, his lips hot and demanding, his tongue tickling my skin.

An involuntary groan escaped me, but I stuck to my guns. "Merlin would be of more use to you than he will be to me."

Ignoring me, he pulled my gown down, letting it pool by my feet, and turned me to face him. "Forget Merlin. I've better things to think of right now. I won't be seeing my wife for weeks, possibly months. I want a night to remember when I'm alone in my bedroll on the hard ground. You wouldn't deny me that, would you?"

Well, of course I wouldn't. I put my arms around his neck and pulled him toward me. "I'll be doing the same here," I whispered. "Only I'll be in our comfortable bed. You'd better remember that too, and hurry back to me. Now, kiss me properly."

I WOKE BEFORE Arthur for once, after a night troubled by dreams of Merlin locked in a high tower like Rapunzel, which was ridiculous as there were no high towers like that in post-Roman Britain. The early morning sunlight filtered in around the shutters on the windows showing me Arthur still sleeping beside me, his dark hair tousled on the pillow.

Sleep had relaxed his features and endowed him with a youthfulness his face rarely had in waking now he was a king. I propped myself up on an elbow and watched him for a while, drinking him in and committing this moment to memory. Who knew when I'd see him again?

Some sixth sense must have told him he was being watched, because his eyes flickered open and he gazed up at me, for a moment still the boy he'd looked in sleep. "Gwen." His hand came up and caressed my cheek, his thumb running over my lips. I opened them and kissed it, closing my lips around the tip and peeking at him suggestively.

He grinned. "Tempting, but no. I have to get ready to leave. But you can stay in bed. It's early yet." Without waiting for an answer, he flung the covers back and got out of bed. Naked, he stretched and looked around for where he'd dumped his clothes the night before – the floor, of course. Where do most men leave their clothes when they undress? No difference there between fifth-century kings and twenty-first-century men. And he'd been in a bit of a hurry the night before.

For a minute, I watched him as he pulled his clothes on, then, as he reached for his boots, I got up as well. Gathering my discarded gown from last night, I went to my clothes chest to find a long day tunic to wear, brushing past him.

It was enough. He caught me around the waist and swung

me into his arms. "You are a vile temptress, and I love you for it."

I rested both hands against his chest. "And you are my knight in shining armor."

"What?"

"Never mind. Wrong time period. I do love you, you know. Promise me you won't do anything reckless. I want you back all in one piece, not damaged."

He bent his head and kissed me hard, and I clung onto him. When he finally released me, we were both gasping. "Damn," he muttered. "I want you right now."

I slid an exploratory hand down and chuckled. "So I see."

Wriggling out of his grasp, I pulled my tunic out of my clothes chest. "Then that should make you get back here all the quicker."

He grinned, readjusting braccae that had clearly become somewhat uncomfortable. "You're incorrigible. I'm going outside before I give in to temptation."

It takes a long time to get an army on the road. Horses have to be groomed and saddled, weapons and saddle bags packed, armor put on, a quick breakfast eaten, food packed, womenfolk and children embraced. The sun was well up by the time Arthur's men were ready to leave.

He strode up from the stables leading Llamrei, his helmet tucked under his arm, to where I stood waiting on the wooden platform outside the hall beside Merlin and Morgawse. Morgana had not appeared. Thank goodness.

As soon as I'd got out there and seen Merlin waiting, with no sign of that witch, I'd set about trying to persuade him to go with Arthur, but to no avail. "He wants me here, in charge. You can't manage on your own."

That response had annoyed me in more ways than one, but I

held my tongue and remained silent. Bloody men.

Most of the men were mounted now, sitting chatting on their horses as the day warmed up, their families standing to one side, waiting to wave them off. After nearly three years these were no longer harsh, alien faces, but men I knew well, men who lovingly dandled their babies on their knees and adored their wives as much as they loved their king. They might look hard and fierce, but without their armor they were farmers, fathers, sons, craftsmen…friends. The bond between them all, between even the men who'd come from other kingdoms, welded them together as one united fighting force. Every man here would lay down his life for his fellow warriors.

A lump formed in my throat, not out of sadness that Arthur was leaving me again, but out of pride for being part of this.

Arthur reached us and held his hand out to Merlin, who clasped it tightly. "Take care of her for me. And of yourself."

My gaze sharpened. Did he perhaps suspect something?

Merlin smiled back. "I will." And did I detect a certain shiftiness in him?

Arthur turned to Morgawse. "Little sister. Be here when I return so I can see more of you, and take care of Gwen for me."

I schooled my face to hide my annoyance that he thought I needed looking after by not one, but two people. Men. Or should that be kings?

He turned to me. "And as for you." His dark eyes twinkled. "Come here and kiss your husband."

Ignoring his rather patronizing tone, I stepped into his arms and he kissed me, long and hard. As we parted he whispered into my ear. "And you look after Merlin…for me."

My eyes widened, but he was turning away, swinging himself up onto Llamrei. With a last grin, he spun her around and jogged down through the mass of warriors toward the gates. Behind him, the riders fell in, and within minutes the courtyard was empty. I stood watching until the last man disappeared through the gates and they swung shut behind them.

How empty Din Cadan felt without Arthur in it.

DETERMINED TO WINKLE Merlin away from Morgana, it had dawned on me during my disrupted night's sleep that a way to do so would be to occupy Merlin so he had little time left for her. The thought of at the same time annoying her appealed to my inner wicked self.

I initiated my strategy as soon as the gates closed behind our departing warriors. "Merlin."

He'd been about to turn away, but swiveled on his heel and came back to me. "Yes?"

I quelled an impulse to demand he fulfill Arthur's orders and "look after me" as if I were an incompetent feeble woman, and instead gave him a winning smile. "I think I could do with some lessons about the Saxons. There're lots of things I don't know. As you're supposed to be here to look after me, perhaps we can begin this morning?"

Oh, the look of indecision and regret in his eyes that told me he'd had plans with Morgana, but I meanly felt no guilt. After the merest moment, his expression changed. "Of course. What do you want to know?"

Morgawse shot me an encouraging glance. The inclination to wink at her blossomed, but I fought it off. "Everything. Perhaps we could take a walk along the walls, and you could tell me then. Now would be good for me." I slipped my arm through his. "I'd like to know why this Saxon leader has a British name and thinks he should have Caer Guinntguic, for a start." No need to tell him I already knew part of this story.

I steered him away from the great hall and down the cobbled road. "It's a beautiful day. It'd be a shame to spend it indoors. And I feel the need for some exercise." Another idea popped into my head. "In fact, I think it would be lovely if you and I rode out every afternoon while Arthur's away. We can inspect the farms like he does, and I'll get the exercise I need. Perfect."

Out of the corner of my eye, I caught a glimpse of Merlin's woebegone expression before he managed to sort himself out. Probably he was thinking about what he could have been doing in Morgana's willing arms.

Poor Merlin, and poor me a bit as well. I learned a lot over the next few days about a lot of different things, primarily the Saxons. To my surprise, Merlin knew they weren't just Saxons but also Jutes and Angles. "Easier to call them by one name only," he explained. "But they come from different areas of Germania, and they have different customs and culture. I daresay they think we're all the same as well, when any fool can see we're not. The men of Dumnonia differ greatly from the men of Alt Clut, for instance."

"So why does this Saxon, if that's what he is, think Caer Guinntguic should be his?"

He was leaning on the crenellations, eyes narrowed against the bright sunlight. "Because his father ruled there. His name was Elafius. He followed the teachings of Pelagius, but converted to full Catholicism when Germanus came on his mission here."

"Germanus who had the Alleluiah Victory? Someone, I think it was Elen at Vindolanda, told me about that."

He nodded. "The very same. They call him St. Germanus now."

There were a few threads I wanted to follow here, but principally the background to the war Arthur was involving himself in seemed most important. "So firstly, how come this man is with the Saxons, and secondly, why is he not already king if his father was? Oh, and who is Natanleod in that case? And how did he get to be king?"

Natanleod had been at the Council of Kings nearly three years ago – young, built like an ox, and covered in tattoos. I'd once considered him a possible husband for Princess Essylt of Linnuis, before her father had packed her off to marry old March of Caer

Dore. Poor girl. Natanleod might have gone some way to consoling her after her separation from Drustans – something white-haired old March had probably never been able to do.

Merlin rubbed his bristly chin. "Elafius's first wife, from Cunedda's line, as many of the royal families are, died when Elafius was himself growing old. He already had a son from her. It was the time of Guorthegirn the Usurper, who, to please his Saxon allies, suggested Elafius should take a Saxon wife." He chuckled. "Put it in a way the poor old man couldn't refuse. But the girl he ended up with was young and beautiful. He got the better part of the bargain. She, poor girl, got a scrawny old man." The chuckle rose again. "But he fathered a child on her – Cerdic."

"I know that name."

"You do?"

Too late I realized my mistake. I couldn't let him have an inkling of my knowledge – that Cerdic was destined to become the founder of Wessex, that would in turn morph into England, in many hundreds of years' time. That in fact our modern British royal family could claim descent, somewhat sketchily, from him. Accepted as historical when Merlin and Arthur would have become just a folk memory, a legend to be recounted around firesides. "I must have heard someone mention his name. Go on, tell me more."

"Cerdic was born in the year Ambrosius defeated Guorthegirn and burned him in his fortress." He swiped at the hair blowing in his eyes. "Arthur's met him in battle before, further east along the coast."

"Where? What happened? When?"

"Llongborth."

I knew a bit about this. Llacheu and his friends had been reenacting the battle of Llongborth the very first time I'd met them, bringing an odd expression I hadn't understood to Arthur's face. But where was Llongborth? Coventina had mentioned something about it once. From her description I'd guessed it might have been Portchester, where even in my day a substantial

Roman fort remained. Now was my chance to learn more about it from someone who might actually have been there.

"Tell me about it."

"It's a long story. Shall we sit down?"

I nodded, and we lowered ourselves to sit on the edge of the wall-walk, legs dangling over the grassy bank.

When I was comfortably seated, Merlin continued. "Ambrosius was ten years dead. Uthyr was High King in his place. Prince Geraint ruled at Din Cadan for Uthyr, and Arthur was a boy of thirteen."

"And you?"

He grinned. "I was at Viroconium, working for Uthyr. Instructing his children. Much as I do here with the boys of the fort. Only Uthyr wanted me to teach his daughter as well..." His eyes took on a faraway look.

"Go on." I was impatient.

"The Saxons landed in force along the southeast coast. There's a harbor there with a sizeable Roman fortress set within it. The Romans called it Portus Adurni but we call it Caer Peris now."

Aha. I'd been right in my surmise. Portchester castle, in the huge bay that in my time housed the extensive Portsmouth docks. We'd sailed from the docks on a ferry to France when I was at school.

He kept going. "Back then, a garrison held it, but loosely. It's large. The walls are high, but you need a lot of men to man them, and there just weren't enough."

Merlin had once told me that after the Romans left, a plague that decimated the population had racked Britain, reducing the manpower available to defend her shores, and her towns and cities. Part of the reason so many townspeople had migrated to the countryside and into the old hillforts left over from the pre-Roman days.

"The Saxons were led by the same general Arthur's gone to face this time – Aelle. With him he brought Cerdic, just a young

FIL REID

warrior back then. After her husband, Elafius, died, Cerdic's mother took her son back to her own people. I think Aelle was her brother. Who knows? Perhaps she feared that Natanleod's father, who had inherited the throne of Caer Guinntguic from Elafius, would kill her son. It's what kings often do – eliminate the opposition when they take the throne."

"Not very civilized."

His teeth flashed white. "You said your scholars call this the Dark Ages – don't expect us to be civilized."

"So what happened next?"

He kicked a foot against the grassy bank. "Uthyr and Cadwy were in Gwynnedd, miles away, fighting Irish raiders. Arthur received the news at Viroconium and took it upon himself to ride with what remained of his father's forces to Din Cadan to tell Prince Geraint – his cousin."

My eyes widened. Coventina had told me a little of this, but it had been hard to believe. "At *thirteen*?"

Merlin nodded. "A budding warrior and leader, even then. Geraint took his men, and Arthur's, and rode to Llongborth. They found Aelle and Cerdic in possession of the fortress. Cavalry aren't much good in a siege, but neither Saxon general had any intention of sitting it out inside their new fortress."

I touched his arm. "Were you there too? You seem to know the story well."

"I was. I came with Arthur from Viroconium and fought by his side." He paused. "Cerdic led the charge out of the main gates. The battle took place close under the walls. Our men fought bravely, but we were outnumbered. Prince Geraint was slain – by Cerdic himself. Right in front of Arthur. He'd have killed Arthur too, if I hadn't snatched him away. My powers have their uses. That wasn't Arthur's day to die."

It was on the tip of my tongue to ask him when that day was, but I stayed silent. Not something I really wanted to know.

After a moment's reflection, perhaps remembering that day and the death of that Prince more clearly than he wanted to

264

describe to me, Merlin went on. "We retreated. Arthur didn't want to, the young hothead, but I reminded him of my teachings – a good general recognizes when the odds are stacked against him and retires to fight another day. He learned a lesson that day. But he's never forgotten that Cerdic killed his cousin, a man the boy admired above all others, and now he has the chance for revenge, I think he'll take it."

Somehow, this wasn't the comfort I'd expected it to be.

Chapter Twenty-Six

C ONTINUING WITH MY plan to keep Merlin away from Morgana, I rode out with him the next morning. A blue sky dotted with cottonwool clouds promised a warm day, as we descended the road that curved around the hillside between the high defensive banks of the fortress. We rode in single file and in silence, three warriors ahead of us and three behind as escort.

From Merlin's rigid back I sensed him brooding, probably due to the fact that Morgana had emerged from her house to stand and watch us pass, her lovely face inscrutable. I'd taken the opportunity to give her a dazzling smile, which I felt pretty sure she'd interpreted correctly. She wasn't stupid.

We rode all morning, mainly at a walk with a few short canters. It wasn't the sort of day for hurrying. Intent on taking as long as possible, I insisted we stop at many of the farms to exchange a few words with the farmers about the crops and animals, and for me to chat with their wives about their children. Polite as ever, Merlin hid his boredom and impatience to be back at the fortress well.

At last, after eating a plain but tasty mid-day meal with one of the farmers' families, we turned back toward Din Cadan. I waved our escort away, and they fell back a respectful distance to give us chance to talk in private.

I edged Alezan in closer to Merlin's horse until our knees rubbed together. She laid her ears back rather unsociably, and I tightened my reins. She could be very mareish at times. How to start the conversation I hadn't been looking forward to having? In at the deep end, maybe.

"I know what's going on between you and Morgana."

He'd been staring ahead toward the rise of the hill, but now his head snapped round and he stared at me, a look of alarm on his face.

I ploughed on. "You may think you've been careful, but if I know, then you can bet others do too. Even Arthur."

He opened his mouth, but shut it again without speaking, and glanced over his shoulder as if to check no one rode within listening distance.

I went on. "She doesn't love you. You realize that, don't you?"

His eyes snapped fury. "How would you know that? Are you inside her head?"

I'd never seen him so angry, except perhaps when Arthur had decided to fight Melwas himself. But I refused to be daunted. "No, you know I'm not. But I do know women like her. I've met enough of them in my old world." Difficult to explain how I'd learned this – at school and university, where there are plenty of bitchy users. "She doesn't love anyone but herself, and she doesn't do anything without an ulterior motive."

"You've got her wrong."

Oh, the foolishness of the lovesick. And Merlin's infatuation was of the worst kind – probably stoked by some kind of magical influence. Once, I'd never have considered this as a possibility, but I'd traveled to the fifth century by magic and straightaway been able to speak and understand their Celtic tongue, not to mention Latin, like a native. Who was I to question magic being used to kindle a love as blind as this? Maybe she'd first used it on him years ago, keeping him dangling on her line until she needed him. I clung onto that, as preferable to the thought of him falling for his young pupil for any other reason.

I rubbed my jaw. "I haven't. It's you who have her wrong.

You who know her, and should be able to see what she's doing to you, but are blinded to it. By her magic."

He shook his head, eyes angry. "No. She loves me, Gwen. Can't you be happy for me?"

I swallowed the longing to tell him *yes, she loves you,* and *I wish you both well,* because it wouldn't have been the truth.

Instead, I dug myself in deeper. "How can you think that? You've known her all her life. You know what she's like. We have a saying in my old world – a leopard never changes its spots. That's true of her. She's no different now to the woman who helped Cadwy with his plot to ambush Arthur and execute Euddolen's womenfolk. She's pure evil."

For a moment Merlin's eyes clouded, then his brows flashed together. "She's not. She's changed. She's seen the error of her ways. And I don't want to talk about this. It's my business, not yours."

Anger welled in me. Anger for his stupidity. For an intelligent man, he seemed to be keeping his brain in his braccae.

"On the contrary," I snapped back. "It *is* my business because it's my husband's business. Morgana isn't some warrior's or farmer's daughter – she's Arthur's sister, a royal princess. And you've been having sex with her. Don't look so surprised. I had you followed. You were seen. Just the once, but no doubt that wasn't the only time."

Now he really was angry. Worse than when he'd shouted at Arthur, by a long chalk. "You had me *spied* on?" The words shot out like bullets from a gun.

"With good reason," I spat back. "You've been behaving like a fool, Merlin. You've had sex with a high-born lady, a princess, without a thought for the consequences. Arthur could have you executed and Morgana thrown into a nunnery."

His mouth worked for a few moments as he struggled to get the words out. "I-I couldn't help myself." He shook his head. "You must know what it's like when you want someone. I know you love Arthur. Can you resist him? And she's his sister – she has the same allure."

My turn to be shocked. Was there something not quite normal – some *allure,* as Merlin put it – about Arthur as there was about his sister? Some magic clinging to him that made him irresistible to me? Yes, his mother and sister had the Sight, but did he share some small part of their magic? Perhaps manifested only in an animal magnetism, a charm, an indefinable something that drew people to him. That made me ache with longing for him whenever we were apart.

"She's a witch," I said bluntly. "You know she is. You taught her yourself." Inside my head, Eigr bent over her scrying glass in a small dark hut. "And you know what her mother's like. Both of them are witches. Morgana has powers like yours – but different. How do you know she's not using her powers on you right now?"

Consternation filled his eyes. "She isn't. She can't be. She told me she loves me. That she feared to speak before her father died, and then Cadwy's cruelty held her silent. She loves me, Gwen. She always has."

Bloody men. I'd once thought Merlin to be different. How wrong can you be?

I sighed. "She doesn't. Merlin, she's using you for some foul reason all of her own. She's a witch all right. Cadwy's witch. You mustn't trust her."

Sadness replaced the consternation. "I'm sorry, Gwen, but I love her so much it hurts. Here." He tapped his chest. "I never thought she'd look at me. I was content to love her from afar. And now, here, away from Cadwy and his court, she finally came to me and told me of her love. I can't help it. She has my heart in her hand. I'll accept any crumb she throws me from her table."

What could I do? I'd tried to send him away with Arthur, and that hadn't worked. And now persuasion hadn't either. He was well and truly hooked.

HAVING FAILED WITH the besotted Merlin, my next plan was to tackle Morgana. I hadn't been looking forward to the confrontation with him, but the thoughts of facing down his lover had me quaking in my boots. But, on the day following my not-so-cozy chat with Merlin, and buoyed by Arthur's faith that I was more than a match for her, I girded up my proverbial loins and set off to find her.

She and her maid occupied the guest lodgings in the courtyard beside the hall, in the house beside Theodoric's. Nervous that Morgawse might unwittingly interrupt the forthcoming showdown, I went into her house first and found her playing with little Medraut.

She looked up, smiling. "Gwen, come and play with us. Where's Amhar?"

"Maia has him." I sat down on a stool beside her while Medraut shunted a little four wheeled wooden cart about the floor. The uneven wheels made it rattle and bounce over the flagstones.

She smiled lovingly down at her son. "I asked Devin to make it for him after I saw the one Amhar has."

Amhar had a lot of wooden toys, thanks to me. Devin only needed a sketch and he could make them – a jointed wooden doll Maia had stitched warrior clothes for, his building blocks, his cart, a wooden top to spin, a wooden tool set, the list was endless. Arthur had insisted on a tiny wooden sword and shield, but Amhar preferred his wheeled vehicles. Just like a little boy from the twenty-first century with his toy cars.

My gaze rested on Medraut's curly head for a moment. I couldn't help it, but every time I saw him the thought that he might bring about my husband's end clawed its way to the surface. I dusted it to one side. "I'm going to speak to Morgana and try and warn her off."

Morgawse's eyes widened. "You're brave."

I swallowed. "I know."

"Wouldn't it be better to speak to Merlin? He is your friend, after all."

"I tried."

She put some round pebbles into Medraut's cart. Delighted, he pushed it off in a circuit of the hearth. "I take it you didn't succeed?"

I pulled a face. "I didn't really think I would. He's a man possessed."

Morgawse grimaced in return. "I rather imagined he would be. She's done this before – led someone on because she wanted something. She's good at it."

I heaved a sigh. "I only came in here to warn you not to come bursting in when I'm talking to her."

She snorted in derision. "Like I'd want to. You're on your own there. I'll stay put even if I hear screams."

I got to my feet. "Don't joke. She's a witch, remember."

Medraut tipped his load of stones out and began shunting his cart back to his mother. She clapped her hands at him, but her eyes were on me. "As if I could forget. Good luck."

Leaving Morgawse, I emerged into the sunshine, not at all looking forward to the next bit. The door of Morgana's house stood open, letting the fresh air inside. I rapped on the silvered wood.

After a moment, Morgana's sly-faced maid came to the door.

I managed a not very sincere smile that she didn't even bother to match. "Good day, Deoch. Is your mistress inside?"

Deoch squinted at me suspiciously. "She is."

How rude. "I'd like to see her then."

Deoch looked me up and down for a second before turning away and leaving me standing on the doorstep. Fuming already, I waited.

Morgana came to the door. Clearly I wasn't to be invited inside. Well, I had refused to let her see Amhar, so it was only reasonable that she didn't want me in her house. Not that it was really hers. She'd better not be thinking of taking up permanent residence.

She regarded me with cold eyes. "Gwen."

By rights she should have called me "my lady" as she was only a princess, and I was a queen. I let that go. Even nearly three years as a queen hadn't quite erased the equality of the twenty-first century from my nature.

"Morgana. I'd like to speak with you in private if I may." Lurking behind her inside the house, Deoch clearly had an ear open for our conversation.

Just for a moment, Morgana's eyes narrowed, then her face resumed its cold, expressionless normality. "Very well. Perhaps a walk along the wall?"

In a place as crowded as Din Cadan, the wall, despite guards every forty yards or so, was always the place for a private chat. I nodded.

We walked in silence, Morgana stately in her flowing gown, me, as usual made to feel the country cousin, having to hurry my steps to keep up with her long strides, conscious that I only wore a workaday tunic dress. Too late it crossed my mind that I should have dressed more like a queen for this showdown.

I led the way to the steepest steps I could find. It worked. She had trouble climbing them in that beautiful gown and had to hitch it up awkwardly around her knees with one hand while she held the rail with the other.

I skipped up the steps behind her in my calf-length tunic.

She halted halfway between two guards and turned to face me. "What is it you need to talk about? Hints about how to care for your child? How to keep your husband from straying?" She looked me up and down. "How to dress, perhaps?"

Clearly this was no-holds-barred territory. I fixed her with what I hoped was a stony stare. "I know your game."

She raised one eloquent eyebrow. "You do? And what would that be, pray?"

"You're after Merlin."

Her beautiful mouth, which could look so cruel, curved into a mirthless smile. "And what's that to you? Are you jealous?"

She was so near the mark my cheeks heated, and my consciousness of them doing so only made them hotter. "He's my friend," I snapped, furious with myself. "I care for him."

She laughed, a tinkling, brittle sound. "A little too much, it seems. Well, he's mine now."

What I really wanted to do was scratch her eyes out, pull her hair, and chuck her off the wall-walk – and not on the inside. Instead, I smiled sweetly. "I think it's time you left Din Cadan."

She set an elegant hand on the top of the wooden crenellation we stood beside. "Really? And who is going to make me? You?" Her lip curled a little in unmistakable scorn.

My own hands involuntarily balled into fists, and I had to forcibly straighten them out, well aware that she'd seen. "Yes. Me. You have until tomorrow to organize your men for your departure. After that I'll kick you down the hill myself."

Her lip curled in a bigger sneer this time. "You think you could? I'm not surprised – dressed like that you could be taken for a tavern girl, and they're well known for their drunken fighting."

Refusing to rise to the bait, I set my hands on my hips. At least there they couldn't make angry fists again. "I've no desire to come to blows with you myself, but if you don't leave, I *will* make sure my warriors escort you from the fortress. Tomorrow morning. Is that understood?"

Her gaze sharpened. Was that a smile of triumph that glinted for a moment in her eyes? "Very well. I will leave." She turned away from me and, presumably because descending the steep steps would have done nothing for her dignity, strode away along the wall-walk in the direction of the main gates.

Relieved the awkward interview was at last over, I climbed down the steps and went in search of Morgawse to relay the news.

NOT WANTING ANOTHER confrontation, and having decided to allow Morgana plenty of time to organize her departure, I remained in my chamber the next morning with Maia and Amhar, playing with him while she sat stitching at more shirts. A toddler his age got through a lot of shirts even if you kept toileting him.

Midday was fast approaching when the side door flew open, and Llacheu burst in upon us, tousle-headed and red-faced. "Gwen!"

Amhar was sitting on my knee chewing at a bone teething ring, his dribble running down the front of his shirt. I looked up, surprised at his urgency. "Yes?"

"She's gone!"

I nodded, pleased. "I knew she was going. I told her she had to. Don't worry."

He shook his head, small chest heaving. "You don't understand. She's taken Merlin with her."

"What?" Lifting Amhar, I plonked him on the floor and got to my feet. "She's taken him? When? How?"

"This morning. First thing. He was supposed to be teaching us boys today, and he didn't turn up." His anxious eyes regarded me. "The other boys were glad – a morning off to do as they wanted. But Rhiwallon and me, we knew something was wrong. So we went to look for him." He wiped a hand across his sweaty brow. "We ran all over the fortress, searching every corner. Then we went to the stables. His horse has gone."

"He could just be out riding." Faint hope. That bitch had stolen him. Now I knew what that smile of triumph had been for.

"He's not. We asked Goff the smith. He didn't know, but his boy, Corann, one of Rhiwallon's friends, was in the forge early this morning, getting the fire going for his father. He saw Merlin leave. He had stuffed saddle bags. Corann said he followed him out of curiosity once he saw the bags. Merlin met Morgana and her warriors down by the gates, and they set off together at first light."

I chewed my lip. That was hours ago. By now they'd be miles away. And anyway, sending men after them would be of no use. It didn't sound as though Merlin had gone with her under duress.

My heart sinking, I patted his shoulder. "Well done. Thank you for this. You're a good spy."

He looked up at me out of his father's eyes, gold flecked, charming. Magical? "She's snared him, hasn't she? Used her magic on him?"

I nodded. "She has indeed. A woman's magic. No man can withstand that."

He shook his head with all the sagacity of extreme youth. "I'll never fall for that sort of magic. Not never."

I stared over his head and out of the door he'd left open. What was Arthur going to say to this?

Chapter Twenty-Seven

TEN DAYS LATER a rider came with news from the east. Llacheu, who'd taken his remit to spy for me to heart, came running into the great hall to tell me, eyes shining with excitement. Together, we went to the front doors and stood waiting for the man and his exhausted horse to reach us.

He slid to the ground and unfastened his helmet with one hand. A grubby bandage covered the other. "Milady." He bowed his dusty head.

"Anwyll." The warrior I'd shared my incarceration in Vindolanda with. "What news do you bring? Is my husband well?" My most important question.

He nodded. "He's well, have no fear. There's been a great battle. At Caer Guinntguic itself."

Relief washing over me, I remembered my manners. "Come inside, and I'll have food and drink brought. You must be tired."

"My horse is in a worse state than I am."

I waved forward a servant. "Can you give Anwyll's horse the best of care, please?"

Anwyll handed his horse's reins over and followed me inside, Llacheu, bursting with curiosity, bringing up the rear.

If Arthur was alive, I could afford to wait for the full story, so I sent Llacheu running for cold meat and cheese, bread and wine.

Anwyll sank to one of the benches at the nearest side table, leaning heavily on his forearms, head hanging. Had he ridden here non-stop?

When the food arrived, with Llacheu and a servant girl, I let him eat his fill. He made short work of it, washing it down with several cups of watered wine.

At last, he looked up.

"Can you tell me about the battle?" I asked.

His eyes scanned the hall. "Won't Milord Merlin want to hear?"

I pursed my lips. Of course he'd think that – he was a man and I just a feeble woman with no mind for battle. *Ha-ha.* "He's not here," I said. "You'll have to tell me."

He sighed. "We headed for the south coast where a broad river comes down to meet the sea in a tidal estuary. The Saxons had drawn their ships up on the foreshore and left them under heavy guard when they moved off inland. We didn't attack them – the Dux said he wanted them to be left with a way to retreat, not get stuck here. So we headed inland toward Caer Guinntguic to aid King Natanleod."

He took another swig of the watered wine, washing it around his mouth. "We found them inside the town, looting. The legions left it with good defenses, but the walls are long, and Natanleod's men were few." He wiped his mouth on his sleeve. "Natanleod had enough time to move his people up to the old hilltop fort to the south of the town. It's defended by good earth banks topped with a stout palisade wall. I did hear it were old Elafius had it refortified for just such an emergency,"

If Caer Guinntguic was Winchester, did he mean the old ring work on top of St Catherine's Hill? It was the only one I could think of that fitted his description. I sat down on the bench beside him.

He rubbed his red-rimmed eyes. "Of course, once we arrived, Natanleod led his men down from the fort, and the battle began. Aelle and Cerdic didn't stop inside the town for long. They'd've had the same problem as Natanleod – too long a run of walls for the men available. They must've decided their best bet was to meet us face to face rather than weather a siege."

My restless hands worked the soft fabric of my skirt. "How many men did the enemy have?"

"Hundreds, but none mounted. The Saxons are not given to cavalry." He grunted. "They meant business, but so did we."

"How did the battle go?"

"All day, that's how. Then the Saxons retreated back inside the gates of the town. We camped outside. They'd have seen our campfires clearly from their walls."

I shifted my position. "And the next day?"

He shrugged. "They sat it out and waited. Natanleod wanted to scale the walls but that would have been suicide. Arthur said no." A wry smile flitted across his face. "That Natanleod was a hothead. Eager to risk his men's lives in useless fighting. Arthur sent some of our men to seal off the aqueduct, so they'd have no water in the city. Better by far than losing men for no good reason other than to show you're brave. Brave and a bit foolish."

"So is Cerdic his uncle?"

Anwyll nodded. "Natanleod's grandfather was old Elafius, Cerdic's father. But Natanleod was all British. The people of Caer Guinntguic don't like Cerdic because of his Saxon mother."

"Cadwy has a Saxon mother."

Anwyll shot me a grin. "And do you know anyone who likes him?"

True. I didn't need to answer that one.

I tapped my foot on the flagstones. "So how did Arthur defeat them?"

Anwyll shook his head. "They're not defeated."

I sat up straighter. "What d'you mean?"

He poured himself another cup of wine. "We sat outside the town after that first battle for a week before they showed their noses again. Probably the lack of water drove them to us. We fought under the city walls in driving rain. The ground underfoot turned to a morass – Caer Guinntguic's built on land prone to flooding."

That sounded like Winchester – the crypt under the cathedral that stood there in my time was usually underwater.

"We fought the next day too. Cerdic wanted that town, and was determined we wouldn't take it from him. Natanleod was just as determined that he shouldn't get it. To his downfall." He paused. From over the dividing wall came the sound of Amhar wailing. "Late on the second day, Natanleod fell. He's dead."

My mouth hung open.

How could such a young man, with his muscular physique and flamboyant tattoos be dead? Was he as old as Arthur, even? Relief that he'd been the one to die came galloping in hard on the heels of my shock. At least it hadn't been Arthur.

Anwyll kept going. "With Natanleod dead, the Dux called a truce. He and Lord Cei met with the Saxon generals. Aelle and Cerdic. Theodoric translated. It's not quite his language, but he knows enough of it to be of use."

"And what did they decide?"

"Cerdic rules in Caer Guinntguic now. He's a strong leader, and he's half British."

Who else was there to take over Caer Guinntguic but Natanleod's nephew, Cerdic, despite his Saxon blood? I understood Arthur's turn to diplomacy instead of violence, but coming to an agreement with the man he hated must have rankled.

Anwyll went on. "Aelle wisely agreed to retreat back to the coast and his ships, but he's not gone far. His retreat made the people keener to accept Cerdic's rule. The people still remember his father fondly."

"Probably not his mother, though."

He nodded. "I saw him. He's dark, not blond, and wiry strong, not big boned like his mother's people. His British blood has triumphed over his Saxon blood, at least in looks."

Well, that would be a help, for now. But it might not continue to be if he ever felt the need to surround himself with Saxon warriors. Every native Briton would harbor the suspicion that they were here to steal the property of the townspeople and the farmers who lived around the town. This didn't have the makings of a peaceful settlement to the war.

"And when will my husband be back?"

Anwyll picked the last crumbs off his plate. He must be very hungry. "I can't say. He's not hurrying away. There's all those Saxon warriors to see loaded back into their ships and gone, for a start. I believe Cerdic's kept a few, and Aelle is taking the rest back to the east where they came from. He's Cerdic's uncle, or great uncle – something like that."

So I wouldn't be seeing Arthur just yet. Frustration at everything gnawed into me, more particularly because there seemed nothing I could do to relieve it. Despite my best efforts, Morgana had stolen Merlin away, and Arthur had been forced to make a treaty of sorts with a man he hated. I'd have liked to have been a fly on the wall in that meeting.

ARTHUR DIDN'T RETURN for another ten days, by which time we were into mid-summer. All around the fortress the fields lay green and lush with growing wheat and barley. The trees had sprouted tiny green apples, and in the vegetable patches dotted all over the fortress, tasty things like cabbages were growing. Yum.

With the loss of Merlin, I'd stopped riding out to visit the farms, and instead had taken to patrolling the length of the wall-walk every morning for my exercise, leaving Amhar with Maia. It gave me time to think without his constant baby chatter, away from the responsibilities of ruling the fortress in Arthur's stead. I'd had some interesting cases to rule on in his absence, and been glad I'd sat in on his judgements so many times.

I was on the walls when the shout came that the army had been spotted. With no one to see me, I hitched up my skirts and ran to the main gates, then climbed the ladder to the look-out platform. The two warriors on duty there, both familiar to me, bobbed respectful bows and stood back to let me peer out over the plain.

Close to the fortress, small fields, flushed with the green of growing wheat, dotted the view. Beyond them lurked the dark shadow of the forest, and beyond that the small hump of the Tor at Glastonbury, where Gildas currently resided with the monks. At first, I couldn't see the army, and one of the men, Dynod, had to point out the faint dust cloud rising behind them. I peered down his pointing arm at the small flashes of light reflecting off their armor and the tiny banner rippling in the breeze.

Arthur was back.

They made slow progress, most likely keeping their tired horses in a walk, drawing ever closer to the hill of Din Cadan. Soon, the rearing bear on the white banner they carried became clearer, and the pale coat of Arthur's horse stood out amongst the bays and chestnuts.

Excitement had me hopping from one foot to the other, like an impatient young girl, and I had to force myself to behave more like the queen I was.

Dynod grinned at me. "Don't fuss yourself for us, Milady. We know you're happy to see him back safe and sound. Just as we all are."

I shot him a smile. He was a man with seven daughters, so he ought to know about women by now. His poor wife had just produced her eighth child – a long awaited son, convinced that by asking me to intervene with the goddess of fertility, Epona, she'd conceived a boy. No matter how much I'd told her I'd had no hand in it, she refused to believe me.

At the foot of the hill, the road dipped out of sight, and it wasn't until the column breasted the summit that I had sight of them again. Arthur rode in front, his helmet and shield hooked on to his saddle, Cei's ginger head visible behind him. And there was Theodoric. Not that I felt overjoyed to see him, but Morgawse would be ecstatic.

Arthur glanced up toward the gate towers, his face breaking

into a smile as he saw me waiting. Abandoning my post, and hitching up my skirts again, I clambered down the ladders to the ground just in time to meet him coming through the gates. I didn't care one bit if this was conduct unbecoming for a queen.

He threw his leg over the pommel and slid to the ground, scooping me up into his arms. The familiar smell of horse, leather and sweat enveloped me as I clung to him. "I've missed you." He spoke into my hair as he pressed me against his body.

I hugged him back. "And I you."

He bent his head and kissed me, quick and hard, then with his arm around my waist began the walk up the slope toward the stables.

It was only when we reached them that I remembered Merlin and my feeling of elation lessened. Sank into my boots, in fact.

The men led their horses into the stalls, and I followed Arthur into the cool, dark interior, clean straw swishing under my feet. Someone, forewarned by the shouts, had flung armfuls of hay into every manger. Llamrei started tugging at it with gusto, and Arthur hurriedly took off her bridle so she could eat more easily. Swiftly undoing his girth, he set his saddle on the dividing wall and hooked the bridle on one of the horns. Llamrei's white coat glistened wet with sweat, her dark skin showing through.

Keen to put off the moment when I had to reveal to Arthur what Merlin had done, I stood by silently and watched him sponge her down. With a hooked metal tool, he picked a few stones out of her hooves. Pushing thoughts of Merlin out of my head and what Arthur was going to say when I told him, I fixed my gaze on Arthur's bum as he bent over, a delightfully distracting sight.

When he'd finished, and Llamrei was as comfortable as he could make her, he finally turned back to me. "Where's Merlin got to? I didn't see him anywhere as we walked up."

I took his hand. "Come on up to the hall, and I'll tell you."

He frowned. "What d'you mean? You'll tell me? Tell me what?"

"Not here." My voice came out in a hiss even though I hadn't meant it to. "Come on." I pulled him after me, and together we walked up the final rise to the doors of the great hall.

As soon as we were inside, he turned and caught my arms above the elbow, not tightly, but enough to prevent my escape. "Right. Tell me now."

No one else was in the hall. Cei must have gone to see Coventina, and Theodoric to greet Morgawse. I could put it off no longer. "Merlin's left. With Morgana."

His body froze. "What?"

"You heard me. She left, and he went with her."

His fingers tightened on my upper arms. I'd have bruises. "What d'you mean? Why did he go with her? Where to?"

If you'd taken him with you like I asked, this wouldn't have happened.

"He went," I said, enunciating every word, "because he thinks she loves him."

His mouth fell open. "Her? Love someone other than herself? Is he mad?"

"Probably. Or bewitched."

His fingers flew to his chest as he crossed himself. "Couldn't you have stopped him?"

I sighed. "Don't you think I tried? I wanted you to take him with you, but you wouldn't. Then I tried talking to him, but he's really convinced she loves him and wouldn't believe me when I told him she was playing with him for a reason." I took a deep breath. "So then I went to her and told her I knew what her game was and that she had to leave. I gave her a day to prepare, or I'd have her thrown out. She left very early the next morning – and she took him with her."

Arthur shook his head as if to clear it. "Of his own free will?"

I nodded. "Can you not hold me so tight – you're hurting me."

He released his hold. "Sorry. I just can't believe this. He knows her too well – he's seen her wiles. He saw what she did two years ago. Why would he fall for her tricks?"

Men. Such idiots sometimes.

"Have you never seen the look on his face when he was watching her?"

He frowned. "Ye-es. But I thought it just infatuation. And she clearly didn't return his...his love. She's a cold hearted, cruel bitch, incapable of love."

At least we shared the same opinion of her. No rosy tinted spectacles for Arthur.

"Capable of fooling him, though."

He turned away from me, strode a few strides up the hall, spun on his heel, then returned. "I just can't believe it. He's my most trusted adviser. Has she taken him to Viroconium? She must have. Will she use him against me? Oh God, Cadwy will have both of them."

He kicked the nearest table leg, most likely out of the same frustration I'd been feeling. "You knew about this before I left? Why didn't you tell me?"

"Because I was worried about how angry you'd be with Merlin."

He stiffened. "You thought I'd be angry with *him* rather than her?"

I nodded. "He was...er...with her. I saw them..."

"Oh."

The clattering of the penny dropping echoed loudly in my head. "Yes. Very much oh." I put my hand on his arm. "She's a royal princess. I didn't know what to do. I thought...no, I feared...that you'd punish Merlin. I couldn't have cared less if you'd sent her off to a nunnery, but Merlin's my friend."

He sighed. "My friend too. Or I thought he was. And yet he's thrown all that away to chase after that...that witch."

I squeezed his arm. "If it's any consolation, I don't think he could help himself. She's very beautiful in a cold kind of way, and he's been infatuated for years. Like a drowning man, when she threw him a twig, he clung onto it, and she exploited that. She came here expressly to steal him away. That must have been her plan all along."

He stared down into my eyes. "Well, we have to get him back."

Chapter Twenty-Eight

C EI MARCHED UP and down our bedchamber, his shaggy red hair standing on end where he'd run his hands through it. "Is he an idiot?" He swung on his heel and strode back again, past where Arthur leant against the table, arms folded, brows furrowed in a perpetual frown.

Sitting on the bed, I chewed my lip, my hands clasping and unclasping in my lap. After my revelation, Arthur had gone to the hall doors and bellowed for Cei, loud enough that had Cei been ten miles away at the Tor he'd still have heard. Without waiting for him, he slammed through the door into our bedchamber and ordered Maia and a wailing Amhar out of it. She scooped our child up in her arms and hurried away, eyes big with fear.

It hadn't taken long to fill Cei in on what had happened.

He stopped his pacing in front of Arthur. "She's done it for a reason." His hand went to his sword hilt. "And Cadwy is that reason."

Arthur nodded. "We'd worked that out for ourselves."

I stilled my hands. "She doesn't really want him. Not for the reasons he'd like. She wants to curtail his power. That's why she's done it. She wants to be the only one with power." Like Nimuë in the legends. But she'd been some kind of fairy woman, and Morgana was as human as me.

Arthur nodded again. "I think it's high time we paid Cadwy a visit."

Cei half drew his sword, the blade winking in the torchlight. "I'd like to give him a taste of this metal." He grimaced. "And lock our sister up where she belongs – in a nunnery. Although I fear she'd not take long to corrupt the sisters."

Pushing himself off the table, Arthur put his hand on his own sword hilt. "As would I."

I looked up at them both, standing there grim faced and angry. Wasn't this the reaction Cadwy wanted? Weren't they playing into his hands?

"What if Merlin doesn't want rescuing?" I said. "What if you go there and find him part of Cadwy's court, doing his bidding, because *she* wants him to?"

Arthur scowled. "How could he? She might have him fooled, but Merlin's known Cadwy since my brother was a boy. He won't be fooled by him."

"You think not?" I said. "Love can be very blind."

Cei turned for the doors. "Shall I tell the men to prepare to ride immediately?"

For a moment it seemed as though Arthur might say yes, but then he held up his hand to stay Cei's impetuosity. "No. They're exhausted. They need to rest, and I need to think. Going off now, unprepared, will make no difference to Merlin. He must have already been at Viroconium for days, so one more day, or two, will make no difference. We'll let the men rest, be with their wives, restore their strength." He paused. "Go back to Coventina. Forget Merlin for the moment. Go on."

Cei glanced at me, and I gave him a reassuring nod. With sagging shoulders he departed, leaving Arthur and me alone. Arthur sank back down onto the table edge, legs outstretched. He thought I didn't know it, but his leg still gave him trouble after long periods in the saddle.

I got to my feet. "Are you sure it's wise to go after them?"

He pursed his lips, regarded his travel-stained boots for a moment, then looked back up at me. "Probably not, but what else can we do? If I thought for one single moment she truly loved him, and there was no ulterior motive behind this, I'd leave him to it. But I don't. I think he's walked blindly into terrible danger. And he's my friend. He needs rescuing."

"Cadwy probably did this to make you come to him."

He nodded. "I know that too. But forewarned is forearmed, as they say."

I managed a tiny smile. "They also say that fools rush in where wise men fear to tread."

He returned my smile. "Well, I'm not rushing in. I'm taking my time and considering my options. But I *am* going there, and I will get him back. And if I have to face Cadwy, then so be it."

I folded my arms to match his. "And I'm coming with you."

THE JOURNEY NORTH to Viroconium in the heart of Cadwy's kingdom of Powys was one I'd made before. But back then, I'd been a frightened, confused visitor from another world, adrift in time, lost and lonely. Now, I was a powerful queen, wife of the Dux Britanniarum, riding at the head of his full army, a woman who'd seen battles and killed a man herself.

We marched with a large part of the army at our heels. Arthur had decided not to travel light. Leaving a garrison at Din Cadan, he'd elected to make a show of force for his brother's benefit.

Consequently, we were too big a group to house easily, and instead of the hospitality of the various towns, villas or way stations along our route, we made camp every night and slept on the hard ground. But it was summer, and the weather held for the entire journey. Although Arthur didn't force the pace, we made good time, and a week after we left Din Cadan, the substantial walls of Viroconium appeared, hugging the banks of the wide Sabrina River.

Of all the places I'd visited in my time with Arthur, this was by far the most splendid – and the most Roman. From living with a father steeped in post-Roman history, I knew that from the fourth century, most Roman towns in Britain had been in decline, and from Merlin I'd learned first-hand the history of many of them. Here, at Viroconium, not far from the modern Welsh border, the Roman way of life still continued almost unbroken. Although where the old forum's open market had once stood, now a decidedly British hall had taken its place. The hall where the Council of Kings was held, and where the round table stood.

We descended the road from the hills to the east of Viroconium slowly, giving the guards on the city walls chance to spot us and warn Cadwy of our imminent arrival. This wasn't to be a surprise visit. We must have been kicking up a sizeable cloud of dust behind ourselves, spread out as we were to either side of the graveled Roman road. Not for the first time did I feel glad of the fact that as Queen I got to ride at the front beside Arthur.

It had taken some argument to get him to agree that I could come. But I'd pointed out that if Cadwy saw me there, he'd be less likely to think Arthur had come with violence in mind. Not that that was true. However he and his men presented themselves, violence was definitely the thing foremost in Arthur's mind, and in Cei's.

They rode to either side of me, serious-faced and somber, as we approached the walled city, passing between the prosperous farms, the orchards, the fields of standing wheat and barley tinted, as yet, with only the faintest dusting of gold. At the sight of so large an army, the laboring farmers dropped their tools and ran for their homes, to watch us pass through cracks in their closed doors. Up ahead, the solid city gates stood firmly closed.

Raising a hand, Arthur brought the column of riders to a halt a little more than a bow shot's length from the gates. No reason to put himself at risk of a marksman up on the walls. He still steadfastly refused to ride any other horse but Llamrei. Stopping well back had been my suggestion, thanks to a memory of how Richard the Lionheart had met his end outside a chateau in

France – or rather, would one day meet his end.

We waited. Wary faces peered at us over the battlements. From down in the willows by the riverside a flock of crows rose in a tatter of black wings. The hot sun beat down on our backs.

At last, one of the two gates swung open to allow three riders to emerge. One of them bore Cadwy's banner, a red dragon on a green background – the emblem of the Pendragons. On the battlements, the audience, now grown larger, of townspeople and guards craned to watch. A murmur of voices ran through the ranks of our warriors, before a hush descended.

The three warriors walked their horses halfway across the open space that stretched between our ranks and the walls, and halted.

I glanced at Arthur. He sat immobile, eyes on the riders. I liked his strategy of letting them wait. On my other side, Cei shifted impatiently, and his horse stamped restless feet, its tail swishing at the flies.

Arthur made them wait a good ten minutes. Impossible to see their faces and who they were from this distance, even if I shaded my hand from the sun and squinted. If one of them had been Cadwy though, we'd have recognized his bear-like bulk.

"Cei, would you care to ride over to see what they want?" Arthur said, at last. "I fear if I go, they might have someone on the battlements ready to pick me off."

Cei grinned. "With pleasure, brother." With a tap of his heels he set his horse jog-trotting toward the three waiting riders under our watchful gaze.

We didn't hear their conversation, of course. The sun beat down on the back of my neck, broiling me in my mail shirt. I fidgeted, sweat sticking my undershirt to my body as we waited. Not a breath of a breeze disturbed the willows lining the riverside, nor touched the wheat and barley in the fields to the left and right. Alezan tossed her head to rid herself of the cloud of flies surrounding her, with no success.

Time stretched out. For how long was Cei going to talk to

those riders? Not for the first time, the thought surfaced that bringing a watch back from the present might have been a good idea. After what felt like forever, but in reality was no more than another five to ten minutes, Cei swung his horse around and jogged back toward us, showing no haste. The three riders stood their ground.

Cei brought his horse in beside Arthur's, with a grin that didn't travel as far as his eyes. "Dubricius and two others I didn't know. They wanted to know what we want, for a start," he said. "Accused us of coming looking as though we mean war. So I told them. Our adviser back, unharmed. Our adviser who's been kidnapped." His blue eyes flashed. "So of course, Dubricius denied they had him. But Morgana's there. I got that out of him, so Merlin must be too." He paused. "Of course, it's possible Dubricius might not know he's there. Cadwy might have him hidden away. Or she might." He chuckled mirthlessly.

Arthur frowned. "That seems very likely. Did you demand entry?"

Cei shook his head. "Didn't need to. He offered it. They – Cadwy, that is – want you in there. A bad sign if ever there was one."

I'd have told him it was the lion's den he was being invited into, if I'd thought he'd have known what a lion was.

Arthur glanced along the line of warriors to either side of us. "He sees I have my full army with me. He knows I mean to have my way. And yet he invites me in. That's clearly part of his plan. If I go, it will be to play into his hands. Yet if I don't, we won't get Merlin back."

"He's not inviting our army in," Cei said. "Just you."

"Don't go," I said. "Sit here and let him come to you."

Arthur glanced at me as his hand strayed to his sword hilt. "If I go, it won't be alone." He squinted against the sun at the three riders. "Go back and tell them that if I come in, I want a valuable hostage out here with my men. Tell him to send his son. That should work – as far as I know he only has the one."

His son? I hadn't known Cadwy had one. A wife, Angharad, yes, but not a son. He'd once been horribly keen to put aside this wife so he could marry me, the Ring Maiden, and take for himself all the things he thought the prophecy would give him.

Cei snorted. "I can try." He wheeled his horse, and this time cantered briskly back to the three riders. He was gone a shorter time than before. One of the riders cantered back to the city gates and was let inside. The other two sat waiting in the hot sun, their banner hanging limply on its pole.

We waited as well. Cei stayed with the remaining two riders, facing the gates. Eventually, one side again swung open, and this time two riders emerged, one smaller than the other. They walked with no hint of haste toward the little group on the no-man's-land between our rival factions. There, they paused, then Cei and the newcomer turned and rode toward us.

As they drew nearer, I saw that the newcomer was a boy of about eleven, with the dark eyes and curling hair of the Pendragons. Cei drew rein in front of Arthur and me, and I stared into the eyes of Cadwy's son.

"Custennin," Arthur said. "Good to see you."

The boy glared at Arthur from under heavy brows – he had the Pendragon scowl as well. "My Lord."

"I'm afraid I have no time for conversation," Arthur said. "And you must remain our prisoner to guarantee the safety of me and my men inside your father's city." He nodded to his men. "Keep him safe in the middle of our army. Guard him with your lives, but do not hurt him. He's just a boy, and he's done me no harm." He paused. "However, if you should receive news of my death, you have my permission to execute him and hang his body up so those within these walls can see it."

The boy's eyes flew wide open in alarm, but he said nothing, his lower lip jutting rebelliously. He was just a child, after all.

Arthur looked at him. "Let's hope for all our sakes it doesn't come to that."

I wanted to say something, but shock, and caution, held my

tongue. That Arthur could so casually order the death of a child had rocked me to the core. But then, he'd also threatened Caw with Gildas's death. Had he truly meant it then, and did he mean it now? Probably. I had half a mind to stay to make sure the boy went unharmed, but the urge to accompany my husband overrode it. I pushed Alezan forward as Arthur and Cei set off toward the waiting riders. And Arthur didn't stop me.

Chapter Twenty-Nine

THE GATES OF Viroconium swung closed behind us with a thud, shutting out all possibility of rescue by our army. Ahead of us, the principle street stretched toward the forum, straight as when the Romans built it. And very empty.

On either side, the houses stood shuttered up and silent, as though the inhabitants, fearful of what might be about to happen, had retreated away from it. They were either on the wall, or, like ostriches, had their heads buried in the sand, hoping that if they didn't see, it wouldn't happen. The news of our large army camped outside their gates must have flown around the city like wildfire.

Ahead of us rode our three-man escort – Dubricius, Cadwy's grey-haired archbishop, and two men I didn't know.

Cei leaned in close to Arthur and I caught his whisper. "I don't like it one bit that it's just you, me and Gwen."

Arthur glanced sideways at him. "Theo has the boy."

"He was a sight too eager to hand him over, if you ask me," Cei muttered.

"Well, I didn't."

There must be something Cadwy valued above his son's life at stake here.

The road opened up into the forum where the market stalls stood empty and abandoned, the bulk of the thatched hall looming threateningly over everything. Here, the mid-summer heat seemed more oppressive than it had out on the plain. My back itched and the flies buzzing around my head made me want to scream. Dubricius halted his horse in front of the hall, and we three drew rein behind him.

Forty yards from the hall, in the middle of a large open space, the rock still stood where Merlin had planted it nearly three years before, the hilt and part of the blade of the sword protruding from it. Merlin had somehow created this overnight during the Council of Kings, and every man then present had tried their hand at pulling it out. Except Arthur, who'd wisely taken note of the inscription declaring that it would only be drawn "when the time is right". None had succeeded. Now a guard stood beside it, watching our arrival with little interest.

The double doors of the hall swung open, and Cadwy stepped onto the cobbles. Half a dozen burly warriors followed him out, like a pack of tame pit bulls.

I hadn't seen him in nearly three years, and time hadn't improved him any. A big man anyway, he wore a huge, black, bearskin cloak that increased his bulk and gave him the presence of a giant. His thick dark hair, liberally streaked with grey, hung in tangled, greasy curls down his back. His face, a bloated caricature of Arthur's, every feature an exaggeration, wore an expression of distaste as he looked us up and down.

"So," he said. "You came."

Arthur didn't dismount. "I've come for Merlin. Give him to me, and I'll be gone."

Cadwy's upper lip curled into a snarl. "Not so fast. I don't have him."

Arthur shifted in the saddle. Perhaps his leg was paining him. It had been a long ride up from Din Cadan. "But you have Morgana."

Cadwy nodded. "I do."

"Then return Merlin to me, and I'll be off."

Cadwy smiled, a not-at-all nice smile. "I can't give you what I don't have."

Cei bristled. "You lie. We know Morgana brought Merlin with her."

Cadwy's sneer returned. "I don't need to hear what you think."

Being close to Cei, I put a restraining hand on his arm. "Ignore him." I kept my voice low, but Dubricius shot me a sideways look as though he'd heard me.

Keeping his voice level, Arthur spoke again. "Then let me speak with my sister. She can tell me where Merlin is."

Cadwy jerked his head at one of his warriors. The man disappeared inside the hall and a moment later re-emerged, walking beside Morgana. She must have been listening from behind the door. Sneaky cow.

She wore a cream gown that swept the floor, girdled with her golden chain, and her long dark hair hung loose down her back, smooth and silky as a shampoo advert. Her pale face, looking as though it had never seen the sun, had a small smug smile plastered onto it.

"Arthur." Her gaze ran over him then slid to me. "Gwen. How lovely to see you."

For a horrible moment I was reminded of Melwas's greeting to me after Arthur captured him and before he died. He'd spoken very similar words, pretending to a link of friendship, or more, that had never existed. Now she had done the same.

I fixed Morgana with my hardest stare. "I wish I could say the same about you. No, that's a lie. I don't wish it at all."

"Ladies, please." A matching smug smile lit Cadwy's face, half hidden by his heavy beard. "Let's keep this polite, shall we?"

Like he'd be familiar with polite.

Morgana stopped beside Cadwy, hands demurely clasped in front of her, eyes fixed on me.

Arthur eyed her up and down. "Where is he?"

The smug smile intensified. "Where you cannot find him." She glanced at Cadwy. "The King spoke the truth when he told you he doesn't have him. I do."

"What is it you want from him?"

She licked her lips suggestively. "Oh, I've had that all right." One hand slid to her belly, cradling it.

My eyes must have been bulging. No, she couldn't be. That wasn't in any of the stories I knew.

Her laughter echoed around the empty forum, across the roofs of the market stalls, bouncing back at us, multiplied many times. The laugh of a madwoman...or a witch.

Arthur was a man, but even he got her implication. "You're not?" he gasped. "What have you done?"

"The same as you. Got myself an heir." She stared into his eyes. "Only *my* heir will be all powerful, the child not only of me, but of Merlin. My child will be...*exceptional*."

"What?" Cei was slower on the uptake. "You're with child?"

From the lack of surprise on Cadwy's broad face, he already knew. A grin of triumph lit his eyes. "And that child will be adviser to me, and then my son. With him by our sides, we will rule the whole island of Britain from Vectis in the south to Din Eidyn in the north, from Caer Lundein in the east to Maridunum in the west."

"With *her* by your side," Morgana said. "This child will be a girl."

Silence fell over the forum. Overhead a skylark sang, far above us, whirling on hidden air currents. Down in the forum the heat throbbed.

"Then give me Merlin, now you've got what you want," Arthur said. Llamrei stamped her feet, as impatient as her master.

Cadwy shook his head. "Not mine to give. I don't even know where he is."

Morgana's eyes narrowed. "You will need to deal with me, *brother*. Merlin is mine, and I don't intend to give him up lightly." She licked her lips again, like a snake scenting its prey. A surprise to see her tongue wasn't forked. "To hand him over to you, I shall want something in return."

Fury bubbled so high in me, I could barely sit still. Where did she have Merlin hidden that Cadwy didn't know about? Maybe not even here in Viroconium. We were wasting our time.

"What is it you want?" Arthur asked.

Morgana's and Cadwy's eyes slid past us toward the sword standing proud in the huge rock. "The sword," Cadwy said. "We want the sword."

Revelation rocked me. She hadn't just wanted a child; she'd wanted Merlin to give her the sword. The image of her trying to touch it on the day it appeared returned to me, of her jumping back as though electrocuted, and saying she couldn't because it knew her. Of Cadwy laughing and trying his hand at pulling it out of the rock, and failing in front of all his people.

It seemed despite his humiliation, he hadn't given up and still coveted it and the power he thought it would bring. Written on the stone were the words *When the time is right, he who draws this sword from this stone shall be the true born High King of all Britain.* Back then, Arthur had said the time wasn't right – was it, even now?

An awful thought followed on. Had Morgana been trying to force the secret of the magic in that stone and sword out of Merlin? In our lack of haste to get here, thinking the time we spent on the road would make no difference, had we left him with her, being tortured perhaps? That she'd not succeeded was evident, or these two wouldn't be asking for Arthur to draw and give them the sword in return for handing Merlin over.

Arthur turned to regard the sword, as though remembering it was there for the first time. It wasn't ornate or special looking – just an ordinary warrior's sword, the hilt like that of any other, and yet, it *was* special. It was the sword in the stone made world famous by legend, and made real by my hasty words.

Arthur turned his gaze back to Cadwy. "And what makes you think *I'll* be able to draw it out?"

Cadwy gave a snort of derision. "It was Merlin's magic that put it there. He clearly intended it for you alone. But to get him back, you must draw it and hand it over immediately to me.

Because it's my destiny, not yours, to become High King."

"No." Arthur shook his head. "I won't do it."

Cadwy's eyes, sunken into the plentiful flesh of his broad face, widened as far as his bloated cheeks would allow. "What d'you mean, no? Don't you want him back? Your friend, your adviser? Or shall we let Morgana and her followers do what they want to him? He's served her purpose now. She has the child. His life can end, like this." He snapped his fingers.

"How do I know he's even still alive?" Arthur asked.

I kept my eyes on the sword for a moment longer, transfixed by it. Would it come out even now, when this was the reason? Was the time right for it to be drawn?

Morgana's dark eyes snapped. "I can assure you that he is."

Arthur's turn to snort with derision. "You'll excuse me when I say that your word isn't good enough for me. I'll need to see him."

She looked at Cadwy, and he gave her a slight nod. He wanted that sword badly.

"I'll have him brought here," she said, her cold face barely showing her annoyance. Perhaps she'd wanted to hang onto him as long as she could, inflict more pain than she already had. "For tomorrow."

Arthur shortened his reins, and Llamrei danced across the cobbles. He had to twist his head to keep his gaze on Cadwy. "I won't give it to you." His eyes met those of his hated older brother, the bully who'd made his childhood a misery, who'd tried to poison him, and me, nearly three years ago. "But I'll fight you for it. The winner to take Merlin and the sword. That's my only offer."

My breath caught in my throat. He'd once before fought in single combat against an enemy, and now he was prepared to do it again. For Merlin's sake. Or was it just for Merlin?

Indecision flashed across Cadwy's broad face. Arthur was younger than him by ten years and considerably lighter, but Cadwy's reputation as war leader for his father and a fearsome warrior was not without justification. What he lacked in agility, he made up for in bulk and strength. He must have been weighing up his chances.

The longing for the sword won. He nodded. "Agreed. To-morrow. At midday."

Arthur grinned, teeth white against the seven days growth of beard on his chin. "And I'll bring all my men. It's not that I don't trust you. Just that...I don't trust you."

He spun Llamrei on the spot, and Cei and I fell in behind him as we turned our backs on Cadwy and Morgana, and headed back to the gates.

WE MADE OUR camp on the farmlands outside the city that night. Arthur set up an iron ring of sentries around the camp, wary lest Cadwy might be planning some treachery, but nothing happened. Our sleep, although fitful, remained undisturbed. After all, attacking us would not have got the sword for him, so even Cadwy must have seen the sense in that.

I awoke early, my back cold in the dawn chill, because Arthur, who'd slept holding me curled against his body, had already risen. Pulling his discarded blanket over me made little difference, so I sat up and stretched, surveying what was going on. Some of the men were feeding the campfires ready to cook themselves breakfast, others sat polishing their weapons or oiling their saddles. A few slept on. Arthur was nowhere to be seen.

Across the plain a chest high mist had drifted, thicker down by the river, the tips of the willows only just visible.

Throwing aside my blankets, I headed for the horse lines to check on Alezan. As I'd expected, Arthur was there, rubbing Llamrei's ears and whispering sweet nothings to her. With her fine summer coat, the dark grey, almost black of her skin shimmered through, and on her ears, she looked touched by a light powdering of soot.

I watched him for a minute, as he stood there fussing over her in only his boots, braccae and loose undershirt. He was a curious conundrum. A fierce warrior who would put his life on the line not just for his wife but also for his friend. A man who could execute an enemy in cold blood and order the death of a child. Yet a man who loved his wife, his son and his horse. Possibly not in that order.

He turned away from Llamrei, and seeing me, his eyes lit up. "Come to check on Alezan?"

I nodded. "She's happy enough. Which is more than I am."

"Don't you start," he said. "Cei's already had a go at me."

Last night he'd refused to talk to either me or Cei about what he'd agreed with Cadwy.

I huffed. "Not without reason."

"You won't change my mind. I know I can beat him. He's an old man."

"Not so old as all that. He's only got ten years on you. What's that? Thirty six or seven? He's still in his prime."

"Have you looked at him closely? He's got fat. Fat and old. His hair's going grey already."

I shook my head. "Half of what you think is fat is clothes. He overdresses even in this hot weather. Underneath all that he's probably hard as nails."

He started back toward the campfires. "And so am I. I'm a little offended that you think I might get beaten by that great fat oaf."

I grabbed his hand. "It's not that I think you'll get beaten – it's that I think he'll cheat." Hamlet's last fight in Shakespeare's play came leaping into my mind, with the poisoned tip to the sword. "He'll see it as not just the opportunity to get hold of the sword and with it the High Kingship, but also to kill you."

He shot me a grin. "We'll be fighting first. If he wants that sword, he'll have to leave me alive. If he wins, that is, and I don't intend to let him."

Back at the campfire, Cei was cooking smoked bacon, the delicious smell rising toward the brightening sky as the sun burnt off the morning mist. We sat down on lumps of wood we'd found for seats, and Cei forked the bacon onto our plates. But I couldn't eat mine. Despite the alluring smell, it turned to sawdust in my mouth, and I offered it to Arthur.

He took it with no sign of the nerves I was feeling, eating with relish.

Cei sat down beside his brother. "A good thing you specified you were bringing all our men. I wouldn't trust Cadwy as far as I could throw him, and quite frankly, I doubt I could lift him off the ground."

As my stomach tied itself in knots, I had to agree with him.

Chapter Thirty

THE FORUM THRONGED with people. Clearly Cadwy wanted his warriors and citizens to witness his triumph over Arthur and the claiming of the sword. The majority of our warriors had ranged themselves along one side, on foot, crammed in together. We'd left a few guarding our camp and horse lines, but little danger threatened them, as on the opposite side of the forum, Cadwy had all his own men lined up. The rest of the space was taken up by the population of the city – the tradesmen and craftsmen, their families, their slaves and servants. A hum of noise like a hive of angry bees vibrated around the forum.

A large space had been left clear in the center, around the sword in the stone and in front of the hall doors. Here, Cadwy stood, resplendent in his armor, not quite so big as he'd looked before, but still built along the lines of a bear.

Beside him, a little closer to the hall doors, Morgana stood, and near her, held between two burly warriors, Merlin. Although Arthur and I were not close, it was easy to see he looked very much the worse for wear. His clothing hung torn and dirty, blood had crusted on his face and in the beard that now adorned his chin. His head hung down as though he couldn't bear to watch. From his appearance, it was clear someone had been working hard to get him to give up his secret and release the sword from its resting place.

Arthur, who'd ridden Llamrei into the city at the head of his army, swung down from the saddle. He wore leather braccae and wrist guards, and his mail shirt glimmered in the sunlight. The padded tunic underneath added bulk, but he still looked slight beside his brother, even though he wasn't at all.

Cei dismounted as well and handed his brother his helmet. Arthur put it on, fastening the straps with steady hands. Unlike mine, which I'd had to bury in Alezan's mane to stop them from shaking. Both Cei and I had come on horseback, but I had no intention of dismounting. The view up here was far better than from the ground. Cei slapped Arthur on the back, and they clasped hands, face to face for a moment, jaws set, eyes alight with something indefinable. Lust for battle, perhaps. Hatred of Cadwy for certain.

A few ranks back, the boy Custennin stood between two of our older warriors, firmly sandwiched in a position from which he couldn't escape. This morning, I'd heard Arthur order his men to kill the boy if Cadwy showed any sign of treachery. Half of me had recoiled at his words, but the other half had considered doing it myself if Cadwy betrayed our trust, even though Custennin was so young. He had a heavy-browed look of Cadwy about him that I didn't like.

Alezan fidgeted under me, restless because she knew I was too, and I put a hand down to soothe her, stroking her warm shoulder. Touching her steadied my nerves a little. I had to remain calm.

By the hall, Cadwy strapped his own helmet on. It wasn't like Arthur's. Instead of the leather head piece studded with metal plates, Cadwy wore something that might have been more at home on a legionary, solid, with well-polished metal and a horsehair plume on the top. A relic of one of his ancestors' Roman past, no doubt. Could his great grandfather, the Emperor Constantine III himself, have worn that helmet?

Archbishop Dubricius stood beside Cadwy, a pudgy hand on his arm, whispering instructions and advice. Cadwy gave an impatient shake of his head and threw off the hand. Being a churchman in this day and age didn't preclude the possibility that Dubricius had been a warrior earlier in his life, and his advice might have been warranted.

Arthur and Cei stepped toward the center of the open space, Arthur carrying his shield with the black bear rearing up on it, his sword naked in his hand.

Cadwy approached with Dubricius, halting half a dozen paces from Arthur. Dubricius held up a hand. Slowly, the noise in the forum died away as every man and woman present, and every child too, fell silent. Excitement crackled around the eclectic mix of Roman and British buildings, from broken pillars to thatched hall, from the remains of a stone fountain to the rows of empty market stalls.

When he had total silence, Dubricius finally spoke. "You are here today to witness the creation of a new High King." His voice, no doubt honed by many years of preaching in his church, echoed around the forum. "Whosoever wins this fight will take possession of the Sword of Destiny."

So they'd given it a fancy name. Interesting. Could it be Excalibur?

"And whosoever loses here this day will acknowledge the other as victor and High King. The message written here on the stone says this sword is for the hands of the High King only. Today is the day when we discover who that will be."

He stepped back.

Cei also stepped back, leaving Cadwy and Arthur facing one another, swords already drawn.

Sword fights are vicious things, exhausting for those who take part, and terrifying for those who have to watch. The shields are heavy, the swords well balanced but heavy too. The longer the fight goes on, the heavier they become. I'd done enough sword practice myself by now to know this. But these two were strong men in their prime and well-matched. This fight could last a long time.

They circled one another, boots shuffling across the uneven

flagstones, swords raised, each never taking his eyes off the other. Arthur was the lighter on his feet, but Cadwy probably the stronger of the two. And despite his bulk, he turned out to be surprisingly agile.

As I watched, Cadwy struck at Arthur. Their blades clashed, sparks flying. The hammer of staccato blows that followed rose to the hot, cloudless sky. Neither had the advantage, both using their shields adroitly to fend off the other's blows. Great dark gouges like gaping mouths opened in the wood.

My gaze strayed past them to Merlin, who'd lifted his head now to watch the fight with intensity, still held between those two warriors. Did they have orders to kill him if Arthur looked like winning? I wouldn't have put it past Cadwy to do that. After all, Arthur had said the same to his men about Custennin.

Cei had come to stand by Alezan's shoulder, his hand on her neck, fingers twisted in her mane. I leant down. "Can you get some warriors closer to Merlin? I don't trust Cadwy not to have him killed if he looks like he's losing. Just to prevent Arthur getting both him and the sword."

Cei raised worried eyes to meet mine. "You're right. I'll see to that." He turned to the man holding Arthur's horse, muttering a few words in his ear. The man handed over the reins and slipped away, melting into the crowd.

The fight went on, blow after blow raining down, then a break while they circled one another and got their breath back. The watching crowd stood mesmerized and silent. Impossible to tell who they might be rooting for. Cadwy rained down blows like a blacksmith striking iron. The blows must be jolting not just up his own arm but up Arthur's too as their swords met.

They fought back and forth across the wide-open space, and as they did so, the crowd moved like the tide, shrinking back as the fight came toward them, surging forward when the combatants moved away.

My grip on Alezan's reins whitened my knuckles, and my stomach and legs felt turned to jelly. Cadwy didn't want Arthur dead, or he wouldn't get the sword, but wounded was a possibility. Arthur only needed to live long enough to pull the sword from the stone and give it to Cadwy.

In front of the hall doors Morgana stood upright as a young pine tree, her arms by her sides, her clenched fists the only thing betraying her trepidation. She had her eyes fixed on the two fighting men – her warring brothers. Her tongue came out and licked her lips, which might have been because they were dry, but I doubted it. The gesture had nothing of necessity about it, rather a deliberate act of enjoyment. She was deriving pleasure from this fight.

I remembered the night Uthyr Pendragon had died, when Cadwy and Arthur had almost come to blows in his death chamber. She'd wanted them to fight then, and now she'd got her way.

Behind her, Merlin stood rigid between his captors, his hands bound behind his back, his face a picture of impotent rage. Did he love her still, after all of this? Surely by now he must have realized that she'd only seduced him to get what she wanted. A child, his power, and the sword for her brother.

I turned my head to look at Custennin, a few rows back, held between two burly warriors. Too short to see the fight, he could only listen to the clash of swords and the occasional hiss or gasp from the audience. Had Morgana been happy to send him as a hostage because she didn't care what happened to him? Had she used her power to persuade Cadwy to put him in such danger? Perhaps because she wanted her own child to one day sit on Cadwy's throne, the throne of her father?

My gaze shot back to Morgana. A small, satisfied smile had crept across her face, and her right hand came up to cradle her belly, as though somehow she knew my thoughts. She turned her lovely head and stared back at me out of eyes cold as a bottomless black lake, yet sparkling with triumph. Did she hope they'd kill one another?

Arthur and Cadwy had sprung apart, Arthur at one end of

FIL REID

their makeshift arena, Cadwy at the other. Their labored
breathing came hard and fast. Their faces under their helmets had
flushed red with effort and sweat shone on every inch of exposed
skin.

With any luck Cadwy would have a heart attack. He looked
the sort. My own heart raced like a galloping horse.

Cei glanced up at me. "Cadwy's tiring."

I nodded. "But so is Arthur."

They circled warily again, in their shuffling dance of death.
Slowly around, until they'd swapped ends and Cadwy was nearer
to us. Then they advanced again, and their swords met. Arthur
pushed Cadwy backward a few steps, hammering home a slight
advantage, and Cadwy's back came up against the rock, the
longed-for sword rearing up above his head like a miniature
Calvary.

As Arthur struck, Cadwy swung his shield up and the hard
edge caught Arthur's sword arm. The sword came down awry,
striking the rock with a jarring clang that must have rebounded
right up Arthur's arm. For a tiny moment the sword held
together, and then three quarters of the blade sheared off,
clattering to the flagstones like breaking glass.

Arthur leapt back, only the stub of his sword in his hand, and
Cadwy, eager to follow up his advantage, charged after him, eyes
glinting in triumph. His sword swung. But Arthur was too quick
for him. He dived forward underneath it, the only thing he could
do. The blade swept harmlessly over his back, and Arthur kept on
going, carried onward by his charge. Cadwy smashed into the
ground, Arthur on top. He ground his shield into Cadwy's sword
arm, pinning it down, striking out with the stub of his sword, the
pommel catching Cadwy under his jaw.

Cadwy's head snapped back, but his shield swung round,
slamming into Arthur's head with enormous force. Enough to
send him spinning. But Cadwy had lost his grip on his own
sword. It skittered away across the flagstones to end up on the far
side of the rock. Out of reach of either of them. They staggered to

their feet, Cadwy's eyes on the fallen weapon.

Hurling away his shield and broken sword, Arthur dived at his brother before Cadwy had chance to lunge for his sword. They went down again, rolling across the flagstones, punching wildly at each other with their bare fists now. Cadwy's helmet came flying off, the strap hanging broken, and rolled away to land by Morgana's feet.

Arthur was on top, punching Cadwy. He had the advantage even though in a fist fight he was the lighter, and less likely to win. Cadwy's hands came up, his fingers gripping Arthur's throat. Arthur hit him again but the hands didn't loosen. The thick, fleshy fingers dug deep into Arthur's skin.

I reached out and grabbed Cei's large hand where he had tight hold of Alezan's mane. This was personal. All the years of being bullied by Cadwy were taking their toll. Arthur seemed not to notice Cadwy trying to choke the life out of him as he hit him again and again. Blood spurted from Cadwy's broken nose.

The crowd of watchers had surged forward, nearly at the sword in the stone, where it stood above the two fighting men like some kind of sentinel. A symbol of what they were fighting for.

And then Cadwy's hands dropped from Arthur's throat. Arthur hit him once more, then stopped, head hanging, blood dripping from his own battered face. His panting breaths sounded loud in the hushed silence. "Do you yield?" He spat blood.

Cadwy lay still, eyes only half open. Arthur seized the front of his mail shirt and shook him hard. "Do you yield?" Cadwy's head rattled against the flagstones.

His beaten brother opened the only eye he could. "I yield." The words came out slurred and broken. He couldn't very well say anything else.

A sudden commotion from over by the hall drew my eyes. The men who'd been holding Merlin lay prostrate on the ground. Allwyn and three others of our warriors were dragging Merlin into the crowd. Morgana still stood, motionless, her furious gaze fixed on her two brothers.

Arthur pushed himself off Cadwy, into a kneeling position beside him, shoulders slumped, breath labored. The crowd watched, fascinated, as though collectively they held their breath. With an immense effort, he struggled to his feet and straightened, drawing himself up tall. With unsteady fingers covered in blood, that probably wasn't all his own, he undid the strap of his helmet and took it off, letting it drop to the ground.

His hair clung in damp curls to his head. Blood and dirt streaked his face. He turned to look at me. Our eyes met for a long, pregnant moment.

My heart swelled. This was my husband, the man I'd sacrificed everything to be with. The man who'd stood up against the bully that was Cadwy and saved his friend. Suddenly I wasn't Gwen the librarian pretending to be a Dark Age queen, profoundly disturbed by what I saw. I was Guinevere, wife of a Dark Age warlord, proud of the way he could fight to defend those he loved.

From a bruised and swelling eye, he winked, then turned slowly on his heel to fix his gaze on the sword, where it still stood, upright and challenging in the center of the old forum.

With determined feet, he crossed the few paces to the stone. It rose three feet above the flagstones, so to put his hands on the hilt he had to step up onto it.

My heart full of pride and glorious triumph, I watched him do it, eyes for no one else but him.

Ever the showman, once there, he paused to gaze around at his audience, gathering them in, letting them participate in this moment with him. In the thick and heavy silence, not even a bird called.

I held my breath, my love for him beating like a drum in my heart.

He set both hands on the sword's plain hilt. "The time is right." His words echoed around the forum, and a ripple of excited murmurs rose to the heavens.

His grip tightened, he set his blood-streaked jaw. Every man there knew how many others had tried this and not succeeded, but from the expectant silence it seemed that they were just as sure the time was now right, and this man would be the one.

His muscles flexed. He pulled on the hilt.

The sword slid out of the stone, silent and smooth. The gasp of a thousand indrawn breaths sibilated through the air.

Arthur raised the sword above his head.

"Long live the new High King," shouted Cei.

A huge cheer went up. From our warriors, from the inhabitants of Viroconium, and even from Cadwy's own men. Only Cadwy, lying on the floor with one eye swollen shut and blood all over him, and Morgana, standing coldly watching, didn't join in.

Over the heads of the crowd Arthur sought me out, a triumphant grin on his face.

The sword was out of the stone.

To be continued...

About the Author

After a varied life that's included working with horses where Downton Abbey is filmed, riding racehorses, running her own riding school, owning a sheep farm and running a holiday business in France, Fil now lives on a widebeam canal boat on the Kennet and Avon Canal in Southern England.

She has a long-suffering husband, a rescue dog from Romania called Bella, a cat she found as a kitten abandoned in a gorse bush, five children and six grandchildren.

She once saw a ghost in a churchyard, and when she lived in Wales there was a panther living near her farm that ate some of her sheep. In England there are no indigenous big cats.

She has Asperger's Syndrome and her obsessions include horses and King Arthur. Her historical romantic fiction and children's fantasy adventures centre around Arthurian legends, and her pony stories about her other love. She speaks fluent French after living there for ten years, and in her spare time looks after her allotment, makes clothes and dolls for her granddaughters, embroiders and knits. In between visiting the settings for her books.

Social Media links:
Website – filreid.com
Facebook – facebook.com/Fil-Reid-Author-101905545548054
Twitter – @FJReidauthor

www.ingramcontent.com/pod-product-compliance
Lightning Source LLC
Chambersburg PA
CBHW070756190726
48292CB00002B/552